The Button Girl

SALLY APOKEDAK

Paraklesis Press
5252 Barrett Parkway #39
Marietta, GA 30064
www.paraklesispress.com

Printed in the United States of America

First Edition 2017

ISBN: 978-1-947446-00-7

21 20 19 18 17 / 10 9 8 7 6 5 4 3 2 1

For Nikki, the joy of my heart. The lover of laughter, the willing worker, the never complainer, the finisher of ...

PROLOGUE

Repentance Atwater stood beside her little sister, Comfort, studying the damp ground where all the mushrooms grew.

Comfort trudged into the patch. "I found a good one!" She bent down to grab it.

"Careful," Repentance said. "Don't get your bib and britches dirty." Repentance, in her sixth year, was the older sister. It was her job to keep Comfort out of trouble while they waited for Destiny—the big girl from down the creek who was coming to take them out of Mama's way for a while.

Repentance studied Comfort's mushroom. "That's a good start. But let's keep looking. We have to find the fattest ones." The mushrooms would be a nice surprise for Mama. They would cheer her up.

Trying to back up, Comfort tripped over her own feet and landed in the muddiest spot.

"Comfort! You've made a mess." Repentance threw a

worried glance toward their cave, hoping no one was watching. "Now Mama's going to be mad."

Something was wrong with Mama lately. She'd been crying all week. And that morning she'd gotten really bad—sobbing so hard she hadn't been able to speak. Repentance had run to the swamp-squash harvest to fetch Daddy.

She pulled Comfort up and brushed at the mud on the seat of her britches, smearing it around, making it worse. "Daddy will help Mama," she said ... to herself more than to Comfort. "Don't worry. It will all come out right in the end."

Hearing a noise on the trail she looked up to see a figure coming—moving fast. It was too foggy to see who it was, but then she heard the familiar whistle. "Destiny!" she shouted.

Destiny ran up to the cave, poked her head in behind the thick leather curtain that closed off the opening, and hollered to let Mama and Daddy know she was there.

"You're late," Daddy said, stepping out.

"I'm sorry, I was—"

"It's not important. Just hurry and take them."

Destiny looked at Comfort's muddy britches. "Come on you two," she said. "I suppose we'll have to go to the swimming hole to get you all cleaned up."

"Yippee!" Repentance said. "I'll get Trib."

Daddy grabbed her before she could enter the cave. "Tribulation can't go."

Repentance stopped, confused. Three-year-old Trib loved to swim. And he wasn't ill. "Trib is hale and hearty," she said. "Why can't he come with us?"

Before Daddy could answer, the morning erupted with scratching and scrabbling sounds as birds and bunnies skittered off the path that led through the swamp.

Dark shapes came toward the cave.

They pushed through the fog—took form. Two overlords and a goat cart with a willow-branch cage in its bed. One of the overlords had a dragon stick slung over his shoulder.

Repentance automatically put an arm around Comfort and crouched down, wanting to be small. She'd seen an overlord shoot a dragon stick once. The fire was so hot it had set a soaking-wet tree on fire. There had been a puff of steam as the water burned off, and then the tree had exploded into flames.

The men stopped in front of the cave. "We're here for the weanling."

"He's is in the house," Daddy said. "I'll get him." Then to Destiny he said, "Too late, now. Bring the girls inside and keep them busy."

Destiny tried to herd them into the cave, but Comfort ducked out of reach. "You said we could go to the swim hole."

One of the overlords took a square of cloth, about the size of the handkerchiefs that Daddy used, from his pocket. Only this cloth was glowing. Bright yellow light was coming off it as if it was a candle. Repentance had never seen the likes of it.

So it was true what everyone said: The overlords had magic.

Comfort, eyes big, reached for the cloth. Destiny snagged her collar and pulled her back.

"Let the little swamp rat be," the man said, dangling his magic hanky in front of Comfort. "I'm not going to hurt her."

While the man was distracted with her little sister, Repentance studied his strange, pale eyes. She'd never been so close to an overlord before.

Daddy ducked back under the curtain holding Tribulation, who was squirming and fussing.

The overlord shoved his yellow, glowing cloth into his pocket.

Daddy, his face gray, planted a kiss on Trib's head and handed him to the man.

Handed him to the overlord!

Just like that!

Blood rushed into Repentance's head and pounded in her ears. Time seemed to slow down.

A sob broke from Daddy, and he slipped into the cave.

The overlord stuck Trib into the cage.

Tossed him in.

Like Trib wasn't anything more than a possum or a piglet.

He hooked the door of the cage. Turned the goat around. Began down the path.

"Meany!" Comfort threw her mushroom at the overlords. It fell far short. Landed on the muddy path. Harmless.

Trib stuck his arms through the willow-branch slats. Reaching out. "Pentace!" he screamed. "Pentace!"

Crying.

Sobbing.

Wailing.

Repentance could see the tears clinging to his eyelashes.

She could see his chubby, wet, red cheeks. She could see his tiny, white, baby teeth. And then she couldn't see anything at all.

He was gone.

Swallowed by the fog.

She made to follow, but Destiny held her back.

His wailing was quickly muffled, absorbed by the swamp, with its sopping trees, its thick moss, and its moldy earth.

The outdoor noises came back. Frogs croaking. Wart-lizards hissing. Trees dripping.

A fat blob of water fell from a tree and splatted onto her face. Repentance swiped it off with the back of one hand. "He didn't break any of the rules," she whispered. Fear rose in her throat like a purple-fruit pit—a thick knot that made it hard to swallow. "They aren't supposed to take us kids if we don't break the rules. Why did they take Trib?"

"It's Grief Day," Destiny said. "Keeping the rules doesn't count on Grief Day."

Sorrow crouches at the heart's door,
   like a cat, waiting the perfect moment to spring.
     ~Lawful Atwood II, during the first year of the captivity

CHAPTER 1

Repentance Atwater sat still as a rock, clenching her hands in her lap to keep them from trembling.

She glared at her reflection in the shiny, wet, black stone before her. She was acting like a child—not like a girl who had seen sixteen years. She was full grown, for the love of Providence. Old enough to button.

Or to refuse to button, if she so chose.

Old enough to choose her own fate.

Still, no matter how bravely she attempted to paste a happy expression on her face, she only managed to get the terrified look of a rabbit caught in torchlight.

Mother stood behind her, gently raking her fingers through Repentance's freshly washed hair. She hummed a lively buttoning tune as she worked, oblivious to the pain that would come with the night.

A weeping and a wailing.

There would come a weeping and a wailing. Repentance had been through plenty of Grief Days and failed button ceremonies. She knew what it felt like to stand helpless before the overlords as they loaded up the slave carts.

Mother began to plait Repentance's hair. All the button girls wore braids to keep their hair from frizzing in the humid air.

Repentance closed her eyes, trying to focus on the tune her mother hummed, but she could not shut out the sound of the steady drip from the fog-drenched trees. Even sitting in the back of the cave, through thick stone walls and two leather curtains drawn down, she could hear the incessant drip, drip, drip.

A weeping and a wailing.

She didn't want to be the cause of it. But what could she do? Inside she'd been weeping and wailing all her life.

She could go along with the buttoning, that's what she could do. She could learn to be content like everyone else.

But she was not like everyone else. She tried to be. She wanted to be. She had practiced the precepts of Providence since she was no bigger than a swamp rat. *To be discontent is to complain against Providence himself, to call him a liar, to say he has not provided as he ought.*

And yet, Repentance Atwater was not content living in the breeder village. She was not content with the fog that clung like a burial shroud. She was not content with the muggy, oppressive heat, which threatened to smother her. And, most assuredly, she was not content to be buttoned to Sober Marsh and to bear sons for the overlords to take as slaves.

"You're too quiet," Mother said, after she'd finished one braid and started on the second.

"What is there to say?" Her voice sounded high-pitched and desperate.

Mother seemed not to notice. "I know you're worried, but you'll grow to love Sober. Your father and I would never have agreed to the buttoning if we did not think it was so."

"You had no choice. Who else would have me?"

Mother evaded the question. "You are a beautiful girl,

Repentance Joyous Forgiveness Abounding Atwater. A beautiful girl."

Repentance cringed at the use of all of her front names. No one in remembrance had four front names. The closest was Grace Renewed Springside, so named because a week before her birth her father had captured a second milking pig after her mother, in a fit of pregnancy fever, had gambled the first one away. It was rare for most families to own even one sow, let alone to gain a second after the first was lost. Grace Renewed, indeed. It was a fitting name for the baby, even if it was a two-parter.

"And you're a smart girl," Mother continued. "Sober will learn to appreciate that."

"A beautiful and smart girl that no one wants." Repentance said.

She knew she wasn't wanted. She was different from the others. It wasn't just her name. She looked different, too. Everyone else had black hair and dark brown eyes. Repentance had hair the color of dried marsh grass and eyes a shade lighter—almost golden—with green flecks that flared up when she was agitated.

"I don't care that they don't want me," she said, "I don't want any of them, either." She looked at herself in the reflecting wall and her eyes spit green sparks back at her.

Why would she want to be buttoned to boys who thought she was cursed?

She'd heard the whispers all her life. It was largely supposed that Providence cursed her for the sin committed by her mother before her birth. And, truly, it must have been a terrible sin. What else would have required that her mother give her such a lengthy name? Repentance Joyous Forgiveness Abounding—it must have been a great sin for her mother to gush so over the forgiveness of it.

The villagers didn't think it forgiven, though. They assumed Providence had demanded payment from the mother by cursing the child. Why else, they wondered, would Repentance have such odd coloring?

When Repentance was little she often tried to discover what

her mother's sin was. If she bore the curse, she had right to know the cause, she figured. But never would her mother speak of the deed.

Mother finished the last braid and bent to kiss the top of Repentance's head. "Sober wants you. He was desperate to have you. You are taking the biggest button price this year at five hundred beads."

"You're right, of course." What was the use of arguing? Mother would believe what she wanted. She had no problem with contentment. She put a good light on everything. That was how she coped with her harsh world. Even Repentance understood that. And it was one reason she wanted out. *Providence desires us to be honest, merciful, and joyous.* Perfect! Except you couldn't be all three at once. Honesty sucked all the joy right out of a body.

"Don't be so glum, Repentance," Mother said, giving her shoulders an encouraging squeeze. "I know you've heard people talking. Saying that Sober is stuck with you. He's failed at four buttonings and if he fails this one it's the slave cart for him, true enough. But look at how good Providence is. Sober needs you and you need him. It is Providence at work. It has to be. He's saving both of you from the overlords."

Repentance met her mother's gaze in the reflecting wall. Tired eyes made Mother look older than her thirty-two years. All that faking of contentment wore a soul out, apparently. But there was love in those dark eyes, too.

Guilt flooded through Repentance. She wanted to tell her mother that she loved her. She wanted to tell her goodbye. But she couldn't steal the afternoon's joy from her. Night would come soon enough, bringing the sorrow with it. "Yes," she said softly. "It must be Providence at work."

Mother smiled. "The other boys are missing out. But the best buttonings are made from necessity. Look at your father and me. See how happy we've been?"

"Why did you two need each other so much?"

"It was his fifth year, too."

"I knew he needed you. I didn't know you needed him.

Didn't any other scarf boys want you?"

"He would have gone to the overlords. That's necessity enough for one button match." Mother blushed and absently tucked a strand of dull black hair back into the bun on her head. "Of course other boys wanted me. I was young and beautiful once myself. Just like you are now."

Repentance twisted around on the bench and hugged her. "You are still beautiful. And I love you." And she hated to hurt her.

She closed her eyes, remembering Trib's howling as the overlords took him away.

And her mother's weeping.

And Comfort, her little sister, clinging to her night after night while Mother sobbed and Father shushed and their world wobbled out of whack.

It fell completely off its axis the following year when the overlords came back for Devastation.

But then the little boys had been born. And joy returned. Mother was happy. She'd given her two sons already. The overlords only ever took two. The little boys were safe.

But Mother was about to have her world tipped upside down again. At the button ceremony. "I have always loved you," Repentance whispered, wanting to keep holding her forever.

Mother patted her back. "There's a good girl. And don't worry. You'll love Sober, too. He's a good man. It will all come out right in the end."

Repentance nodded, though she knew Mother was wrong. Nothing was going to come out right. She'd known that from the day Trib disappeared into the fog. She'd known then that she would never button. Never breed. Never give her children to the overlords.

Repentance found Comfort sitting on the mossy bench in the main room of their cave with a parchment book on her lap. She held a char-stick in one hand, eyes closed as if she was trying to picture, in her mind's eye, the image she wanted to capture. Repentance stared, determined to etch every line of her sister's face into her brain permanently. She would think of Comfort forever in this peaceful pose—leaning back against the wall with the dim light washing over her features.

No one ever accused Comfort of being cursed. She was beautiful in every way. The blackest hair; the smoothest complexion, like cool brown tea; high cheekbones; and the darkest, deepest eyes, dancing with secret joys.

As if feeling Repentance's gaze traveling over her, Comfort opened her eyes. "Pentance!" she said. "You scared me."

"What are you drawing?"

Comfort tipped up the parchment to reveal a blank page. "Haven't started yet. And you couldn't see if I had. I'm thinking on your button present. I want it to be perfect."

A tremor ran down Repentance's spine. "Everything you draw is perfect." She sat down next to Comfort. "I can't believe I'm leaving tonight. I'll miss you."

"It's not like we'll never see each other again. I'll walk to the marsh and visit you every day."

Repentance nodded.

Comfort twisted slightly to look at her. "If you want me, I mean. If you're not too busy taking care of Sober. And then the babies. Pretty soon you'll have babies and you'll be too busy to miss any of us."

"I'll never stop missing you, Comfort, you're my best friend."

"And I'll always be." She smiled. "Even when Aggravation and I are buttoned."

There had been no waiting until the last minute for Comfort's buttoning particulars. The Mossybanks had paid over beads to purchase Comfort for their son years earlier. Both Comfort and Aggravation were well pleased with the arrangement. Repentance smiled thinking about the two as button mates. They were the handsomest couple in the village—their children would be adorable.

And Repentance would never see them.

"You'll have Aggravation for a best friend, Comfort. I'm glad of that."

Comfort set char-stick to parchment and began sketching. In moments Aggravation's face took shape on the paper.

"Are you afraid?" Comfort asked without looking up from her work.

"A little," she lied. She concentrated on the soft scratching of char-stick on paper and forced herself to relax.

"Because you don't know Sober?"

"I know him." Not well. He was older and he lived on the far side of the marsh. He'd left school five years earlier.

"I haven't thought about Sober much. I'm not really afraid."

Her little sister lifted her eyebrows in disbelief.

"Really," Repentance said. "Now I'm going to leave you so you can get to work on my button present." She tapped the picture Comfort was working on. "Don't you dare give me a picture of Aggravation. He's a handsome fellow, but I don't want him hanging in my main room."

Comfort laughed, her cheeks tinged with the rosy hue of embarrassment. "I didn't even realize I was drawing him. I do it without thinking."

Repentance squeezed her tighter. "I'm glad you have someone to love, Comfort. And who will love you back. He'll take care of you."

Comfort leaned against Repentance's shoulder. "He'll take care of me, and Sober will take care of you, and we'll have lots of little girls and they'll be best friends just like we are."

Repentance kissed Comfort's head. Sweet, happy Comfort. It was just like her to imagine that they'd only give birth to girls. If only there was a way to have such a guarantee. The mothers in the village would give their milking pigs and their weaving hands, too, for a promise of only girl babies.

Repentance shoved that little bit of hope down. She could not depend on Providence to give only girls.

It wouldn't do any good even if he did. If he started giving only girl babies, the overlords would start taking girl babies instead of leaving them to breed.

No, the only way to keep the overlords from stealing her children was to not have any in the first place.

The girls are safely promised.
The boys have all found mates.
Slave carts shall stand empty.
Come drink and fill your plates.
Gather 'round. Let joy abound. We'll drink and fill our plates.
~From an old buttoning song

CHAPTER 2

Fire glowed in the village center, its smoke acting as a discouragement to the biting flies. Repentance wilted before it. If the fingers of flame had clawed a hole in the fog she would have embraced the heat, but the sticky mist clung as always, threatening to choke her.

She sat on the ground with her back to the blaze—she and five other girls all in their sixteenth year.

Repentance ignored the chatter from the others. She held a char-stick and hunched over her small parchment pad, trying to think of some way to explain to Comfort. Nothing came.

People began to fill up the village center. They sat on logs facing the girls.

She quickly wrote *I love you, and I'm sorry,* ripped the note off the pad, and tucked it under one leg. Later that night, or maybe in the morning, someone would find it and give it to Comfort.

And Comfort would cry her eyes out.

Repentance slipped her parchment pad and char-stick into the pocket of her blouse with a sigh. Nothing she could say would ease the pain.

She looked up to see Confusion Pondside taking a seat up front. Cursed lot! Repentance had been born three days before Buttoning Day and Confusion had been born three days after. So, though Repentance was only a week older than Confusion, she was to be buttoned this year and Confusion would wait until next. Of course, Mother would say that was a kindness granted by Providence. Next year there would be no desperate fifth-year boys willing to take Repentance as a mate.

Goodwoman Marsh would likely agree with her mother.

Repentance scanned the audience. She found Sober's mother on the left, in front, leaning forward anxiously. Her features were fuzzy in the dim light, but Repentance could still make out a guarded look of longing directed toward her. If she would save Sober, she'd have Goodwoman Marsh's undying devotion. She lifted her eyes from the crowd, saw the dark slave cart hunkered just outside the circle of villagers, and a wave of nausea swept over her.

She wouldn't be condemning Sober alone, though. She would share his fate. Boys had five chances to find a button mate. Girls had only one—they were either buttoned in their sixteenth year or they were sent off on the slave cart, never to see their families again.

Often one or two were sent away. There were not enough boys one year and not enough girls the next. So button ceremonies were full of mixed emotions. The relief and joy felt by those who had found mates was tempered out of pity for those who had not.

This year was different. The crowd didn't hold a single weepy face. All the boys and girls of age had been promised. Beads had changed hands and blouses and scarves had been sewn amidst a jolly feeling of wellbeing. The girls were especially happy. Buttonings made on years that took no slaves were said to enjoy special blessings from Providence.

The button girls wore blouses with different colored

buttons. Repentance had gray buttons. A large heart-shaped one at her breast, a round one at her wrist, and a square one at her hip. To her right, Blamed Backwater had the same shapes in brown, and to her left, Sovereign Gumtree had green. It was supposed to be a surprise—the identity of the button mate—but that tradition had long passed out of practice. Each girl knew which boy would carry the scarf that matched her buttons. Some had known for years; others had only just found out. In the end, they were all promised and they were all happy.

All except Repentance.

Drums began to play and the crowd hushed. The buttoning ceremony was officially started. Repentance gave her sweaty forehead a swipe with the heel of her hand.

Angered Springside came out from behind the fire. He danced along the line of button girls swirling his tan scarf in and out around their heads. Up the line he went, weaving a tan trail in and out, in and out, while the drums beat and the trees dripped and the fire flared. And back down the line he went. Slowly, rhythmically, dancing, weaving, keeping beat with the flames and the drums and the dripping.

Time slowed down. The air felt heavier than ever.

Repentance thought she might throw up.

Or scream.

Or both.

Couldn't they hurry? She sent a quick prayer to Providence, begging him to keep her from fainting. If she lost consciousness, she would wake up to find herself buttoned to Sober Marsh. Destined to live in the clinging fog until she choked to death on it.

Of course, Providence probably wouldn't listen to her prayer. She was a malcontent, after all. And lacking in mercy. What she planned to do to her family and to the Marsh family was by no means merciful. Why would Providence listen to any prayers she offered?

On Angered's third trip down the line, Benefit Underfall, grinning flirtatiously, caught his scarf. She hung on while he pulled her into a standing position. Then she pushed the heart-shaped button on her blouse through the first hole on the scarf and began her vows. The round button at her wrist went through the second hole and the square button at her hip went through the third. She buttoned herself without looking—all the girls had practiced this maneuver for weeks and could easily do it by feel—so she could gaze into Angered's eyes as she recited her vows:

> *With my heart, I'll love you,*
> *With my hands, I'll serve you,*
> *By your side, I'll abide, forever and always.*

Angered then buttoned the scarf onto the corresponding buttons on his shirt and, looking deeply into Benefit's eyes, he answered:

> *With my heart, I'll hold you,*
> *With my arms, enfold you,*
> *Beside you, I'll guide you, for now and for always.*

Using the scarf, Angered drew Benefit close and kissed her.

The crowd erupted into cheers. Repentance added hers, halfhearted as they were. One down, five to go. But maybe she wouldn't have to wait until the end. Maybe Sober would come out next.

Angered and Benefit moved behind the fire.

The drums picked up the beat.

Repentance held her breath.

Consternation Mossybank came out trailing a green scarf. On her left side, Sovereign emitted a little squeal of excitement. Repentance sagged a little—torn between disappointment and relief.

Why did Providence make her wait? Was He giving her time to change her mind?

Too late.

She closed her eyes, remembering Trib with his chubby arms

outstretched. "Pentace, Pentace."

And she couldn't save him.

He called to her because she was the one he could see. His mother—their mother—had hidden in the cave.

A mother and father were supposed to protect their children.

If they couldn't protect their children, they shouldn't have any. No, she wasn't going to change her mind. She'd never breed for the overlords.

When Consternation headed up the line for a second time, Repentance dug her elbow into Sovereign's side. "For the love of Providence, don't keep him in anticipation," she whispered. She was feeling sicker by the minute and didn't know how much longer she could hold on.

And then Sovereign was reciting her vows and Repentance, trying to calm down, studied the audience. Her father sat tall and proud with his family gathered around him—his first daughter about to be buttoned. Her mother wore her ever-present look of contentment. But they were no better at obeying Providence than Repentance was. They were not merciful or honest. It was not merciful to give your first two sons to the cruel, pale-eyed overlords without a fight. Nor was it honest to pretend to be content about it later.

Peace washed over her. She was making the only decision she could make. Surely Providence wouldn't fault her for that.

Applause erupted for a second time and Sovereign and Consternation, beaming at one another, slipped behind the fire.

The drums picked up their volume; the crowd fell silent once more.

Sober Marsh came out, a gray flannel scarf in his hands.

You've rushed into trouble again.
And Providence frowns.
You'll never be free among men.
And Providence frowns.
And Providence frowns.
And Providence always frowns.
~Repentance Atwater, *Slave Cart Compositions*

CHAPTER 3

The peace Repentance had felt only moments earlier fled as quickly as a swamp-slinker on fishing day. Once again the heat and the drums and the dripping fog weighed down heavily.

With his loose, shoulder-length curls scrubbing his collar, Sober danced up the line and down, weaving his gray scarf around the girls.

Repentance, studying him with a sideways glance, was suddenly aware that he was not only five years older than most of the other scarf boys. He was also five years stronger. Maybe he had a bad temper. Maybe he'd kill her.

No, he wouldn't. Two overlord slavers stood in the shadows behind the crowd, dragon sticks at the ready. They wouldn't let Sober kill her. Live slaves were as good as beads in their pockets. Dead slaves were worthless.

She needed to get on with it.

Way back, a provision had been made for a girl who chose

not to button. Such a girl would turn her back on the audience and on the scarf boy, signifying her choice to never button but to go into a life of service to the overlords instead. In refusing to give the overlords her first two sons, she would forfeit herself.

And if the scarf boy happened to be a fifth-year boy? She'd forfeit him, too.

She was sorry about that. But Sober was grown. Much better for him to ride the slave carts than for the babies they'd have if they buttoned. He was a big man. He'd have to look after himself.

Sober wove by her for a third time. She glanced up, mouthed the words, "I'm sorry," and turned her back on him.

A gasp went up from the crowd and for the first time in her life, the incessant dripping of the trees faded from her consciousness. She searched for the familiar sound, but couldn't hear it above the moanings and the groanings of the people.

Someone shrieked—probably Goodwoman Marsh.

Repentance heard her father's voice rise above the din, "It's a mistake, a mistake. She doesn't understand. It's a mistake, a mistake." He kept repeating himself, the words churning in place like a cart wheel stuck in mud.

"No, Father," Repentance whispered toward the fire, "repeating a thing over and over does not make it so."

"Why have you done this?" Sober leaned over her, livid. "You *are* cursed. And now you have cursed me! When did I ever wrong you?"

She offered another prayer, this time asking Providence to let her faint. She couldn't bear their anger. Never mind that she didn't make the rules. Never mind that Providence put them in a swampy hole and forgot them. Never mind that the overlords enslaved them. Never mind all that. With Providence they were content and with the overlords they were resigned, but with Repentance they were angry. Come the morrow, when what she'd done had fully sunk in, she'd be the most hated person in the swamp. They'd all blame her for any sorrow that came their way for the next ten years.

Comfort, her sister, was crying. Wailing.

A weeping and a wailing.

Her mother she did not hear. She was humming to herself, no doubt.

Strong arms lifted her from behind. One of the overlord slavers set her on her feet and prodded her toward the waiting slave cart. Beside her, Sober stumbled, going down on one knee. The slaver grabbed a handful of hair and dragged him up.

Goodwoman Marsh grabbed their captor. "You cannot take him. I've given two sons already. He's all I have left."

The man's fist made a cracking noise as it connected with her face.

Repentance's legs went weak at the awful sound.

Wisdom Marsh hit the ground and lay still. Maybe alive. Maybe dead.

Repentance went numb. Did she kill Goodwoman Marsh?

Sober dove toward his mother.

Repentance twisted against the overlord. His grip tightened. "I've changed my mind," she said. Her words melted, unheard, into the chaos. She tried again, "I want to stay here."

The overlord lifted her and threw her into the slave cart.

Goodman Marsh squatted on one side of his fallen button mate, with Sober on the other side.

One of the overlords pointed his dragon stick toward the sky and pressed the ignition. A fountain of fire, six feet tall, whooshed from the stick, followed by a loud boom.

Repentance threw herself flat in the bed of the cart and covered her head with her arms. When the echo from the explosion subsided, the world was silent.

"As Providence is my witness, I am on the edge of hauling you all away for rioters." The slaver spoke loudly enough to be heard, but softly enough to let them know that he was in complete control. "There are three more couples waiting to be buttoned. Proceed with order or forfeit them to me."

Repentance peered over the edge of the cart. Without a

whisper of complaint, the people pushed themselves off the ground, brushed dirt from their sleeves and stomachs, and faced the remaining button girls. The overlord aimed his dragon stick at Sober's face.

Sober, keeping his gaze on his mother, climbed into the cart.

A drumbeat began. In front of the fire, three rumpled button girls sat, angry tears cutting tracks down their dirty cheeks. Wrathful Mudflat stepped from behind the fire, streaming an ochre scarf.

Repentance scooted close to the overlord who stood next to the cart. "I want to change my mind," she whispered. "Please, may I change my mind?" She had made a mistake. Her mother had always told her that she'd come to no good end if she couldn't learn to be content with her place in the world.

She'd finally done it. She'd come to no good end.

She'd thought through what would happen when she refused Sober, but the reality was so much worse than the way she'd imagined it. "I change my mind," she said a little more loudly.

Sober turned his attention away from his mother. Repentance couldn't see his expression in the dim light, but she could feel him looking at her.

He stood and moved toward her end of the cart. "She wants to change her mind," he said. "She was afraid. She knows better now." Standing in the cart, he towered over the slaver on the ground.

The man pointed his dragon stick at Sober. "Sit!"

He sat. "She wants to button."

The slaver swung the butt end of the dragon stick out, catching Sober on the side of his face. He landed in the bed of the cart like a clubbed catfish.

"Too late," the slaver said to Sober's unmoving body, his cold, pale eyes full of disgust. "She made her choice."

That button ceremony concluded more quickly than any Repentance had been to. The girls grabbed hold of the scarves right away, as if desperate to be buttoned before their scarf boys could change their minds. Less than half an hour later, the crowd dispersed, women keening, men cursing, and Comfort sobbing like a weanling. Wisdom Marsh groaned as men picked her up to carry her to the healing cave.

"Chain them," one of the overlord slavers said to the other before he headed down the road toward the gatehouse.

The man clamped heavy iron shackles to her ankles and chained her to the driver's seat.

Sober moaned and rolled over. He cried out, grabbing his head.

Repentance scooted back into the corner of the cart, making herself small, not wanting to face Sober's wrath.

The slaver pulled a leather pouch from his pocket. "Give me your hand," He said to Sober.

He dumped some powder into Sober's palm. "It's healing powder. Your head will feel better and you'll sleep."

Sober hesitated.

"I'm not going to kill you. You're worth nothing to me dead. Eat the powder."

Sober licked up the powder and lay down in the bed of the cart.

Repentance let out her breath, relieved. She could face him later. After he slept. When his head wasn't hurting so much.

The slaver sat under a tree to keep watch.

They would pull out as soon as it got light enough to see the road. Repentance had watched many carts depart. She was always half afraid for the poor villagers being taken and half excited, wondering what they would see outside the fence that surrounded the village.

Her father came and tried to talk to her during the night, but the watchman warned him off. "The girl has made her choice. Go home and forget her."

Father thanked the man, telling him, loudly. "I'm so thankful that Goodwoman Marsh lives and she will heal. I wanted to tell my daughter about that, and also I wanted to tell her that her mother and I love her. But, of course, I don't want to do anything that breaks the rules, so if I can't talk to my daughter, I'll just go back home. Thank you very much."

Tears welled in her eyes as her father walked away slowly, his shoulders hunched.

The village lay muffled under its thick cloak of fog and Repentance sat in the cart bed, hugging herself and rocking and wondering and worrying.

She jerked awake when they moved out the following morning with two overlords up front and Sober, sleeping still, in the bed of the cart.

Sitting up, she looked to see where they were.

Still inside the fence.

Ahead, people lined the cart trail, as they always did when the slavers pulled out. Only her neighbors hadn't gathered to proclaim their undying love and to encourage her. They usually talked about how brave the poor unbuttoned girls were. Even when they weren't brave. Even when their eyes were red and their noses were swollen from crying all night. Still, the sorrowful villagers called the girls brave.

They wouldn't speak that way about Repentance.

They'd come to curse her.

Women spat as the cart rolled past the first of the onlookers. Children stood ready, balls of mud in their grubby hands.

Sober's father stood in front, straining for sight of his son.

Repentance looked at Sober, asleep in the cart. He wasn't even going to have a chance to tell his father goodbye. She nudged him with her toe, thinking to wake him so he could see his father one last time. Nothing. She pushed harder against him, jerking against the heavy iron shackles clasped onto her ankles.

"She's kicking him, now," the newly buttoned Sovereign Mossybank shouted. "Did you see her kicking at him as he lies injured in the cart?"

Repentance shook her head. "I didn't—" A gob of mud smacked into her chin and splattered into her mouth.

When you've made a bad choice, there's but one thing to do. Welcome the consequences without whining. Mayhap some good will come eventually, but if you're stooping and drooping, looking at your boots and moping in your soup, you won't see the good if it does decide to show up.

~Meticulous Mudslide, *An Old Man Remembers*

CHAPTER 4

With a wild cry, all the boys let loose with their mud. Repentance dodged and ducked, trying to keep from being hit herself and also batting blobs away before they could land on Sober.

A dragon stick exploded from the front of the cart and the mud attack ended immediately. "The next one to throw mud at this cart will come along for a ride," the overlord driver said.

Repentance wiped her muddy hands on her button blouse and scanned the crowd looking for the faces she loved. Her gaze crossed over Goodman Marsh, taking in the pain that was clearly etched into the deep frown lines in his face. He was broken more than angry, and that cut her deeply.

Moving on, Repentance searched for her family

The whispers she'd heard all her life were louder than ever, and they had a new insistence to them.

"Cursed."

"Wicked, selfish, child!"

"May Providence look upon all your days with scorn."

Her gaze flitted past the midwife, who shook her head sadly; skipped over Comfort's scarf boy, Aggravation Mossybank; and finally, she found her sister, in the very back, all alone, sagging against an oak tree. On seeing Comfort with her dark eyes full of anguish and tears, Repentance forgot why it had been so important for her to refuse to button. She wanted to bury her face in her hands and cry, to hide from the reproach and hurt in her sister's look, but she wouldn't. She couldn't turn away. She gazed at Comfort, willing her to forgive. Willing her to be strong and well and happy.

She twisted as the cart went along, keeping her sister in sight as long as she could.

The angry shouts died down as her neighbors fell behind.

Comfort, too, was finally swallowed up in fog.

Numbly, Repentance kept staring toward where she'd last seen her sister, hoping for one more glimpse.

They followed the familiar road down past the healing house at the hot springs where the overlords went when they were ill.

And then came the poisoned river that surrounded the village.

Repentance took a deep breath as the cart pulled onto the barge. A thrill of fear ran through her. She'd finally see what the world looked like on the other side of the river.

It took a half an hour to cross the river. There was no current in the wicked, poisoned water, but it was wide.

Too wide. Repentance had heard tales about villagers who had tried to cross. Their wooden rafts were eaten by the acid in the water long before they could reach the other side.

The barge the slave cart pulled up onto wasn't touching the water. It was hanging over it. And the overlords who ran the barge didn't dip any paddles into the water. They pulled the barge across with pulleys and ropes.

The cart bumped off the barge and Repentance looked around with a sense of disappointment. For some reason she had thought that things would look different on the far side of the river.

Maybe it had been the pictures she'd seen in her schoolbooks. She'd imagined that all the world outside her village would be sunny, but even after the river was an hour behind them, all that lay on either side of the road was foggy swamp.

Mud and marsh.

The cart swished along the sandy track, harness leather creaked, and the foggy, fuzzy world slipped by. Exhausted, sorrowful, and lulled by the swaying and swishing, Repentance lay down next to Sober and slept.

Some time later the sun woke her. She groaned and stretched. Every bony place ached from being bumped arou—

The sun! The sky!

Repentance lay still and gazed at the huge blue dome above her. She got dizzy staring at it. Not a wisp of fog. And cool air. She breathed deeply. The pictures of blue skies and sunshine in her schoolbooks didn't come close to the real thing. She sat up, threw her head back, and stretched her arms to embrace the sky.

"Is it worth it?" Sober, sitting behind her, sounded bitter.

She turned. One side of his face was swollen and purple. She dropped her hands and bowed her head. He couldn't understand. She didn't really understand it herself, but she somehow felt as if she'd been made for the sunshine and the crisp, cool air. "I think I might have died if I'd stayed in the swamp," she whispered.

"Well, how nice that you have escaped then. How nice for you."

Anger flared, making her cheeks hot. "I didn't do this so I could escape that Providence-forsaken swamp. I would have stayed forever under those drizzling trees if I could have. Do you think I would have hurt my sister, simply because I wanted to see the sun?"

"I didn't think it yesterday, obviously. But today? Yes, I think you're capable of the most harsh and unfeeling acts."

Her anger melted into a messy puddle of shame under his reproach. "I'm sorry, Sober. I never wanted to hurt you. I didn't know my father was negotiating with you. If I'd known I would have told him I was never going to button and breed. By the time I found out it was too late for you. All the other button girls were taken." She looked him steadily in the eye. She owed him an explanation. "Since the day the overlords took my brother, Tribulation, I've been glad to know that all the boys in the village thought I was cursed. I was sure none of them would button me, and that was fine with me. I couldn't bear to button and breed sons to be given to the overlords. How was I to know you would pay over beads for me? I never expected any such thing."

"You have destroyed my family and yours. You've—" he choked on his words. "You've killed my mother, probably." He turned sideways, leaned back, and closed his eyes as if the sight of her was more than he was willing to bear.

He didn't want to talk to her? Fine! Then she wouldn't bother telling him what she knew about his mother.

But no. He wasn't to blame any more than she was. They were both trapped by the overlords. She looked at Sober's swollen face and winced. He should hate the overlords, not her. They were the ones who hit his mother. They were the ones who ran the slave carts. But she didn't blame him for his anger. "Your mother lives," she said.

Sober twitched but didn't open his eyes.

"My father came in the night and told me she would heal."

No answer.

While she'd slept the sandy track they'd set out on had been replaced by a hard-packed roadway, which wound up a mountain.

As sick and sorrowful as Repentance was, she couldn't keep herself from looking at the world she'd so long wondered about.

Meadows full of wildflowers, in vivid reds and blues and purples, lined both sides of the road. Repentance had never seen so much color at one time. Here and there trees gathered in small clumps, splashing puddles of shadow across the grassy slopes. Oh, Providence was good after all. He had not made an ugly world. He had made beauty and light. In such a world, even Repentance might learn to be content.

The sun was not quite at the top of the sky when buildings came into view. Barns made of tan and red stone squatted behind a low stone wall. In corrals outside the barns, horses nodded and snorted as the cart rolled past. One, a comical, knob-kneed colt, shied and tripped over his own gangly legs. Repentance couldn't stop smiling. How her little brothers would laugh at the baby horses wobbling about. And Comfort ... oh, how Comfort, with her artist's soul, would love to see sun on satiny flanks. She would so enjoy the lights and the shadows in this mountain world.

At the thought of Comfort, her heart clenched as if a dried hook briar was twisting into the middle of her chest.

Repentance swallowed hard, and prayed.

When the cart came to a breach in the wall, they turned into a wide drive, which circled around in front of a big building also made of red and tan stone. The driver halted the horse at the front steps where two uniformed men waited.

"Hancock from Hot Springs," the driver said to the men, as he and the slaver jumped from the cart.

One man nodded. "Yes sir. Will you need your wagon now, or will you be stopping for lunch?"

"Lunch." The driver took off his hat and wiped his forehead with a kerchief. Repentance stared. In the fog, overlord hair always looked dull and had a grayish cast, but in the sunlight it looked golden.

"Transfer the slaves and guard them," the slaver said, dropping several beads into the servant's hand before following the driver into the building.

Repentance turned her attention to the servants. They wore hats, but she could see black hair underneath. And their eyes were brown.

The shorter of the two headed toward the barns.

The cart lurched forward as the other man led the horse to a water trough, which stood on the side of the drive. The horse drank while the man rubbed his neck and whispered to him in a soothing voice. After a minute the man threw Repentance an uncomfortable glance. "What you looking at? I've grown horns atop my handsome head?"

He *was* handsome and Repentance blushed at being caught staring. "It's just that ... just that ... you're not an overlord," she stammered.

"What's it to you?"

"But you're not a slave. I saw the overlord pay you."

"Even slaves can earn beads if they work hard."

"Really?" That was hopeful news. "Can a slave earn enough to buy his freedom? How long have you worked here?"

"Buy his freedom!" The man laughed. The horse finished drinking and nuzzled him with a sloppy, wet face. "We've lived here all our days prior, and we'll live here forever after, won't we Bargess, old man?" he said patting the animal. "There's never freedom for a slave. But we can't complain, can we old man? For we've a kind master as compared with some." Looking back at Repentance, he added, "Leastways, I'd much rather be down here than in the ice city where some are headed, and that's speaking straight."

At mention of the ice city, the collar of her button blouse suddenly felt too tight. Repentance tugged at it. "What's an ice city?"

"A city made of ice. What else?"

Repentance had never seen ice. She'd read about it in school. Frozen water. It was said to be very cold.

"What's wrong with the ice city?"

"I'll give you a trickle of advice, young babbler, 'cause I hate to see any living thing suffer no matter how ignorant it is. Talk a lot less, and you'll do a lot better in the ice city. Or anywhere else, for that matter." He turned his attention back to Bargess, the horse, rubbing his nose and crooning to him, obviously done with Repentance, the babbler.

"There's a good, old, tired fellow," he said. "Don't you fret. I'll fix you up with a bag of hot oats." The horse whickered, and the man purred. "That's right. I give you my word, old man, and you know when Rebuke says a thing, his word is as strong as a steel bit."

Sober, who had appeared to be ignoring everyone, gave a small gasp. "Rebuke? What's your back name?"

"None of your concern."

"I have a brother named Rebuke. Rebuke Marsh."

Repentance caught the man's look of surprise, but he quickly pulled down a mask of indifference. "That can't be me, can it?" he said. "I've lived here since I were a wee colt. I've never had me a Mam, nor a Pap, nor any brothers or sisters."

Looking from Rebuke to Sober, Repentance saw that both men had the same chin—square and dimpled. Rebuke's eyes were round while Sober's tilted up slightly at the outer corners, but Repentance remembered that Goodman Marsh had round eyes, too. The noses clinched it. They were identical, leaning a little to the left as they did. She finished studying them and gasped. This was Sober's brother. And ... what about her brothers? If Sober's brother was here— "Do you know any boys named Tribulation or Devastation?" she blurted out.

Rebuke glared at her. "If you've lost boys, let it lie. If you didn't keep track of them when they were babies, you hardly have a right to ask after them now."

Her cheeks burned as she remembered Tribulation calling out to her. She had done nothing to save him.

Bargess shifted and the cart jerked forward, as the other servant returned, driving a wagon that was half the size of their long-bed slave cart. Repentance shifted her attention from Rebuke to the new wagon. There was nothing to drive in the smaller wagon—no horses—and no wheels. It skimmed along just above the ground. Repentance had never seen anything like it. She looked at Sober to see what he made of it.

He seemed unaware of its arrival—his eyes were trained on Rebuke's face. "Our parents loved you," he said softly. "They didn't give you up easily. It's not like they set you down outside one day and forgot where they put you."

Color flamed in Rebuke's cheeks, and a look of longing

31

came and went, very quickly. Then he said loudly to the wagon driver. "You can always tell the ones fresh out of the swamp, eh, Woeful? So talkative."

"Is that how you tell?" Woeful gave an exaggerated sniff and waved his hand in front of his nose. "I always thought it were the smell as gave them away." He laughed and added, "Calling them *fresh* out the swamp is not really speaking straight, is it?"

"How can you make fun?" Repentance demanded. "We're slaves. Just like you."

"I'm never like you." He gave her a hard look. "There's slaves," he gestured toward himself and Rebuke, "and then there's swamp scum." His glare traveled from Repentance to Sober and back again.

Then his look went from angry to slimy. "Of course *you* may do well in the ice city, little girl. Once they scrub the stink from you. You'll not be sold as a seamstress or milkmaid, I'll judge."

The greedy look on his face made Repentance feel like she'd fallen into the scummy end of the swamp.

Woeful jumped down from the wagon and approached the slave cart. "Rich overlords will line up to exchange beads for an hour in your bed, or I'm a blind man."

He climbed up on the wagon wheel and grabbed her by one wrist. "How about you come with me and let me teach you how to give them good value for the beads they put on your pillow?"

Carefully chosen routes don't always bring one to the desired destination. Ruts, washouts, and armed men are but a few of the things that may waylay or divert the weary traveler. Worse still is to get to your map's end only to find that the promises of riches, far out-spoke the reality.

~Babbcocc the Cartographer, *Journal of My Journeys*

CHAPTER 5

Repentance yanked her wrist back, but the slave tightened his grip.

"I'll break you in, little filly," he said.

"I don't need to be broken in, thanks all the same." Her heart was beating like a herd of stampeding hogs.

He laughed. "Already been ridden a time or two, eh? No matter. One hour with me and I'll break you of the bad habits the ill-bred swamp boys have taught you."

Rebuke placed a friendly arm around the man's shoulders. "Hold yourself back, now. We've been paid good beads to guard these two."

Repentance yanked on her wrist. Yes, she belonged to the overlords. Surely a slave wouldn't dare—

"Right you are." Woeful shrugged off Rebuke's arm. "But I got a burning in my loins what's worth all the beads in your pocket."

"Oh, I can give the beads back, I guess," Rebuke said. "You

think that will satisfy the slavers? Or do you think they'll beat us and take us from our master, and sell us on the slave dock, if we damage their property?"

"Damage her? Rebuke, my boy, I don't intend to damage her. I plan to educate her and increase her worth. It's likely the overlords will reward me for my services." He made to step into the cart.

"Besides," he added, "the overlords need never know. Who's going to tell them? The girl? They won't listen to a word she says."

He released his grip slightly as he spoke, and Repentance wrenched her wrist free. She scooted all the way back in the cart, bumping into Sober.

He moved to the side, slipping out from behind her. "You chose this life, *little filly*," he said angrily.

Rebuke grabbed Woeful from behind, taking hold of his collar and his belt. He hauled him to the water trough and dumped him in. "As payment for saving your life, I'll keep your share of the beads."

When Woeful began a protest Rebuke shoved his head under the water. "None of that noise, now. You're upsetting Bargess."

Woeful climbed out of the trough, dripping and sputtering. "I've got but one change of clothes," he said, the pitch of his voice rising to a whine.

"Thank Providence for that, then," Rebuke replied, and he shooed the little man away.

Turning his attention to Sober and Repentance, he said, as he unlocked their ankle shackles. "Into the skim wagon, then, and not one word do I want from either of you. I've done my good deed for the day. You'll get no more from me than that."

In the quiet, a dark dread seeped into Repentance's heart like fog slipping into a hollow.

She gazed desperately out past the barns and prayed. Oh, please Providence. If only she didn't have to go to the ice city. If only she could work for a kind master and live in a sunshiny meadow dappled with shadows and dotted with wildflowers.

She could learn to be content as a slave. She *would* learn.

If only.

The overlords came from their lunch, sat up on the cushioned front seat of the skim wagon, and the journey continued up the mountain. There were no horses and the driver guided the wagon using a stick that came up from the floor. Repentance and Sober bounced along on the hard bench in the open back bed of the wagon.

As they went up the road, the slavers passed a canteen back and forth. Repentance's stomach rumbled and her mouth watered at the sweet smell that escaped the uncorked canteen. No one offered her anything to drink, though.

No matter. She looked over the side of the wagon and feasted her eyes on the colors of field and sky.

They skimmed up the mountain, passing several side roads. A few other skim wagons passed them going down. They also saw wagons pulled by horses and, as they got higher up the mountain, some pulled by yaks. Repentance counted fifteen farms, some with goats grazing, some with workers tending crops. In the afternoon, shaggy meadows of wildflowers and cultivated fields alike, gave way to a rolling carpet of snow, which sparkled like sugary frosting on a birthday cake. Repentance had never seen anything so clean and bright.

"Close your worthless swamp eyes halfway," the driver said over his shoulder, "else you'll be blind inside of an hour." He and his partner pulled the brims of their hats down, but kept their pale eyes wide open.

The overlords wrapped themselves in blankets. Repentance shivered in her thin swamp clothes. She glanced back at Sober, her teeth chattering. He sat on the floor of the wagon with his arms wrapped across his chest.

After a time, the sun slid behind jagged mountains on the left, painting the snowy ridge on the right with a peach-colored brush as the sky faded from blue to pink to pearly gray. Repentance, in spite of being numb from cold, stared at nature's canvas in bliss. The driver stopped the skim wagon in a field beside a small, stone cabin. "Perfect timing, as always," he said, glancing at the nub of sun still visible between two peaks.

"Chain them," the slaver said over his shoulder as he headed for the cabin, apparently unimpressed by the driver's punctuality.

"There's no chance they'll make it down the mountain if they run," the driver said. "Not in this cold."

The slaver turned around, his hand on the doorknob. "But they may be foolish enough to try, and frozen corpses bring no beads on the slave market, do they?"

The steel bands of the shackle burned into Repentance's ankle when the driver clamped it on. She cried out.

"Use the blanket," the man growled. He threw a scrawny piece of material over her. "Better drink something, too." He tossed a canteen so that it fell between Repentance and Sober.

Sober grabbed it up and sucked down a long draft.

Repentance waited.

Finally he finished drinking and she held out her hand. He shook his head and tucked the canteen under his leg.

She gaped at him. What a warthog! But he was too big to fight and it would be pointless to beg. Fine. If he wouldn't share the drink, she wouldn't share the blanket.

As she had done the night before, Repentance again turned her back on Sober Marsh.

She scrunched under the blanket, cocooning her body against the cold. The strange material was thin but heat radiated from it, like steam rising from the hot springs, and within a minute she was all toasty—even her shackled ankle.

She turned over to lie on her back and saw, for the first time in her life, stars sprinkled across the darkening sky. She gasped. Let

Sober keep the canteen if it made him feel better to punish her. She didn't need to drink. She was drunk on the beauty of the night sky, the nectar of Providence, Himself.

On his side of the wagon, Sober shivered.

He blew on his fingers.

He rolled over.

He scrunched up in a ball.

His teeth chattered.

Repentance sighed. She couldn't let him freeze. "Lie over here."

He hesitated.

"I'll share the blanket with you."

He didn't move.

"Your choice," she said. "Either share or go without. You're not getting it from me to keep for yourself."

He stared at her, maybe trying to decide if he should take the blanket by force.

"You can stop blaming me," she said. "You had five chances to button and you failed every one. I shouldn't have to take all the blame simply because I was the last to turn you down."

He didn't answer. He lay on his side of the cart, his teeth chattering like woodpeckers.

"You hate me so much? Didn't you hear the overlords? They said this cold doesn't just feel bad. It can kill you. You'd rather die than share the blanket?"

He scooted over next to her.

She covered him with one side of the blanket.

After a minute his shivering stopped. A moment later the canteen landed beside her face.

"Did it ever occur to you that I wasn't trying to get buttoned the first four years?" Sober asked. "Did you stop to think that I might have been waiting for someone?"

She took a swig from the canteen. Milky, frosty liquid ran down her parched throat. "Oh, that's rich," she whispered.

"That's rich? That's all you have to say?" He turned his back to her and pulled the blanket up over his shoulder.

Repentance took another drink. What was Sober carrying on about? Her heart gave a little trip and stumbled against her ribs. He'd waited for her?

She glanced over at his back, solid and unmoving. No. He was waiting for someone else. He only settled for Repentance when his true love turned him down. Still, the fact that he'd waited for someone *was* kind of romantic.

She drank again. And again. And then she lay down to let the stars lull her to sleep and when she slept she dreamed a gray flannel scarf swirled around her like a thick fog. It wrapped around her nose and mouth, smothering her.

The next day Repentance and Sober rode side by side, the blanket wrapped around their shoulders. The slavers gave them a little to drink. Nothing to eat.

The scenery was not as varied as the day before. Snow. Lots of it.

The wagon swerved and jostled Repentance against Sober. Without looking, he gave her a shove with his shoulder.

"Sorry," Repentance said. "At least the skim wagon is not bumpy like the cart was. How do they make this thing go with no horses, though?"

"Sunlight," Sober answered.

"How can sunlight make a wagon move?"

"I don't know how. All I know is that I saw four men pushing this wagon from a dark barn and the minute it got out into the sunlight, it began to hover, like a dragonfly over water. Then, last night when the sun went down, the wagon set itself down on the ground."

"You saw it being pushed out from the barn? But you weren't looking. You were talking to Rebuke."

"I'm not blind, Repentance, or stupid, much as that may

surprise you."

"I never said you were stupid."

He threw her a scathing look.

She quit arguing. He was right. She did think that all the people in her village who were content to keep breeding slaves for the overlords were stupid.

The wagon wound its way up the mountain. Several times it rounded curves and revealed something ahead, glinting in the sun. The overlord city of ice.

The sun was still high when they drew close enough to see the city sticking out of the fold between two mountain peaks.

"Behold your new home," the slaver said over his shoulder. "You will work there in Harthill until you drop and die."

The city shimmered, all silver and shine. Repentance shielded her eyes, as she stared at the peaks and spires poking the sky. They drew closer and saw houses with thick walls of white, blue, and purple ice and with windows made from thin, clear slices.

And this was the city of the overlords—they lived in such beauty but had hearts full of mud and muck. She shook her head, amazed.

Around the city ran an ice wall some ten feet high and several feet thick. The wagon pulled to, at a wooden gate. "Slaves, failed at buttoning," the driver called up to the guard on watch.

Once inside they followed a narrow road clotted with carts and wagons and overlords walking. The road was cut between houses of ice. On the outskirts, small, two-storied houses overlooked the lane. As they progressed the dwellings grew taller and finer, with towers and pinnacles and with intricately carved walls.

Half an hour after entering the city, they came into a deserted square at the center of which stood a frozen fountain—a wild spray of blue and green and purple ice. Off to one side of this fanciful sculpture was a wooden frame upon which three bodies hung. The bodies were slave men. No ... they were boys. Younger than Sober. The eyes had been burned out and the fingers and toes cut off. The bodies, stiff and gray, hung naked but for thin loincloths.

Repentance stared without understanding what she was looking at. They looked like real people, but they couldn't be. What could boys have done to make the overlords kill them in such a gruesome fashion?

No, they couldn't be real.

She looked from the ice fountain to the boys and back again. What was wrong with the overlords that they would want bodies, fake or not, hanging in their sparkling city?

The driver halted the wagon right beside the wooden frame.

A drip sounded.

One drip.

Repentance looked around. There was nothing wet or drippy in the frozen city.

Another drip.

Her gaze darted toward the sound. The next drip splashed into a reddish-brown spot, which stained the ice under the foot of the boy nearest to her.

The horror dawned. The boys were real. And they were not long dead for the blood in one had not yet frozen.

The little bit of drink Repentance had been thanking Providence for all morning, roiled in her stomach, threatening to come up.

The slaver shoved the first corpse with his dragon stick. It swung over and bumped into the second, which, in turn, bumped into the last. "You see these things that used to be slaves?"

Repentance bent her head down refusing to look.

"Get an eyeful, girl." The slaver pointed his dragon stick at her.

She lifted her head but lowered her eyes, trying to veil the evil sight. The ropes creaked as the boys swayed.

"This is what becomes of any who think they can cheat us by running away," the slaver said. "We catch the runners and we hurt them and we hand them over to the swingman. After that we go down and take their family into service." He paused, maybe wanting to let his words sink in.

Repentance couldn't really hear him. Her ears were filled with the dirge that the ropes were playing. What she wouldn't give for the sound of the swamp—the whisper of insect wings, frogs plunking into water, her mother's constant humming—she would welcome any of those noises. Anything to drown out the creaky, screaky sound of dead boys on ropes.

Washed and dressed, polished and pressed,
    the mistress has spit on me and offered me up for sale.
Good or bad, happy or sad,
    which master will bid on me, with bead-strings in his pail?
       ~Repentance Atwater, *Slave Cart Compositions*

CHAPTER 6

Horrified, sick from hunger, and achy from the long ride, Repentance dropped over the side of the wagon. Sober landed beside her, massaging the small of his back. The overlord slaver led the way across the courtyard toward a building on the north side.

Desperate to escape the gruesome square with its dead boys, Repentance stumbled after the man, moving as fast as her trembling legs would take her.

They entered the building through a wooden door set on metal hinges, which were frozen into an ice doorjamb. Repentance was surprised to feel a wave of heat as she passed through the door. She stopped for a moment to let her eyes make the adjustment from the blinding-white of the courtyard to the gloomy interior of the building.

Sober plowed into her from behind, knocking her off her feet.

Her knees and hands sank into a plush carpet from which

radiated warmth.

"Enough nonsense!" the slaver said, as he grabbed a handful of hair and yanked her up.

She clenched her teeth to keep from screaming.

"Two from Hot Springs for processing," their keeper told a man sitting behind a desk just inside the door.

"Name?" The man looked up at Repentance. Then he glanced over at Sober. "A boy and a girl? What's their crime?"

"Failed buttoning," the slaver answered.

"How can you fail a buttoning when you have one of each available?"

The slaver laughed. "She refused him."

The desk clerk looked at Repentance again, his eyes large behind round glasses. "Not too bright, then, eh?" He didn't wait for her to answer. "Name?" he asked for the second time.

"Repentance Atwater," she whispered.

The man spun his chair around to face a bank of file cabinets. Cabinets made from some honey-colored wood Repentance didn't recognize and polished to a high gloss. Because of the heat in the room, Repentance expected to see a few drips running down the ice wall behind the cabinets, but it was smooth and dry.

The clerk stood and pulled out the top-most cabinet drawer on the left. "Atwater, Atwater, ah, here you are. Repentance Joyous Forgiveness Abounding Atwater?"

She nodded.

"Hmmm, fancy name. Maybe that's why you can't think too well. Brain gets a little tired carrying around such a heavy name, no doubt." He chuckled, as he pulled several sheets of parchment from the file and shoved them across the desk. "Take them into the first room on your left. The attendant will help you."

Repentance looked back at Sober as she pushed through the door. He was the last familiar thing in the world, and all of a sudden she was terrified to let him go. He wasn't looking at her; he was talking to the clerk. The door swished closed, blocking him from view.

43

"Come along then, child," someone said.

Repentance turned from the door to face the attendant. She was not an overlord. Her dark hair and eyes pegged her for a slave.

"Take your clothes off," she said. "Put them in the basket there to be burned."

Repentance took her parchment book and char-stick from her pocket and unbuttoned her britches with fat, numb fingers. Her mind felt as sluggish as her fingers. She couldn't stop thinking about the dead boys swinging outside.

"Hurry up, child. I've not got time to dally with you."

"I'm going as fast as I can." She yanked her blouse over her head. The thought that leaving the swamp had been a terrible mistake crawled into her heart and settled down like a holler frog digging into a mud bank for winter. Cold and heavy.

She tossed her blouse in the basket. It landed with the heart-shaped button on top. Fishing the blouse back out, she asked in a trembling voice, "May I save my buttons?"

The lady squinted at the blouse Repentance held. "You have a button blouse? You thought you were going to be buttoned?"

"It's a long and tiresome tale."

The attendant reached into her pocket and pulled out a small pair of scissors.

Repentance snipped off her three gray buttons. She'd keep them to remind her of why she left. Gray buttons to remind her of her gray home and the gray tunes her mother hummed and her baby brothers' gray faces as the overlords carried them off. If she hadn't left, she'd have drowned in the gray.

"Where are you from?" the attendant asked.

"Hot Springs." She handed back the scissors.

"I'm from Crooked Crick, myself," the woman said. "But it's been many years since I've been there." She directed Repentance toward a sunken pool in the middle of the room.

Repentance crossed the floor, this one covered in thick, red carpet, and stepped into the pool. Three steps down. She sat on a shelf, steaming water lapping at her neck. "What brought you up the mountain?" she asked the attendant. The woman seemed friendly enough. Not like Rebuke and Woeful.

The attendant laughed causing two deep dimples to form in her cheeks. "What brings anyone up the mountain? The slave wagon, of course. Ain't no other way to get up here, is there?"

"What did you do to be taken by the slavers?"

"No one to button. Short on boys, our village was. Tilt your head back, now. If I don't get the dirt off, you'll not fetch a high price at market. And then it's the strap for my back." The woman poured water over Repentance's head, and followed that with a healthy dollop of sweet smelling soap, which she worked through her hair. "Hey, now, what's this?" she asked scrubbing at a spot on Repentance's neck just behind her left ear.

"Ow! Leave a little skin if you're willing."

"You've got some smudges of dirt here that don't want to come off."

"Not dirt. That's a birthmark and it's not coming off no matter how hard you scour. Would you please stop?"

The woman bent to look. "Ah, a birthmark," she muttered. "An unfortunate blemish, but with a fortunate placement, anyway. No one will see it. That's alright, then." She set in again, scrubbing Repentance's scalp.

They didn't like birthmarks on the mountain? Repentance didn't want to ask. She was happy the attendant had quit scrubbing her neck raw and didn't want to set her off again. A tremor went through her, though, at the thought of how ignorant she was of the ways of the mountain. Birthmark blemishes and skim wagons and ice cities. Everything was strange and dangerous.

"You're trembling, poor child," the attendant said. "I'll tell you what I tell every new girl what gets off the slave wagon all big-eyed and shaking. Work hard. Obey your master. You'll be fine as a sunny day in Harthill Square."

Repentance remembered the three bodies swaying on the frame not fifty feet outside the building. "And don't run away, right?"

"What's that?"

"Work hard, obey your master, and don't run away."

"Oh well, that goes without mention. Don't never run away. It's the swing frame for the runners."

Suddenly Repentance was filled with an urge to run. Suddenly she realized it was not the fog that she'd been choking on down in the village. It was the fact that she was owned by the overlords. She could never be content under their rule, whether she was in the swampy village or on a sunny farm. She was going to have to run one day.

She'd found a way out of the swamp and one day she'd find a way out of the ice city. One day she'd live in a sunny meadow with no fog and no overlord rulers.

And no dead boys.

After the bath, she put on a clean flannel nightdress and followed the attendant to a small cell with ice walls a foot thick. The floor was covered in the same heat-producing carpet she'd seen in the rest of the building. Against one wall was a small cot and in the opposite corner, a waste stool. No windows and just the one door.

The attendant left, locking the door behind her, and leaving her in pitch darkness.

Repentance curled up on the cot and pulled the thin, warm blanket around her.

Maybe she wouldn't have to run away. Maybe, by the will of Providence, a kind master would purchase her and she could forget that she was owned and living under the threat of the swing frame. She might get a job on the mountain tending horses or goats. So far she'd met three slaves. Two took care of horses, and one gave baths to other slaves. Those jobs didn't seem so horrid.

She'd made the right decision when she'd chosen not to button with Sober.

She would miss her parents and Comfort and the little boys—she missed them already. Missing them made a gaping hole inside her. She crossed her arms over her chest and pressed as hard as she could, trying to squeeze out the emptiness, but it didn't help.

All alone in her dark cell she found no distractions from the fears and no strength to hold her tears back. She broke down—rocking herself and sobbing and wishing for her mother. But she had no mother to hum and to hush and to promise that Providence would make it all turn out right in the end.

Later, after the sobbing had slowed into heavy, lip-trembling sighs, she dried her face on her blanket. She felt better. No, she felt empty, not better. But now that she had the cry out of her system, she would *get* better.

In the pocket of her nightdress she found her three gray buttons and worked them around in her fingers so they clicked against each other. They almost sounded like water dripping from trees. *Click, click, click.*

She had done the right thing. *Click.* She would get a good master. *Click.* She'd had no choice. She'd done the right thing. *Click, click, click.* She'd get a good master.

Somewhere in the back of her mind she heard a little voice say, "No, Repentance, repeating a thing over and over does not make it so."

Her windowless cell was as dark as ever when a rattle at the door woke her. A slave boy entered with a bowl of thin soup. Warm water, really, with half a potato in it. It tasted like muddy creek water, but she was too hungry to care. The boy left a lamp with her, so she could see to eat. The strange lamp had a clay base that looked like a bowl, and in the bowl was a cloth that shone with yellow light. She poked at the cloth with her spoon, expecting flames to shoot up from underneath. No, the cloth itself shone with light, and the base of the lamp was an ordinary bowl.

She had seen something like this long ago. In the swamp. The day the overlords took Tribulation. She was still examining the lighted cloth when an old slave woman, her brown face as wrinkled as a dried pear, came for her.

"Come. Time to dress."

She was given another bath, scrubbed with sweet soap, and after that lathered with buttery balm that smelled of mangoes and melons. For a moment, as the old attendant massaged the balm into her arms and legs, Repentance relaxed and dreamed that the woman was her old-mother—her mother's mother who was always gentle, not her father's mother who was prone to crankiness and impatience. She dreamed that her old-mother was washing and dressing her, preparing her to be guest of honor at a grand feast.

The slave dried and brushed her thick hair until it shone then piled it up on her head with ringlets dripping down. "Interesting color," she said. "When it's clean and brushed it's almost more like overlord hair than lowborn."

The old woman stripped her of the towel she was wrapped in and draped a robe of heavy, maroon velvet around her. Repentance ran her hands down the cloth. She'd never felt anything so soft. Instead of buttons, the robe had strings set at regular intervals. The old woman moved from top to bottom, tying the robe, but leaving gaps so skin could peek through and the smell of body lotion could escape.

"Beautiful," she declared when she was done. "You'll go for the refreshment of royalty I'll wager. I wouldn't be surprised if Lord Fawlin himself took you ... If he were able, I mean."

Repentance shivered. "Lord Fawlin is still alive?"

"You heard that he was ill? He rarely makes it to market anymore. Mayhap his nephew will buy you."

"Lord Fawlin, the king? He's not dead?" Repentance couldn't believe it. She knew her history, and Lord Fawlin was the king who had enslaved her people two hundred and fifty years earlier. Surely he wasn't still alive.

"No, he's not dead. Nearly died many years ago. Went down to the hot springs for a cure and came back in a deep sleep. Doctors could not wake him. But he come out of that dreamland of his own strength and by the grace of Providence, and he's lived all these years. Not much of a man, though, if you get my meaning. Not able to keep a button mate or a concubine. So say those what whisper about such things."

"He's lived for two hundred and fifty years?" That must be why the overlords were able to keep the lowborns down, then. They had such long lives. There must be thousands of them. Tens of thousands.

The woman grimaced. "Hold still. You're shaking your curls loose." She reached up to give Repentance's hair a tuck and a pat.

The door of the bathing room burst open. "Merry, are you in here talking?" A tall overlord woman strode in, her long satin skirts swishing along behind her. "I might have known. We wait on the docks for her." She landed a slap on the old slave's face with such force that the woman crumpled to the ground.

Repentance jerked as if she was the one who had been slapped. She reached to help, but the old woman, bowing before the overlord with her forehead to the ground, didn't see the hand Repentance offered.

"Oh, do get out of here before I kick you," the overlord woman said. "You tempt me so when you snivel like that."

The slave scrambled from the room.

The overlord woman turned to Repentance, taking in her outstretched hand, then looking into her eyes. "If you offer help to a slave being disciplined you will receive the same fate." Her glance slid from her face, down her neck, and kept on going. Repentance blushed.

"My name is Madam Cawrocc. I own you. You will obey me."

Repentance nodded. So this was the way Providence answered her prayers for a kind owner. She wasn't surprised.

"Yes, you'll do," the woman said. She moved close to Repentance. "You will not speak. You will drop your eyes out of respect for the buyers. You will hold your chin down. And that blush of yours will do nicely. It makes you look quite innocent and alluring."

She opened the top tie of Repentance's robe and retied it so more skin showed. Then she pushed her over to the counter on the reflecting wall and spritzed her neck and into the top of her robe with water laced with golden dust. After looking Repentance over one more time, she spit on her fingers and smoothed a stray curl into place.

Repentance trembled. There was still the market. Someone would buy her. Surely. She would be respectful to the buyers as Madam Cawrocc had instructed. She would find a woman with kind eyes who needed a nanny for a rosy-cheeked baby. Or maybe a rich old woman who needed a companion to go with her on trips to foreign lands.

"Overlords will line up to pay over their beads for a turn in your bed," Woeful had said. She looked into the reflecting glass and felt like retching. *Please, Providence. A nice old woman in need of a traveling companion.*

Squeeze his muscles, check his teeth,
    lift her skirts and look beneath.
Try his ear, test her eye,
    come on boys, we've a slave to buy!
        ~A slave dock ditty, from *Mountain Lore and Folk Music*

CHAPTER 7

Repentance stepped from the building. Thank Providence, the bodies were gone. The square was flooded with sunshine and overlords, but no dead slave boys. Several living overlord boys played skipball beneath the empty hanging frame.

Keeping her head down and her eyes half closed against the glare of the morning, she followed Madam Cawrocc onto a wide, covered porch. Several slaves were there ahead of her, standing with their backs against posts. Their hands were lashed to the posts, and packets of parchment hung on hooks above their heads.

Sober was there. His glossy curls combed back, away from his face. He was shirtless, but he had his button scarf wrapped around his neck.

Next to him, a girl was staked. She wasn't dressed in a velvet robe. She wore a gold shirt and brown britches with sturdy boots made of leather and sheepskin. There was nothing pretty about the girl. Nothing ugly, either. She was just a girl, unremarkable in every way. When Repentance saw her, a stab of fear ran through her. That girl was going to be her downfall. That girl wasn't meant for the refreshment of royalty. That plain girl would get the job as nanny for the tired mother, or companion for the rich old woman.

Repentance scanned the rest of the slaves. Seven boys, all younger than Sober from the looks of them, stood in long pants, chests bare in the chilly mountain air. Of the nine girls, only one other was richly robed, as Repentance was. The other eight wore working clothes and braids.

Madam Cawrocc handed Repentance over to the dockmaster. "Up front, with this one," she said to him. "Let the poor men wish and the rich men bid."

The dockmaster staked Repentance a couple of posts away from Sober, who was also in the front row. His swollen face had gone down a little, but he still had a purple bruise covering one cheekbone. Guilt flooded over her. For all her fancy dress and sweetly-lotioned skin, she felt as dirty as a pig on slaughtering day.

Sober caught her looking and he nodded as if to say, *Yes, Repentance, it is your fault. Take a good look at your handiwork.*

The sun climbed slowly as buyers came and buyers went. The men buyers strode right up to poke and prod the other girls—to look at teeth and peek into clothing. The women buyers stood to the side and let their brothers or male cousins or servants check the merchandise over. But no one poked at Repentance. With her they were almost shy.

Finally, one man approached, bent close to look at her face. Then he studied her hair and lifted her chin so he could look into her eyes.

She looked back, into the pale overlord eyes, this particular pair, light green and full of lechery.

Her knees went squishy.

"My good, great dragon guano!" the man exclaimed. "I'll be hanged for a runner if your eyes aren't golden. I've never seen such a remarkable color." He shook his head in amazement. He smiled at Repentance.

She didn't smile back. She trained her eyes on one knee of his tan, suede breeches and stood perfectly still, afraid to move. Afraid to breathe.

"And your hair!" He curled a bit of it around one finger. "It's delicious. Such a lovely color. I could almost pretend I was in bed with an overlord woman."

Madam Cawrocc, leaving a customer on the other side of the slave dock, came swiftly, her skirts sweeping the icy deck. "Lord Carrull, I'm so glad to see you today. How is the last girl working for you?"

Glancing over, Repentance found Sober looking her way with a disgusted expression on his face. She hung her head, her cheeks burning.

The overlord man bowed to Madam Cawrocc. "There's not a thing wrong with the last girl, Mertina. Not one little thing. But I've been thinking lately of giving her to my brother-in-law and buying another for myself—I'm hankering for something new."

"Good plan," Madam Cawrocc said. "Let me show you some nice girls over this way." She took his elbow to steer him toward some of the "britches and braids" girls.

He pulled back. "But I like this girl, Mertina."

Madam Cawrocc laughed. "And well you should. You have good taste, and no one can tell me different. However ... " She leaned close. "She's quite out of your price range, my lord," she said quietly. "I fear that few outside of the prince himself will be able to afford this treat."

The man gave an embarrassed giggle. "Oh, yes, I see. I had no idea. Her coloring makes her worth so much, no doubt."

Madam Cawrocc nodded, as she led him away.

Repentance blew out the breath she was holding. But she barely had time to take another breath before she was confronted with another potential buyer.

An enclosed skim carriage pulled up in front of the dock. A woman disembarked and approached. She took Repentance's parchment packet down and flipped through it. "A sister in her fourteenth year? Is she as pretty as you?"

Repentance dropped her gaze and said nothing.

The woman leaned in. "When I ask you a question, you answer."

"I don't know how to address an overlord lady," Repentance said.

"Look at me."

She was beautiful. Creamy skin, pale blue eyes, and silver hair. She smiled displaying a row of straight, white teeth.

"I am no lady," she said. "You are to call me Jadin. That's my name. And you are to answer when I ask a question."

Repentance nodded.

"Is your sister pretty?"

Repentance thought of Comfort, rosy–cheeked and with a constant sparkle dancing in her merry brown eyes. "Not pretty, I'm afraid," she said, without really knowing why she lied. She merely felt a need to protect Comfort from this woman who showed too much interest in pretty slave girls. "An unfortunate birthmark covers half her face."

The woman gave a soft chuckle. "This once, I will let that go. Once, you lie to me and live. Once, because I admire your bravery. A second time and I will think you are stupid and obstinate rather than brave."

She waved the parchment she held. "I have a sketch right here. I cannot easily tell if she is pretty or not, but I can see that she has no birthmark. So then, I assume she is pretty, since you felt the need to lie to make her ugly. That means you have one pretty sister and ... "She paused, looking at the papers again " ... two little brothers. Hmm. Sometimes little boys are wanted. If not, I can always trade them."

Repentance gaped in horror.

Jadin stood back, studying Repentance.

She nodded.

Stepping closer, she examined Repentance's face and looked into her mouth.

Madam Cawrocc swished over. "Jadin! Is she not what I promised?" She tapped the parchment Jadin held. "And this one has a sister."

"Maybe," Jadin said noncommittally.

"She's beautiful! She's perfect!"

"She's alright."

"Alright?" Madam Cawrocc sounded shocked. She began untying Repentance's robe.

Repentance shook her head and tried to back away but the post to which she was tied gave her no room to maneuver.

Madam Cawrocc paid no attention, her hands following Repentance as she moved. "She's worth every bit of 25,000 beads, Jadin, and you know it. There's not a blemish on her entire body." She worked her way down the robe, undoing more and more of the little ties. When she had untied half of them, she pushed the robe back. It slipped down, stopping at the place where Repentance's hands were tied behind her. She stood naked from the waist up before Providence and all the world.

Repentance squealed and hunched her shoulders forward trying to hide herself.

Madam Cawrocc scowled at her. "Stand up straight, girl. How can anyone see your beauty if you slouch over?"

In horror Repentance saw Sober staring. A second later, he looked up at her face, his cheeks flaming, and then he mercifully turned away.

From across the dock Lord Carrull stared, a huge smile plastered across his lecherous face. A buzz of sound and movement penetrated her senses. People seemed to be drawing toward her. Three boys in the square stopped their skipball game and approached the dock.

Jadin laughed. "Look at her blush."

"Yes, quite fetching, isn't it? She's obviously never serviced anyone before. The prince will be pleased, don't you think?"

Jadin reached behind Repentance and took hold of the robe. "What *I* think, is that we need to cover the poor girl up." She hung the robe around Repentance's shoulders and tied the first few ties so it would stay up. "Yes, I'll take her," Jadin said. "Have her sent to me at the Hot Springs healing house."

Repentance gasped.

Jadin glanced over toward the other robed girl. "Two beautiful girls failing at the button ceremonies. Providence smiled on you today, eh, Cawrocc?" She crossed over to inspect the other girl.

Madam Cawrocc finished tying Repentance's robe. "I made a tidy sale," she said. "A tidy sale." She gave Repentance a dirty look. "No thanks to you, what with your whining and hunching over like a deformed troll."

"I'm to go back down to Hot Springs?" Repentance asked.

Madame Cawrocc either didn't hear or chose not to answer. She headed off to convince Jadin of the other girl's worth.

Repentance's knees went weak. She would go back to the fog and the gray. Apparently the healing the overlords sought in her village entailed more than soaking in the hot springs. Apparently it was a brothel of some sort. She'd seen overlord women walking in the woods near the Hot Springs healing house often enough. She'd always assumed they had come down for healing. Maybe they were providing services rather than being served.

This was Providence's idea of a joke, no doubt. She should have known that she could not rebel against her assigned place in life. He had made her a breeder and planted her in a muggy, gray village, and no matter how much she was willing to sacrifice to escape, to the swamp she would return.

She bowed her head. She had given up her beloved Comfort and the sweet, funny, little boys for nothing.

No, not for nothing. She lifted her head and stared defiantly at Jadin's back. She would never have children. She would never have to watch as her bawling weanlings were taken away in the slave carts. The prince wanted refreshment and Repentance understood what that meant. It did not include children. When he was ready for children, he'd leave his concubines behind and button with a royal overlord woman.

An old man—a slave—shuffled across the dock, followed by a fat overlord woman. They stopped by Sober's pole. "He's a big, strong, healthy fellow," the slave said.

He felt Sober's muscles. "Yes, indeed, Providence has smiled upon us this day. I never hoped to find such a fine one after Buttoning Day. Usually them as fail the buttonings are weak or sickly."

"Maybe something else is wrong with him, Calamity," the fat woman said. "I don't want a mean one, remember. Providence knows disciplining the spoiled ones takes so much time and energy, and we're not in a position to spare either commodity just now."

The slave nodded. "That's true, Mistress Merricc."

"What's wrong with his face, then? He's been hit. He's probably disobedient."

The old slave chuckled. "That's nothing on his face, there," he said. "I still remember the day I stood on this dock—what was it?—sixty years ago or thereabouts."

"Yes, Calamity, but there's no need to go back all that way, is there? Can you tell me why his face is bruised or not?"

"As I was saying, Mistress, if you are real big and strong, like this lad is, and like I once was, the slavers hit you even when you never provoke them. They do it to prove to the buyers that you can take a beating. They do it to show that they can mistreat you and you won't hit back." He paused and guided his mistress around the back of Sober's pole. "See his back, here?"

The woman gasped. "Do you mean they beat him like this and he'd done nothing wrong?"

Repentance, horrified, looked over at Sober. The slavers who guarded Hot Springs never beat anyone. They left you alone as long as you minded your own business and didn't try to run away.

Sober lifted his head and Repentance flinched, expecting to see hatred in his eyes. Instead she was met with only sorrow. He held her gaze until she had to look away, as waves of shame and despair crashed over her.

Never is a man so rich that he needs no help from others. Humble yourselves, therefore, and accept the blessing, though it be offered by the hand of a fellow you hate. It's all from Providence, in the end.

~Precepts of Providence, 34.6

CHAPTER 8

Mistress Merricc stood on the slave dock inspecting Sober's back and tut, tut, tutting. "This is not the way. Not the way to treat a man. Are you sure he did nothing to deserve this?"

"This young man is gentle, Mistress," the old slave said. "I'm speaking straight. If he'd hit back when they beat him, he wouldn't be standing here now. They send the ones as hit back over to the fighting ring."

The woman held one hand over her mouth as she continued to stare at Sober's back. "I had no idea."

After a moment, she walked around and faced Sober. "My name's Mistress Merricc. I own a farm down the mountain a ways. Grow a little bit of everything, but potatoes are my bead crop, for the most part."

She paused.

Sober kept his eyes respectfully averted and said nothing.

"I am in need of a young man," Mistress Merricc continued. "My man, here, has gotten old and while I have several other workers, none of them are quick enough to take on the job as overseer."

She paused again. Then sighed. "And I suppose you are not smart enough either. Why do you not look at me when I speak to you?"

"He's not allowed," the old slave, Calamity, said quickly. "Mistress, maybe you'd best leave the talking to me, this being your first time at a slave market and all."

She scowled, but stepped back.

Calamity moved in front of Sober. "Now boy, look at me."

Sober looked.

"I am old and I been a slave on Mistress Merricc's farm for sixty years. I served her father until he died last year. Now I serve her. It's a good place to live. Hard work, good food and never a beating unless you deserve it."

Sober nodded.

"We need a smart man, you understand?"

"Yes, sir," Sober said.

"You smart?"

Sober threw a quick glance at Repentance. "I make my share of bad choices, but I try to gain some wisdom on the other side of each one."

Repentance winced.

The old man cleared his throat. "We'll soon find out how wise you are, young man. Answer me this:

When dragon breath and Harthill meet,
Icy tower, searing heat,
I roll down the city street,
And make my enemies stumble.
What am I?"

"What is that supposed to be, Calamity?" Mistress Merricc asked. "You ask him a riddle to test his intelligence? Wouldn't it be better to ask him how many chignets of potatoes are in a bashful? Or how many beads he'll earn if he grows eighteen bashfuls of potatoes on each of thirty parcels of land? Something along those lines?"

"All due respect, Mistress, but I'm not interested in the boy's mathematical ability. I been here with your daddy many a time buying slaves. Let me do my job."

She held up her hands in surrender and stepped back, again.

Repentance checked Sober's expression trying to see if he knew the answer to the riddle. His face held no emotion as he stared at the ground.

He didn't know.

He had to know.

If Repentance could see Sober on a farm working for Mistress Merricc—she offered up a quick prayer. If he had a fair mistress, he might be able to forgive one day and Repentance might find her load of guilt a little lighter. Besides, he deserved to have a good position on a farm with a mistress that wouldn't beat him. He'd done nothing wrong. He was suffering through no choice of his own.

She stared at Sober, willing him to know the answer to the riddle.

The old slave shifted his weight from one foot to the other.

Mistress Merricc, looking skeptical, opened her mouth as if to speak, but closed it again when Calamity shook his head.

"Give him a trickle of time to work it out, Mistress," Calamity said. "It's good that he pauses. A wise man does not rush."

Repentance tried to work out the riddle herself. When dragon breath and Harthill meet—icy tower, searing heat.

She didn't know what would happen if a dragon breathed on Harthill's towers, because she'd never been around ice. Or dragons, for that matter. Maybe chunks of ice would crack off and crash down onto the street to make men stumble. More likely, rivers of water would flood the streets.

She was so intent on the riddle that she didn't notice the two troopers until they stood in front of her.

The big one set to untying her hands.

Her legs trembled. This was it. She was headed back down the mountain. Back to the gray life. Only her new gray life would be even worse than the old.

She, the one who hated the overlords so much, was destined for their entertainment. If it weren't so sad, it would be funny. It *was* sad, though. The thought of an overlord man touching her, turned her stomach sour.

"Repentance," Sober said.

She couldn't look at him.

"May Providence give you a torch for your right hand and cast a solid path before your feet," he said.

Repentance didn't understand. She heard Sober pronouncing the ancient blessing on her, but it made no sense. He hated her. Didn't he? She glanced up to search his eyes.

He smiled a sad sort of smile.

The trooper, one giant hand encircling her upper arm, yanked her away from her post.

"May thick fog hide you, Repentance," Sober said. Then he turned to look at Calamity and continued, "even as it causes your enemies to stumble."

"You see!" Calamity shouted. "I knew he was a smart one."

"Is he? How do you know?" Mistress Merricc asked.

"Fog, Mistress. The answer to the riddle is fog."

A fat grin spread across her face and her chins wobbled as she nodded.

Repentance reluctantly pulled her gaze away from Sober. He was safe. That was something. And he'd forgiven her. Her heart lifted at the thought. He didn't hate her. She hurried after the trooper trying to catch her body up to the arm he was yanking.

He pulled Repentance off the slave dock and turned into an alleyway which ran beside the building. "Why are we taking this one so early?" he asked.

The other one turned to answer, and Repentance saw that he was missing an ear. "Dockmaster's afraid she'll come to harm," he said. "She's bought and paid for and he don't want anyone messing with her."

Repulsed, Repentance tore her attention off the earless side of his head. It had probably been bitten off in a fight. They were no better than animals.

The trooper yanking on her arm smiled at—no, he leered—at her. "Who's the lucky fellow with the pocket full of beads?"

"The pocket that *was* full of beads, you mean. His pocket is a trickle lighter after paying for this one, I can guarantee."

"Whose pocket are we discussing?"

The big trooper tripped on a crack in the ice. He jerked her arm while regaining his balance and Repentance cried out.

"Careful with her," Earless said. "She's going to the whore house ... I mean the healing house at Hot Springs, but I don't think Jadin bought her for regular service. I hear this one is reserved for the prince himself."

"Yoiks!" The big one jerked away from her as if her arm had become a hot coal. "I hope I haven't left a mark."

"Your life's not worth two beads if she's bruised."

Repentance rubbed her sore arm and shoulder. If it wasn't for the bit about the prince, she wouldn't mind going back. She hated the gray swamp but from the healing house she might be able to catch glimpses of Comfort and the little boys every now and again. And she wouldn't have to worry about having sons. Ever. She could almost make herself feel glad about her fate.

Almost.

Except for the prince.

If Providence was fair He wouldn't send her to the healing house.

Was he fair? Every fiber of her lowborn soul screamed the answer. Providence favored the overlords. She could expect no help from Him. If she was to escape the prince, she had to find her own way. She dropped her hand into her pocket and worried her buttons around in her fingers as she considered her situation.

It came down to making a choice, really. She could walk docilely along beside the troopers and let them take her down to the fog, down to Jadin, down to the prince. And she'd be no better than the girls in the swamp, breeding for the overlords like a herd of dumb cows.

Or she could run.

The troopers were afraid to bruise her. What could they do if she ran? They wouldn't dare beat her as they had done to Sober.

She dropped the buttons, extracted her hand from her pocket, and picked up the skirt of her robe. She didn't know what kind of distraction she was looking for, but when it came, she'd be ready.

If they caught her—and they probably would—what then?

She saw in her mind's eye the dead boys on ropes and shuddered.

Determined, she clutched her skirts tighter. She'd rather die than entertain an overlord prince.

She tested the ground, dragging her feet, trying to slide. The ice was dry and sticky. Fine for running. She took that as affirmation from Providence that her plan was a good one.

Halfway down the block, the troopers stopped next to a skim carriage, this one very different from the open-bedded wagon that had carried her up the mountain. She climbed in to find cushioned seats covered with buttery-soft, warm material. She sank into the seat by the door. The troopers took places up front—the big one, moving levers, sat looking out the wide, front window, and Earless, holding his dragon stick at the ready, sat by the side window.

The carriage lifted off the icy street and set off with a whisper. Repentance pulled aside the curtain and peered out. As they turned into an alley in back of the slave market and approached an intersection, a boy darted from behind a stairway, screeching.

Both troopers tensed. The driver banked to the right while Earless took aim. A second boy charged out from a gate across the alley, hitting the first boy with ice pellets shot from the muzzle of a toy dragon stick.

Earless cursed, but relaxed. "Get on out of here, you alley dogs," he shouted out his side window. "You came this close to losing your heads this day."

The next street their narrow alley crossed was a wide, busy thoroughfare. The driver stopped the wagon. Repentance blinked at the sunny scene. A man on one corner played a mountain pipe, a bowl in front of him. Men walked by, few stopping to give the man any attention at all. Some women stood, swaying to the music. One, her hair tucked into a fur-lined hood and her body sheathed in a velvet cloak, dug in a handbag, extracted some beads, and dropped them into the bowl.

Skim carts of varying shapes and sizes sped up and down the street, swishing back and forth to pass one another. The movement made Repentance dizzy. She'd never seen so many people at one time.

One wagon seemed to be disabled just in front of her alleyway. It blocked the street partially. Two men lay next to it, studying the underside. A tendril of smoke twisted out from underneath on the street side.

Repentance's driver leaned out his side window. "Move that pile of dragon dung! I'm on the king's business."

One of the men crawled out from under the disabled wagon and approached. "Sorry, sir. We're trying." He leaned around the driver slightly so as to get a view of Repentance. He was a handsome overlord with sky blue eyes and a scar across one eyebrow.

"Mind giving us a hand?" the man asked the troopers. "We'll push our piece of dragon guano back into the alley and be out of your way."

The wind shifted and Repentance smelled something delicious. Juicy broiled meat, perhaps. Or maybe a thick, hot stew. She spotted the source of the smell across the street. An eatery—The Plump Partridge. A sign in the window claimed they served the most succulent squabs and cheepers on the summit—flash-fried to sear in the juices.

She sniffed greedily. Her stomach felt all caved-in.

And that made her mad. They hadn't even fed her but one bowl of thin soup in two days.

The troopers had their attention on the man with the broken wagon. Repentance grabbed the lever on the door. But where would she run too? She couldn't go home even if she did know the way, and she had no friends on the mountain who would take her in.

The big trooper and Earless, both cursing, climbed out and followed the man with the sky blue eyes.

Repentance sat alone in the wagon. If Providence wasn't giving her the perfect chance to run, what was He doing? Maybe He'd changed His mind and was going to be nice to her for once. Maybe He'd show her feet the way to go, if she'd only start out. She whispered the fifth Guidance Precept to herself. *Walk and you will see what's around the bend. Stay still and you will never know the places Providence would have taken you.*

She opened her side door, sprang from the seat, and took off running.

She ran past the man playing pipes, knocking a smartly-dressed overlord lady on her rear end, as she flew by. She ran past a shopkeeper who was raking a grid-pattern into the ice on his front stoop, past a nanny with a baby stroller, and around the corner into an alley.

Angry shouts followed her, drowning out the sound of the pipes.

Repentance ran.

Where she was going, she didn't know. She wanted to head toward the small houses on the edge of the city. Once she found the wall, she'd figure out how to get over it and away. But she was running too fast to be able to study the houses.

She bolted out of the alley. Turned on a busy street. Darted into the next alley on her left. Zig-zagged across another street. Into another alley.

Behind her, shouts gave indication that she was still being chased. She didn't slow down to look.

Her lungs burned. She ran on. Twisting, Turning. Taking whatever path opened in front of her.

"Stop running, girl." The voice sounded right behind her.

A hand touched the back of her robe but didn't manage to get a firm grasp. She put on a burst of speed, darting out of the alley and into a sun-flooded square. A square with a frozen fountain in the center. She skirted some boys playing skipball.

Repentance looked wildly around. The slave market sat at one end of the square. Sober was still at his stake. Her heart slammed against her chest.

All for nothing.

She was right back where she'd started.

She ducked into an alley on the right.

Feet pounded the hard ice behind her.

This time the hand, instead of grabbing at her, slammed her between the shoulder blades. She stumbled. She was recovering from that when something hit her behind the knees and she went down. Hard. Her bare hands hit the ice, and she felt an immediate burn. One shoulder crunched against the ground.

Big hands grabbed her. She squirmed and kicked as she was thrown over a broad shoulder. She beat on her captor's back.

He ran down the alley carrying her as if she were no more than a sack of grub roots. He turned a corner and skidded to a stop behind a staircase. "For the love of Providence, hold still," he said. "My first rescue and it's all gone wrong."

She stopped hitting him.

Rescue?

It was a lie.

She set to beating his back with renewed vigor.

The man set her feet on the ground and, taking hold of her shoulders, he shook her until her eyeballs hurt.

"Listen to me," he said. "You have to be quiet. You'll bring the troopers down on us. What made you run back to the slave market?"

She stared, trying to focus her blurry vision.

Holding her with one hand, he removed his cloak and threw it over her shoulders. "Pull the hood up, and walk with me. Quietly. Or we'll both meet the swingman before the week is out."

She stared at him, weighing her options. That's when she saw the sky blue eyes and the scar above one eyebrow—he had been working on the wagon that blocked the alley. He wasn't a trooper, then.

She pulled the cloak shut to cover her robe.

They wound their way through alleys, slipping from shadow to shadow. At busy streets the man peeked around corners, studying the traffic for signs of troopers before quickly leading her across, back into the relative safety of the dim alleyways. She followed along quietly, hoping more than believing that he was trustworthy, and memorizing every turn, every block, every alley. If she had to run again, she'd not run back to the slave market.

She kept an eye on the buildings, too, wanting to see them get smaller. Looking for the city wall. But they were still surrounded by ice towers, when her guide stopped at the back alley entrance of one. She leaned back, peering up, trying to count the stories on the structure. A flag, with a red background and an orange triangle in the middle, waved from a flagpole at the top of the building.

The man knocked on the door, and a moment later a small slave woman let them in.

Thick carpets, fine tapestries, and the slave's purple satin dress, attested to the wealth of the house. The woman opened a door off the hall and ushered them into a great room, the size of which astounded Repentance.

In the swamp she had lived in a cave with several rooms, so she had grown up with sleeping quarters of her own. Others had considered her family rich, and they were, by village standards. It never occurred to her, though, that anyone would live in a house with rooms the size of her entire village center.

The high ceiling was hung with cloths, like clouds, which glowed with the same kind of yellow light she'd seen in the bowl lamp that morning. A slight hum came from them. The carpet radiated heat. The ice walls were carved and painted—full of pictures. Repentance, without really looking, vaguely registered pictures of meadows with streams, overlord hunting parties mounted on yaks, and portraits of regal overlord women and men.

The old slave woman led them across the room, in the center of which stood a table, twenty feet long, made out of a honey-colored wood and shining like a reflecting stone. Tall vases of flowers sat at both ends and in the center of the table. At the far end of the room a fire blazed. In front of the fireplace sat a grouping of chairs and settees. It was to that end of the room that the slave led Repentance and her rescuer ... captor ... the man.

Another man, sitting in front of the fire, looked up from a book he was reading, a smile on his face.

Repentance gasped as she took in the tan breeches and pale green eyes. It was the lecherous Lord Carrull from the slave dock.

The man who acts without considering the effects of his actions on others, ends life alone and never understands why. "I never hurt a soul," says he. "I simply tended to my own pursuits—minded my own business." But all along behind him, people lie bleeding—trampled 'neath the boots of his ambition.

~Kindness Firtree, *Meditations on the Precepts*

CHAPTER 9

The man focused his gaze on Repentance and shot from his chair. "What have you done?" he shouted.

At Lord Carrull's fierce glare, Repentance stepped back and crossed her arms in front of her chest.

He wore the same clothes he had worn at the slave market, but he didn't look like the same man. He wasn't giggling, for one thing. His face was red with rage. "What is this about, Dagg?"

"It's not my fault." Dagg started frantically patting Repentance's hair back into place.

She ducked out from under his hands. He was no rescuer. He was a kidnapper, delivering her to the lecherous Lord Carrull.

"She ran away from the troopers," he said. "Ran back to the slave market! Like a demon. I almost didn't get her at all. But she's fine. Just looks a bit rough. Nothing a bath and a new gown won't cure."

"Not her! Not her!" Lord Carrull yelled. "You weren't

supposed to bring her."

"You told me to bring her. The girl in the robe."

"Scarlet, I said. Are you color blind? This girl is wearing maroon."

The rescuer, or rather the kidnapper, studied her robe, a confused look on his face. "But you never even looked at the other girl. This one here is the one you liked."

Anger burned in Lord Carrull's eyes. "You do not show a great interest in the object you plan to steal. Not if you have a trickle of sense."

Dagg worked his jaw, but no sound came out.

Repentance took the opportunity to jump into the conversation. "Since I'm not the one you want, I'll leave you to your business."

"You stay where you are." Lord Carrull sank into his chair. Then, looking at Dagg, he said, "Go see Compassion in the kitchen. Tell her to feed you. I need time to think."

Nodding and bobbing apologetically, Dagg scuttled out.

Lord Carrull turned toward the fire, leaned over, and rested his head in his hands.

Repentance took a couple of silent steps backward toward the door.

"Sit down and let me think for a minute," Lord Carrull said, patting the seat beside him.

"I'm comfortable where I am." She would sooner sit next to a muckback snake that hadn't eaten in two weeks.

"Sit!"

She jumped.

And she sat.

In the chair farthest from him.

She looked at the rich furnishings. A wooden table in a city that had no trees. And flowers. It must have cost a bucket of beads to have them brought up the mountain. So, if Lord Carrull was so rich, why would he steal slave girls? But Madam Cawrocc had intimated that he didn't have much money.

"When did you last eat?"

She jerked at his question. "Not counting the potato water they gave me this morning, it's been two days."

"I'll have dinner brought."

"I'd rather join Compassion and Dagg in the kitchen, if you don't mind," Repentance said.

"Stay where you are." His voice was firm—gone was the silly man who had stood on the slave dock a few hours earlier. This man was not one to simper and be led around by the likes of Madam Cawrocc.

A few minutes later, Compassion set a dinner plate on the small table beside Repentance. Lord Carrull brushed her off when she asked if he'd like a dish, too. He stared moodily into the fire while Repentance ate. There was some kind of meat she'd never eaten before. It tasted something like lizard—brown and tender and juicy. A mound of boiled potatoes and gravy snuggled up to the meat on her plate but not for long. She ate with gusto, washing the lot down with the same cold, milky beverage the slavers had given her on the trip up the mountain.

When she was done, Compassion took her dinner plate and set a steaming berry brick in its place. "Fresh from the oven," she said, as she slathered thick cream over the flaky crust.

Rich. Ripe. Really, really good. The sweet berries slid down like fruity velvet.

Repentance finished and sat back sipping from a cup of hot coffee, satisfied, for the moment, to stare into the fire and wait for Lord Carrull to explain himself. There was nothing else to do at present. She might as well enjoy her full stomach.

She wasn't greedy. She didn't need riches. She didn't need power or beads or clothes or jewels. She would be content with a good meal every now and again. Was it such an evil thing for her to think she deserved to eat as well as the overlord masters?

The back of her neck prickled and the fine hair there stood up. She looked over to find Lord Carrull studying her.

"You've had enough?" he asked.

71

"Yes, thank you."

He raised his eyebrows in surprise. "Such manners."

She shrugged. "My future is no more grim than three hours ago, and my stomach is full, which is more than I ever expected. So, yes, I thank you. We lowborns know how to give thanks when it is due, unlike you overlords who take what is not yours and offer no thanks for it at all."

Lord Carrull sighed. "A fine speech. I do hope you learn to shut up, though. Else you'll not live long here on the mountain. And you're wrong, of course, to think your future is not more grim than a few hours ago. Your situation is quite grave."

Her heart skipped a beat, then set to rat-a-tat-tatting like a woodpecker. "If you let me go I'll run away, and the prince will never know you took me. I'm not going back to tell on you."

"You belong to Jadin, and I have to return you. There is no other way."

Repentance thought of what waited for her in Jadin's keep. Death if she was lucky. If not that, then down to the hot springs she would go. Down to the fog. Down to the humiliation. Down to await the overlord prince.

No, she had no desire to go back. Better to stay with Lord Carrull. A rich house. Fine food. A master with a guilty and dangerous secret she could exploit. "I can stay here," she said. "I'll never go out of the house, and no one will ever know you took me."

Lord Carrull looked on her with disgust. "You would stay, wouldn't you? Selfish child."

Her mouth fell open in shock. "You keep slaves. You *steal* slaves. And you call me selfish?"

"You may hate me all you like, but you have your own sins to answer for. You had no pity for the young man you were supposed to button. No pity for his family, either. Or your own family, for that matter."

Repentance winced.

"Yes, you have so far proven to be a headstrong, selfish girl. And now you want to hide here instead of going back to do your duty."

Repentance couldn't believe what she was hearing. "You think I have a duty to give myself as a concubine to your filthy prince?" He could kill her for all she cared. She would never agree that she had a duty to serve the overlords.

"You have a duty to your family." His eyes were hard—angry. "If you do not go to Jadin, your entire family is forfeit."

She stared without seeing him, her mind clicking through all she'd seen and heard since she came up the mountain. The slaver had said something when they first pulled into the square at the slave market. He'd said they caught the runners and hurt them. And something else. She hadn't really heard him properly. All sound had been drowned out by the deafening drip of blood on ice. She cast her mind back. He's said something about taking the runners' families into service.

That's why Jadin had been so interested in her sister. Comfort would be the compensation if Repentance ran.

She sank back into her chair.

"You didn't realize," Lord Carrull said softly. "I'm sorry. I misjudged you."

She didn't answer. They were going to take Comfort? Oh, holy Providence.

"I'm afraid you must go back," he said. "We have no other choice."

She stirred. "If I go back, my sister will be safe?"

"I think I can convince Cawrocc to say nothing of this event. But I need you to swear not to tell anyone you've been here."

"This event ... what is it? Why would you kidnap the other girl and not me? The girl in the scarlet robe?"

"She has no family. When she runs, no one pays."

She shook her head. "Why would someone who kidnaps slaves for ... for ... to be used as concubines care about the families of the girls he steals?"

"I don't kidnap girls to be concubines! That is a part I play. I have a reputation for having a huge appetite for new girls. I buy them and I smuggle them out to other states where they can go free. To Montphilo, first of all. But many move on from there. The Deliverance Day people help me move some."

Repentance studied his eyes. He looked sincere. "So ... there are cities where lowborns walk free?" she whispered.

"But the fancier girls—the ones dressed as you are—I cannot often buy. It isn't that I'm too poor. I have enough beads in my pocket to compete with Jadin. But Jadin will remember you. She studies you all carefully. If I beat her out on too many sales, she would wonder what I was doing with you all. It would bring scrutiny upon the whole undertaking."

"So you steal us instead. You steal girls like me and set us free."

He shook his head sadly. "No Repentance. Not girls like you. I only steal girls with no families. Girls like you, I'm sorry to say, I cannot help."

The yak-drawn carriage wound through the dark streets of Harthill. Repentance didn't open the curtains. She cared nothing for the evil city and had no wish to see any of it. Not the alleys, not the street entertainers, not the hanging frame. She wondered, briefly, if Sober was still tied at the slave dock. Of course not. That was ridiculous. He was on a farm with a fair mistress. She would always picture him, though, as she'd seen him last, tied at the dock but with an earnest look of forgiveness on his face.

He had forgiven her. She didn't know why, but she was grateful for that and happy that he had found a place on a farm. That relieved much guilt, which was good, because when she lay with the disgusting prince, she would have enough shame to deal with.

The driver halted the yak team rather abruptly, jostling Repentance into Lord Carrull. The iron collar the Lord had put around her neck chafed against her skin and the chain, draped down from the collar, clinked against itself with an empty, hopeless sound. One tear escaped and slid down her cheek.

Lord Carrull patted her knee. "Courage, child," he said, "I'll protect you from the worst of it."

He descended the carriage first, holding the chain.

Inside the slave market, a disinterested clerk looked up from his book. His eyes popped wide open at the sight of Repentance.

"I'm here to see Madam Cawrocc," Lord Carrull said.

"Yes, indeed," answered the clerk. "She's in the dining room. Top of the stairs. First door on your right."

"She's dining? Perhaps I'll wait." He had reverted back to the indecisive, weak man Repentance had first taken him for.

"Oh, I shouldn't think so, sir," the clerk answered. "I'm thinking she'll want to be interrupted. In fact, let me lock my desk and I'll escort you."

He smiled greedily, obviously looking forward to Madam Cawrocc's response to their arrival.

Repentance shivered. It seemed she was destined to entertain men one way or another, no matter what she did.

Madam Cawrocc looked up crankily as they entered. When her gaze hit Repentance, she gave only the slightest reaction—a tiny twitch in one eye. She finished chewing, swallowed, and took a long drink from her mug.

"Lord Carrull," she said at last, "what are you doing with my slave?"

He giggled, once again the simpering, lecherous nincompoop. He played the part so well that Repentance, even knowing he was acting, hated him.

"I found your little bird, lost and alone," he said. "And I determined to bring her back to you. I knew you'd be worried about her."

"Do I look worried?"

"You didn't know?" Lord Carrul giggled again. "The troopers who lost her never reported it, eh? They and their families are halfway to Montphilo by now, I'll wager."

Madam Cawrocc gave a look to the clerk who stood at the door. He left quickly, going to send someone to search for the troopers, no doubt.

"Thank you for returning her," Madam Cawrocc said. "Will you stay and share my meat?"

He giggled again. "I was hoping for some little reward. But perhaps something a little more filling than a meal."

"What exactly did you have in mind?"

He pulled Repentance's chain so she had to step next to him. Running one finger over her cheek, he said, "I was sorely tempted to keep this one. Sorely tempted. I only returned her knowing I held your life in my hands. I knew if I didn't return her you'd swing before the week was out." He smiled sweetly. "So I brought her back to you, convinced you'd be happy to trade her for the other girl. The one in the scarlet robe."

"I'd hardly swing. If you'd have kept her, Jadin would have had to make do with her sister, is all. It would have cost me a few beads refunded and no little amount of embarrassment, I grant you, but that's a far cry from swinging."

He shrugged. "Oh, good great happy day, then." He started to turn. "I'll keep her." He was almost drooling when he looked at Repentance.

"You drive a hard bargain," Madam Cawrocc said. "I'll trade you, you old thief. But not for the girl in the scarlet robe. She's sold."

"Buy her back."

"I won't. You'll have to be satisfied with one of the others."

"I don't want a homely girl," he whined. "I think I deserve a beautiful girl this one time."

"I'll make sure you get a pretty girl."

"I'll keep this one." Lord Carrull made as if to leave.

"Don't be ridiculous. Walk out of here with the prince's girl and your life is forfeit."

"I found her. By law she's mine." He was still whining. "I brought her back as a friendly gesture, but you, Madam, are not being friendly."

Madam Cawrocc stood, her back straight, her jaw clenched, and her eyes filled with hate.

Repentance shrank back.

"Very well," the lady said. "You shall have the girl in the scarlet robe."

She crossed the floor. "And as for you, my sweet," she said to Repentance, "I will personally tuck you into bed tonight." She reached for the chain.

Repentance sought protection behind Lord Carrull.

"Oh, yes, a good idea," Lord Carrull said, yanking the chain forward. "You take care of this one yourself. You can't be too careful." He handed over the chain. "I made sure no mark was on her." He giggled into his hand. "Had to inspect her, you know. For I knew your business would suffer if you delivered damaged goods to Jadin."

Madam Cawrocc gave him a dirty look, then turned her attention to Repentance. "Don't feel any relief, Miss Repentance Happily Forgotten Atwater. I may not be able to beat you, but that pretty little sister of yours is a different thing now, isn't she?"

Repentance gasped.

"That's right. I'll take the price of Lord Carrull's girl out of your sister's back."

"No," Repentance screamed. "You leave Comfort alone!"

Madam Cawrocc laughed. "She'll work for me until she dies. It should take a couple of weeks, give or take a day. And every day, as she's being beaten I'll make sure to remind her that she has you to thank."

Repentance lunged at the woman, wrapping her hands around Cawrocc's neck, intent on choking the life from her.

Lord Carrull squealed like a girl. "You mustn't!"

Something cracked into her skull and everything went black.

Actions have repercussions. Toss even a tiny pebble into the still morning waters at the swimming hole and watch the water move aside to accommodate the pebble's new place. The ripples go on and on. Likewise, when I move, the person next to me has to shift over to accommodate my new place, and the person next to her has to shift over, and on and on the ripples go. Oh, dear Providence, I didn't know.

~Repentance Atwater, *Healing House Journal*

CHAPTER 10

"What's wrong with her?" A woman's voice filtered its way into Repentance's fuzzy consciousness.

"She's asleep." A man.

Fingers massaged her skull and hit a sore spot. She winced.

"She's concussed." The woman again. "She has a lump as big as a cumquat on her head."

Repentance took a deep breath.

The air felt hot and heavy.

She opened her eyes.

Fog.

A woman bent over her. White hair, gleaming teeth, brilliant eyes. Jadin. "Do you know who I am?"

She pushed herself up.

And fell back down, grabbing her head and gagging.

"Holy Providence," Jadin swore. "Who did this to her?"

The world seemed to be spinning. Repentance looked to her side, trying to focus on something that would stabilize her. She was lying in the bed of a slave cart, with Jadin leaning over the side.

Slave cart. Fog. Sore head.

A man's face came into focus beside Jadin's. "Lord Carrull hit her. She was about to kill Madam Cawrocc."

She remembered.

"I've got to go!" She tried to jump from the cart. The man pushed her back, then jumped into the cart and wrapped steely arms around her. She fell back against him, dizzy and nauseous.

"You don't go. You do as you're told," Jadin said.

"My sister, my sister!" She'd tried to yell, but it came out more like a croak. "I need to warn my sister. Please!"

"Warn her about what?" Jadin's voice was steady like the voice the midwife would use to calm a fussy babe.

"Madam Cawrocc is going to kill her."

"She's going to do no such thing."

"She is. She told me." Repentance squirmed weakly against the man, her head throbbing as if it would split open.

Jadin's eyes narrowed. "What did you do?"

"Please."

"You tell me right now what you did to pull that threat out of Cawrocc, or I swear I'll get your sister and both brothers and kill them right here in front of you."

Repentance sagged back against the man. "I ran," she whispered. "I'm sorry. I'm sorry. I didn't mean it." She looked up at Jadin. "Please help my sister."

"Your sister is fine," Jadin said. "At present. It's up to you if she's to stay that way."

"I killed her. She's dead already."

"Oh for the love of Providence," Jadin said. "What good is she to me in this condition?" She looked at the man. "I paid for perfection and Cawrocc's given me a lunatic."

"You can hardly blame Cawrocc. The girl was crazy from the start. Refused a buttoning, and chose the slave cart."

"I don't want to live," Repentance said.

"I want you to tell Cawrocc I hold her responsible for this.

First she lost control, so the girl needed to be hit on the head, and then she obviously chose to withhold any healing powder or potion. She thought she'd make the girl suffer, no doubt. Only she has no business deciding how to punish my slave."

"I killed my sister," Repentance said, tears coursing down her cheeks. "Give me a dragon stick. I'll do it myself. I don't want to live anymore."

"You stop talking," Jadin said, sternly.

"Kill me now!" Repentance screamed.

Jadin slapped her. Hard.

Her head exploded in pain and her face went numb.

She put one hand to her cheek, wondering what had just happened.

Jadin got right up close to her. "Now you listen. Your sister is fine. Madam Cawrocc will not harm her. I know this because when I bought you, I bought rights to your family. They are mine if you misbehave. Cawrocc doesn't own them, I do. Do you understand?'

"Comfort is alive?"

"I am going to have this trooper let you go in a minute," Jadin said. "Do you know where you are?"

She looked past Jadin. The healing house stood behind her. She was back in Hot Springs. Back in the gray. Back in the swamp. But Comfort was alive. Maybe.

The trooper released her, and she scrambled down from the cart. Her legs buckled. She landed in a heap at Jadin's feet, the foggy world spinning crazily before her eyes. And darkness fell.

She woke next on a comfortable settee with her head on a soft pillow. Gray light filtered into the room through wide windows. She was in the healing house, she supposed. In all her years, she'd never been in the building. The villagers were not allowed to use the hot springs. That privilege was for overlords only.

"You live," Jadin said, entering the room like a cool breeze.

Repentance nodded. And winced. Her head ached with a dull pounding.

Jadin handed her a small cup. "Drink this. It will help your head."

"How long have I been asleep?"

"An hour."

"My sister?"

"Is still fine."

"May I see her?"

Jadin examined her for a long moment. "I suppose you are no good to me unless I can convince you she's alive."

"If she's alive I'll do whatever you want."

Jadin considered. "I'll let you see that she's alive. And I'll give you my promise that if you give me any trouble after that, she won't be alive long."

Repentance pushed herself off the settee, and Jadin put out a hand to steady her. "First you need to get cleaned up and give that healing potion time to work. I'll have the cook make you some food while you bathe."

Two hours later she stood, fed and bathed and dressed in light-weight britches and blouse, in front of the healing house with Jadin and a big overlord man called Lok, who carried a dragon stick. A dull ache pounded at the base of her skull, but she could walk without feeling like she needed to throw up, and she desperately wanted to see Comfort, so she said nothing about the pain.

"The girls will be picking their nets in another half hour. Take this one and hide in the bushes by her family's set-net site." Jadin pulled a burlap sack over her head. "Just in case you run into anyone."

Repentance could see through the burlap. And she could breathe, though the sack was dusty and made her sneeze.

Jadin poked her with a slender finger. "No noise. No one is to know you're here. If they find out, your family will suffer."

Lok laid a giant hand on Repentance's arm to lead her into the woods. He kept Repentance off the main paths, stopping and cocking his head often, listening for villagers.

Each time he stopped, the musty, marshy smell of home came in through the burlap bag which covered Repentance's face. And the sounds of the woods filled her ears. The small animals digging, the bugs buzzing, the constant drip, drip, dripping from the trees. But she heard no villagers moving about.

What would people do if they knew she was so close? What would they do if they knew that outside the fence there were states where lowborns did not live as slaves? Should she call out when she saw her sister? Should she tell her to try to escape?

No, her people were not interested in fighting. They were content to give up their first two sons and to go on with their lives.

She walked silently beside Lok.

The canopy of leaves above her wept.

The set-net site was empty when they arrived, and Repentance and Lok had no trouble finding a spot in the dense woods and undergrowth where they would be able to see without being seen. They couldn't see well—the fog was as thick as cotton—but she would be able to know if Comfort was well.

Repentance, squatting beside Lok, was overcome with homesickness so strong she felt like she might not be able to breathe. She longed to see Comfort again. To hear her laugh. To sit by the river while her little brothers swam and while Comfort sat nearby, drawing.

Sweat covered her scalp and face, and she struggled to breathe in the bag. She pulled the bottom of the sack open to let in fresh air, but the swamp air was hot and humid, and she gulped it in without feeling much relief. She was about to ask Lok if she could take the bag off, when she heard someone coming along the path.

Repentance heard Comfort's voice before she saw her.

"Why do they blame me?"

Repentance strained to see her.

"I'm sorry," Aggravation answered Comfort.

"You aren't sorry!" Comfort said. "You could fight if you wanted."

The two of them came into view, passing a few feet from where Repentance hid.

"I've got to think of my little brothers," Aggravation said. "If my family aligns with yours now—"

"It would prove that there's nothing to be afraid of. When people saw me keep my promise to you .... If you don't trust me, you who know me better than anyone, then no one will. I'll ride the slave cart."

"Someone else ... a fifth-year boy—"

"No one! No one will ever trust any of us. I'll ride the cart and so will both of my brothers."

"You can't blame me for that. It's Repentance—your cursed-from-birth, selfish sister. She's the one you can thank."

Repentance jerked as if she'd been slapped. No, no, she didn't do it to be selfish. She'd only wanted to save—

Lok grabbed her, maybe afraid she would jump up.

"I'm sorry," Aggravation said again. Then he fled like a coward, running away from the girl he had been promised to for years.

Comfort squatted and pulled the set net in, her tears falling on the fish as she picked them.

Repentance gulped and gulped trying to get rid of the lump in her throat and keep herself from breaking down sobbing. She wanted to go to Comfort. She wanted to wrap her arms around her sister as she had done through every crisis since the overlords took Tribulation. But all she could do was watch Comfort through the burlap and through the fog, knowing this picture of her sister crying over the fish net would haunt her for the rest of her days.

Finally, after eternity and more, Comfort threw her net back out into the river, picked up her pail of fish, and headed down the path.

Lok kept hold of Repentance, forcing her to remain still.

Pain thudded against the base of her skull.

The trees dripped.

A small animal splashed into the swamp.

Insects thrummed through the heat.

And Repentance sat in her burlap sack, quietly weeping.

After a few minutes, when no one approached, Lok released her. She followed him in silence. In shock. Oh, Dear Providence, what had she done?

If she obeyed Jadin, if she pleased the prince, she could keep them from taking Comfort right away. But in two years, Comfort would still make her way up the mountain in a slave cart—an unwanted, unbuttoned girl.

Repentance left Lok at the bottom of the porch steps. She pushed open the door of the healing house and stepped into the large room with the settee, where she had woken up earlier that morning.

A young woman—a beautiful, pale, overlord girl a few years older than Repentance—sat on the settee with a book.

She looked up and lifted her upper lip in a sneer. "How did you get in here?"

"I walked," Repentance said, still distracted by her worry over Comfort.

The girl's pale eyes—perfectly matched to the light blue of her satin gown—opened wide. "Did I ask for your sarcasm? Why are you here?"

Repentance dropped her eyes, not willing to anger any more overlords. "I'm looking for Jadin."

The young woman shook her head and her short blonde hair swung around her face. "You can't march in here like this. For the love of Providence, do we need to hire troopers to protect us, now?"

Jadin came through the archway. "Ah, you're back," she said to Repentance. "And you have seen that your sister is alive?"

Without waiting for a reply, she looked at the young overlord woman. "Tawnic, this is Repentance. Would you give her a tour of the place, please? And then give her the bed Mek vacated last week."

"A lowborn?"

Jadin winked at Tawnic. "Take good care of her. If she pleases the prince, he might leave you alone."

"The prince with a lowborn?"

"He does like his forbidden fruit, Tawnic. You know that."

Repentance shivered.

"Oh, well, then," Tawnic said. "I wouldn't mind a trickle of rest. In truth." She shot Repentance an ugly smile. "He's got more energy than a hyena, that one."

Repentance wasn't aware that hyenas were especially energetic, but she understood the point perfectly. She would have hated Tawnic, with her ugly smile and nasty personality, only she was too tired to muster up the anger.

Tawnic led her through the archway, grabbed a torch from the wall, and proceeded down a narrow stone stairway. They were going underground. The healing house was not the wooden building it looked like from the outside. That building stood in front of a huge cavern in a cliff. In the cavern, walls had been erected to make separate rooms and a second story had been built.

Repentance, even in her light swamp clothes, began to sweat as they descended. She understood why when Tawnic threw open a door at the bottom of the stairs.

"The hot spring," Tawnic said in a bored voice. "This water is for healing." A large pool—easily four times the size of the swimming hole in the swamp, bubbled in the floor of the cave.

"Is it boiling?"

Tawnic rolled her eyes. "How would people swim in boiling water? It's bubbling out of the underground spring."

Along one wall of the cavern were several doors. Tawnic waved toward them. "Those are the guest rooms."

There were three more large pools, two were warm-water springs and the third was fed from a cold mountain stream, which came down through the cliff.

Behind the last pool were more doors.

Tawnic threw one open to reveal a small, dark, damp, stinking-of-mold-and-sweat room with furnishings consisting of mats on the floor. Plus nothing. Three mats, each one with a small pile of night clothing folded up where a person's pillow normally lay.

"The slave quarters," Tawnic said, a nasty smile marring her beautiful face.

Repentance stepped into the stinking room where the slaves slept. "Which bed is mine?"

Tawnic stared at her, unanswering.

"Jadin said I was to have a bed. Which one?"

The overlord girl rolled her eyes. "Wouldn't I love to leave you down here? You'll get your stench all over the upper floor." She turned and led the way back up the stone stairs.

Repentance followed.

On the next level Tawnic pushed open a door in the back of the room with the settee. "The kitchen," she said.

Repentance had already seen the kitchen. She'd eaten a bowl of soup there before she'd gone to see Comfort.

"Jadin's quarters." Tawnic waved down the hall, then turned the other direction and led the way up a flight of wooden stairs which ended in a wide hall with rooms on both sides. She threw open the third door on the right.

Repentance slid past Tawnic, who didn't bother moving out of the way.

The room was huge compared to the slave quarters downstairs. Bright yellow walls. A bed—off the ground and with a thick mat—was shoved against the far wall. Against another wall stood a desk with a reflecting stone above it. A wardrobe stood in one corner.

Repentance swelled with a tiny feeling of hope.

Yellow walls.

When the prince came, she'd deal with him. Until then, she had yellow walls.

I gaze into the midnight gloom; an evil fast approaches.
I steel my heart to face my doom; a devil now encroaches.
But lighting rends a peaceful morning,
with ne'er a sound or hint of warning.
A danger bursts forth from a quarter unseen.
And I am undone.
~Repentance Atwater, *Healing House Poetry Collection*

CHAPTER 11

"The prince is coming, the prince is coming!" An excited chattering and nattering swelled through the halls of the healing house.

From bits of overheard conversation, Repentance understood that the girls were happy because the food and wine always improved when the royals visited.

Tawnic, especially, was looking forward to the visit. She'd apparently not been able to enjoy the festivities on prior occasions because of the prince's strenuous demands on her. She'd taken every chance, over the previous three weeks, to let Repentance know how much she was looking forward to the next royal party.

Repentance pulled her blanket over her head trying to drown out the whispers in the halls.

Despite Tawnic's cruel gloating, life had not been hard on Repentance the past few weeks. She and Jadin had come to an understanding. Jadin had complete control over her life. Repentance had gagged on that truth but finally choked it down.

It had been driven home the last time she worked in the kitchen. The potatoes she was paring had put her in mind of Sober on his potato farm. She wondered how he was doing and tried to picture him working in a sunny field. She remembered his earnest face and his sorrowful smile.

Thinking about Sober, remembering his eyes and his kind look, instead of concentrating on the task at hand, she'd slipped and jabbed the paring knife into the center of her palm.

Jadin had quickly slathered ointment—onion milk and hog's grease—on the wound.

"Clumsy girl," she'd said. "Don't you dare damage the merchandise, or I'll be forced to take sweet Comfort."

Repentance had cringed. Jadin had been treating her well—teaching her how to eat at an overlord table and how to drink and walk and sit. In the end, though, Jadin was an overlord slaver, same as any other. Repentance heaved a world-weary sigh.

"Oh, surely it isn't as bad as all that," Jadin said. "You have the richest of foods and the softest of beds."

"I was merely thinking how different my life would have been if I'd been ugly. Had I known what my beauty would cost me, I'd have scarred my face on the day before the Button Ceremony. Then you would not have purchased me. I'd have gone for a lady's maid or a nanny, perhaps."

"Hmm." Jadin studied her. "Yes, I do believe you would have taken a knife to yourself. You're that stubborn. But you *didn't* scar your face, and I *did* buy you. Your job now is to take care of yourself so I get a good price from the Prince. If he buys you outright—Oh please, dear Providence, let it be so—if he should buy you outright, then you can scar yourself all you want. Let him deal with your stubborn spirit. But as long as you stay with me, you will take care of my merchandise so I might exact a top rental price."

"I'm not really your merchandise, you know," Repentance said, selecting another potato from the basket on the floor. "You can't tell me what to think. What's inside is the real me, and that's between me and Providence. You can't own that part."

Jadin burst out laughing. "You are welcome to your insides, Repentance. I cannot package and sell them. No man cares to buy the thoughts of a silly girl."

Repentance felt as though she'd been slapped. Determined not to let Jadin see her cry, she swallowed down the tears, but she vented her anger by stabbing her knife deeply into the potato she held.

Jadin had gasped. "Give me that!" She'd snatched the potato and knife out of Repentance's hand. "I'll tell you what. You and Providence may have full control of your insides. But, know this: If I wanted your thoughts, I'd have them. Because I make the rules, not you. Is that understood, or should I send for Comfort so she can explain it to you?"

Repentance pulled her hand out from under her blanket and studied the white scar on her palm. It barely showed. Jadin had taken her off kitchen duty that day. She'd done no work of any kind after that, in fact.

She swam daily in the cool spring. Jadin encouraged her to exercise as long as she never went outside.

She pulled her robe on and headed down to swim.

Tawnic was in the hall at the foot of the stairs. She bowed. "Oh, pardon me, your highness," she said, "I didn't mean to breathe the same air you were breathing."

Repentance ignored her and headed for the pools.

"Jadin's girl," Tawnic said. "But not for long. The prince rides hard and you're too soft. Once he breaks you, you won't be worth two beads to anyone. See how much Jadin loves you then."

Repentance kept walking. She didn't need to listen to Tawnic. She'd heard it all before. Nineteen pleasure girls in the healing house—all overlords. And she, a slave, had a room on their floor. They all hated her.

She was sure Providence was laughing about that. When she'd left the swamp, she'd consoled herself with the thought that at least she'd be away from the foggy swamp and the villagers who hated her and whispered behind her back, calling her cursed. And there she was back in the heat, back in the fog, and more of an outcast than ever.

She dropped her robe, dove into the spring, and swam.

And she cried, letting the water wash her tears away.

She swam until her tears were spent and all the knots were gone from her muscles and until she was too tired to worry about how awful her night with the prince was going to be. Tawnic was lying about that, anyway. She had to be.

The dining room was empty by the time she got there. She always swam first so she could eat in peace.

Jadin entered, a bounce in her step and a sparkle of excitement in her eyes. "Had your swim? Good, you have to bathe and get dressed for the prince."

Repentance took a bite of scrambled egg cooked with ham and peppers and onions.

"And for the love of Providence, be sure to clean your mouth with mint. He's to arrive this afternoon. Why are you eating onions?" She pulled Repentance's plate away. "You don't need more, anyway. You'll eat dinner with the prince in a few hours. And you won't forget your manners." It was half question, half threat.

Repentance nodded.

"After dinner you'll go with him to the royal suite."

"Not the healing pool? Doesn't he come to soak in the hot springs?"

"The royal suite has a small healing tub. Plenty big for two."

Repentance's stomach clenched at the thought. "But then I'm not in need of healing," she said. "So it only needs to be big enough for one."

"I'm warning you, Repentance. One complaint from the prince, and I'll have Comfort brought over for breakfast tomorrow. And I don't mean she'll be here to dine."

"I can't help it if he complains. I don't know what to do." She looked at Jadin, pleading with her eyes. "I won't know what to do."

Jadin smiled, showing perfect white teeth. "Don't worry about that. The prince likes it that way. He'll teach you." She waggled her eyebrows.

"What if I displease him?"

"I'm telling you, girl, let go of any schemes you have in that foolish head."

"I don't have any schemes. I'm afraid I'll cry. The girls say he's ... he's ... he causes pain."

Jadin visibly relaxed. "Don't worry about that. Crying doesn't displease him at all. I don't think he feels finished until the girls cry."

Repentance trembled. "How long do I have to stay with him?"

"Until he's done with you."

Repentance went to her room and took out her parchment pad. She poured her hatred onto the page.

The warthogs steal and take and take and take.
I hate them when I sleep and I hate them when I wake.
They threaten and snarl and bare their teeth,
but one day, I'll be above, and they'll be beneath.
Tomorrow is another day. Tomorrow I might run away.

She read her poem back. Not her best work and she had no time to rework the lines. But it had served its purpose. The hatred kept her from crying. If she cried her nose would swell and turn red, and the prince would think she was ugly. She had to please him, or Comfort would pay the price.

Thinking of Comfort, she tore the parchment out of her book and crumpled it. She had to stop pretending. She would never run away.

Numb, she headed to the bathing room to prepare for the prince.

The slave knows well that he has no power over his fate. He is passed from master to master through no fault or merit of his own. But there is One who sits above slave and master both. It is the wise man, then, who holds his own plans loosely and bows to the interfering will and wisdom of Providence.

~Steadfast Atwater, *Lessons Learned at My Father's Knee*

CHAPTER 12

He looked nothing like the monster she had imagined. Sitting in the feasting hall, laughing with his friends, he looked quite pleasant. He was not young, but not ancient either. Maybe he'd seen thirty summers. When he lifted his gaze to her, she saw his pale blue eyes widen in surprise just before a glow of approval lit in them. Suddenly, her thin lowland gown felt too thin, and she blushed.

Jadin led her to the seat beside him. "Lord Malficc, I'm happy to introduce Repentance. She'll minister to your needs tonight."

He gave a slight nod without taking his gaze from Repentance.

She sat, relieved to be off of her shaky legs.

Around the table sat eight overlord men, all dressed as royalty, in fine satin shirts, brightly colored, and with their hair wrapped in silk turbans. To her left sat an older man, a lock of white hair escaping his head covering.

Repentance caught him studying her. She took a quick look at his eyes—pale blue. Lighter than the prince's, even. A little washed out from age.

A smile crinkled the corners of his eyes. "What year are you in, child?" he asked.

"My sixteenth."

"Indeed," the old man said. "Indeed. I would have guessed precisely that, had I been forced to venture an opinion." He twisted toward her and reached one hand up to her neck. "Your hair is an arresting color," he said, brushing it back behind her left ear and letting it fall through his fingers.

She nodded politely, and then angled her seat a bit so that her back was slightly toward the old man. She was, after all, supposed to be entertaining the prince, not conversing with everyone else.

The prince smiled at her. A nice smile. Lots of shiny, white teeth. Maybe the girls were lying. Maybe he was nice.

Some of the other girls sashayed in, dressed as Repentance was, in thin lowland gowns and with their hair piled in curls on top of their heads. Each one carried a covered serving dish. They looked the overlord men in the eye, giggling and mincing as they went. As they circled the table looking for empty spots for their food dishes they swung their hips and brushed up against the men, and as they put the food down, they bent low, letting their gowns gape open.

The men grinned—some chuckled—and pulled chairs out, bidding the girls to sit. As they fought for the chance to pour drinks, Repentance finally understood why the girls liked it when the royal party came. Of course the farmers and the owners of the eateries who came every week worshipped the girls. But to be so desired by royalty was another thing altogether. The greater the men, the greater the honor for the girls.

She glanced over at the handsome prince. Hers was the greatest honor of all, then.

He couldn't really be mean. The others were just jealous. How could a man with such a face be as cruel as they said he was?

Jadin surveyed the table. "Everything is to your satisfaction, your highness?"

The prince nodded.

"But not to mine," the old man said.

"Your worship?" Jadin looked stunned.

The noise in the room suddenly dimmed.

"I have been given no girl," the old man said.

"But, King Fawlin, you have ... never required a girl before. I was ... unaware ...."

Repentance twisted in her chair to see the old man better. King Fawlin. This, then, was the man who had beheaded his button mate and enslaved the lowborns two hundred and fifty years earlier. How could he still be alive? The hot springs must have amazing restorative powers.

"I am not assigning blame," the king said. "You need not stammer out a defense. Simply rectify the situation."

"By all means, your worship. I'll have a girl sent immediately."

"I'll take this one," he said, indicating Repentance. "I'm sure Lord Malficc won't mind."

She gasped.

"Oh," Jadin said, looking at Repentance in a daze. "Oh."

"Woman!" the king said. "Retrieve another girl for my nephew."

Jadin jerked. "Oh, of course. Of course. Another girl for Lord Malficc."

Lord Malficc was smiling. With his mouth. Not with his eyes. "It's just as well," he said. His eyes, Repentance thought, burned with an anger that belied his words. "I was hoping for Tawnic tonight anyway. She knows how to take care of a man. Let my uncle break in this new girl. It's about time he did some work."

The other men burst into laughter.

The king smiled and lifted his glass in salute to the prince.

Jadin bowed and backed out of the room.

Repentance's mouth went dry. Two hours earlier if anyone had told her that her fortune was going to get worse she would have thought it impossible. She was glad Jadin had taken away her breakfast because her stomach, the one she thought couldn't tie itself any tighter, clutched in fear.

The king set to his dinner, completely ignoring her.

She drank. And drank. And still her mouth felt dry.

Tawnic came in, bathed and dressed and smiling, but Repentance, as she scooted her chair over to make room, smelled fear on the girl.

"Tawnic, my old friend," the prince said. "My uncle has stolen the new girl from under me and I'll have to drown my sorrows with you." He grinned at her. "But we'll survive it, and even enjoy it, I dare say."

Tawnic smiled, her lower lip quivering. "Of course, my lord."

The king put his fork down, burped softly, and coughed a couple of times into his napkin. He pushed his chair back and rose. All the others quickly stood with their heads bowed.

"Go on with your party," he said. "I'll take my old bones to bed." He looked at Repentance. "I trust you will accompany me, my dear, and tuck me in."

Several of the men snickered.

Not the prince. A muscle along his jaw twitched, but he didn't crack a smile.

Repentance took the king's arm, her knees weak, her stomach churning, and her mind wondering if she'd make it to the suite without throwing up on her velvet slippers.

At the top of the narrow stairway, a slave took a torch from the wall to light their way down.

They were going down to the guest rooms by the hot pool. Down to the dark, damp heat.

The king disengaged himself from Repentance, and, turning his thin back to her, he followed the slave with the torch.

She could push him. He was feeble. The steps were stone. It might work. And Providence knew he deserved it. He was evil.

Hatred rose in her chest until she felt like she might scream.

All her trouble, all the pain she had ever born, all the pain of her family, and of the village, and of every lowborn for the last two hundred and fifty years could be laid at the feet of the wicked man in front of her.

The slave carts.

The dead boys on ropes.

All of it.

His fault.

And there he was, tottering down stone steps, practically begging her to give him a shove. But the slave in front would break the fall.

She clenched her hands into fists, and followed, her feet moving somehow, even as her mind screamed out in protest.

The lower level, usually dim, was lit by torches poked into holes in the walls. Apparently, the royal party gave Jadin enough beads to make it worthwhile for her to light up the cave like noonday on the mountain. The slave left them, heading back to wait for the next overlord noble who needed him to light the way down the stone steps.

The king led Repentance through the door to the largest, hottest pool and entered the first private room. As soon as the door closed behind them, he let out a strangled cough—as if he'd been holding it back. That first cough opened a floodgate. He fell into a coughing fit and dropped onto the bed, terrible spasms racking his chest.

Repentance watched, unsure of herself. If she did nothing, he might die. But if she did nothing and he didn't die .... She stepped forward thinking she'd pat him on the back, then stopped. A slave girl couldn't hit a king.

Instead, she filled a glass of water from a pitcher on the table, but when she offered it to him, he knocked it aside. Gasping for breath, he pulled a small, silver flask from his pocket and took a slug. Then another. The coughing subsided.

"Better," he said, exhaling slowly. He unbuttoned his silk shirt, revealing a wrinkly, pale chest.

Repentance thought about touching that withered flesh and fought down a gag.

The king slipped his shirt off. "Make yourself useful then, and unwind my turban."

She obeyed in silence, freeing his shoulder-length, white hair.

"Now," he said, pushing himself off the bed with some effort and tottering for a moment before he gained his balance, "we will soak in the hot pool before we sleep. Before all the revelers finish their drinking and come down to invade our quiet. Get my robe." He waved toward the wardrobe in the corner of the room.

Repentance took a silk robe from a hook behind the door and turned around. The king stood with his back to her, naked, his pants in a pile at his feet. She focused her gaze on the back of his head—she couldn't bear to look at his shriveled body—and managed to slip the robe on him without touching him.

The king led the way out of the room.

The pool was lit like the passageway with torches closely spaced in the walls, making the whole cavern bright and warm.

The king stopped at the top of the steps, which led into the pool, his back to Repentance. She stopped next to him.

He sighed. "You are to help me off with my robe." His tone was tinged with irritation.

She stepped behind him and gingerly pinched the shoulders of his robe, lifted it, and slid it down his arms.

He walked sideways down the steps, balancing carefully, testing each step so as not to slip. He moaned with pleasure, when the water was deep enough to cover his chest. "Yes, that loosens me up," he said, softly. Then he turned to Repentance who still stood at the top of the steps.

"I don't care if you swim, or not," the king said, "But for appearances sake you must get in the water with me." He coughed into his fist then bent his face forward and took a deep breath from the steam rising off the pool's surface.

He turned and started paddling slowly toward the other end of the pool.

Repentance draped his robe over a nearby bench. She unbuttoned her gown, dropped it off her shoulders so it slid to the ground, and hurried into the bubbly water.

She found the bench cut into the side of the pool and sat with her back pushed against the wall.

He reached the end of the pool and turned to slowly paddle back.

Going up and back several times, he completely ignored Repentance. His breathing came regularly with an occasional cough echoing across the water.

Finally, he stopped his paddling and climbed out of the pool. He stood dripping, his back to Repentance.

She stayed where she was, rooted to the spot, hoping—no matter how unreasonable the hope was—that he'd pick up his robe and head into their sleeping quarters without her.

It has thus far worked out that each time I've reached the end of my strength and lost all hope of rescue, Providence has sent a hero. Why does He wait so long? I suspect it is because His heroes are always so unsuitable in my eyes that I would never accept their aid, had I any other options.

~Meticulous Mudslide, *An Old Man Remembers*

CHAPTER 13

Standing wet beside the pool, the king sighed loudly. "You should now get out of the water and help me on with my robe. You must watch me and anticipate my needs."

She crawled up the stairs, keeping her body in the water as long as possible. Reaching the second step from the top, she made a dash for her gown. It didn't want to go on her wet body. The sleeves stuck and twisted. She yanked violently, desperate to get it on before the king turned around.

"I am a sick old man and I stand here dripping. But you have no sympathy. How about this, then? I am your king and master. You will attend to my needs before you attend to your own. If you are smart, that is."

She yanked her gown down and grabbed his robe. "I'm sorry, your highness."

He shrugged his arms into his loose sleeves. "And tonight you must sleep in my bed. The maids will chatter otherwise. It's a nuisance really."

Repentance gave him a sideways glance. If he didn't like to share his bed, why had he taken her? Apparently his mind was like his body—old and wrinkled. That happened. Her father's old-father was always confused and forgetting things. This king was in his two hundred and fiftieth year. Maybe he had forgotten what men were supposed to do to girls in their beds. A fragile strand of hope drifted her way, and she made a desperate grab for it. "I could sleep on the floor, so as not to bother you in your bed, Lord."

He considered that for a moment. "You could at that. I'm sure my nephew throws the girls out of his bed when he's done with them. Why shouldn't I? Excellent idea!"

The hope slipped through her fingers, blown away by his cruel words. He didn't want her to *sleep* in his bed. That was all. He didn't mind sharing his bed for other purposes and kicking her out when he was done.

He walked her to their room. "You mustn't discuss our sleeping arrangements with anyone. You understand?"

She gaped. Who did he think she might discuss the matter with?

"But, by Providence," he continued, giving her a cranky look, "it is a huge inconvenience. I can't have a servant because you should be serving me, and it's clear you know nothing about serving. I daren't hope you know how to help a man bathe?"

She shook her head. "I was never told that would be one of my duties."

"Yes, I suppose they thought you'd need different talents this night. Mayhap I should have left you for my nephew." His expression softened. "But, no, that would not have been kind."

She stared. He considered himself kind? He really was crazy, then.

"Go to sleep on the floor, child. I'll bathe myself."

Surprised, she jerked, but she recovered quickly and wasted no time. She threw herself down and lay as still as the warm stone beneath her. Afraid to move. Almost afraid to breathe, lest she call attention to herself and cause the king to change his mind.

Sounds of bathing drifted to her from the other room, interrupted every once in a while by muffled coughs. Maybe his condition was agitated by his effort to wash himself. Repentance saw the flask sitting on the table by the bed and wondered if she should take it to him, but his coughing subsided.

He reentered the room.

Repentance breathed deeply and evenly, keeping her eyes shut.

She tensed as she felt him walk toward her.

His robe landed on her. She heard his labored breathing as he bent down, then she felt him pull the robe up around her shoulders.

He doused the lantern and got into the bed.

Repentance relaxed. It was unfathomable, but the king had decided not to use her ill that night. Before long, soft snores floated down from the bed. She offered a prayer of thanksgiving and gave herself over to sleep.

The following morning Repentance woke stiff and achy from sleeping on the stone floor.

She stretched, then rose, stifling a groan, and looked toward the bed, from whence came the sound of snoring. The king looked frail in sleep. He was ancient. The surprising thing was that he looked so ... so ... normal. Like a nice old-father. Not like a murderer.

Fifteen minutes later, when she finished in the bathing room and re-entered the sleeping quarters, the king was sitting on the edge of the bed.

"Ah, you're an early riser," he said. "That's good." He stood, swayed, and steadied himself. "Here we must be careful. Once we're at the palace, it won't matter. You'll have your own quarters there. And no one will expect you to be in my bed, of a morning."

"You're taking me to the palace?"

"Of course, I'm taking you. I can't very well leave you here to be used ill by any man who takes the notion."

Repentance sat, stunned.

"Besides," he added, "it's about time I took a concubine." He toddled toward the bathing room. "Go up and tell Jadin I require Catlinora to wrap my turban."

"Child," he said, as she reached the door. "Remind me of your name. If we are to be famous lovers—and we shall, of course, have all of Harthill's tongues tattling—I should at least know your name."

She almost cringed at the thought of being the king's lover but fought to control her face. "Repentance," she answered calmly.

He grimaced. "Ah. How could I have forgotten? Let's hope I don't end up repenting this foolishness of mine."

"Surely your highness has never been foolish."

"Saving you from my nephew was foolish."

"You took me in order to save me?"

"You think I need a child to care for at my old age? Maybe being king doesn't keep me busy enough? Of course I was saving you. What do you think I was doing? "

"I thought you ... I thought you took me ...."

"For a concubine? Good. Let the world think as much. Why should they think I am too old and infirmed to enjoy the pleasures of a concubine?" He coughed into his hand and sucked in a wheezing breath.

Repentance took a moment to catch her own breath. He was saying that he wouldn't ... he couldn't use her as a concubine? "I don't understand. Why would you care to save me from the prince?"

"You are so young. And you ... " He drifted off, staring at her for a moment—giving her a kindly look. "You remind me of someone I once knew."

Did his eyes mist up? Or were they merely old and rheumy? Repentance couldn't be sure.

He sighed. "The prince has a reputation for being very cruel."

Heat rushed into her cheeks. "I've heard rumors of the same."

"Good. Then you will pay attention when I say this: As long as my nephew thinks you are my concubine, he will leave you alone. If he suspects you have not been in my bed, he will take you to his." He gave her a hard look. "To all of Harthill, we will be lovers. And you will not disabuse anyone of that notion. If you do, I'll give you to the prince. And you will not find the change in circumstances to be to your advantage."

"I understand." She didn't understand much, but she understood enough. For the moment, by some unexpected good will from Providence, she was safe.

They stayed for three more days at the healing house and the king never laid a hand on her. Repentance took three meals a day with him, but the other girls didn't often dine with the royals. They were present for dinner, but not invited to breakfast and lunch. Repentance also noticed that the men traded companions back and forth. She and Tawnic were the only girls who were never traded. She, because the king had purchased her outright from Jadin, and Tawnic, because the prince apparently didn't like to share.

At the table, the king treated Repentance as if she were his guest and not his slave. Well, maybe not a guest, exactly. He treated her like a possession, expecting her to obey him. But he *asked* her do things instead of ordering her about. And after Madam Cawrocc, and Jadin, with their constant threats to abuse poor Comfort if Repentance stuck one elbow too far out, the king seemed like an angel of Providence Himself.

He'd saved her from the prince, and he didn't even require her presence in his bed. Short of freedom, she couldn't have landed in a better place.

Still, she was surprised by the warmth she felt toward the king when he took her hand and helped her into the carriage after lunch on the fourth day. It made her feel a little sick to her stomach. He showed her the merest trickle of kindness, and she was almost ready to forgive him for the evil way he'd treated her people. She thought of her little brothers, howling as they were being carted off by the slavers. She thought about the slaves at the healing house, scrubbing the pools, cooking the food, sleeping, after long days of labor, in cramped, hot, smelly rooms. She remembered Sober, beaten and tied to a post on the slave dock, and the dead boys swinging in the courtyard, and she pulled her hand away from the king and wiped it on her gown.

The prince, standing beside the carriage, saw. He looked into her eyes and smiled before he climbed into the carriage behind his uncle.

"Lord Malficc," the king said. "Why do you not ride with your friends?"

"We have business, your highness. Nothing you need to worry about. Just papers for you to sign."

A frown flicked across the king's face, but he said nothing.

The prince settled into the seat facing the king and Repentance, and one of his friends, Lord Garresh, took the spot next to him.

Repentance gave a last look at the healing house, wondering if she'd ever see the swamp again or if this time she was leaving it for good. The other girls stood on the porch, laughing and waving and telling the noblemen to hurry back. Tawnic was with them. She wore a forced smile.

Turning away, Repentance thanked Providence for her reversal of fortune. She couldn't feel sorry for Tawnic. The girl had shown no pity, and her curse had fallen on her own head, while Repentance had reaped a blessing. That was fair. Amazingly, Providence had sided with her for once, but she was surprised that her victory over the snotty overlord girl didn't bring her any satisfaction. Instead of wanting to gloat, she felt empty and old and tired.

Escorted by at least thirty troopers on horseback, which

hemmed them in before and behind, the carriages rolled away.

The king looked at the prince. "What do you need?"

The prince held out his hand and Lord Garresh pulled a thick pad of parchment from a leather pouch and passed it over.

"We've gotten the census from the breeder villages."

He placed the parchment pad on the king's lap.

"You'll see there all the numbers, and you'll be pleased to know that Providence has blessed us with more boys."

Repentance stared out the window and bit back her anger. Providence blessed them with more boys. The lowborns were no more than chickens who were suddenly laying twice as many eggs.

The king grunted and Repentance heard the sound of parchment pages being turned.

"Well, there's no need for you to read the whole packet," the prince said. "The numbers are up in every village. Just sign the bottom page, here—" More shuffling of parchment. And then the scratching of a charstick.

"Ah, very good," the prince said. "And now we have one for you to sign in regards to your troopers."

Repentance looked over to see the prince taking up the parchment pad and replacing it with a single sheet.

The king picked up the sheet and read it. "Five thousand beads! It's criminal."

"They're here for your protection."

"My left elbow! Here for my protection. No one is trying to assassinate me. I'm the best loved king in three-hundred years."

A look of hatred crossed the prince's face. "I'm aware of that, Uncle. Yes, I am. But it's because you are so loved, that we need to pay your troopers more. You are too precious to the people for us to take chances with your life."

"My troopers? You are the one who orders them about."

"Yes, Uncle. I order the troopers about, I take care of the imports and exports, I watch over the labor issues, I attend to our foreign wars, and you? You sign papers. That is how we have done it for a long time and that is what keeps the people happy. You smile and sit on the throne and I run the kingdom."

The king glared. "You forget yourself, Malficc."

"No, sir, I do not. I have not forgotten the kingdom and its needs. You are the one who seems to think everything will run itself while you're constantly down at the healing house. It is because of my work that the people love you so dearly."

The king squinted at the prince. "No. You'll not give the troopers a bonus in beads. I'll give the bonuses myself. I'm old, Lord Malficc, not stupid. Yours will not be the hand that feeds the watchdogs." He crumpled the parchment.

The prince nodded. "As you wish, your highness." He took another stack of parchment sheets from Garresh. "One more signature, then."

The king grabbed the pile. "What is this?"

"Provisions for various ministries." The prince tapped the top sheet. "More desks requested by the Ministry of Education." He lifted the page. "Rope for the Ministry of Jus—"

"Oh, for the love of Providence!" The king jerked the pile back. "I can read for myself." He flipped through the sheets, scanning the contents of each, then turned to the bottom one and signed his name.

The prince took the parchment book back and handed it to Garresh.

Repentance thought the look he gave Garresh came very close to the one her little brothers would exchange when they'd succeeded in slipping slugs into the pocket of Comfort's shift when she wasn't looking.

Why use your sons to till the soil?
    Why give their strength to sweat and toil?
        Why send your sons to fight in war,
            when slaves can do all these and more?
                ~Captain Karrnidge, *Stratagem for Success*

CHAPTER 14

The carriage followed the sandy road up the mountain. "Wake me at the farm." The king put his head back against the seat cushion and closed his eyes.

Repentance looked at the old man, then chanced a sideways glance at the prince and his friend Lord Garresh who sat across from her. In the back of her mind, a thought began to form. It didn't matter how much she hated the king. If she pleased him she might be in a position to help Comfort when her buttoning failed. He had saved Repentance. Maybe he'd be willing to save Comfort, too. Thank Providence the king was well loved and no one wanted to assassinate him. As long as he was alive she was safe from the prince.

But then a horrid thought hit her. The king was ancient. How much longer could he live?

And when he died ....

She glanced again at the prince's handsome face. He caught her looking and gave her a broad smile.

She smiled back, with a grin that she hoped didn't look as sickly as it felt, and then quickly looked out the window. He scared her more when he smiled than when he frowned. She would have to pray that the king wouldn't die.

By the time they turned in to the farm where they would trade their horses for two skim carriages, Repentance had counted seventy-eight birds flitting between trees, and three wild hogs in the creek that ran alongside the road. And she'd managed to keep from looking at the prince the whole way.

The king disembarked and held up his hand for her. She took his hand, this time letting it linger after she'd gotten down. She had to forget his past and worry about her future, and Comfort's. And that meant she had to make the old king happy.

"We'll stay the night here and leave early," the king said. "We'll make it to the palace by tomorrow afternoon." He led her up the steps.

Repentance breathed out a sigh of relief. The following day, the prince would be traveling in the other carriage, Providence willing.

Woeful's eyes nearly popped from his head when he saw her. He actually bowed as she passed. She couldn't resist giving him a little smirk. There were advantages to being the king's concubine. She hadn't landed in an unbearable position, considering how bad it could have been. Strange, to be sure, but not unbearable.

But none of the strange occurrences that had tumbled, willy-nilly, into her life over the previous month prepared her for her first view of the palace grounds the following day.

After traveling through the ice city for almost an hour, passing block after block of tall houses, the skim carriages paused at a tall iron gate in the middle of a long ice wall.

The prince, who had been traveling in the front carriage, climbed out, and the carriage pulled off, down the road.

The king's carriage pulled forward and stopped beside the prince. He climbed aboard and sat opposite Repentance. She stiffened. But maybe he didn't live in the palace. Maybe he was just going to visit or he had some work to do there.

On either side of the gate, two ice statues towered over the carriages. Giant men with crossbows, surveying the sky.

"What are they hunting?" Repentance asked the king.

"They're guarding against dragons."

"I've never seen a dragon."

"Nor will you. They were annihilated in the Dragon War. Once, they were a threat to us, though, so dragon hunters were highly regarded."

The drive wound through grounds filled with mist and magic. Colored ice fountains were abundant. And from hot water fountains, ice fog lifted and settled on pine trees, clothing them with thick, frosty shawls.

Repentance put her hand out of the carriage window, feeling the warm day. "Why doesn't the ice melt in the sun?"

"It can't melt. One of the gifts of Providence, you know."

No, she didn't know.

"Like the cloths and the hot springs," the king said, as if that would clear it all up for her.

She nodded, not wanting to press him for an explanation lest he grow exasperated with her.

Off to one side, a patch of slick, smooth ice shone like gold, and several children slid across the surface.

Repentance laughed. How much fun her brothers would have had sliding there.

She looked closer. "But it looks wet, there, where the children are sliding,"

"It is wet," the king said. "It has a constant sheet of hot water running over it to keep it slippery. Otherwise it would freeze, dry and sticky, like the streets."

"And would you like to know what's really funny?" the prince asked.

Repentance looked shyly at him.

"Me?" she asked.

"No, you're not funny," he answered looking at her with a

kind of strange, hungry look. "I can assure you, you're not funny."

She blushed. "You were asking *me* if I wanted to know something funny?"

"Oh, you are funny, after all. Yes, I was asking *you*. Who else? You don't suppose my uncle likes to laugh, do you? Can't you see what a sour face he has?" He cocked an eyebrow.

His insolence was shocking.

He continued, apparently feeling no reproach from her shocked expression. "What's really funny is when someone turns off the hot water that washes over the top of the frozen pond. The children come to a screeching halt in seconds. The water freezes and they are stuck solid."

Repentance tried to picture such a scene.

The prince was laughing. "Small children waving their arms around and screaming hysterically." He waved his arms around to demonstrate. "Help, help!"

"Their mothers didn't find it as entertaining as you did," the king said. "The cook quit."

"But Uncle, you have only yourself to blame for that," the prince said. "A king shouldn't allow his servants to quit."

"When the prince freezes a child's feet to a pond so they get ice-burned, it would hardly be fitting for the king to make the mother continue to cook for the young ne'er do well."

The prince frowned. "I don't see why not. The king owns the child's feet. He should do as he pleases with them."

"Yes, and the king was pleased to provide healing treatments for those feet. Do you question my rights in the matter, or only my wisdom?"

"Neither, Uncle," the prince said turning away to gaze out the window. "You are all sovereign and wise and ever may you receive honor and glory," he muttered.

The king's eyes narrowed, but he said nothing. He pulled out his flask and took a swig.

As the carriage approached the palace Repentance ducked down and looked out the window, so she could see the top of the palace towers, which soared into the blue sky like giant icy cliffs. "So tall!"

"The palace is five stories," the king said, "with the towers going up four stories beyond that."

The face of the building was carved in elegant scrolling patterns, while sculpted dragon hunters guarded the main doors.

The carriage halted and the king stepped down first. He waved the footman away and turned to help Repentance down himself.

The prince tucked his leather pouch under one arm and stepped out in front of Repentance. "Thank you, Your Majesty," he said, taking the king's hand.

As he let go, he gave the king a little jerk, pulling him off-balance.

The footman caught the king and steadied him.

The king slapped the footman away, as if offended that anyone would think he needed help standing on his own two feet. Then he helped Repentance from the carriage and led her up the wide palace steps.

"Here's Provocation," the king said indicating an old slave woman standing in the doorway, dressed in a fine gown. "She is head over the affairs of the house. If you are in need of anything, you may go to her."

The prince brushed past the woman and into the house.

The king squinted at the prince's back for a moment, then turned his attention to Provocation. "I've brought home a friend," the king said. "This is Repentance. She's to have the queen's chamber."

Provocation's eyes widened for a moment before she bowed her head serenely.

Repentance was much less composed. The queen's chamber!

"And, send Biased to me," the king said. "I want to get out of this dratted turban. Makes my head itch." Turning to Repentance, he added, "I'll expect you for dinner." Without waiting for an answer, he strutted down the hall to the left with an energy Repentance knew did not come easily. He was acting like a strong and healthy king.

"Follow me." Provocation looked as wrinkly as an old-mother, but not half as friendly. She marched ahead of Repentance, her back as straight and hard as Hatcher's Cliff, back home.

They turned to the right. As they rounded the corner, they almost stumbled on the prince who was squatting in the middle of the hall. A boy, who looked to be in about his seventh year, sat on the floor in front of the prince. Parchment pages were strewn around the two.

Provocation stopped abruptly and Repentance barely stopped in time to keep from knocking the older woman off her feet.

"I'm sorry," the boy said.

Repentance couldn't see his face. His head was bowed. He began to collect up stray sheets of parchment.

"You know better than to run in the hallways, Tigen," the prince answered angrily.

"I have been told many times," the boy said. "I keep forgetting." He scooped up a page and glanced at its contents.

Provocation and Repentance both stooped to help collect stray papers.

"No," the prince said to Provocation. "Leave them."

The boy picked up another page. "You are going to take slaves my age?" he asked, reading from the sheet he held. "Will they come to the palace?"

"Give me that!" The prince said, grabbing the sheet.

"It says you're taking all the boys—"

"Provocation," the prince said. "I'm sure my uncle's new concubine is tired. You should take her to her quarters. Tigen is capable of picking up the pages he knocked loose."

Provocation bowed. She and Repentance skirted the mess and continued down the hall.

Tigen's voice followed them. "That page said you were taking all the lowborn boys from their sixth year to their fourteenth year."

Repentance gasped. That would include both of her little

brothers.

"Will any of them come here?" Tigen continued.

Provocation and Repentance took a right-hand turn and Repentance stooped down to fiddle with her slipper.

"Can you not read?" the prince said. "That was a provision for the Ministry of War. They are going to the trooper camps to be trained for front-line soldiers. I've told you before that I don't want you playing with them, anyway, Tigen. Your interest in slaves is unnatural."

Provocation looked around. Repentance jumped up and trotted to catch up. The two continued a long ways, taking several more turns. Repentance, thinking about her brothers being trained as front-line soldiers, couldn't concentrate on the path they took or the countless doors they passed.

Finally the old slave woman stopped and threw open the door to a big room, its floor covered with thick, soft, buttery-colored carpet. In the center was a bed piled high with quilts.

Repentance stood in the doorway, closed her eyes, and breathed in, trying to regain her balance.

But the prince was going to take Fullness and Restoration. There was no balance in the world. It was hopelessly tipped in favor of the overlords.

"Well go on." Provocation said. "I can't stand all day in the hallway with you. Some of us have work to do."

Repentance opened her eyes and stepped into her new quarters. The room was richly furnished and smelled sweet and spicy. A hearth sat in one corner. It would be lovely and homey once a fire was lit. In front of the fireplace sat several stuffed chairs with small tables in between. On the wall to the left were three windows.

She crossed the room, approaching one window, and looked over the grounds toward the front gates, wondering where the trooper camp was and who the overlords were at war with. What made them need to take lowborn boys for soldiers?

Warmth flooded through the window and Repentance reached out and touched the clear ice pane.

Pain bit at her fingertip as if she'd touched red-hot iron.

She yanked her hand away and stuck her finger in her mouth.

"A good lesson," Provocation said, her voice deep and scratchy. "The ice is so cold it burns the skin."

Yes, she'd discovered that. It would have been nice if Provocation had warned her a little earlier.

She crossed to the opposite wall. Carved in relief, with bright paint frozen on top, was a city scene, depicting houses and markets and streets full of wagons. On the sidewalks were merchants raking their stoops or hanging signs, and fine ladies in colorful gowns. The detail was incredible. She would love to show Comfort.

She turned away with a sigh, holding her stomach. Missing Comfort felt like a physical pain. And now to hear that the little boys ....

She crossed to the bed and sat. She wanted to lie down and cry. She felt sick and dizzy and a little bit like she wanted to throw up.

Provocation glared at Repentance, as if offended by her presence. She turned and threw open the doors of the wardrobe which stood in the corner opposite the fireplace.

Empty.

"I didn't know you were coming." She said it like a rebuke. "I'll send for the seamstress tomorrow."

Fear prickled Repentance's scalp. The housekeeper was as cranky as an old-mother with fish nets to pick in mosquito season.

Provocation closed the wardrobe and continued acquainting Repentance with the room. "Your desk." She pointed to an oak desk, its top polished to a shine.

"Your bathing room, here." She opened a door revealing a large room with a small pool in the floor. "You share with the king. His sleeping chamber is through that door, there." She pointed across the bathing room. Repentance leaned forward to see.

"I'll send Generosity to help you get ready for dinner. She'll be your maid."

"I'm to have a maid?" She looked at her huge bed, covered in soft, fluffy quilts. Draped overhead, hanging down around the bed, was gauzy material. Repentance rubbed it between her fingers. The material oozed warmth. Everything about the room was rich and comfortable. Of course she would have a maid.

Provocation studied her. "How old are you, child?"

"I am barely in my sixteenth year."

The old slave shook her head and clucked her tongue. "What possessed him to take a concubine now? At his age!"

Repentance gave a slight shrug.

"Yes, you have a maid." Provocation said. "Poor child. You know nothing of the ways of the mountain, I'll wager."

"I would not be opposed to someone sharing the particulars with me."

Provocation nodded. "You will grace his dinner table. You will go with him to parties. You will laugh at his jokes and hold on to his arm and gaze into his face as if there is nowhere you'd prefer to be."

She smiled sadly at Repentance. "You'll dance with him. And when he requires it, you'll go to his bed and keep his old bones warm."

Repentance said nothing. What could she say to such an embarrassing statement? But she was happy that, at least in one particular, Provocation was wrong. The old king did not like to share his bed.

"You'll eat well. And you'll not do any work. You won't even dress yourself. But don't get used to it, child. It won't last. It never does with these nobles. A summer. Maybe a year. Another one will take your place and you'll be sold to another man or put into service in the household."

Repentance's heart jumped. "How long has the king kept his other concubines?" She had to keep him happy, at least until Comfort came up in the slave cart.

"And why now?" Provocation asked, ignoring Repentance and apparently speaking to herself. "He's never taken a concubine before." She looked at Repentance as if to see what it was about her that would make the king act so uncharacteristically. "We all assumed he was unable to ... unable to ... well, with his illness, we assumed he'd never take a concubine. Why now?"

He said he was trying to save her, but she couldn't tell anyone that. She had to convince this old woman that the king really wanted a concubine.

Provocation stood staring, as if waiting for an explanation.

"Maybe he was waiting for the right girl," Repentance offered, meekly. "Maybe he was being careful and that's why it took so long for him to choose. Maybe now that he's found me, he means to keep me."

Provocation harrumphed. "Yes, well, that's a lot of maybes all strung prettily together like gemstones on a necklace. In all my life I've yet to see a situation hanging on so many maybes turn out for good in the end."

She left then, thank Providence, and took her grim predictions with her.

Still, Repentance couldn't help but notice that the room was a little grayer and colder than she'd first thought.

The old housekeeper had been gone only a moment when the door swished open and the prince stuck his head into her room. Without knocking!

"Ah, getting nicely settled?" he asked.

Fear coursed through her. She stared at him mutely.

He smiled. "You are far too young and pretty to be stuck with a smelly old man like my uncle."

She hadn't noticed an odor on the king. "Thank you, your highness," Her voice was no more than a whisper. "But I cannot accept such a compliment. It is untrue, and it comes at the expense of my master, besides."

"And you're loyal as well." He nodded. "An admirable quality in a concubine. Very good. He can't live forever, can he? And then I'll inherit his throne. And his concubine. And I'm not sure but I'll enjoy the one as much as the other."

He bowed and left her.

She collapsed onto the floor in despair. The prince was apparently going to take her brothers and make them go to war. He would put them up front like peons in a game of Kings and Conquest, to be sacrificed for a cause they had no part of. And she could do nothing to stop him. She was stuck with an old king who did nothing but sign papers like an obedient child. And when he died?

As hard as it was to comprehend, when the king died, things would get even worse for Repentance and her family.

A harsh word, rashly spoken, can't be snatched back once it's been released upon the world. Consider carefully, then, before you open your mouth to instruct others.

~Mercy Atwater, wisdom passed on from
mother to daughter and largely ignored

CHAPTER 15

Repentance had one hope. She might please the king and make him want to save her and her family. Surely he could tell the prince not to take Repentance's brothers. They were just two boys. The prince could live without two little slave boys. And the king could save Comfort, too, when she came up on the slave cart.

If he lived that long.

And if he lived long enough and she served him well enough, he might even let Repentance and her family go to one of those places Lord Carrull had spoken of. One of those states where slaves went free. He could do that before he died.

Repentance pushed herself off the floor, went to the bathing room, and washed her face. She would work hard for the king and make him want to help her.

She was leaving the bathing room when the maid arrived and drove the prince and his evil plans from her mind.

Generosity was everything Provocation was not. She was

young—in her eighteenth year—and jolly and talkative. She'd been sold as a slave when she'd failed to button. She told Repentance all about it as she bathed. Her intended button mate had died in an accident—they were from a logging village halfway up the mountain on the other side from Hot Springs—and all the other potential button mates in the village had been spoken for.

Repentance found it harsh that Providence would take Generosity's button mate two months before the ceremony. If He'd waited until after the ceremony to take the young man, Generosity could have lived out her life with her family and cheated the overlords out of slave children. It would have been the perfect life. Sometimes Providence made no sense.

But Generosity seemed not to mind. Her warm, brown eyes were quick to smile and she seemed genuinely happy to be taking care of Repentance.

"I'll braid your hair for you when you go to the Moonlight Festival next month." She steered Repentance into a chair by a sunny window. "But for dinners here, you'll wear it long and loose."

"Moonlight Festival?"

"You didn't keep the festivals to Providence in your village?" Generosity asked as she began to brush her long, wet hair.

None that had to do with moonlight, anyway. Or sunlight, for that matter. But she didn't feel like explaining about the fog generated by the hot springs and how she'd grown up without heavenly lights. "Not the Moonlight Festival, no," she said.

"We have the Moonlight Festival to thank Providence for the gift of mooncloth."

"That's why we never had the Moonlight Festival. We never use mooncloth in Hot Springs."

Generosity took a small snatch of cloth from the wide front pocket of her work tunic and looked at it fondly. "This is made from mooncloth my mother wove. It's all I have to remember her by." She sniffed and held it out to Repentance. "I'll wager you've never seen finer."

Repentance had never seen any, let alone any finer. She

rubbed the satiny material between her fingers.

As Generosity stashed the cloth back in her pocket, Repentance thought she saw a flash of light. "Let me see that again."

Generosity complied.

"That was strange. I thought I saw a blue light as you stuck it into your pocket."

"It's mooncloth. It shines in the dark."

Repentance frowned. She was so ignorant. When she'd offered herself up to the slave cart in hopes of cheating the overlords out of her babies, she'd never dreamed there would be so many oddities filling the wide world on the other side of the river. Cloth that lit up in the dark. Houses made of ice that were never cold. Horseless carriages with no wheels. She blew out a breath and looked out the window at the cloudless sky. "Windows made of thin plates of ice that never melt in the sun."

"What's that you say?" Generosity asked.

"Nothing. I was thinking out loud." She reached up to feel her hair. Almost dry. "So are there more festivals I should know about? Sunlight festivals, perhaps?"

Generosity looked at her as if she were a two-headed toad. "You jest."

Repentance gave a tight-lipped smile. She was not anxious to look stupid in the eyes of a maid. Especially not in the eyes of one as talkative as this one. "I don't know how you celebrate up here on the mountain. Tell me about the festivals."

"Oh, I see. You wish to test me. My knowledge? Or my devotion? You need not worry, my Lady. I'm not like so many today that claim devotion to Providence but never serve Him. I know all the festivals, and I attend them."

Repentance sucked in her breath when Generosity called her "my Lady" but she controlled her face. "I'm sure you're devoted. I truly want to know if the people here celebrate the same festivals we did in my village."

Generosity set the brush on the small table next to her and began ticking the festivals off on her fingers. "In winter we have the

Snowfrost Festival to thank Providence for the snowcloth woven in Velvet Valley. In spring is the Lavaheat Festival. For the lavacloth, you know. From Smokey Peak." She paused, glancing at Repentance.

Repentance nodded as if she were well aware of Smokey Peak and knew exactly how to locate it on a map.

"In summer there is the Sunlight Festival for the suncloth." She waved a hand at the cloths that hung on the walls. The ones farthest from the window, in the shadows by the bathing room, glowed with yellow light and emitted a soft buzzing noise.

For the love of Providence! What was going on with all these cloths? And why was it that every slave village but hers seemed to weave some kind of special material?

"Fall is the time for the Moonlight Festival, as I've already said, and a few weeks later there is the Dragonbreath Festival."

"Of course. For the dragoncloth," Repentance said confidently.

Generosity frowned. Then she laughed. "Oh, you're having a joke on me. You looked so serious, you had me fooled for a moment. Dragoncloth indeed."

Repentance felt a headache coming on. She would never learn it all. She forced a chuckle. "I'm pleased that I've been given a maid with a good sense of humor. If you'll leave me, now, I'll go to bed. I'm tired from my travel."

"What will I tell His Highness? He's having an early dinner. You're expected."

Sighing, Repentance stood. "Then I'd best go, hadn't I? What shall I wear?" Preferably something the prince wouldn't like. She shivered.

Generosity helped her into one of the thin lowland gowns she'd brought from the healing house then led her through a maze of hallways, as she gushed forth on whatever topic caught her fancy. She stopped at the door of the dining room, ending with her thoughts on having Repentance in the palace. How nice it would be to have another young woman to talk to, Generosity said, and how boring life had been, what with all the other maids being much older and then with crusty Provocation lurking about and scolding at every opportunity, and how much fun they were sure to have now.

As much as Repentance liked Generosity's open friendliness, she wasn't sad to part company with her at the dining room door. All that chatter couldn't be good for the digestive system.

When Generosity left, Repentance patted her hair into place, smoothed her gown, and entered the room with what she hoped was a peaceful expression on her face. She wouldn't show the prince how much he had shaken her.

It turned out not to matter. The room was empty, save for a manservant—a slave—loitering in one corner. She breathed out in relief.

As soon as she entered, the slave sprang forward and pulled out a chair from the far end of the table.

Repentance sat.

As the slave poured her some of the milky drink she liked so much—yak's milk, she'd learned it was, thinned with mountainberry wine and sweetened with honey—she studied the room. Ice walls, thick carpet, like every other room. The carpet was a deep maroon, which matched the dark wood of the dining table. She bent forward to study the grain. Mahogany.

On the wall opposite her, a painting was carved in relief on the wall, like the cityscape in her room. This one was a man on a yak. A nobleman—she could tell from the turban—it looked like .... She leaned forward. It looked like the king. At his side, a woman stood, her back to Repentance. She was a slave woman—black hair. But she was dressed in a fancy gown. His button mate, probably. Before she'd lost her head.

Repentance stared at the picture trying to reconcile the king she'd been with for five days, with the king who had beheaded his button mate and enslaved all the lowborns in a fit of rage over her infidelity. She was guilty, if history books were to be trusted. But the history books were written by the overlords, so who knew if they could be trusted. And even if she was guilty, how was it right for him to cut off her head and take her people captive? And to still be punishing them two-hundred-and-fifty years later? The punishment hardly fit the crime. And now her brothers were to be sacrificed in an overlord war they knew nothing about.

The door swished open, and the king came in.

Repentance stood, wiped the glare off her face, and bowed her head.

The slave seated him then reseated Repentance.

The king raised his hands toward heaven.

Repentance bowed her head. He hadn't prayed in the healing house, but apparently in the palace he did things differently.

"For all you have provided, we give you thanks," the king said.

A serving woman came in with a silver tureen and ladled soup into their bowls.

"Will we begin without Lord Malficc?" Repentance asked. At the healing house the table was full for every meal. She had a vague idea that a king's table would always be crowded with friends and pretenders.

"He doesn't dine with us."

Joy swept through her. "Doesn't he live in the palace, then?" That was good news, indeed.

"He does. But he dines with his goodwoman and their four boys in their family quarters. Oh, no, you'd not catch me dead, sharing a table with those four boys."

"He's buttoned?"

"That surprises you?"

"He was with ... with ... " Repentance felt her cheeks burning.

"With?"

"Why does he go to Hot Springs? Why does he have Tawnic service him when he has his own goodwoman right here?"

"Oh, the men in your village have only one woman. Is that it?"

She blushed again. "We button for life."

"As do we. But our button mates don't have exclusive rights

over us. We used to do it that way. It's an old-fashioned idea. I didn't know any of the villages still practiced it."

Repentance let her spoon fall into her bowl and stared at him in horror. Such a thing for him to say!

"But you decapitated your button mate for that very thing! That exact same thing. That's why you took all the lowborns into slavery, you hypocrite. You ... you warthog!"

"Warthog? Warthog!" His face had turned maroon.

"You've punished us for two-hundred-and-fifty years because you believed you had exclusive rights over your button mate, and now you say this idea of exclusive rights is old fashioned?"

He pushed himself to his feet, shaking with weakness and rage. "How dare you? And you a slave!" He glanced at the servant who stood by the wall, his face a mask of disinterest.

"It cannot be left to stand unpunished," the king said through clenched teeth. "You will go to your room and wait for me to determine your fate."

All the anger drained from Repentance.

What had she done?

Had she yelled at him?

Called him a name?

He glared down at her.

She slid her chair back. "I don't know the way to my room," she whispered.

When the lowborn grows too old to do your bidding, it is your responsibility to call in the swingman. When the slave can no longer provide you with pleasure, his purpose in life is gone. It is cruelty to keep him alive then, an unhappy, useless shell.

~Doctor Durr Raynjed, *The Care and Feeding of Animals*

CHAPTER 16

At the king's command, the manservant took Repentance to her room. He said nothing along the way and left her without a word.

Repentance sat in shock on the edge of her big, soft bed.

What had she been thinking?

She absently took her three gray buttons from the pocket of her gown and placed them on the bed.

She hadn't been thinking. That was what caused her trouble. Speaking first, thinking later. Her mother had always said her mouth would land her in a puddle full of trouble one day.

Picking up the heart-shaped button, she rubbed it between her fingers.

This time she'd done damage that no amount of prayer would be able to undo.

His face had been so red! Maybe he would hand her over to the swingman.

For certain she'd lost her comfortable room in the palace. "Gone the cushy bed." She whispered. She stood the heart button on its edge and flicked it off the bed.

"Gone the comfortable palace." She flicked the round button.

"Gone the concubine's head." The third button followed the first two. "The king lopped it off with malice."

And all she could do was sit and wait to die. If she tried to run, the king would take Comfort.

Of course, if he did hang her, he'd take Comfort anyway. The law stated that if you disobeyed and were killed, the master could take a member of your family to replace you.

So why should she wait for him to kill her? Maybe she could get down the mountain and get Comfort and the little boys before the troopers did. Or maybe she could get to Lord Carrull. Maybe he would help her. Or those Deliverance Day people he mentioned. They helped slaves.

She slid off the bed, scooped up her buttons, and headed for the door.

Just to check.

Just to peek out and see if a guard had been posted in the hall.

Silently, she twisted the knob ... cracked the door open ... and ... found herself staring into the king's face.

She slammed the door and raced to her bed.

The king entered. "You were going someplace?'

"I was just looking."

"Just looking. Just talking. Just unwilling to live wisely. That's the manner of girl you are. You rush into trouble. Am I right?"

She hung her head. "My mother has told me I have a bad habit of speaking rashly."

"Your mother." He crossed to the chairs by the fire and sat down with a sigh. "Your mother was a beautiful woman."

Repentance shot a glance at him. "How do you know that?"

He paused for the smallest of moments. "I've seen you. It's

not possible that you came from an ugly mother. Besides, I have a sketch of her in the paperwork Jadin gave me. But is your mother wise as well as beautiful? That's what I can't see when I look at you." He twisted in his chair to look at her. "She scolded you for your rash tongue, you say, but she failed to train it out of you."

He patted the chair next to him. "Come here so I can see you without straining my neck."

Why was he sitting before her fire as if he'd come to tea? She couldn't figure this old king out. She went and sat.

"Tell me about your family," he said. "How many young? And how does your father occupy his time?"

She stared at him mutely, not sure what to say. Not sure how to best protect her family.

"When you should be silent, you spew forth unfettered. And when I command you to speak, you refuse. Your mouth needs instruction. That much I can see." He held up one finger. "Lesson. When the king asks a question, you answer. Respectfully."

She knew that. Jadin had taught her that rule.

She'd forgotten.

"Shall we try again?" the king asked. "Tell me about your family."

"My father fishes in the winter when the water cools and the holly pokes come downstream. He sells them two-fer-a."

"Toofurah?"

"Two-fer-a-bead. Two fish for one bead."

The king nodded. "And what does he do in summer when the holly pokes aren't running?"

"He builds things."

"Such as?"

She thought for a moment. "One summer he made a cooling system for our cave. Then he made several more and sold them."

"The cooling system must have worked well if he was selling it."

"It did work. Cold water from the cliff runs through a pipe on the ceiling. The pipe is full of holes so the water drips down like the curtain of a waterfall. It falls into a trough a couple of feet off the ground at one end and runs down the trough to land on a paddlewheel. The paddlewheel turns a fan, which blows air across the curtain of water. It cools the whole cave." She finished and felt her face flush as she realized her father's invention was childish and crude compared to the wonders of the mountain. Besides, the king had never asked her for a detailed explanation of how the system worked. She'd gotten carried away. Again.

"Your father is a smart man. What about the youngsters? You have one sister and two brothers, your papers say,"

"Plus the two boys taken as weanlings."

"Their names?"

"Tribulation and Devastation."

"Those are your parents?"

"Those are the boys taken for slaves when they were babies."

He gave her a hard look. "If they are gone you would do well to forget them. Tell me about your family as it is now."

She might as well tell him. If she lied, he'd be able to find the truth easily enough. "Comfort is after me. She's in her fourteenth year. Then there were the two boys taken from us—Tribulation and Devastation. They would be in their thirteenth and twelfth years." No, she would not forget them as her parents had. They were still part of her family.

The king flushed red, and Repentance pushed quickly on. "After that, Mother had two more boys—Restoration is in his eighth year, and Fullness is in his seventh."

"And did any of you go to school?"

"Of course we went to school!"

"Respectfully!" He reached out and rapped his knuckles on the top of her head.

"Ouch!" She scrunched back into her chair.

"Did any of you go to school?"

"Yes, your highness. We all went to school."

"And you learned in your history class that I'd killed my

button mate and taken the lowborns captive?"

She nodded mutely.

"And believing me to be this kind of man, you dared rebuke me?"

"I didn't dare," she said quietly. "It wasn't that I thought you were a ... a ... murderer, but I yelled at you anyway, just because I was feeling brave. I spoke in anger. Without thinking."

"You need to learn to start thinking. If I allow you to hurl abuse at me, it won't be any time at all before someone else will do the same. And will they stop with verbal assault? No, they will not. They will refuse to pay taxes. Refuse to obey the laws. Chaos will reign. Do you see that?"

She nodded, considering his words.

"You not only rebuked me, you did it in front of a servant. And by now it is all over the palace. It cannot go unpunished." He gazed at her with a kindly look, like he really didn't want to punish her, and added, "I want you to know I've never killed anyone."

"I remember reading it in the fourth-year history book. You're saying the story was made up?" Maybe they made the whole thing up to intimidate the lowborns.

"I am saying that I am King Fawlin," he said. "As was my father before me and his father before him, and all the old-fathers, back to the ancients."

"Old-fathers?" She frowned, thinking.

"Your face, child. What a sight." He laughed. "Did you never get past fourth-year history?"

She thought back to her school. A damp, dark cave. Without the overlord teacher most days. More often than not he took the big boys out to the swamp and made them fish and hunt so he could sell meat and skins to the troopers who guarded the village.

The smaller kids never cared. Better to be alone than to have the teacher who loved to punctuate his lectures with knocks on their noggins. Her face grew hot. She was ignorant. She had always prided herself on being a trickle smarter than the rest of the villagers with their ambivalence and their superstitions and their beliefs in curses and such, but she was just an ignorant village girl in the end.

"You're not in your two hundred and fiftieth year?" she whispered.

They had few books in the school. No science. Nothing with maps. And only a couple of history books—all of which told stories of overlord victories and fierceness. She'd read all the school books. Several times over. She remembered nothing about the overlord kings all having the same name. She only remembered one overlord King. Sometimes the book called him King Fawlin the Dragon Slayer and sometimes King Fawlin the Wise, and sometimes King Fawlin the Banisher, and so on.

She put her hand to her mouth. Oh, she was so stupid.

"I must look to be in my two hundred and fiftieth year to a young girl, like you." The king said, chuckling. Then he broke up laughing. He laughed until he fell into a coughing fit.

He dug into a pocket, came up with his silver flask, and took a swig. The coughing subsided. "Ah. Better. Now where were we?"

"You didn't kill your button mate."

His eyes sparkled. "I'm not in my two hundred and fiftieth year, and I've not yet killed a single person."

She tried to sort through the information she had about him. He was still the overlord king. The sound of the ropes creaking in the courtyard in front of the slave market played in her mind like a badly-tuned lute. He did kill people.

"A slave is a person," she said.

He looked at her, confusion written on his face.

"You have killed a person. More than one person."

He shook his head. "I've always treated my slaves well. Never killed one." He gave her a hard look. "Never had one so unruly so as to need killing. You should tread carefully, Repentance, lest you be the first."

She scooted back in her chair, wanting to get away from him.

"What now? Your schoolbooks told you something else? Who did I supposedly kill this time?" he said, his voice held a tinge of anger.

"The day I entered Harthill on the slave cart, three bodies hung in the courtyard by the slave market." Her cheeks burned at the memory. "Three young men—boys, really. Hanged for runners."

His eyes narrowed. "I didn't kill those boys. Their disobedience killed them. They broke the law, knowing the consequences full well. You'll not paint my hands with their blood."

She looked at him, silent.

"Say it," he said. "I see you thinking something evil of me."

"You could change your law, your highness. Free the slaves."

"It's not *my* law." Exasperation filled his voice. "I didn't order it into effect. You've always been slaves. How can I change that? Our industry and commerce would likely collapse. I'd be assassinated, for certain, and slavery would continue. You are an ignorant child. You have no understanding about affairs of state. And you keep speaking out of turn."

Yes, she kept speaking out of turn, but that was only because slaves never got a turn. There was never a right time for them to speak. She hung her head and answered very softly. "We haven't always been slaves. Two hundred and fifty years ago we were not slaves."

"Do you think I can wave my hand and take away two hundred and fif—" He broke off, coughing.

"And now you will take my two remaining brothers into slavery. You say you don't kill anyone, but my brothers will be killed fighting your war and that will kill my mother as surely as if you pointed a dragon stick at her and hit the ignition switch. Please, your highness. Forgive me for speaking out of turn. But please don't take them. Surely your army can do without those two little boys."

He swigged on his tonic and got his coughing under control. "What are you babbling about? War? Where would you get such an idea?"

"The prince dropped the parchment pages you signed in the—"

"You read pages that are none of your concern?" Anger

131

burned in the king's eyes.

"But my brothers are my concern. When you take them to put them on the front lines of your war, I am very concerned."

"Your rumors will ruin me! We are not at war. Don't you dare breathe one more word of this nonsense."

She pressed back into the seat, trying to get away from his anger.

"What parchment did you read? I signed no parchment about war."

"I didn't read it. The prince was talking to a boy in the hall. He had dropped the parchment pages you signed in the carriage yesterday. He said something about a provision for the Ministry of War. He said all the boys between their sixth and fourteenth years would be taken to the trooper camp and would be trained for the front line."

The king's nostrils flared. "I signed nothing of the sort. We are not at war." He swallowed several times as if trying to calm himself.

Repentance waited.

The king sighed. "The kingdom is not at war, anyway. The prince and I? Oh, yes, we are at war."

Relief flooded her. There was no war.

"You needn't look so relieved," the king said. "The fact that my nephew is so bold as to slip a sheet of parchment into the provisions I signed for is all the more reason for me to punish you severely. I must show myself strong. I cannot allow your outburst to go unanswered. The thought that a slave could call me a warthog at my own table, and live, is unthinkable." His face looked gray and weary. "No wonder my nephew thinks he can get away with such a scheme. I've been too lax. Too willing to let him run the kingdom. Too kind to insolent servants. Well ... no more."

"And that's why I was relieved, your highness. I could see that you will not let the prince get away with this. I can go to the swingman in peace, knowing you will keep my brothers safe from the prince."

His face softened. He pushed himself from the chair, grimacing over painful hips or knees, she supposed. Maybe both. "I must needs take my weary bones to bed. It's been an exhausting week. And now it looks as if my nephew is going to give me no rest in the immediate future." He paused, thinking, then looked at her. "And you? What will I do with you? Rescuing young women from virile young princes is no easy task for a man of my advanced years. And the thanks I get for my efforts? You insult me to my face in front of the servants. I'll pronounce judgment on you tomorrow."

He toddled out.

An hour later she lay in her bed, the suncloths on her walls filling the room with artificial daylight. How was a person to sleep?

Her head ached. Her heart felt tight and sore. And she kept going over in her mind the words of the king and thinking about the arguments she'd made. Maybe she should have said less about slaves and murder.

But her brothers were safe. For the time being. So she couldn't be too sorry for the whole exchange.

Still ... she should have told the king she was sorry even if she wasn't.

Had she even apologized for calling him a warthog?

It hadn't come up.

She should have at least apologized for that.

She should have apologized to others, too. She spent the night thinking about her family. Remembering mean things she'd said to the people she loved best and wishing she could tell them how much she loved them.

She even thought about Goodwoman Marsh.

And Sober with his earnest expression as he pronounced the blessing on her. It hadn't worked—the blessing hadn't—but it had been a nice thought all the same. She would have liked to have been able to tell him that she was sorry.

Sober.

Why didn't he fight back when the overlords beat him before they sold him on the slave dock? Why didn't any of the villagers ever fight back? Maybe they were not as stupid and cowardly as she had thought. She pictured Sober as he was on the slave dock, forgiving her instead of hating her. That took strength. Sober wasn't powerful, but he was strong. She had never thought about that before. She had always thought that the overlords were strong because they were powerful and the lowborns were weak because they were powerless. But maybe it took more strength to live without power than with it.

The light from the suncloths melted into the morning light, which slipped through her window. Repentance gazed out at the sky wondering what her punishment would be. The king hadn't seemed too angry with her when he'd left. He'd been more angry—or worried—about the prince.

But he'd also been determined to stop being lax. He would make an example of her.

And he had said it was unthinkable that she could call him a warthog and live.

The music filled me with peace. Like a bucket overflowing with second chances, graciously being poured from the hand of Providence, melody washed over my soul.

~Lady Timminn, an essay
The Value of Music in the Education of Children

CHAPTER 17

Generosity burst through the door. "Good morning," she said cheerfully, settling the breakfast tray on the bed. "Did you sleep well?"

Repentance looked at the fruits and cakes on the tray. The thought of eating made her stomach cramp, but she reached for the cup of steaming tea.

Generosity studied the suncloths on Repentance's wall. "You didn't drop the night covers? Ach. I'm sorry. I was afraid to come last night. Provocation told me to keep away as the king was in here with you."

Repentance looked at the rolled up material above the suncloths. Oh. Night covers. She wouldn't have slept, anyway.

"But all is well this morning," the maid continued, happily. "You will break fast every day in your room, my Lady," Generosity said, shaking a napkin out and laying it on Repentance's lap. "Provocation instructed me to tell you."

Repentance looked at the girl, trying to focus on what she'd said. Break fast every day in her room? She wasn't going to swing?

"And you are to lunch in the kitchen with Provocation and Skoch," Generosity continued. "You are to be there at noon." She paused, frowning. "Are you ill, my Lady?"

"I didn't sleep well."

"I'd better tell Provocation. She said I was to teach you how to take down the suncloths and wash them." She stopped smiling then and gave Repentance a hard look. "I may be speaking as a fool, but I have to say it's an easier punishment than you deserve. What would possess you to call the king a warthog? And him being so good to all his servants."

"What's an easier punishment than I deserve?"

"Washing the suncloths on the whole fifth floor. You'll have to do them on your own, and it will take a year at least. I'm sorry about—In truth, you do not look well. I'd better tell Provocation."

"No! I'm fine. I want to work." Thank Providence! She was to remain in the palace. The boys were safe for the time being and there was still a chance that the king would save Comfort. She was going to do nothing to jeopardize that. She threw back her covers and climbed out of bed.

Generosity provided her with a work smock—one with a big pocket in the front, like the maids wore—and showed her how to take the suncloths from the walls without burning her fingers. A yak bladder filled with water and lavacloth gloves were the only tools needed. The cloths were frozen directly to the wall at the two top corners. One squirt from a pinhole in the bladder melted the ice tack for a split second—just long enough to pull the corner of the fabric away from the wall.

Hanging the cloths back up was done in the same manner. Squirt the corner of the suncloth and stick it up quickly where it would freeze-dry to the wall immediately. During the reattachment process the lavacloth gloves were of the most importance, Generosity explained. They kept fingers from being burned or frozen to the wall.

"When I arrived at the palace I saw maids hanging suncloths downstairs," Repentance said. "Do they get dirty fast? How often do they need to be washed?"

"Those maids weren't washing the cloths," Generosity said. "They were moving them from inner rooms to outer rooms."

"Why would they do that?"

"To enliven them," Generosity answered. "They draw their light from the sun, so they must be in the rooms with windows every three days. They are rotated on schedule."

So that's why she'd never seen suncloths at the healing house. There was no sun there to enliven them.

"None of the cloths up here on the fifth floor need rotation," Generosity continued. "They are all in rooms with windows."

Repentance looked out the windows on one side of the room in which they worked and saw that the fifth floor was made up of a ring of rooms. In the center of the ring was a courtyard, built on the fourth-floor roof, which was carpeted in lavacloth. And in that courtyard were settees, and stuffed chairs, and tables. There were also evergreen trees in big pots, and fanciful ice sculptures—dragons and goats and rabbits and squirrels, all scampering among the trees and furniture. Repentance had never seen anything so lovely.

Once she had the suncloths down in one room, Generosity took Repentance to the washroom in back of the kitchen downstairs. A vat that was as big as her washtub back home sat over a fire pit. Boiling water roiled inside the vat, pouring out steam.

Generosity taught her how to wash the cloth, using a paddle to stir it in the vat and then to flip it from the boiling water into a basket, which sat on the floor. From there she took it to the drying rack in the back of the washroom.

And then, with many apologies and much good will, Generosity left Repentance to wash the rest of the cloth herself.

She set to work with earnest, stirring her wash loads, heaving them from the water, and dragging them to the drying rack.

Hunched over the boiling water, she could almost imagine

she was back home in the swamp. The windows were open but the work was still hot, and mist rose, engulfing her as she stirred with the long wooden paddle.

Backing away for a quick break in the middle of her fifth load, she wiped her damp brow with the hem of her work smock. She sighed and stretched her aching shoulder muscles. The work was hard. And she had a year of it stretching before her. But at least she got to smell the cool air, which came in from the windows. And she was alive. That was something. And she still might save Comfort.

Digging the paddle back into the vat, she began to wrestle the heavy panel of cloth from the water. Halfway through the process she heard a familiar voice.

"When I prayed for fog to hide you from your enemies, I'd no idea I'd get a literal answer."

Sober!

Balancing her loaded paddle on the edge of the vat, Repentance turned to look.

It *was* Sober.

"I almost didn't see you under all this mist," he said. "How fortunate that I was raised in Hot Springs and can see through fog as thick as swamp mud."

Her heart made a happy little bounce at that familiar phrase spoken in the Hot Springs accent. It made another bounce when she noticed the smile in his eyes.

"What are you doing?" he asked pointing to the vat behind her.

She turned back, following his gaze, and the load of heavy material fell off her paddle into the boiling water. "Rats!"

"Where?" Sober peered into the boiling water.

She bumped him with her shoulder. "It's hardly funny. That was a heavy load. Now I have to dig it out all over again."

He took the paddle from her and, with one quick flick, plunked the sopping load into her basket. Hot water streamed out of the loosely woven sides and ran toward the ice pit where it would cool and freeze and, eventually, be shaved off and carted away.

Repentance bent to retrieve the load.

"I'll get it." Sober scooped up the basket.

She felt a rush of affection for him. A face from home. He looked different than she remembered, though. What had changed? Same square chin. Same curly black hair. Same crooked nose.

"Lead on," he said.

She knew. His shoulders seemed broader. Or his waist narrower. Work on the farm suited him.

He smelled good, too. She closed her eyes and breathed in the scent of soil and sunshine.

He cleared his throat. "You were right. This is heavy. Are you inclined to show me where to take it?"

Her cheeks flamed with heat. "Sorry. Right back here." She led him to the drying rack.

"This is amazing material," he said, dropping the basket. "And the mooncloth. Have you seen that?"

She nodded.

He grabbed the wet suncloth, but she pulled it from him.

"I have to do it myself."

"Why are you doing this at all, let alone by yourself? I assumed the prince would ... I assumed you'd have other duties."

"The prince is not my master." She smiled, happy to share her trickle of good fortune with him.

Sober stared. "Well," he said after a moment, "it does seem as if Providence is answering my prayers. But if the prince is not your master, what are you doing at the palace?"

"I came yesterday from the healing house at Hot Springs." Yesterday? It felt like she'd aged ten years in her first night.

"I've looked for you here these two months. I often imagined you were up in one of the palace windows looking down. And all that time you were in Hot Springs?"

"What do you mean you've been looking for me for two months?" she asked. "You can't live at the palace. That farming woman bought you."

"I come twice every week to deliver potatoes. And on

Fridays I bring greens, as well, for the yaks." He motioned to the frozen courtyard outside the windows. "You can't grow vegetables here on the mountain."

"Sober!" An old voice called out. "What are you doing, boy?"

Repentance looked over her shoulder. Calamity, the old slave from the slave market, stood at the kitchen doorway.

"Will you be at lunch on Friday?" Sober asked. "Cook feeds us on Fridays, because it's our long day here. I usually eat on the dock at the lake."

Repentance shivered. The lake was cold and shrouded in ice fog. Not a place she liked to visit.

"But if you can make it to lunch, I'll eat in the kitchen," Sober added.

"Come you along, young man," Calamity said, "My whiskers sprout as you loiter."

"See you Friday?" Sober asked, walking backwards toward the kitchen as he looked at her.

She nodded and grinned at him.

He winked and turned to join Calamity. "I'm coming, old man, tell your whiskers to cease and desist."

A few minutes later, as she stood watching out the window by the drying rack, a skim wagon loaded with produce emerged from the front of the palace, and headed down the drive. Sober looked back from the driver's seat and waved.

As Repentance lifted her hand, the prince rounded the corner of the palace and looked back as if to see who Sober was waving at.

Repentance ducked behind the hanging suncloths.

At noon she entered the kitchen for lunch to find only Provocation and a young, overlord tutor by the name of Skoch at the large wood table. Generosity wasn't present—the maids and the groundsmen ate last, Provocation explained.

The smile Repentance had worn since Sober left, disappeared. He would eat with the groundsmen, no doubt, when he came on Friday. So be it. If he was on the grounds, she would find a way to visit with him.

A few minutes into her meal with the housekeeper and the tutor, she was missing Generosity's chatter. Provocation was too busy eating to speak more than a few words, it seemed, and Skoch didn't speak at all—just nodded when Provocation introduced him.

Still, Repentance sipped her onion and potato soup slowly. She was in no hurry to go back upstairs and get more cloth to take to the washroom. There were a hundred and fourteen rooms on the fifth floor, but she had the rest of her life to get them done.

And Sober would come again on Friday.

There was that.

She sighed, content to be alive.

"I hope that sigh doesn't mean you're too weary to p-p-pay attention to my lectures this afternoon, my Lady," the tutor said.

Repentance eyed him skeptically. His yellow hair stood in short spikes all over his head, reminding her of a porcupine. And why was he eating lunch with two slaves?

"Lectures?" This was the first she'd heard about any lectures.

"History and de-p-p-portment," he answered.

She shook her head, stupefied. Who would pay a stuttering man to give lectures?

"You're to sit in classes with the young p-p-princes. Did no one tell you?"

"You're telling her just fine," Provocation said. "No need to tell people things before they have need of knowing."

"I'm to go to school with little boys? I've already finished my schooling." And she didn't have any desire to go to school with the young princes. That would increase the likelihood that she would bump into their father, and she was not anxious for contact with the handsome, cruel Lord Malficc.

The tutor dropped his eyes, his cheeks a shade pinker than a moment before. "It seems the king thought your g-g-grasp of history was not all it should be."

Heat rose in her cheeks. Was there anyone who hadn't heard? But it made sense that the king would tell everyone that she thought he was half way through his third century. If she looked like a foolish child, others would think him kind, rather than weak, when he spared her from the swingman. He was a smart man, her king.

"And as for the deportment classes, if the king had not suggested them," Provocation said, "I certainly would have. You'd best learn manners, before the whole palace is in an uproar. The Moonlight Festival is next month, too, and you're not fit to be seen at the King's side."

"I'm going to the festival with the king?"

"Did I not tell you, Skoch? Ignorant as a block of ice."

Lectures started right after lunch. Skoch showed her to the schoolroom.

There were four other students—Lord Malficc's sons. Three of them were small replicas of their father with pale blue eyes, golden hair, straight noses, and perfect chins. The fourth, the youngest, had hair that was more orange than golden and eyes the color of jade.

"She's sitting in on our lectures?" the biggest one asked, in an offended tone. "Why is she not in school with the slave children the king insists on educating?"

They stood at the front of the class, by the tutor's desk, staring at Repentance.

"Boys," Skoch said, "it's imp-p-polite to stare." Then looking at Repentance, he introduced them. The tallest—a boy eleven or twelve years—was Gaylor. Next came Baeler, then Tigen, and finally, little redheaded Rrow.

Tigen, she remembered was the boy who had been in the hall with the prince.

"Boys," Skoch said, when he was done naming them all,

"meet Lady Repentance."

"Lady?" Gaylor said, with disgust. "Are you mad?"

"Her p-p-position requires the title."

Gaylor turned a cold eye on the tutor. "She's my old-uncle's whore."

Skoch blushed. "For deportment today we'll discuss how to address p-p-people.

"And she's a slave, besides." Baeler nudged his older brother. "Do you call a slave, lady?"

"I don't," Gaylor said. "I call slaves, *scum*." He laughed at his little joke. Baeler and Rrow joined in.

Tigen, second from the smallest, gazed on her with serious eyes and said, "I think she's beautiful."

Baeler rolled his eyes. "She's a slave, dragon dung. Slaves can't be beautiful. Not really. Even if you clean up their outsides, they still have dirty innards. Like animals, is all they are."

Repentance wanted to slap him, but she looked at her red, chapped hands and remembered that she was on a new path. She wasn't going to strike out rashly anymore. She had to stay with her plan to save Comfort. The king hadn't sent her to the swingman, but the Prince ... she wasn't about to test him by slapping one of his sons.

"Dirty innards," the littlest one sang.

"Sit!" Skoch said.

"I am not sitting with a slave," Gaylor said.

"The king, has commanded her to attend lessons. Sit or l-l-leave."

Gaylor and Baeler turned toward the door. Tigen scuttled over and sat in the chair next to Repentance. Little Rrow stood looking between Tigen and the other two.

"If you go, I'll have to t-t-tell your father."

"You won't have to t-t-tell," Gaylor said. "I'll t-t-tell him myself. And I can promise you, he's not going to like this." He grabbed Rrow by the collar and yanked him out of the room.

I tried to walk on Providence's road and found the going hard. The rewards were little to none. Or is it that I haven't been on His road, after all, but on a man-made road all along?

~Repentance Atwater, *Mountain Journal*

CHAPTER 18

Skoch lectured for two hours—one hour on deportment and one on history—amazingly without the stutter. He seemed to forget to be nervous once he was teaching. Repentance heard very little, though. Gaylor's sneering voice played over and over in her mind. Her cheeks burned, the soup in her stomach turned sour, and her neck muscles ached from holding her head up, high and defiant.

When the lectures ended, she shot out of her chair and made for the door.

Tigen jumped up, too. "Where are you going, my Lady?" His voice held a hopeful note as if she might invite him along.

She glanced down at the boy. He was in seventh year or maybe his eighth. Around the age of her brothers. But he looked so much like his hateful older brothers and his father. She left the room without answering him. It was the kindest thing she could muster.

She went to the washroom, as if to collect her dried suncloths, but slipped from the palace through the back door.

The sun was sliding toward the peaks in the west. Chilly air bit at her nose and made her eyes water, but it felt good. It felt free. She could breathe on the mountain in a way she never breathed before. They didn't really own her. She might have to bow down on the outside, and drop her gaze as if she weren't good enough to look them in the eye, but on the inside she was cursing them, and they were powerless to stop her. She just had to remember to keep that cursing from bursting out of her mouth and getting her in trouble.

She walked past the kitchen courtyard and past the outbuildings—the dairy and a freeze barn. After that were three more barns—one for sows and two for yaks. She stopped when she reached a bluff overlooking the city only because she could go no further.

She stood by the lone pine tree on the cliff, using it as a shield against the wind, and looked out over the land.

Below her, Harthill lay in a half circle, snuggled in against the face of the mountain, in a series of rings. The outer wall and the houses built against it, formed the lowest ring, and each street was a little higher as the city worked its way up to the palace. She gazed out at the wall, hazy in the dying light. She was safe in the palace—for a while, for as long as the king lived—but she was not free.

Out past the wall was the freedom she longed for. No, not past the wall. Sober was past the wall. And Rebuke. And her family. None of them were free. She looked at the ridge of sharp-toothed peaks behind the valley. Maybe on the other side of that range. Lord Carrull had said he smuggled slaves to other states. Montphilo, he'd mentioned. A place where overlords and lowborns were equals.

Repentance sighed and tucked the thought of freedom away. She needed to be content where she was—content with a hateful little boy saying she was no different from a yak—and she needed to make the king content with her. Because in two years, Comfort would be coming up to the slave market.

She headed back. A chill wind snatched snow from the ground and blew it against her back and down her neck. Shivering, she picked up her pace. If she hurried she could have a bath before dinner. She would present herself as the perfect companion for the king.

Two hours later she entered the dining room, shyly.

The king was already there. He looked up from some parchment he was reading and nodded his approval. "Ah, I see you wear your punishment well," he said.

She raised an eyebrow as the manservant seated her.

"The work has done you some good, I think," the king continued. "Your face is peaceful. Dare I hope you are a little more mature tonight than you were last night?"

"King Fawlin, I'm sorry for my outburst last night. And I want to thank you for being lenient with me."

"Well, in the end, by the grace of Providence, it worked out for the best. If it hadn't been for your outburst, I might not have learned of my nephew's scheme for training an army of slaves and attacking Westwold in ten years' time. But I did learn, thank Providence."

He smiled. "But I do hope you learn some wisdom soon, young Repentance. You've been here but two days and you've thoroughly worn me out."

The serving woman scooped a plump cheeper onto her dish.

Repentance cast a sideways glance at the king. "I am surprised to hear you say that I'm wearing you out, your highness. You are looking quite lively to me."

He laughed. "It's true. It's true. I'm finding that I enjoy our encounters."

He set his fork down and laughed some more. "I'm quite sure that many people have cursed me behind my back, but never has anyone called me names to my face. Not even my nephew."

Her face burned. She didn't see anything funny about it.

He looked at her face and let his laughter taper off. "It's just this, Repentance. You don't know how to lie, do you? You always speak what's on your mind. And even if you kept your tongue in line, your face would give you away. You would never make a good statesman, but at least I'll always know where you stand. I must tell you, it's not altogether unpleasant to have someone speak honestly to me." He took a bite of his cheeper.

"Oh," she said. "So shall I—"

"Don't you dare!" He pointed his fork at her. "Never speak disrespectfully to me again."

After dinner he walked with her to her room. He brought along a bottle of wine. They spent the evening before her fire, reading.

At ten o'clock, he rose and approached her chair. "I must get to my bath and bed." He bent down and kissed her forehead. "Goodnight."

He left before she could snap her slack jaw shut.

She touched the place where he'd kissed her.

She couldn't understand him. But praise Providence, the king seemed bent on being kind to her and she was not going to tempt him to change his mind. No more outbursts.

She was still by the fire, reading and listening to the king splashing in his bath, when her door flew open. The prince glared at her.

She darted a look at the bathing room.

The prince followed her gaze.

"He can't help you," he said quietly. "If I wanted to kill you right now, I could. And there wouldn't be a thing he could do about it."

She stared at him, trying to swallow her terror.

"I warn you. He's not going to live much longer."

"You're going to ... kill him?"

"Not if I can achieve my goals in a less drastic manner. The people love the good king. If I killed him I would have a rebellion on my hands. And why should I bother to kill him when he allows me to run the kingdom as I see fit?"

She couldn't believe he would speak so easily about killing his own uncle.

"But think about this, little concubine. If the king keeps interfering with me, I will be forced to rethink the risks involved in assassinating him. So you might try to encourage him to rest, to go the hot springs, to go back to sleep. I will be your master for many more years than he will be. Maybe you ought to rethink where your loyalty lies."

"I don't know why you tell me this. What influence do I have over the king?"

"Apparently enough influence to make him deny me the right to take more slaves from the villages." He pointed a finger in her face. "I need an army to invade Westwold and I intend to get an army. Whether the king is alive or dead when I gather my troops makes little difference to me."

"But surely you don't need my brothers for your army."

"That's what drives you?" He gave her a measuring look. "I'll do this for you, then. You make the king keep his peace with me and I'll leave your two brothers in the village with their mother."

She nodded.

He flashed a nasty smile. "Oh course, you know, when I take the other boys and your brothers stay, they will be hated by all the rest of the villagers."

He left without waiting for an answer.

The little princes weren't at school the next afternoon.

Or the next.

Or the one after that.

Not even Tigen.

Repentance wasn't sorry they were absent. She didn't want to bump into their father. She didn't even want to see their faces—didn't want to be reminded of the prince. She told the king nothing about Malficc's threat. The last thing she wanted was for the king to push the prince. She had no doubt about which man was stronger. She determined to do her best to keep the king calm and happy so the prince would let him live.

Her life settled quickly into a new routine. Mornings she

washed suncloths from the fifth floor, afternoons she was in lectures with Skoch, and evenings she spent with the king, reading, talking, and sipping wine by her fire.

She found that Skoch, as irritating as he was with his blushing and stuttering every time he looked at her, had a passion for history, so his lectures were interesting.

He was teaching ancient history that year, he told her. He'd already covered how Providence created the tribes, the Windsong Ceremony where He cut the Precepts into the face of the cliff at Seaport, and the great eruption at Pernick. Repentance was familiar with those events, but Skoch spent the first three days of her schooling giving abbreviated lessons on them. Then he moved on to the next major world event, the granting of the gifts.

"You mean Providence granted gifts to all the people?" Repentance asked, wondering why she'd never heard of such a thing. No doubt the village tutor had cut facts out of the lessons the same way he cut maps out of the books. Allowing lowborns access to certain pieces of knowledge would prove dangerous to overlords, she guessed.

Skoch nodded. "He gave gifts to all the tribes. To the eastern tribes He gave the ability to weave suncloth. To the western tribes, mooncloth. To the north, snowcloth and to the south, lavacloth."

Repentance frowned. Snowcloth. They could have used some of that in Hot Springs.

She wasn't good with directions, but she closed her eyes and tried to remember the map she'd seen in the library at the healing house. Which tribe had she belonged to? Her village had gotten nothing. Providence had left them out. Forgotten them. He seemed to make a habit of it.

"And there were more gifts, for the cities and villages. Your people received the dragon breath."

"Dragon breath?"

"The fog rising from the hot springs. It keeps you from disease and gives you long lives."

So Providence hadn't forgotten them after all.

"The people from Gatling Woods make boats capable of riding the wildest seas. The wood will not sink. The Harthillians, as you've seen, were given ice that refreezes faster than it can melt. Sutherland was given the ability to harness the sun to move their wagons."

"So Providence gave all these gifts, why?"

"The legends teach us that Providence gave gifts to all so no one city could claim supremacy. All would have something of value to offer the others."

Repentance frowned. His plan hadn't worked. One city ended up with all the gifts and one city did claim supremacy. "Legends?"

He shrugged. "Stories, myths."

"They are not true?"

"Who can say? They are the way some men have chosen to interpret history. Others choose another way. They believe the stories about Providence are merely stories and the gifts belong to whoever has the power to take them."

"Who is right?" Repentance asked, waves of anger and relief fighting for control of her emotions. She knew who was right. Now it made sense—the conflicting precepts and the unanswered prayers. "There is no Providence," she said simply.

"Of course there is," Skoch said. "He lives in the hearts of people. He's not real, like us. But he's as real as love and joy. He's an idea. A noble idea. And it would do the world good if more people believed in him."

"But if he's made up—simply some people's interpretation of history ...." She shook her head. "Who decides?"

He must have heard the anger in her voice, because droplets of sweat gathered on his brow, and he started stuttering again. "Who decides w-w-what?"

"What we are to do. I think it's wrong to take slaves. Young Lord Gaylor thinks it's wrong to let slaves live in the house. He thinks they should be in the barn. Who is right?"

"You are r-r-right."

"How do you know?"

"M-m-my heart tells me."

"What makes your heart a better judge than anyone else's?" she blurted out in anger. "I feel ill." She fled and slipped down to the washroom and out the door, heading away from the palace in search of a place to breathe freely. She strode past the dairy, her head ringing with questions about Providence and the power that belonged to people who cared nothing for him or his precepts.

When she reached the yak barns, she heard the animals grunting inside and decided to go in and hide out until her lecture time was over. Skoch would never tell anyone she'd left early, she was sure. He was too busy feeling guilty that his people had enslaved her people. But she didn't want to be discovered and questioned about her absence from class.

She shouldn't have run out. Skoch was on her side. Why was she angry with him?

Because if Providence wasn't real, then she had no one to blame for her troubles, maybe.

The yak barn was dim and cool, the beasts' breath hanging in misty clouds above the occupied stalls. Two things stood out for their absence. No lavacloth carpet and no suncloths. The floor was made of rough planks, but with the heat from the yaks' bodies and breath, the barn was warm enough.

Light spilled into the barn through narrow windows high in the walls—just enough for Repentance to see the shaggy animals in their stalls. She wandered down the center corridor, peering at yaks on either side, afraid to get too close lest the animals gouge her with their sharp horns.

One, a black fellow with friendly round eyes, grunted at her as she passed.

"What are you saying?" she asked, approaching cautiously.

The yak didn't answer.

"You can pet him." The voice came from behind her.

She spun around to face a boy—a slave, maybe a couple of years younger than she—exiting a stall, a pitchfork in his hands.

"You scared me," she said, holding a hand to her chest. "I didn't know anyone else was here."

"I'm always here," the boy said. "These yaks and me, we've been together as long as I can remember."

"Are they friendly? I'm afraid of the horns."

The stable boy smiled. "That's Bramble. He'll never gore you. Worst he'll do is chew the pocket from your work smock, looking for something to eat." He rested his pitchfork against the wall and walked over to scratch Bramble's forehead.

Repentance shivered.

The boy laughed. "You're that scared?"

"It's a little chilly in here," she said, defensively.

He nodded. "No lava cloth in here to warm things up."

"It would make it too hot for the yaks?"

He laughed again. "It would make the floor too messy. Yaks don't care much where they do their business."

"Speaking of cleaning stalls, my pitchfork and I are itching to get done before dinner." Reaching into his pocket, he pulled out a small bunch of wilted broccoli, and offered it to Repentance. "Feed him this, and old Bramble will be your friend for life."

"What's your name?" she asked, happy to have someone willing to carry on a friendly conversation.

"I'm Shamed. And I know who you are, already. Everyone does, my Lady." He left her.

She held out the broccoli and gave a little squeal when Bramble lipped it from her hand, almost sucking in her fingers with it. As he munched she reached out tentatively and touched his quivering neck.

"Gaylor says I'm a dirty animal," Repentance whispered to the beast as she moved her hand around and scratched his forehead. "In truth I'd rather live in the barn than the palace. I'd rather live with the dumb animals who can't tell the difference between an overlord and a lowborn."

Yaks, she quickly decided, would be better company than overlords, on any trail in the swamp. Better than lowborns, too, for that matter. Bramble was calm and kind and he listened to everything she said, staring at her with his big round eyes. Even when she told him about how she often thought dangerous things in her heart, he didn't judge her. "But sometimes those things slip out of my mouth before I can snatch them back," she whispered. "Like when I yelled at the king. I never plan such things." The yak lowered his shaggy head and offered a sympathetic grunt.

"And this time I really need to plan," she said. "But whichever way I look at it, I'm doomed. If the king finds out I've been talking to the prince and I haven't told him about it, he'll banish me, or worse. But if I tell him the prince is threatening him, and the prince finds out I told ...." She sighed and leaned her forehead against Bramble's neck.

Repentance was still worried when Generosity woke her the following morning.

She let the maid's chatter fly by without paying attention. But it did little good for her to worry over what the prince and Providence had planned for her. If the prince was determined to kill the king, she couldn't do anything about it. She had only one hope. She might as well focus on trying to keep the king calm and alive and let the rest of it go.

And if Providence did turn out to be real? All she ever got from him was a frown. So she might as well let him go, too. She didn't need to bother with him at all. She would make her own way.

"And Merit has been eyes-only for Favor ever since." Generosity's words broke into her thoughts.

"Why would she be eyes-only for him? Why should slaves bother falling in love? They can't button."

"Of course they can button. What's to stop them? Especially since the king owns them both. He's always willing to have his slaves button. Says they make better workers when they're happy. And he never sells one button mate without the other."

Repentance turned this over in her mind.

"What if they don't belong to the same owner?"

Generosity blushed. "It's still possible. One owner has to be willing to buy the other slave, is all. And the other owner has to be willing to sell. It happens."

Repentance studied her maid's pink face. "You're in love?"

"Not in love." She shook her head, but she quickly followed her denial with a smile. "However, there is a mighty handsome farmer who's been coming around the last couple of months."

Repentance jerked a little, and her heart did a little stutter-step. Generosity was in love with Sober?

And why not? He was handsome. And Generosity was pretty and sweet.

The knowledge that Generosity was eyes-only for Sober, or heading that way, did nothing to dampen Repentance's excitement at the thought of seeing him at noon. Generosity could button him for all she cared. She only wanted him for a friend.

She hummed her way through the morning's workload, but put on a sad face at the lunch table.

"What ails you, child?" Cook asked as she slid a potato cake onto her plate. "You've not said a word since you sat down."

Repentance liked the cook. Spare with words and generous with food, she seemed to enjoy her job. She'd failed at the buttoning, as had every other woman on the mountain. Well, almost every one, anyway. Provocation had come up as a baby. Her parents had escaped from their village. They'd been quickly recaptured and hanged for runners.

"It's not like you to not greet me in my own kitchen, child," Cook scolded.

"I'm sorry," Repentance said. "I'm not feeling well today." She was determined to stay for the servants' lunch so she could see Sober, and that meant she wouldn't be going to Skoch's lecture that day.

"I hope," Skoch said from his seat across from her, "that your illness will not deprive me of your company in the schoolroom this afternoon."

He hadn't said anything about her behavior the day before. Still, she didn't like him. He reminded her of a slug—no backbone. No convictions. He believed in Providence but not really. He thought it was wrong to keep slaves, but he'd never say so in front of another overlord. She tried to glare at him but one look at his pink face and shy eyes drove the meanness out of her. Hating a weak person, even if he was an overlord, wasn't all that much fun. "I'm afraid I won't be able to make it today," she said. "I'm not feeling well enough. I hope you'll excuse me."

"Rest and get well, then," he said. "And I, since I shall have no students, shall visit the market."

"No students?" Provocation asked. "Where are the young princes today?"

"They no longer attend school with me in the afternoons. Their father is hiring another tutor."

Provocation lifted an eyebrow. "How long has this been in effect, and why wasn't I notified?"

Skoch turned bright red and began his stammering. "I believe Monday was their last d-d-day."

"Monday," she said fixing a glare on Repentance. "That would be the day you started. What did you do? Call them warthogs?"

Repentance stared guiltily at her potato cakes.

"She did no s-s-such thing," Skoch stammered out in her defense. "They refused to sit in the s-s-same room with her. She d-d-didn't say a word."

"We'll see what the king has to say about this. That's what." Provocation muttered.

"No!" Repentance dropped her potato cake. "Please don't say anything." The less the king knew about what the prince was doing, the better.

"I most certainly shall. He has the right to know what goes on in his own palace."

Piggetty, jiggetty, light the fuse.
    Paggetty, jaggetty, close eyes and choose.
        This or that? Both ways I lose.
That children's sing-song rattles in my head.
     One man is deadly. The other will be dead.
           ~Repentance Atwater, *Mountain Journal*

CHAPTER 19

The others left, and Repentance, worrying about Provocation stirring up trouble but not being able to do one cursed thing about it, moved over to the high-backed wing chair in front of the kitchen fire. She took a book from her pocket and opened it, pretending to read. She wasn't reading, though. She was praying—her foot falling upon the well-worn path, irrespective of her recent decision to disregard Providence. She was praying that the king would leave the prince alone.

Cook put a cup of hot wine on the table at her elbow. "Good for the gray mood," she said.

Repentance reached into her pocket and pulled out her three gray buttons. They felt cool and smooth in her hand. She stirred them in her palm. She was used to gray moods.

Ensconced in the big chair in the corner by the fire, she heard the kitchen door swish open behind her. Several people entered, laughing and talking.

She heard Sober's voice among the crowd. "Cook! Friday is my second favorite day of the week. Your potato cakes are unmatched on the mountain."

His voice drove out all thought of the king and the prince.

She remembered his earnest face at the slave market. And his comical expression on Monday, when he winked at her.

"What's your first favorite day, then?" Cook asked Sober.

"Monday of course, when you slip me a mug of your onion and potato soup to take in the vegetable wagon with me."

Several people laughed.

Repentance started to rise from her chair to join the others at the table.

"Good thing the palace uses so many potatoes, then." It was Generosity's voice. "And you have to come twice a week."

Why she did it, Repentance didn't know, but she settled back into the chair so she wouldn't be seen. She had a vague idea that she needed to listen for a minute to see how Sober would answer Generosity.

Maybe he would button Generosity and live at the palace.

Her heart beat with a funny little stutter again.

No, it didn't.

She was being silly. She could never button—she was the king's concubine—and Sober and Generosity would make a good match.

A young man spoke next. "Unfortunate for you that you aren't required on Wednesdays, though. Cook's pork pie would spoil you for any other meal."

"We'll have to talk Cook into buying more vegetables so he can come up Wednesdays, too," Generosity said, with what sounded like a flirty tone.

"I'd like to come more, anyway," Sober said. "I have a friend who lives here now. I'd like to come visit her."

Repentance flushed with pleasure. He was her friend. She'd never had friends.

"And who might this friend be?" a man asked.

"The new maid. She's from my village."

Plates and silverware scraped and clanked.

"We have no new maids," Cook said.

"You do. I saw her Monday."

"I think I'd know. Only fresh belly I've had to feed for quite some time is Master's new concubine. Oh ... she's sitting right—"

"This was no concubine," Sober said. "She was in the washroom scrubbing suncloths."

Several people laughed.

"That'd be the new concubine," Generosity said. "She's a bold one. Scolded the king for killing his button mate. Called him a warthog. To his face. I do not jest."

Cook said, "She's sitting—"

"The king killed his button mate?" Sober asked.

"The new concubine thought he was in his two-hundred-and-fiftieth year," said a male voice.

More laughter.

Repentance shrank down in her chair, her cheeks burning.

A woman said, "And he let her off easy. For punishment all she has to do is to wash the suncloths on the fifth floor. But that's enough to bring the fine Lady Arrogance—erm, I mean Lady Repentance—down a rung or two on the ladder of self-importance."

Repentance stiffened in her chair.

"That's enough," Cook said.

"She's not arrogant," Generosity said. "And she'll get all those suncloths washed, too. You watch. She's a tough one, is the king's new concubine."

"Repentance is the king's whore?" Sober asked in a dazed voice.

"Hush," Cook said. "She's a slave same as you and me. We don't get to choose our duties."

"But she's different from most," Sober said. "She did have a choice. She *chose* to come up the mountain."

"How did she do that?" Generosity asked.

"She refused to button."

Still more laughter.

"She was promised to me, and she refused me at the ceremony."

"She never, Sober Marsh," Generosity said. "Lady Repentance is too smart. And you're too handsome. You'll have to come up with a better story if you want to have a joke on us."

"Well, either Lady Repentance is not as smart as you think, or I am not as handsome," Sober said with a bitter laugh.

Repentance squeezed the buttons she held as if she were squeezing the life out of him. *You are not as handsome, Sober Marsh.*

"No jest, Sober?" Generosity asked.

"Hush now," Cook said. "You don't know what you're about. She didn't choose her job. She's the king's possession like the rest of us. Next one to speak a word about that child loses his lunch."

Repentance rose. "Thank you, Cook," she said, "but I don't need you to make excuses for me."

A collective gasp rose from the servants.

Repentance continued speaking to Cook, "Sober is right. I turned him down. It stings him, but the wound will heal in time, I'm sure."

She walked out the door, her head high and her back straight.

But inside, in the privacy of her own chest, her heart trembled.

She ran down the hall, chased by the memory of their ugly laughter. It seemed that no matter where she went, people would laugh at her and hate her. She wasn't one of the servants—she was lifted above them by her position. But she wasn't an overlord, either. To the overlords she was no better than a yak.

She was nothing.

She fit nowhere.

Sober's words cut her more than all the others. She thought he had forgiven her. She thought he was her friend. His bitter words swirled through her mind like so much fog, dampening her spirits and choking her with gray hopelessness. Once in the safety of her room, she collapsed on her bed in tears.

After a time, the tears washed away the dark, moldy feeling of despair that had seeped into her heart. She dried her face on her blanket.

Sober was nothing to her. She'd never loved him. She didn't care what he thought of her.

But he was her only link to home. The only one who knew what growing up in Hot Springs was like. And he had pronounced that ancient blessing at the slave market. And his face ….

She sat up. She would just have to get him out of her mind.

Taking her parchment pad from her smock pocket she sat in the chair by the windows where the sunlight streamed into the room. She would write a poem. She looked around her room, thinking.

A glint of gold winked at her from the cityscape carved into the wall across from the bed. She rose to investigate. It was the gold roof of the palace, shining in the sun. She looked over the city, which spread down the mountain in ever-widening semi-circles. Several blocks from the palace was the slave market with its frozen fountain in the square. And its swing frame. She leaned closer. There were even little bodies on the frame. Little, naked, slave bodies. A sob broke out of her. How dare they? How dare they make the murder of slaves into art?

She stormed into the bathing room and got a glass of water, then she flicked drops onto the wall and used the handle of her hairbrush to gouge at the carving until the bodies disappeared into lumps of mottled ice.

Standing back, she studied the effect. Surely no one would notice. It was only a small part of a great big map of the city of Harthill.

A map of the city ... she searched the carving carefully. A few blocks from the slave market was a tall building with a red and orange flag at that top. Lord Carrull's house stood as she remembered it, bordered on the front by a main street and on the side by an alley. The map was accurate, then. Maybe she wouldn't always be a slave. One day she might run. She'd wait until Comfort and the boys were brought up. She'd talk the king into buying them. Please, Providence, let him live that long. And then they would leave. All of them together.

She closed her eyes and pictured the carving in her head trying to map out a route from the palace to the outer wall of the city.

She woke to the sound of Generosity opening the wardrobe door. The slant of the sun told her it was late afternoon. She'd fallen asleep on the floor, trying to memorize the map on her wall.

She quickly slipped her parchment book into her pocket. "I was lying in a patch of sunshine, and I fell asleep."

"Yes, my Lady."

For the first time since Repentance had come to the palace, the maid was silent as she worked. She bathed Repentance, and dressed her with hardly a word. By the time Generosity got to her hair, Repentance had had enough of her sulking.

They had been talking and laughing about her behind her back. She was the one who should be mad.

"What is it, Generosity?" Repentance asked. "Do you intend to never speak to me again? Are you thinking to punish me for refusing to button your handsome farmer?"

"No, my Lady. Not that. It's never my place to punish you."

"But you'd like to."

"Not at all. I don't have an opinion on the matter. I'm sure you had your reasons for turning Sober down and taking him away from his family."

"If you have no opinion, why do you refuse to speak to me?" And why did she feel a need to mention that Repentance had deprived Sober of his family?

"I thought you might be angry with me."

"I am and I should be. You all laughed about my thinking

the king was so old."

Generosity hung her head. "I am sorry, my Lady. I didn't mean anything by what I said. We didn't know you were there. We weren't trying to hurt you. None of us."

"Lady Arrogance is a nickname given to one you like, then?"

"Biased fancies herself to have a sharp, wit," Generosity whispered. "I'm sorry, you heard that. None of them really think you're arrogant."

"Like it or not, we have to see each other every day. We might as well speak to one another. I forgive you for laughing at me. And ... thank you for sticking up for me with Biased."

"Oh, my Lady, I'm that happy that you have forgiven. I was thinking about how hard it would be if you were the kind to hold a grudge, but I was sure that you weren't. The others said there would be no living with you, but Sober said—"

"I forgive *you*. But I never said I forgave Sober. I don't ever want you to speak the name of Sober Marsh to me again. Please. I don't care to think any more about your handsome farmer."

Generosity blushed. "If you were to ask my opinion, I'd say he's not *my* handsome farmer. I do believe the reason he was so shocked and upset to find out you are the king's concubine is that he is still, in his own heart, anyway, very much *your* handsome farmer, my Lady."

Repentance scoffed. "But then, I didn't ask your opinion on the matter. A good thing, too, for you are not seeing clearly. You've gotten used to seeing Merit and Favor eyes-only for one another, and now you think you're seeing the same devotion everywhere."

"Time may bear me out, my Lady. I'm content to wait and see."

Monday, after lunch, she was walking to the schoolroom, looking at her feet, lost in thought. Sober would be delivering his potatoes and Cook would slip him a mug of soup, but he wouldn't be eating lunch at the palace, anyway. He'd not be eating with Generosity. Not that Repentance cared who he ate with.

"She doesn't look to be stupid." A man's voice sounded in front of her.

She looked up.

Lord Malficc stood in the hallway by the schoolroom door. He ran his gaze down and back up her body.

She shuddered. "I'm sorry?"

"I said you don't look like you are stupid." He stepped closer to her. "But my uncle is in an uproar over your schooling. I've not seen him so energetic in a long time. You must be good medicine, Repentance Atwater. You've taken twenty years off that old man's life. But I warned you about this."

Her skin turned clammy. "I'm not sure what you mean."

"Oh, I think you know exactly what I mean." He smiled. "You complained to my uncle about my sons."

"I didn't complain. It was Provocation. She found out that you'd taken the boys out of school. I asked her not to tell."

He gave her a long look. "You're using up my patience, Lady Atwater." He turned and walked off.

Skoch looked up and saw her in the doorway. "Ah, good. We're all here, then."

And they were all there. All four of the young princes.

The king, once alerted by Provocation to the situation, had apparently demanded the boys return.

She wished he hadn't. She hated the sight of their faces. And ... the prince was that much closer to deciding that he needed to kill the king.

Skoch launched into the day's lesson. "Now the war between Harthill and Lavalley took place in the twelfth year of King Fawlin the Dragon Slayer. There were dragons then. Lavalley had domesticated the beasts and used them to hold off our attack."

"Where have all the dragons gone?" Rrow asked.

"They're extinct," Skoch said, "That means they all died."

Rrow looked stricken.

"That's a good thing," Skoch added quickly. "When they died so did the last threat to Harthill. Dragons' fiery breath was the only thing that could melt Harthill's towers."

Repentance, cold dread knotted in her stomach, used her char-stick to draw a picture of a scaly dragon in one corner of her parchment. It blew flames at an ice tower. *Melt Harthill, melt.*

Tigen leaned over to look at her dragon and smiled.

She glared at the little boy who was a perfect image of his father.

He picked up his own char-stick and sketched on his parchment, using swift, sure strokes.

She pretended not to notice.

"Why didn't Lavalley send the dragons against Harthill to destroy it?" Gaylor asked.

"They'd never gone on the offensive," Skoch said. "It's assumed they didn't know how. They were a peaceful people, trying to defend themselves."

Gaylor snorted. "A stupid people, you mean. Look at them now! Subjects of Harthill. As soon as the dragons were slain they had no way of defending their city."

"Weak," Baeler added.

Tigen nudged Repentance and shoved his parchment toward her. He'd drawn a boy dragon—obvious from his square jaw, muscular arms, and large size—with one wing wrapped protectively around a girl dragon. The girl dragon had long eyelashes and puckered lips and long dark hair. The boy dragon had white hair. Underneath, they were named. Tigen and Repentance.

Angry, Repentance snatched the parchment from him. He was a small boy, but he might as well learn early that she wanted nothing to do with filthy overlords. Bending over the parchment, she colored over her dragon, making it all part of a bigger dragon—a giant girl dragon, crouching above the little Tigen dragon, with an angry tilt to her eyes and flames spewing from her mouth.

Repentance smirked and shoved the parchment back across the desk to Tigen.

And for the first time since she'd met him, he lost his smile.

"Yes," Skoch was saying, apparently in answer to something Gaylor had said. "The conquest of Lavalley did give him the power he needed to take the lowborns into slavery. With the Lavalley men in the front lines, his troops far outnumbered the lowborns."

Repentance jerked her attention back to the tutor. So it seemed the overlords made a habit of putting other people in their front lines. They were talking about Fawlin the Dragon Slayer—the monster who had married a lowborn and then beheaded her when she was unfaithful, but nothing had changed over the past 200 years.

"And we've had them as slaves ever since," Gaylor said, sneering at Repentance. "Dark and dirty. And all they're good for is scrubbing our waste stools."

She bit her lip. Fawlin the Dragon Slayer sired a son with his lowborn button mate before he'd beheaded her. Gaylor had lowborn blood in his veins. But she wouldn't remind him of that. She had enough trouble with the prince without antagonizing his son.

She glanced at the boy, wondering how she would survive day after day in school with him.

Gaylor jumped up, grabbed a handful of her hair, and yanked her head back.

Repentance cried out.

"Don't you ever look at me." Gaylor said.

Tigen grabbed his brother's hands, trying to pry them from Repentance's hair. "Leave her be, Gaylor," he pleaded.

Gaylor backhanded Tigen, sending him flying. "Sit down, baby, and suck your thumb."

Giving Repentance's hair a jerk, he said, "You were giving me a dirty look. I want recompense."

Repentance moved her head, trying to follow Gaylor's hand as he yanked her hair.

"D-d-dis-m-m-missed," the tutor stammered.

Gaylor gave her head a final jerk, and released her. "My father will hear about this!"

Gaylor gave Skoch a dirty look, then sauntered out the door

with Baeler and Rrow tagging along behind.

We are made for relationship and when we don't find it in the familiar places and faces, we must needs find it in the unfamiliar. Desperation drives us to humbly accept friendship from one we've all along despised.

~Meticulous Mudslide, *An Old Man Remembers*

CHAPTER 20

Tigen stood slowly. Blood dripped from his lip.

Repentance felt a stab of guilt. She shouldn't have been mean to him. He only wanted to defend her.

"My lady," Skoch said, "are you injured?"

She wanted to scream at him. Of course she was injured. The brat Gaylor treated her worse than he would treat an animal. Why would Skoch need to ask if that caused injury? But the last thing she needed was for the prince to think she was complaining about his sons. "I'm fine," she said. "It was my fault. I shouldn't have looked at him."

Repentance watched Tigen collect his char-stick and parchment from the table, hoping he'd smile at her again.

He looked up and saw her. "Why don't you want to be my friend?"

What a silly question. How could she have an overlord boy for a friend? Especially one with a father and brothers who would kill her as soon as look at her.

But he was just a little boy. He couldn't help who his father was. She reached out to wipe the blood from his chin.

He flinched and backed away.

"I'm sorry, Tigen. I was wrong. You remind me of my own brothers. They are kind and brave, just like you."

He gave her a shy smile and left.

The boys showed up to school the next day, Gaylor and Baeler acting as obnoxious as ever. No more, no less. Nothing came of Gaylor's demand for recompense. Apparently his father wasn't going to battle the king just then on whether or not the young princes were to be educated alongside a slave. Repentance took special care not to look at Gaylor or respond in any way to his constant threats and harassments.

The schoolroom was not her favorite place, though. Never knowing what would set Gaylor off put a huge strain on her, and by the end of the week, she was exhausted.

She took to slipping down, often, to the yak barn, to unburden her heart to the ever-patient Bramble. He never failed to calm her nerves.

On Friday morning, when she finished hanging her suncloths a few minutes early, she smiled up into the cloudless sky and made her way to visit the yaks. When she entered the barn, she saw Shamed at the far end, divvying up food. She nodded at him and slipped into Bramble's stall. "Here you go, big boy," she said, feeding him some bits of birch syrup pie she'd saved from breakfast.

He slurped the food up with a snuffle and a grunt.

"He looks for you every day," Shamed said, leaning over the stall door. "You've spoiled him with all the treats."

Repentance rubbed the yak's nose. "I have to bring Bramble treats. What good is it to have a friend in the palace, if she won't bring you tidbits every now and again?"

Shamed went back to work, and Repentance left Bramble and made her way down the corridor, petting noses and passing out treats. "Here you go, Thistle . . .. Now, don't be so impatient, Rose,

I've not forgotten you . . .. Ah, Holly and Hawthorne, calm down you two, I'm coming."

She was at Barberry's stall, when the double doors at the end of the barn scraped open on their icy tracks.

Framed in the open doorway was Sober.

She could only see his silhouette because he was backlit by the sun and the glaring snow outside. Ducking into Barberry's stall, she hoped Sober hadn't noticed her. It would take his eyes a moment to adjust to the dim interior of the barn.

"Ho, Shamed," Sober called.

"Right here, no need to yell."

"I didn't see you hiding behind the bales. I've brought two wagons of greens this week. Do you want it all at this end?"

It was Friday! She'd forgotten.

Barberry ate his sweets and snuffled around Repentance's pocket looking for more.

She pushed against his wide nose. "I don't have any more, boy," she whispered.

He didn't believe her. He pushed against her with his wide forehead.

She stepped back to catch her balance.

He pushed her again.

"This end'll do fine," Shamed said. "I've been pulling the old greens forward to make room for the new."

Barberry gave a snort. He wanted more treats and he wanted them now. He pushed Repentance again.

She fell against the door, which unlatched and fell open. Stumbling into the corridor, she tried to catch her feet up to the rest of her, all to no avail. She landed in a heap in the center of the barn floor.

"Repentance?"

Sober stood over her, concern in his dark eyes. He reached down and helped her up. "Are you hurt?"

She pulled away from him, brushing off her work smock, avoiding his eyes. "I'm fine."

He bent and picked something up, then held out his hand to her.

Three gray buttons sat in his wide, calloused palm. They must have fallen from her pocket.

"Why do you keep these?" he asked.

She pocketed the buttons and touched his scarf. "Why do you keep that?"

"To remind me of home, for one thing."

"Same with me." She turned to leave.

"Repentance?"

She stopped.

"I shouldn't have spoken as I did the other day. I was surprised, is all. I thought you were a maid, and I was upset to find out you were a .... " His voice trailed off.

She faced him. "A whore."

He cringed. "Can you not forgive?"

"What good would it do? I'm still a whore in the end."

He looked away from her.

Her cheeks burned with shame. "You can't stand to even look at me."

She turned and left.

The king would be gone for a week or so. Business in the south, he said, and he didn't want to take Repentance out of school. The Moonlight Festival was fast approaching, and she needed all the help Skoch could give her.

He'd been feeling poorly, and Repentance suspected he might be going to the healing pool at Hot Springs. He wouldn't admit to it—he was always so worried about appearing weak.

Repentance followed him to the front steps to bid him goodbye. "Is it safe for you to go?" she asked.

He gave her a strange look. "Why the concern?"

"I'm afraid for you. What if the prince ... do you think the prince might try to take the throne from you?"

He grimaced. "He'd have done that long ago if he could have. He cannot. The people would storm the palace and kill him. My subjects love me, because I have always treated them fairly. The prince, however, is not well loved. He's in line for the throne, true, but if I die without handing the throne to him—without showing my confidence in him—it will not go well for my devoted nephew. If he wants to assassinate me, and I'm sure he does, he'll have to woo my troopers away from me and make my subjects hate me, first. And that will be a battle fought on uneven ground with me in the upper position."

Relief coursed through her. "Why do you travel with all the troopers, then?"

"Appearances." He sighed. "I must keep up appearances. Traveling with a full skein of troopers gives me power in the eyes of the people. It also keeps the troopers close to me. It keeps them loyal."

Relieved, she watched his skim coach wind down the drive. The prince thought he was smart, but the king was smarter. She offered a prayer for the king's safety, picked up her basket, and headed upstairs to her suncloths.

She was in one of the guest chambers, taking down cloth, when someone came in.

Twisting on the ladder, she looked over her shoulder at the doorway.

Lord Malficc.

She jerked and almost fell.

"Careful, my Lady," he said. "We can't have you breaking your neck just when I have such a wonderful proposal for you."

Repentance glanced nervously at the bed below her. The entire fifth floor was reserved for guests and usually deserted. And here was Lord Malficc making a proposal.

"I've been invited to a feast. An early Moonlight Festival party. I'd like you to go as my guest."

"I'm sorry," she said. "My new wardrobe is not complete yet.

I have nothing appropriate for feasts."

He crossed the room and lay down on the bed, folding his hands behind his head and gazing at her. "I will talk to the seamstress myself. I'll speed her up a trickle. What do you think of that?"

She had to tread carefully. He was a powerful man and a dangerous one. "I'll ask the king when he returns. When is the feast?"

"It is when I say it is. I'm not sure of the exact date, yet. It will most likely be before the king returns from his trip. I have it on good authority that he'll be delayed at the healing house."

She shot him a look.

"Oh yes, I know exactly where he is at all times. And in his absence I am in charge of the kingdom and I give you permission, Repentance, to go to a feast with me."

"If you want him to stop interfering with you ... maybe you should stop antagonizing him. How do you think he'll react when he finds out you've taken me to a feast?"

"That's no longer a concern."

She gasped. The king was wrong. The prince was going to try to kill him. Maybe one of the girls at the healing house would sneak in and kill the king. Maybe Tawnic would do it. How hard would it be to smother him in the night? There were no troopers inside the healing house.

"He's off the mountain," the prince said. "He'll never know what we do."

"Someone will tell him." Whatever the prince was playing at, she wanted no part of it. But she couldn't very well deny him on the deserted fifth floor. It wasn't safe.

She dropped the suncloth into a basket on the floor, stepped down from the ladder, and began to drag both basket and ladder toward the door.

"Where are you going?" the prince asked.

She pointed toward the hallway. "Only 102 rooms to go."

"You'll have a little break soon. I'll have a dress made up for you. When it's done, you and I will have a night out."

Not if she could help it. She would get a message to the king somehow. She turned to leave the room.

"Oh, and Repentance?"

She looked back at him.

"I don't think you should mention our little outing to Provocation, or anyone. Just in case you were thinking that you might. Remember that my uncle is old and weak. He won't be here forever to protect you."

She left her ladder in the hall and fled downstairs with her basket of suncloths. Down to the relative safety of the kitchen washroom.

She spent the next few days avoiding the prince and worrying about how she was to get out of betraying the king without calling the prince's wrath down on her head. It wasn't safe to send a message. She didn't know which servants were trustworthy. Besides, the prince might intercept a written message.

Eating alone in the royal dining room left her exposed to the prince, so she took to eating dinner, as well as lunch, with the housekeeper and tutor in the kitchen. She changed her morning routine, too, and stopped going to the fifth floor. She had no intention of being caught up there all alone. In the mornings she washed the same suncloths over and over. In between times, when she was supposed to be hanging the clean cloths on the fifth floor and taking dirty ones down, she hid out in the yak barns. She had her whole life to get the washing done. When the king came back and she told him what the prince had proposed, he wouldn't blame her for not doing the work he'd assigned. She continued to attend lectures in the afternoons. Her absence there would have been noticed. But she made sure she was never alone. Always she walked with Skoch to and from the classroom.

On Monday, the king had been gone a week. Repentance prayed he'd return soon.

After visiting Bramble, she made her way to the lake, which lay at the back side of the palace, opposite from the barns. It was full of cold, cold water, but it never quite froze because half of it lay in a cavern beneath the palace dungeons—fed by a spring that constantly flowed from deep inside the mountain.

The water, with fog billowing off its surface, was gray and cruel and cold, and that morning it fit her mood. She climbed the steps on the dock and sat down on the bench there. She was thinking about the swamp and Comfort and her little brothers when a man emerged from the fog a few feet from her.

Sober.

He jerked when he saw her and stopped at the bottom of the steps. "I'm surprised to see you here." He looked genuinely startled but quickly recovered his wits. "Do you mind company, or are you trying to be alone?"

She stood. "I was just leaving."

"You have so many friends on the mountain that you can afford to bear a grudge?" He looked up at her, not moving to let her by.

"What do you want, Sober? I thought you forgave me on the slave dock when you pronounced the blessing. You acted like you wanted to eat lunch with me when you saw me in the washroom. And then you ... you .... " tears blurred her vision.

"I did forgive you. I was surprised in the kitchen. That's all. I spoke rashly."

She knew something about speaking rashly. "You want to be friends with a whore?"

"I want to be friends with you."

She sat, scooting to one side to make room for him on the bench.

He joined her. Then sucked in a big breath full of fog. "Ah. Reminds me of home. I come every chance I get."

"I hate fog."

He chuckled. "I think we established that fact in the slave wagon that first day. What was it you said? You felt like you were made for sunshine?"

She shivered and tucked her hands into the front pocket of her smock. "I kind of liked the sunshine further down the mountain."

"It is beautiful. You were not mistaken on that count."

She glanced over at him. "Your farm is beautiful?"

"Very. And I like working in the soil."

"And your owner?" She winced when she said the hateful word.

"She's good to me."

"I'm glad."

"What about the king? Does he treat you well? Everyone says he's fair-minded."

She frowned. If only he would come back. "He's been away for a whole week."

He grimaced. "And that bothers you? You miss him?"

"I do."

Sober pursed his lips and nodded.

"What?"

"Can we talk about something besides your master and how much you miss him?"

If you will wait, friends will find you.

   Common bonds will safely bind you.

As long as you breathe, there is hope for a day of deliverance.

   ~Repentance Atwater, *The Fawlin Palace Poetry Collection*

CHAPTER 21

The mist from the lake closed in around them, muffling the world, and filling Repentance with a deep longing for home. For her family. For a place where people loved her. Comfort had loved her. And her mother and father. She could see that from her new vantage point of being a lady and also a slave. On the mountain, she was more of an outcast than ever.

"I'm sorry," Sober said. "I wasn't going to bring up the king again."

Repentance shifted uncomfortably. It was always going to stand between them—the business of her being a concubine. She thought nothing of it and Sober, apparently, thought of nothing else. "Sober, can you keep a secret?"

He shrugged. "I managed to fool the village through four buttoning ceremonies. In the end, though, I wasn't half as good at keeping secrets as you turned out to be."

She searched his eyes, trying to see if he was telling the truth.

"You never wanted to button those first four times?"

"I told you before. I was waiting for someone."

She blushed. "The king and I aren't ... we don't ... I'm not his concubine, really."

He looked puzzled.

"He doesn't like to look weak. But he's really sick. He coughs every night. Coughs and coughs. He can no more have button relations than a fish can walk."

A look of relief crossed his face. "I'm glad to hear that." A smile broke out and he nodded. "Yes, I'm very glad to hear that."

A moment later, he said, "The king never took a concubine before. Why now?"

She shivered, remembering how sick and afraid she'd been that day at the healing house, waiting for the prince. She'd thought she wouldn't survive. "He took me to save me from his nephew, who has a reputation of not being kind to his concubines."

"Thank Providence. He answered my prayers for your protection."

She looked up at him, startled. "I'm not sure how much Providence had to do with anything. The king said he took me because I reminded him of someone he once knew."

"That doesn't make much sense. How many lowborns could the king have known in his life?" He gazed over at her. "And there I was in the kitchen calling you a whore. I'm so sorry."

"You were right, Sober. I chose badly." There. She'd admitted it. And it felt like a weight had rolled off her shoulders. "If it weren't for chance I would be a whore."

He smiled. "It was hardly chance. Providence has been watching out for you. But about that choice .... " He nudged her with one shoulder. "Do you mean you wish you'd chosen me? You wouldn't mind being buttoned to me?"

She blushed, "Sober!" She hadn't even thought about what it would be like to be buttoned to him. And she wasn't ready to discuss it. It didn't matter what she wanted, anyway. She was concubine to the king. She could never button Sober.

"I'm sorry," he said. "I was teasing."

Still blushing, she thanked Providence for the fog that cooled her hot cheeks, and, looking at the lake, she changed the subject to a less embarrassing one. "Why doesn't the water ever freeze?"

"It's fed from an underground spring—a hot spring. By the time it gets to the surface it's ice cold, but the spring keeps it a trickle warmer than freezing."

"I don't understand how the palace is sitting on top of the water."

"Ah, it just happens, my Lady, that I can explain that to you. Calamity told me all about it the first time I drove up here with him. He's a living history book, that one." He threw one arm across the back of the bench and leaned across her to point to the spot, barely visible through the mist, where the lake disappeared underneath the palace. "The palace sits on top of six feet of ice, which sits on top of the water. Or the ice originally sat on the water, I mean. The water level dropped a trickle each year so now the lake is five feet below the ice on which the palace sits."

She could smell him and feel his warmth. "The lake froze at that end but not at this end?" That made no sense to her but she wasn't sure if that was because it really made no sense or because her senses weren't functioning normally.

"The hot spring is at this end of the lake. The water at that end cooled and froze over, and the palace was built so half of it sits over the lake."

"Why would anyone build on top of a lake?"

"According to Calamity, at this elevation, it was the easiest way for them to get water into the palace."

"Only six feet of ice?" She gazed up through the mist trying to see the top of the towers. "How can six feet of ice hold up such a big building?"

"Ice is strong," he looked at her. "Sometimes things ... people ... are much stronger than they seem. If you look carefully, you may even find that people you thought were not worth your time had more to them than you gave them credit for."

She nodded. "I'm sorry I didn't button you, Sober."

His smile was like sunshine. "I forgive you."

The next few days dragged by. Repentance continued hiding in the kitchen for meals with Skoch and Provocation. She spent the rest of her mornings in the washroom or the yak barn between times. Lord Malficc never went to those places. He didn't like being so close to slaves and animals.

Of course if he wanted her, he could easily send troopers to get her. She knew she wouldn't really be safe until the king returned. Still, as each day passed without incident, her worry lessened, and she found her mind often straying from her problems to settle on more pleasant things. Things like Sober. His smile. His arm around the back of the bench. His shoulder brushing up against hers.

On Friday she told Skoch she'd be late to school and she stayed in the kitchen when he left for his afternoon lectures. She didn't care if the other slaves did whisper or laugh, she meant to stay and visit with Sober.

He walked in, looking fresh and healthy from his work in the mountain air. When he caught her looking at him, his cheeks flushed and his eyes brightened. He made his way over and plopped onto the bench beside her. "Cook," he said without taking his eyes off of Repentance, "the kitchen seems uncommonly bright today. What happened? Got your suncloths rotated last night?"

Cook scooped three large potato cakes onto his plate. "I'm always glad to have your smiling face in my kitchen, Sober Marsh." She lowered her voice. "But you're tempting the swingman with this business. If you two are friends I'm glad to see it. I didn't never want you to be enemies. But friends don't need to get too close to one another. 'Specially not when one of said friends is the king's concubine."

Others began shuffling in and Cook moved around, greeting

them before Sober had a chance to respond. "Calamity here's a 'tato cake for you. Generosity and Shamed, I hope you brought your appetites. "

Repentance scooted over on the bench so as not to be too close to Sober. She was sure Cook was exaggerating about the swingman, but she saw no need to start rumors.

People came one by one, the seats filling up around the table. No one sat on the other side of Repentance. They all gave her a second look and then looked quickly away when she met their gazes.

Generosity sat across from her with a huge smile plastered on her face. "My Lady, would you be so kind as to pass the yak's milk?" she asked, as if there was nothing odd at all about her being there for lunch.

Repentance shot Generosity a grateful smile and slid the pitcher to her.

"Favor," Cook nodded to the footman as he entered. "I have saved the two biggest cakes for you." Then, "Tigen, I think you are supposed to be at your lectures, young man."

Repentance looked around Cook's ample backside and saw the young prince loitering by the kitchen door.

"One potato cake, please, Cook," he said. "I'll eat it on the way to school."

Cook tut-tutted. "Why don't you eat the food your father's cook produces, is what I'd like to know." But she was smiling when she said it, and obviously pleased that the young prince preferred her potato cakes over his own cook's.

Merit pushed by the boy, ruffling his hair as she passed. "Tigen, you'll be here tonight for a game, I take it?"

"I'll be here to give you a thrashing, Merit." He grabbed the potato cake Cook offered and backed into the hallway. "You can bet your best yak on that."

Merit laughed. "Thank you kindly, but I think I'd hold on to my yak, if I had one to hold on to. Since I don't have a yak, I might as well bet my best one, and I'll throw in my best gold necklace as well."

"That boy," Sober said to Repentance, "is the hope of the kingdom."

"How's that?" she asked.

"He has a rich heart. I'm praying that he'll sit on the throne one day." He smiled at her, his eyes lit with hope. "If that were to happen, our people would go free. And you can bet your best yak on that!"

"How can you know that?"

"He loves slaves. He often visits me in the barn when I deliver my greens. He's a good boy."

His smile filled her heart and made her feel rich. But he was dreaming. "Tigen's the third son," she said. "He won't sit on the throne unless both of his older brothers die."

Sober glanced over. "One can always hope."

"They're just boys!" Generosity said.

"Just boys now," Sober said. "Men one day. And men I'd rather not see on the throne if even a trickle of the tales I've heard of them are true. But Tigen ... now, why do you suppose Providence has given him such a fine heart? I think he has a plan for that boy."

He broke off half of a potato cake and handed it to Repentance.

"What's this for?" she asked.

"You eat it. It's a potato cake."

She jabbed a playful elbow into his ribs. "I know what it is. I mean, why are you giving it to me?"

He looked over at her, laughing. "I can't enjoy my lunch with you staring at me with that hungry expression on your face."

Heat rushed to her cheeks.

Merit jumped into the conversation. "Are you saying you want Tigen's older brothers to die?"

Sober chewed and swallowed. "I'm not saying anything about the older brothers. I'm simply saying I think Providence has plans for our young Tigen."

Repentance laid the piece of potato cake back on his plate

"I'm not hungry. I ate lunch right before you got here."

"Hmm," he shrugged. "My mistake. I thought you looked hungry." He popped the whole piece in his mouth and washed it down with yak's milk.

She looked away. Was she that transparent? She was hungry ... for so many things. She was hungry for the freedom to come and go as she pleased. She was hungry for her mother's hug, for her father's laugh, and for Comfort's whispered confessions in the middle of a night. But she wasn't hungry for the swamp. She'd never fit there. What she was really hungry for—she glanced sideways at Sober—was for a place to fit.

Saturday was her rest time every week. Repentance spent the day snuggled in the stuffed chair by the kitchen fire. After deciding to attack the library in alphabetical order, she'd started *Adoration*, the biography of Adoration Hogswallow, an overlord woman who had left the mountain to serve as a doctor in a village called Lumberline. The villagers had given her the front name of Adoration when she'd arrived, and she'd gotten her back name when she'd buttoned with a lowborn widower, Urgent Hogswallow.

Late Saturday afternoon, Repentance closed the book, thinking about what Adoration had given up in order to button a lowborn man. She'd lost everything. She'd given up her right to ever go home again. She was like Repentance, running away, only Adoration had been born free and she'd buttoned into slavery. But how silly! Or maybe they really were alike, she and Repentance. Both living in a society that told them what to do and never asked their preference.

Still! Adoration must have really loved her lowborn button mate to have given up the mountain for him.

Repentance sighed, wondering what it would be like know a man worthy of such love.

After dinner with Provocation and Skoch, she made to go

back to her room, as usual, but since she had finished Adoration's story, she stopped off in the library for another book. It was by the grace of Providence she took that detour. She was returning to her room when she saw Lord Malficc in the hallway ahead of her, several dresses draped over one arm. She drew back into the nearest doorway. He threw open her door without knocking and went right in. She raced back to the kitchen, looking for safety.

The kitchen was full when she arrived. Generosity jumped up as she entered. "Do you need me, my Lady?"

"I thought I'd read here for a while and help Cook clean up later." She sat in her usual chair in front of the fire while the others ate.

After dinner, Repentance jumped up to help several of the maids wash the dishes while the men stretched out on the benches and tamped smoke-weed into their pipes. While they worked, several of the buttoned slaves came in—mothers with children hanging on their skirts and fathers settling in at the table and lighting pipes. When the dishes were done, the women joined the men at the table. Repentance, having never been in the kitchen this late before, sauntered over to investigate.

Several men and women started a game with eight-sided dice.

Repentance watched for a moment before moving on to see what Favor and Merit were doing. They sat across from one another with a large piece of soft suede spread on the table between them. The suede had been painted to show rolling hills covered with meadows and woods and with a rushing stream traveling from one side to the other. Standing at various spots on the surface were small statues of animals, wild and domestic. There were dragons, sheep, pigs, and assorted others.

Repentance watched for a few moments then continued on to see what everyone else was doing.

Tigen, had slipped in at some point. He squatted in the corner with several slave boys, playing some game with shiny stones laid out on a sheet with a grid marked on it. Repentance stood over him trying to understand how the game was played.

The young prince looked up. "My Lady, why weren't you at lectures on Friday?"

"I took the afternoon off," she said.

"I know that, my Lady. I wanted to know *why* you took it off."

She smiled. "Did you miss me?"

His cheeks took on a slight pink tinge. "I did."

"Do you come here every night?"

"Almost."

"Your father doesn't mind you being here?"

Tigen moved a stone from one square to another. "My father doesn't know where I am most nights."

She spent the evening reading by the fire while the others played their games. When they left for the night, she went with them, and then she sneaked back and lay down on the rug in front of the hearth.

The following day was Sunday. Repentance went wearily back to washing the same suncloths that had been washed fifty times already. By noontime she was thoroughly sick of suncloths and thrilled to join Provocation and Skoch for lunch, silent though the two of them always were.

Skoch surprised her by greeting her with a broad smile. "You look like you need cheering up, my Lady. I have just the thing that will make you feel better. Today we will have lectures as usual, but tomorrow ... a big surprise."

"Tell me."

"Tomorrow morning there will be no washing of suncloths for you. Tomorrow, we trade laundry baskets and schoolbooks for the real world."

"Meaning?"

"We go into the city to see some of the oldest buildings. We will tour the original palace in the Old Village Circle, and when we are done, we will dine at the Fin and Feather."

"Fin and Feather?" Provocation said. "Who's paying for that nonsense?"

"The M-M-Ministry of Education." Skoch looked defensive. "It's an important part of the social education."

"A waste of beads, you mean." Provocation said. "Why spend such money on a slave girl and four little boys."

Without regard to Provocation's objections, the carriage dropped them early Monday morning in the old section of the city, where two-storied buildings, gray with age, squatted around a circle.

"That's the Hall of Justice," Skoch said, pointing to one of the buildings. A small gathering of overlords milled around in front, waving signs at folks in passing skim carriages.

"Who are they?" Repentance asked.

"They are always here, m-m-my Lady. They are part of Deliverance Day."

"The group that wants to free slaves?" Lord Carrull had told her about them.

"They buy and free as many slaves as they can afford. Many overlords w-w-want the slaves to be freed. I'm not sure how we can free them, though. If we had to pay the slaves wages, our economy would crumble."

"Better that slave families are ripped apart than that the overlord economy should suffer," Repentance muttered.

"Next to the Hall of Justice, is the Hall of Records," Skoch said. "And the short building, there is the Ministry of Education."

Repentance noted the different style of the buildings on the circle. They were shorter and fatter than the buildings in the neighborhoods by the slave market and palace. And the carvings in their faces looked somehow fiercer—less refined.

"This is the Military Command." Skoch pointed a building just to the left of them. "And this one—" he indicated the building before them "—is the old palace. Now a museum."

"And there's the Fin and Feather," Tigen said, looking next to the museum. "The best eatery in all of Harthill."

Gaylor, Baeler, and Rrow, ran up the stairs, and into the museum, ahead of the others.

Repentance looked back at the Deliverance Day group before she went in. There were overlords who didn't hate her. That gave her hope.

The museum was dark and cold, with its threadbare lavacloth carpets and suncloths. The rooms were not nearly as comfortable as those of the newer palace. But the worst part, for Repentance, were the gruesome carvings, in every wall, of bloody battles of old. She averted her eyes and concentrated instead on the furniture or the dinnerware as Skoch carried on about the importance of this king and that king in the shaping of the present-day Harthill.

After going through all the bed chambers upstairs, and considering how hard life was back before the overlords had lavacloth in abundance, they entered a great room and found one entire wall given to the destruction of a lowborn village. Gaylor, who had gotten there first, stood before the picture chortling. Repentance turned away in disgust.

"Are you feeling ill, my Lady?" Skoch asked.

"I need the relief room."

"Do you recall the one we passed downstairs in the main hallway when we came in?"

She nodded.

"We'll be right behind you. We have only two more rooms up here."

After washing her face, she felt better, but she had no desire to see more of the dark, old palace. She stepped out on the wide porch to suck down some fresh air.

Across the circle, the Deliverance Day people were crowded around an open skim wagon loaded with chignets of potatoes. Repentance strained to see better. The driver looked a lot like Calamity, but she couldn't be sure at such a distance.

"This tongue of mine," quoth the fool, "will take me to the swingman, if it doesn't learn to be still."

"Then you must teach it to be still," the wise man replied.

"Alas, alas, then swing I must, for my tongue refuses to attend lessons. Of an afternoon it can always be found down at the pub, a lapping and a flapping, all fast and free."

~from *The Fool and the Wiseman*, by Lord Kawklin

CHAPTER 22

Repentance wandered down the steps in front of the museum and headed across the circle toward the Hall of Justice.

As she neared the potato wagon, she saw that Calamity was indeed sitting in the driver's seat. He was talking with the Deliverance Day people.

Sober walked around from the back of the wagon, balancing a chignet of potatoes on his shoulder as if it were a small basket of berries. His black hair gleamed blue in the midday mountain sunlight.

He looked up and gaped. Then set his chignet of potatoes down on the seat next to Calamity and walked toward her. "Repentance, you're the last person I expected to see here." His soft flannel buttoning scarf was wrapped loosely around his neck and Repentance had to force down the urge to reach out and touch it.

He'd offered that scarf to her once and she'd turned it down. She'd had a good reason for turning it down. She was sure of it. But as he stood next to her in the sunshine and crisp mountain air, she couldn't remember what that reason was.

"Are you not well?" he asked, leaning forward to look into her face.

"I'm fine. Just surprised to see you. The tutor brought us to the museum. Why are you here?"

"We deliver potatoes to the Fin and Feather," he pointed to the eatery. "And you? Why are you not in the museum with the porcupine tutor?"

She laughed. "The tutor I can tolerate. The young prince Gaylor is another matter."

"You always did have a hard time making friends." He winked. Then his expression grew serious. "Except for Comfort. You always got along with your sister."

"How would you know that?"

"I've known you since you were born, Repentance. How would I not know that about you?"

"But I don't know anything about you. You didn't even go to school with us."

He put his arm around her shoulder and walked her back toward the benches in front of the Hall of Justice. "I did go to school with you for a couple of years. I still remember your first day." His face softened as he spoke. "You burst into class, a muddy little girl with a possum under her arm. You'd caught him on the way to school. And that smile. It lit up the swamp like a thousand torches."

She had a smile? He was confusing her with some other muddy little girl. She was not much for smiles.

Sober sat on a bench and patted the spot beside him. "Sit with me."

"Don't you have to work?"

"Calamity's busy. He'll let me know when we have to go."

"Why is he talking to those people? Aren't they ones that help slaves escape?"

"They buy slaves. They don't break the law. They buy slaves and set them free."

"Is Calamity hoping they'll buy him?"

Sober looked at the old man and smiled. "He'd never leave the Mistress. He's not talking to the Deliverance Day people. He's talking to the mistress. See her there? She walks with them, holding her sign once a week."

Repentance frowned. "But she owns slaves. How can she protest?"

"She pays us. She lets us work off our debt. Then, if we want, we can leave."

Praise Providence! How wonderful for Sober.

A carriage edged around Calamity's potato wagon, slowly.

Repentance sat next to Sober. "So you remember me from school? Why don't I remember you?"

"We remember what's important to us. No one was important to you but Comfort."

She remembered many things besides Comfort. She remembered the other kids whispering about her. Calling her cursed. She remembered that they teased her because she was different. She remembered that she never fit in.

She watched the skim carriage turn in the circle and head back their direction, and wondered if a rich overlord was in the carriage and if he might come back and yell at the Deliverance Day people. But there were carriages coming and going regularly and they mostly seemed to ignore the crowd in front of the Hall of Justice.

"When you were in your sixth year you lost that smile of yours," Sober said. "The overlords took your brother and you changed. You didn't play with the other kids anymore. You hung onto Comfort like she was your only friend in the world. And when you were in your eighth year, I left school. There's no reason you should remember me."

"Then how do you know so much about me, if you left school when I was so young?"

"I kept an eye on you as the years went on."

"Sober," Calamity called. "We're late for our rounds. You should have had this chignet over to the Fin and Feather long afore now."

Sober rose and turned to give Repentance a bow.

She couldn't believe that she hadn't seen how handsome he was before. Surely she should remember something about him from school. But there was nothing.

He remembered her, though.

You remember what is important to you, he'd said.

He met her gaze and she tried a smile on him. Maybe it wasn't as bright as a thousand torches. Maybe it was more like the small, flickering stub of a candle. But it was a start.

And he smiled back.

Repentance wandered back toward the museum and sat on the bench in front, thinking about Sober, trying to remember what he looked like back when she'd first gone to school. Skoch and the young princes finally came out.

"I'm sorry we took so long," Skoch said. "The boys wanted to go out on the roof, and when we went out, the door locked behind us."

"And guess what we saw from up there?" Gaylor asked. "We saw you talking to the Deliverance Dogs."

She ignored him, keeping her eyes on the ground. He always got tired of taunting her when she didn't respond.

"You're better?" Skoch asked.

"The fresh air has done me much good, thanks," she said softly.

"We'll see the Hall of Justice, next."

Skoch had barely gotten the words out when a skim carriage pulled to in front of them. Favor, the palace footman, jumped out and approached them. "The king bids you to return to the palace," he said.

"The king is back?" Repentance asked.

"Just now arrived," Favor answered.

"We are having a tour of the Hall of Justice," Baeler said.

"They have old swing frames in there. And," he gave Repentance a horrid grin, "they have the axe that Fawlin the Dragon Slayer used to cut off his lowborn button mate's head."

"And after we see all of that," Gaylor added, "we are going for lunch to the Fin and Feather."

"I'm told to bring you straight back," Favor said.

The princes continued to protest, but Favor was unbending. The king had given orders. Finally Gaylor and Baeler gave up their complaints and climbed into the carriage.

Repentance got in behind them, glad to be heading back to the palace. She had no desire to see The Dragon Slayer's bloody axe. Besides, she was anxious to see the king. She wasn't sure how much she'd tell him, but she was sure of one thing: having the king home would save her from having to go out to any feasts with the prince. As they swished out of the circle, Repentance looked back at Calamity and Sober's potato cart, which stood in front of the Fin and Feather. She wasn't even sorry to miss out on lunch at the famous eatery. Sober would be delivering vegetables up at the palace in a couple of hours, and she wanted to be there.

They pulled to at the palace steps and Favor opened the door.

"We made good time, thank Providence. The king is that upset. He'd likely blame me for loitering if anyone had slowed us down today."

"Ups-s-set?" Skoch stuttered. "What is he upset about? We didn't go without authority. It was the prince himself who suggested the trip and procured the money from the M-m-ministry of Education."

Repentance stared at Skoch, aghast. If the prince had arranged the trip—

Generosity flew out the front door, wringing her hands. "You're back. I'm to take you to the king."

"What's wrong? Favor said the king was upset."

Giving her a pitiful look, Generosity whispered, "My Lady, he is very angry about something, I know not what. When

Provocation told me to fetch you she told me your tongue could ... your tongue could melt the palace as easily as dragon breath." Her words drowned out the happiness Repentance had been feeling under the glow of Sober's smile. The maid might as well have dumped a bucket of mud into her heart.

"Provocation said that if you lived through this one she'd know for sure you were a blessed one under protection of Providence, for none but he can save you now."

"That's what Provocation knows," Repentance said as she followed Generosity down the hall. She'd done nothing but dodge the prince and mind her own business for two horrible weeks. And for that she was in some kind of trouble. "There are no blessed ones among the lowborns. Providence hasn't bothered himself with us for two hundred and fifty years."

Generosity gasped. "I'm sure you're wrong, my Lady."

She wasn't wrong. She was always in trouble simply for having the misfortune of being lowborn. She hadn't even seen the king, but she'd done something to offend him.

Surely it was some kind of mistake.

Or the prince was up to something.

"Did you call him a name, my Lady? Did you say anything to him?"

"I've done nothing, I tell you. I haven't seen him in two weeks."

"Lower your voice, my Lady." Generosity went pale. She pulled at Repentance's arm trying to slow her down.

Repentance shook her away.

"It's here," Generosity said, motioning toward a closed door. "The king's personal library is here."

Repentance reached for the door handle.

"I'll pray for you, my Lady," Generosity said.

"If it helps you, Generosity, pray as you wish." She opened the door and strode in.

Provocation stood in front of the king's desk, looking at some parchment. The king leaned over to peer around her. Then, looking up, he nodded a dismissal.

Provocation brushed by Repentance on her way out, throwing her a look of disgust.

The king waited, his face livid. As soon as the door swished shut he spoke. "Must I kill you? Will you force me to hang you on the frame?"

"What have I done?"

"As if you don't know." He coughed a couple of times. "Who else have you told? How many of my enemies have you sold information to?" He coughed several more times.

"I don't know what you're talking about!"

He took a flask from his drawer and took a healthy swig. "I saved you, Repentance. I saved you out of pity. And this is the way you repay me? You tell my enemies that I am sick. Too weak to take a concubine. Coughing all the time."

She hadn't told his enemies. "I've told no one."

Only Sober.

Sober!

"There! Your face tells the truth that your mouth will not admit."

But surely Sober wouldn't have told anyone.

"I've nothing to admit to."

"You lie. No one knew that you were my concubine in name only except for you, Repentance. I never told anyone."

"Neither did I tell!"

"Word of your treachery reached me down at the healing house. If you told no one then why is half the palace laughing over the fact that I am too old and sick to take a concubine?"

"I never—"

"Provocation heard it. The tutor told her. My footmen heard it. One of them passed it to the milkmaids, no doubt, who tattled it to Cook. She may have hushed it up at table but not before the stable hands caught hold of it. In one day the whole palace knew. Three days later all Harthill was aware, for the story made its way to the city market to be bartered back and forth with the broccoli and the beads."

Sober!

"The thing that makes me angriest is that I treated you so kindly. I gave you so much. You had the queen's bedchamber. I have paid for a wardrobe full of rich clothing. Above all, you had honor. You were being educated beside my own flesh and blood."

She hung her head.

"I don't believe you told anyone because you wanted to harm me. I believe you did it because you are stupid and impetuous."

She was both of those and selfish besides. She'd told Sober because she wanted him to like her. She'd been ashamed and she'd wanted Sober to know that she wasn't really a concubine. And that had been more important than keeping her word to the king and securing his trust so that she might save Comfort and her little brothers when they landed on the slave dock.

"I *am* stupid and impetuous, my Lord," she said.

"A king must command respect from his subjects or all is lost. You've treated me like your pet potentate. You dance around the palace as if you own it."

"I'm sorry."

"But that doesn't do away with the damage you've done. Had you been working instead of meeting with boyfriends, and shaming me in public—oh no, don't give me that shocked look—I've heard about your fondness for stable boys and farmers. Had you been working, you would not be in this trouble. Your blood won't be on my hands. Your own disobedience has brought this to pass. You've had many chances and you've proven to be obstinate."

So that was it. He would kill her and do it with a clear conscience. She had broken the rules and that justified him in his own sight. Well, if she was going to die .... She stood up tall and gave him the sternest look she could muster with her chin trembling as it was. "You may think you can kill me and not bear guilt, but Providence will decide between us."

He sighed heavily, an exhausted old man. "Providence has already decided, Repentance. He raised me up as king and He made you my slave."

He was right. Providence had picked favorites two hundred and fifty years earlier.

The king continued. "I stupidly thought I could defy the order Providence has set. I thought I could lift you out of slavery and educate you and make something out of you. But apparently you aren't able to be reasonable and to appreciate the good I've given you. You turn, like a wild animal, and bite me."

She cringed. In the end she was no more than an animal to him. To the slaves at the palace she was a lady and to the overlords she was a yak. When Providence created her, he was having a joke on the world. "So you might as well kill me as you would kill a hog that gored one of the stable boys."

"Quit goading me, or I just might do that. Who did you tell? Your maid? How did you get involved with the Deliverance Day group?"

"I don't know anything about Deliverance Day."

"I was in the Village Circle not one hour ago and I saw you with them in front of the Hall of Justice."

"I was there with Skoch and the young princes. I wasn't—"

He slammed his hand on his desk. "Who introduced you to them? Who do you give your information to?" he shouted.

She couldn't hand Sober over. "My Lord, I told no one."

"You are standing firm on that patch of ground, then?"

"I am."

He laughed—not a happy laugh. "Is it to be forever this way, Repentance? Will you always speak when I order you to silence and remain silent when I bid you speak?"

"I cannot tell you what you want to hear." He was so mad at her he was about ready to kill her. And he liked her. A little, anyway. He cared nothing for Sober. If she gave him Sober, he would likely not hold himself back.

Anger burned in the king's eyes. "So you are no longer my concubine. You never were, in fact. There's no need for you to attend afternoon lectures. You are to spend your afternoons washing, as well as your mornings. As soon as I can arrange it you will be transferred to Madame Cawrocc for resale."

The last time she'd seen Cawrocc, she'd tried to choke her. After Cawrocc killed her, if she was lucky, what was left of her would be sold to Jadin to be handed over to the prince. The prince! He was the one who set up the trip to the museum. He knew the Deliverance Day people were there. He must have sent the king there. "Your Majesty, the prince—"

He waved to silence her. "I'll put it into the ears of the tale-bearers that I've grown tired of the game we've been playing. I took you only because I wanted to hurt my nephew. I knew how much he wanted you and I wanted to remind him, in public, that I had power over him. But now I let you go, laughing over the whole thing. He can have you now."

"You can't mean that!"

"You've brought this on yourself. See Provocation when you are done with your work tonight, and she'll show you to the maid's quarters."

"How did word reach you? Your majesty while you were gone the prince told me he wanted to take me to a feast. He had some ... some plan. That's why I didn't do the washing. I've been hiding from him for two weeks. And he's the one who told Skoch to take us to the museum. I wasn't there to meet the Deliverance Day people. How could I have orchestrated a trip into the city? He must have started this rumor to get me into trouble."

"The prince is taking much pleasure in my disgrace. There can be no doubt. He sent word to me to go into the Village Circle. He's been watching you and he's taken great pleasure in telling me of all your many trips to the stables. And he's handing those stories to many others besides me, we can be sure. If the people find me ridiculous and believe he's been running the kingdom, his popularity will grow." He coughed and took a swig from his flask.

"Oh, yes, the prince is making the most of my humiliation. But he's not the one that started the rumor. You told someone. The look on your face when I asked, said as much." He sighed. "I've told you before that your expressions always betray you."

"But the prince—" She pictured his leering face. "You might as well kill me."

"No!" he yelled, pointing a finger at her. His face was red and his hand was shaking. "*You* might as well have killed *me*. In making me look ridiculous, you've given the prince power over me that he never before had. The troopers won't follow a weak leader. And you have done more to weaken me in two weeks than the prince has been able to do in ten years. You've handed me to my enemies."

"I never told your enemies. I swear to you."

Just Sober.

He was no enemy.

The face of the friend and the face of the betrayer often appear the same. Both men will look at you, sincerity burning in their eyes. One is a lover and one is a leech. One is true and one is an actor. And how can you tell between them?

~Lady Dannik, *After the Curtain Call*

CHAPTER 23

It took the prince all of fifteen minutes to find Repentance after the king had dismissed her.

She was on the stairs, heading for the fifth floor with a basket of suncloths.

Stunned. Not sure what she was going to do—how she could convince the king—when she turned a corner on a landing and came face-to-face with the prince.

"I was just up on the fifth floor looking for you," he said, leering. "You can never keep a secret in the palace, Repentance. Now you know."

She hugged the basket to her chest, bracing herself.

He smiled. "But don't you worry. I have no intention of letting you go back to Madame Cawrocc. My uncle is barbaric to suggest such a thing. I'll buy you myself."

"Excuse me. I need to hang these suncloths."

He didn't move. "It's a good thing the truth came out. Now

I don't have to kill you as I'd planned."

She gasped and stepped back. "Me? I thought the king—"

"Well, I wasn't going to kill you myself. I was going to order it done, of course." He reached out and caressed her cheek with his knuckles. "Far be it from me to watch the life drain from such a lovely face."

She shrank back, keeping the basket between them.

He shrugged. "Still, it was a good plan. My uncle would not have said a word against me, for you were to be found dead in another man's bed after a feast where you were flaunting your infidelity. I was going to explain that I'd ordered your execution to protect his reputation. All your hours spent with the stable boy and the farmer worked perfectly for my plan. The more you were seen with them by the other servants, the more believable your affair with a certain nobleman would have been. It was a perfect plan—to kill you two and put you in bed together. I'd have been rid of you both. I've been wanting to kill him for years. An honest man who has never played well with my troopers.

He spoke of murder with such coldness. As if taking life would be no more difficult than squashing an irritating gnat. "But, why kill *me*?"

She backed away from him. Two steps.

He pressed forward. "Well I couldn't very well kill *the king*. I already told you. If I'd have killed him, the people would have rebelled. Though, thanks to you, I'm in a much stronger position now than I was in last week. The king is a laughing stock now."

She cringed.

"And I didn't need to kill him. What did it matter if he toddled around the palace, pretending to be king? I ran the kingdom. But you came and he suddenly got some life in his half-dead carcass. He started to defy me. Told me I couldn't invade Westwold. Where did he get the energy to meddle, all of a sudden, I asked myself."

He reached out and caressed her hair. "What kind of magic did his new concubine work? I thought you were giving him something in the night. I thought you were like medicinal herbs, bringing him to life."

She took another step back.

"It certainly looked like you were his concubine, doing him a service," the prince continued. "He was happier than I've ever seen him. And what, I wondered, would I do if you produced an heir? Half-breed or not, I couldn't chance it. The king loved you and likely he'd love any ill-bred brat you conceived, as well."

Repentance fought down a gag. The king never loved her. She was a slave. He was an overlord.

"But then I found out you were giving him nothing in the night. I found out that there would be no heir. And, happily, I didn't have to have you killed. I simply had to make sure the story of the king's infirmity spread. He looks the fool and you are thrown out. But don't fear, Repentance. I will take you in."

"Thank you, your majesty. I'm happy to go to the slave quarters." Surely Sober hadn't told the prince. But he had to have told someone. The prince must have spies in the Deliverance Day people. "May I leave now?" She spoke quietly, not wanting him to think she was challenging his authority. "I need to get to my work."

He stepped forward, seized the basket, and threw it aside.

Suncloths tumbled onto the floor, landing in a tangled heap. Like her life.

"Now that I don't have to kill you," the prince said, "we might take some entertainment."

She threw her hands up, bracing them against his chest. "I'm too busy for entertainment."

He took her hands and put them on his waist. "You'll be busy, alright."

She pushed against him, backing away.

He followed.

She bumped into the wall.

He bumped into her—pressed himself against her—and, grabbing a handful of hair, he pulled her head back, tilting her face up toward his.

She twisted sideways, moving her mouth away.

"Ah, pretty little ear." He bent toward her.

Then caught his breath.

He pulled her head farther back.

She strained to look out of the corner of her eye.

He had an angry look on his face. He seemed to be looking at her birthmark. All praise to Providence! So he really did hate blemishes, just as the attendant had told her on her first day on the mountain.

Then he kissed her behind her ear. Right on top of the birthmark. When he pulled away, he looked at her as if searching for something in her eyes. "I can't finish this today, I'm sorry to say. But soon, Repentance. I'll be back to make you forget about the King. And the farmer."

He left her.

She slid to the floor, landing in a trembling pile. He was gone. By the grace of Providence, he was gone. Relief and pent-up fear coursed through her. He was gone. He was gone.

But he would be back.

When she entered the kitchen at lunchtime, the other servants stopped talking and looked at their plates as if eating took all their concentration. Generosity scooted over to make room for her on the bench. "Sit by me, my Lady."

"I'm not a lady."

"I'm sorry. The foot falls easily on the well-worn path," Generosity said. "But I'm glad you are still here, my La—Repentance. I feared for your life this morning. And I'm giving it true. I prayed for you, though, and Providence answered."

Repentance sighed. If Providence really did exist, he had an odd way of answering prayers. But she said nothing. She had no need to take Generosity's faith from her. Besides, she'd said a few prayers of her own during the morning, just in case, so she had no room to hold Generosity in disdain.

She ate in silence. As talk picked up around her, she listened with one corner of her mind and worried with another.

Could she tell the King that the prince had planned to kill her? Would he listen to her? The king *had* been kind to her—much kinder than Cawrocc or Jadin or Lord Malficc. But he was kind to all his slaves. The truth was that he was an overlord. He treated his slaves well, yes, but when it came down to it, he saw them as equal to yaks. He gave them the best of barns and the best of food, but Providence forbid that they ever refuse to pull his wagon. He'd carve a yak into roasts if it dared refuse a command. He couldn't look weak, after all.

And she had made him look weak.

But, how had the prince found out? Surely Sober didn't tell him.

Across the table from Repentance, Shamed pushed his plate away and stood. "You have cups of soup for Sober and Calamity today, Cook? I'll take them out to the vegetable shed."

Sober!

It felt like days—not hours—since she'd sat with him on the bench in the Village Circle. She needed to see him. She could ask him why he told. And who.

"Calamity and Sober have already come and gone," Cook said. She glanced at Repentance. "They were early today."

Repentance frowned. He'd betrayed her! She was in trouble, it was Sober's fault, and he didn't even have the decency to talk to her about it.

"Early?" Shamed scratched his head. "I did see them pull to a half hour ago. Same as always. When they didn't come in, I figured I'd take their cups of soup out to them."

"You figured off-center, then." Cook said. "They came and went early today and you've no reason to figure on it anymore."

Repentance spent the next half hour figuring on it, though. Wondering, as she took down her suncloths from their drying rack, what Sober was playing at.

She didn't stop figuring on it until she headed upstairs with her basket. As she placed her foot on the bottom step, fear over what awaited her at the top drove all thoughts of Sober from her mind.

But that afternoon Providence smiled on her. Or something like that. The prince did not return to make good on his promise to drive the king and the farmer from her thoughts.

At the end of the day, exhausted, more from the strain of the worry than the days labor, she made her way to the kitchen, where she ate dinner as quietly as she'd eaten lunch.

After dinner she tucked her chapped hands into her the pocket of her work smock and followed Generosity to her new room. It was a little room with meager furnishings—a bed, a nightstand, a washbasin. No window. No fire. No pictures carved into the walls.

But she was alive.

There was that.

She fell into the bed thinking she'd not be able to sleep for worry over the prince. She planned to think through a defense. She would just rest her head on the pillow for a minute first.

"Time to get up." Generosity shook her gently.

Opening her eyes, Repentance attempted to focus in the dim room.

Generosity tucked Repentance's hair back. "I was thinking," she said. "Maybe this is a gift from Providence. You can button Sober Marsh, now."

Repentance slapped her hand away. "I'm not buttoning Sober Marsh. What would put such a thought in your head?" Generosity. She was so much like Comfort. Blind to the realities of slavery.

"I've seen how he looks at you. And how he looks when he talks about you. Talk about eyes-only!"

"When was he talking about me? Yesterday? He spread

rumors about me quicker than water freezes on a wall."

"I didn't mean that. He'd never spread rumors about you. I'm sure of it."

"Someone did."

She dragged herself from bed, washed with a cold, damp rag, pulled on her work smock, and headed to the kitchen.

Breakfast was good, anyway. Hot pork sausage with fried potatoes. Cook took care of the servants.

Repentance worked all morning, looking over her shoulder at every sound, fearing the prince.

He never arrived.

At lunch, Calamity shuffled into the kitchen.

He never came on Tuesdays, but Repentance didn't care about that. She wanted to see Sober. She couldn't help but hope that he hadn't purposely betrayed her.

Behind Calamity came a young man, slouching into the kitchen on feet too large for his thin legs.

"Who's this one?" Cook asked, eyeing the stranger.

"This here's Belligerence," the old man said.

"Sober is sick, then?"

"Took ill of a sudden yesterday," the old man said. "We're here today to collect Friday's order, since we left yesterday without getting it.

Repentance settled back onto the bench. Sick! He was afraid to face her, that's what. Maybe no good explanation existed. Sober might have just plain betrayed her.

He'd said he wanted Tigen to sit on the throne. And his mistress was one of those Deliverance Day people. Maybe Sober was involved in some kind of plot and Repentance had given information to the king's enemies, after all.

The prince didn't make an appearance in the afternoon. Repentance finished her workday and went wearily, but thankfully, down to dinner. The table was full when she arrived. All the regulars were there. Three stable boys, Reticent, Shamed, and Blustering—all younger than Repentance by a couple of years. The four unbuttoned maids were there as well. Generosity and the three older ones—Biased, Blessed, and Forthright. The footmen, also, Meekness and Favor. And Merit, Cook's helper, who was, as Generosity had said, eyes-only for Favor and was barely aware anyone else was alive.

All the other servants, the ones who were buttoned, took meals with their own families in their own quarters.

Generosity waved to Repentance and motioned for her to sit between herself and Favor.

Favor grinned up at her.

She sighed as she squeezed between him and Generosity. She just wanted to be left alone. She was so tired. Tired of trying to figure out how to stay alive and who she should align herself with in order to save her sister and brothers. Tired of being forced here and there at the whims of others. And she was tired of men grinning and gaping.

"I'm sorry you've fallen on hard times," Favor said.

"What would you know about my times?"

He shrugged. "You've moved from the queen's chamber to the servants' quarters. Things can't be going well. And you sat with a world-weary sigh. But at least the prince is willing good fortune on you." He passed her the bread basket. "Things must improve now. He's a powerful man, and it's always good to have that kind of man as a friend and not an enemy."

"He's what?"

"A powerful man. Didn't you know? He's possibly more powerful than the king, now."

She shook her head. "He is willing me … ?" She took a piece of bread and passed the basket on to Generosity.

"Ah. He's willing you good fortune. I heard him say so when he and his friends left in the carriage today."

She waited while he took a bite of pork roast.

"And?" she asked when he made to take a second bite.

He looked at her perplexed, his fork poised halfway to his mouth.

"What exactly did the prince say?"

"Lord Dahner said it would be simple enough to charge you with a crime and hand you over to the swingman."

His words slammed into her with such force that she almost fell off the bench. Why kill her? The prince knew now she was never going to provide the king with an heir.

"And the prince said he had no intention of letting you swing. He would fix the problem with the king, and you could move back to the queen's chamber." He shoveled in a bite of pork roast.

"Where did the prince go?" Repentance asked. "When he left in the carriage today, I mean."

Favor shook his head but said nothing, his mouth full.

Merit came up behind him and bent over his shoulder to put more roast on his empty plate.

He rewarded her with a grateful smile.

Repentance sat silent while her heart slowed back to its normal tempo. Yesterday the prince had been overjoyed to find that she was no longer the king's concubine. Why would he fix things with the king so she could have the queen's chamber back?

She could be sure of one thing—Favor was wrong to think the prince was willing good fortune on her.

Coincidence or Providence? Which lights my darkest hour?
Does He order my day? Choose my way?
Stoop to save me by His power?
~Repentance Atwater, *The Fawlin Palace Poetry Collection*

CHAPTER 24

After dinner, the slaves settled in for their regular evening activities, bringing out the games and the tatting and the books. As usual, several of the buttoned slaves joined them.

Cook sat at the head of the table, looking like the proud mother of a large brood, pouring mugs of steaming yak's milk flavored with cinnamon.

Tigen showed up, gave Repentance a shy wave, and joined a clutch of boys in one corner.

Repentance rose, thinking to take a wingback chair by the fire. She would sit and read as she had been doing.

But things were changed. She couldn't sit aloof anymore. Now that she was a servant like the rest, they opened their hearts to make room for her.

"Come, Repentance," Favor said. "Have a game of Dragon in the Tower with me."

"I don't know how to play."

He laid his square of suede across the table. "I'll explain it."

They'd been playing for half an hour when Tigen sidled up next to her.

She smiled at him and went back to studying the game. She had two possible moves. She could eat Favor's crow with a polar bear or with a dragon. She hesitated, trying to see what his next move would be in either scenario.

She put her hand on the polar bear.

Tigen gasped softly.

"I heard that, Mr. Tigen," Favor said. "No helping."

The boy giggled.

Repentance looked at him from the corner of her eye. She moved her hand to the dragon.

Tigen gave a contented sigh.

Favor plucked his crow out of the tree and threw it at the boy. "Go away, you. If I wanted to be a laughingstock, I'd have challenged you to a game. I didn't do that now, did I? I asked Repentance."

Tigen laughed. "But the lady doesn't know how to play yet, Favor. She's brand new."

Repentance sighed. "And that's true. Only I'm not a lady anymore, Tigen. I'm a servant now."

"You're still the prettiest lady I've ever seen," he said.

"Tigen," a boy called from across the room. "Come play Tink-tops with us, then."

Tigen threw one more smile her way, then left.

Generosity looked over the top of her book. "Doesn't matter what age they are," she said. "They are bound to adore you."

Repentance thought of the king. And Sober. And the prince. "They don't adore me. Wanting to use someone and adoring someone are different things." Maybe she *was* cursed. Maybe her beauty was a curse.

"Well, our Tigen, he adores you."

But Tigen was just a child. She looked at Favor, sitting across from her. He didn't adore her. He had eyes-only for Merit even as he played Dragon in the Tower with Repentance. He loved Merit. It was as clear as white tea broth.

She sighed. She'd rather be loved by one man than wanted by many.

Life for Repentance, the maid, fell into a pattern. A grueling, hopeless pattern. Her shoulders ached from taking down and hanging up the heavy suncloths, her hands were red and cracking from constantly being wet and cold, but it wasn't the hard work that made her despair. Nor was it the anger she felt toward the overlords. It was the thought of Comfort, facing her Buttoning Day with no one to love her and no one to rescue her.

The one thing that made life bearable was that the prince had not returned to the palace. Favor had promised to tell her the minute he arrived back. So Repentance was able to relax on that count as she worked on the fifth floor, and she occupied her time thinking on how she might save Comfort from being sold as a concubine when her time on the slave dock came.

All day every day, in the mornings when Repentance washed and hung suncloths or in the evenings as she read in her room or sat in the kitchen with the others, her sister was never far from her mind.

Only one other person could knock Comfort from top place in her thoughts.

Sober.

She didn't want to ever see him again, and yet he intruded into her thoughts. It had been over a week and he'd not been back. Sick, Calamity said.

Monday morning she was on the fifth floor hanging suncloths, when she glanced out the window and saw Calamity's skim wagon winding its way up the drive. She felt sick to her stomach thinking about seeing Sober's smiling face again. She didn't want to meet with him and have her fears confirmed. She didn't want to learn that he'd been using her to gain information.

He'd told someone her secret. He must have.

Wondering about it was driving her mad. She had to find out the truth. She tacked up her last suncloth, wiped her face on her work smock, and headed for the kitchen. He probably wasn't there anyway. He probably was still *sick*.

She got to the kitchen too late.

Cook told her that Sober had been there, but he and Calamity had made it in and out quicker than a wolf could eat a piglet.

He was not sick, at least. She would confront him on Friday.

A little before noon on Friday morning, after washing a load of suncloths, she sneaked down to the yak barn to wait. She was taking a huge chance. If the king was watching her ... but the prince was gone and he was the one that liked to spy. And she had to see Sober. She had to know, once and for all, if he'd betrayed her.

She hoped for a better explanation than that. She dared to hope ... he did have a close relationship to the Deliverance Day people. He might help her run away. He might save her from the prince. She couldn't run away, though. The prince was buying her and if she ran, he'd take Comfort in her place. She shuddered at the thought of poor Comfort under the prince's control. Her sweet little sister wouldn't last two weeks under his abuse.

Still, she hoped that Sober might find a way to help her.

While she waited, she talked to the yaks, patting their velvety noses as she made her way down the corridor to the end of the barn where the greens were stored.

She was standing by Goldenrod's stall when the double doors slid open, letting in the brilliant mountain sunlight.

Blinded by the glare, she only saw Sober's silhouette.

He walked toward her, stepping into shadow.

It wasn't Sober. It was Belligerence.

"Something you need?" he asked when he saw her staring at him.

She shook her head. "I'm just ... I was just ... where's Sober?"

"Sick today."

Two Fridays in a row! He *was* trying to avoid her. He was skipping Fridays so he'd not have to eat lunch at the palace.

It didn't matter. She'd be ready for him on Monday, then. The hateful beast. He was avoiding her because he was ashamed. He wasn't going to get away with it.

"He is not trying to avoid you." Generosity sat in front of the reflecting wall braiding her hair. "I told you on Monday he was asking after you."

Repentance lowered herself into the bathing pool until only her head stuck out. They got to bathe every other night, and she and Generosity were on the same schedule. "Say what you want. I know what I know. Sober Marsh is hiding because he's done wrong. I told no one else that I wasn't servicing the king."

"Well, if he told anyone, he had good reason, Repentance Atwater. You can be sure of that. He's a good man. You ought to be ashamed, thinking so poorly of him. And him being so in love with you. What a waste and a pity that is."

Repentance felt her heart give a little tumble. "He's not in love with me."

"Most any fool would see it." Generosity gave her a stern look. "But maybe you're more fool than most."

Repentance ducked her head under the water to drown out Generosity's scolding. Sober couldn't be in love with her and betray her as he had. She had thought that maybe ... she had hoped he might .... But it was becoming apparent that he had been using her. He was either paying her back for refusing to button with him, or he was involved in some plot against the king.

After bathing, she was too wound up for sleep, and she was in no mood to face the crowd playing games in the kitchen, so she pulled on her robe and headed down the yak barn for a word with Bramble. Coming back she looked up at the starry sky and breathed deeply of the cold mountain air. She wrapped her lavacloth shawl tighter and spun around, gazing at millions of brilliant red and green and blue twinkles, lavishly sown across the sky by the hand of Providence.

And she felt a sudden anger well up.

Providence withheld so much beauty from the lowborns in Hot Springs. They were not worthy to look on the stars or the clear, blue sky, apparently.

And he seemed to delight in knocking her down. Every time she had her hopes raised, he would dash them. She dared try to escape the village and fight back against the overlords and Providence had sent her back to the swamp. She dared to hope that the king would help her save her sister and Providence had allowed the prince to make the king hate her. She dared to hope that Sober might be a true friend, and ... Sober believed in Providence. He was doing Providence's bidding, no doubt, when he told the king's enemies what Repentance had said.

A light bobbing up the lane caught her attention. A yak-drawn coach approached and finally disappeared from view as it followed the curving lane toward the front steps of the palace.

She hurried toward the back door, afraid to be out alone in the dark.

Provocation was coming out of the washroom as Repentance approached. "And where have you been?" the older woman demanded.

"I was catching a breath of fresh air."

"Fresh air, my elbow. You were sneaking around. I don't know what kind of scheme you have going, but I aim to discover it. Why is it that Madame Cawrocc won't buy you back?"

Repentance shrugged. The prince had probably paid her to refuse.

"And now you're taken off the fifth-floor suncloths and put on kitchen duty until after the Moonlight Festival. Why does Providence reward you?"

"I'd forgotten about the Moonlight Festival. When is it?"

"Little that matters to you. You'll not be going."

"Little that matters to me. I didn't even want to go."

"Then each one is happy, and the mountain stands strong," A satisfied look crossed Provocation's normally sour face. "The other servants will sit at the slave tables, but the king gave me specific instructions that you are not to attend. It seems he's afraid he'll kill you if he has to lay eyes on you." She sniffed. "I'm not able to guess what hold you have on him, that he takes such pains to protect you from himself."

Repentance held up her chapped, bleeding hands. "I think you may be confusing the word *protect* with the word *punish*."

But the next day she had to admit that she was being protected.

At breakfast Favor told her the prince had returned to the palace the previous night. So the day he got back she was assigned to kitchen duty, instead of being stuck working all alone on the fifth floor. The prince may have been off protecting her from Cawrocc, but Providence, it seemed, was protecting her from the prince.

That day she cut up vegetables and scoured pots and pans.

Cook, bustling and bossing, made it clear that no one was to touch her stove. She would only allow Merit and Repentance, and Generosity who was also on loan to the kitchen, to fill pie shells, pluck and clean birds, and engage in other such activities "what took no skill and little grace," as she liked to say.

To that end she sent Repentance to the yak barn on a mission that took no skill. "Take these left-over taters down to the boys," she said, handing a bowl to Repentance. "They never seem to get enough food, those three."

"Hello to you, Repentance," Shamed said when she entered the barn.

She stood, letting her eyes adjust to the gloom. Finally she saw him, looking over the door of the stall he'd been mucking out. He leaned on his pitchfork.

"Bringing sweets to Bramble, then?" he asked.

Repentance gave him a distracted smile. She liked this boy with his open face and happy expressions. "I'm afraid I have nothing for the yaks today. But Cook sent you a bowl full of garlic potatoes."

"Here, then," he said, reaching into his pocket. "You can't very well go see your lover empty-handed. He'd be crushed."

Her heart gave a quick tumble, and she had to keep herself from looking around for Sober. He was talking about Bramble, she knew that. But that word ... lover ... it brought Sober immediately to mind.

Shamed held out a pickle.

Her cheeks flamed. It was Generosity's fault. All that nonsense about Sober loving her.

She traded her bowl of potatoes for Shamed's pickle and smiled at the boy. The fact that he loved Bramble made her like him even more. If Comfort came up to the palace in two years, Shamed would make her a nice button mate.

Of course that dream was now gutted like a catfish on the block.

"Maybe you'd best give him the pickle quick like and be off back to the palace. It's been a busy place of late, this yak barn has. Never know if someone new is going to show up, what with all the hush hush hullabaloo going on."

"What kind of hullabaloo?"

"Coming in at all hours. They were trying to be quiet and all. But any fool knows you can't sneak into a yak barn in the middle of the night. These animals always get to snortin' and snufflin' when they're worried, and waking them in the middle of the night worries them."

"Who was trying to sneak in?"

"Two of them. One a trooper."

"Were they going on a trip?"

"Not going on. Coming from. Brought two yaks with them." He pointed down the corridor indicating two strange yaks with their heads poking over their stall doors.

"I pretended not to be awake," he said, dropping his voice even further. "It's not my place to interrupt people sneaking around in the middle of the night, is the way I see it."

"No, I would think not. I wonder what they were doing, though."

"This morning, when I'm letting the yaks out for their early exercise, the trooper comes in. He tells me I'll find two new yaks in the barn. He and a nobleman had come in late last night, he says. After sunset. So they drove the yaks in not a skim wagon. And would I please exercise and feed them well. Says we want to take extra good care of them as they belong to the nobleman and him being such a close friend of the prince and all."

A trickle of fear sprang up in her chest and quickly grew to the size of a swollen, springtime river. The prince had some scheme underway.

They hide in the dark—these eaters of flesh—and spring when they think no one is looking. But as long as there are some few left that will fight, against all odds, I will not lose my faith in Providence, who alone is the giver of courage in the blackest of nights.

~Kindness Firtree, *Meditations on the Precepts*

CHAPTER 25

The second day in the kitchen Repentance peeled four chignets of apples for Cook's fluffy pies and cobblers. It took all day and the work was boring, but she didn't mind. She was happy to be in the warm kitchen knowing she was safe from the prince for a spot and a space.

The third day, Repentance was assigned the filling of Cook's puddingpuffs. She bent over the round, flaky pastries, spooning out pockets in the center and dolloping in the pudding.

Tigen, having a love for puddings and pastries of all kinds, had come to visit each day. His family had their own kitchen and cook on the other side of the palace, but Tigen preferred Cook's tender, flaky pastries to Goodwoman Hardscrabble's dry, clumpy crusts. And so he sat, on Repentance's third day in the kitchen, with a little plate of pudding, talking to her as she worked.

"And if I lived in the days of dragons, I'd not hunt them. I'd train them. That's what," he said. "I'd keep them in the dungeon and let them swim in the lake underneath."

"I wasn't aware that dragons liked to swim. Would they eat your old-uncle's prisoners, do you suppose?" Repentance asked.

"They loved to swim," Tigen said. "In cold water, 'specially. It cooled the burning in their bellies. And, there are nary any prisoners in the dungeons to be et. My old-uncle never locks people up. My friends and I like to play down there. You can get onto the lake under the dungeon floor."

Repentance stopped her work to stare at him. "The lake is frozen under there?" She was sure Sober said it wasn't.

He grinned. "No, we go in the boat."

She was stunned. "Why would you go out on that lake in a boat?"

"To fish. There are sawtooth fish way down deep. We drop in a hundred foot line with a slug on a hook, and those old sawteeth can't resist."

Repentance could picture the gray lake, enshrouded in fog. It was warm enough not to freeze, true, but only by a degree or two. To fall into that water would mean swift and certain death. "Tigen, that lake is dangerous," she said with a shiver.

The boy shrugged. "So are dragons dangerous. I'd still tame them if there were any to be had."

"A tall order for such a short person," Repentance said. "How would one go about training a dragon?"

"The same way as the yaks. If you get an animal young enough, it grows up trusting you."

"And how, pray tell, would you get a young dragon?" She thought about her brothers Tribulation and Devastation—taken early. She had hoped to find out where they were, but she hadn't wanted to push too early. "Do you suppose the dragon's mother would give it to you when you asked?" As her own mother had done? If she'd have known she would lose favor with the King, she would have made inquiry about the boys sooner.

Tigen frowned. "I may have to kill the mother of the first litter."

She gasped. If her own parents had refused to give their

sons, they too would have been killed. And then all their children would have been taken.

"That's not right, Tigen."

He sighed. "It matters not. There are no dragons left. My old-father many times back did away with the last of the lot."

"It might not work, anyway," Repentance said. "Look at your own family. Why is it that you like slaves and your brothers don't? You all had slaves taking care of you from the time you were babies. But you alone trust us, out of all your family."

Tigen shrugged, then licked his plate.

Repentance spooned out more pudding for him. "Maybe you take after your mother. I've heard she's kind to lowborns. At any rate, I'm glad you don't hate slaves the way your father does."

"All but one," Tigen said.

"You hate one slave? Which one?"

"No, my father. He hates all but one."

"Which one?" She straightened up, stretched her back, and looked at the boy.

"The one he has hidden in the yak barn," he said.

"What?" She searched his face to see if he was having a joke on her, then bent to ask him quietly, "Why is your father hiding a slave in the yak barn?"

The boy shrugged.

"Shoo, now, Tigen," Cook called from the stove. "You're ruinin' your appetite and Goodwoman Hardscrabble will be glaring icicles at me on account of it. She'll likely complain to the king. You know how she is."

"She's not paying me any mind, today," Tigen replied. "She's too busy cooking for the feast my father is hosting tonight."

The kitchen door opened and the stable boys flooded in, rosy cheeked and hungry for their lunch.

Tigen quickly licked his plate, slid off the bench, and scampered out.

218

In the afternoon, Repentance told Cook she needed a short break.

"What for do you leave me now?" Cook stepped back from the pot of pork gravy she was stirring.

To look around the yak barn, of course. "I promised the boys that I'd take pudding down to the barn if I had any leftovers." She held up a bowl full of pudding.

"Did you settle the pans of pastries in the freeze?" Cook asked, wiping her sweaty brow.

"I delivered twelve flats of thirty-six puddingpuffs to the freezing barn this morning. And another six flats after lunch."

"I need you back here to peel my boiled potatoes. I'll be ready to fill the pork pies in two hours."

"I'll peel you a chignet of potatoes before you need them, I promise you that."

"Promises so easily made, young Repentance, are usually not so easily kept. You remember that when you're wanting a break from peeling."

Repentance ran down to the yak barn and found Reticent mucking stalls.

"Take a break," she called cheerily. "I brought you some pudding."

He smiled. "Put it in the tack room, would you? I'll wash my hands first."

"Where's Shamed?"

"Out back, ministering to a calf."

Repentance dropped the bowl of pudding on the table in the tack room, and headed out.

Shamed had a young yak cornered in a corral and was putting drops in its big, round eyes.

"I brought you some pudding," Repentance said loudly. In case anyone was listening.

When she got up to him she asked, "What are you doing with the yak?"

"He's got glare burn. Blind, he is. The drops will fix him up."

"Poor fellow." Repentance reached out to pet the baby.

Then she whispered. "Shamed, that trooper that came in the other night? Did he hide someone in the barn?"

"Haven't seen anyone." Shamed whispered back. "Or heard anyone, either, for that matter."

"If you wanted to hide someone in the barn, where would you put him?" Then she said out loud, "Don't be so scared, little fellow. Shamed is taking good care of you."

Shamed looked at her from the corner of his eye. "You want me to give you all my secrets? So you can interrupt me when I take girls there, no doubt. I've always suspected you were the jealous type, Repentance."

"You've found me out. Think on this, my comical friend: I'm working in the kitchen for the next three weeks. I have it in my power to bless your stomach or curse it. Which will it be?"

"I'm having a joke on you. No need to get mean. There's a secret room. Back of the feed bins. In the old days the troopers used it to store a cache of crossbows and arrows. If the dragons attacked the palace, well then—"

"No, no, calm down, little yak," she said out loud. "The big mean boy is almost finished torturing you."

"Who do you think is listening?" Shamed whispered.

"Finish the story."

"The barns would be the last to be attacked. So any trooper escaping the palace could come to the barns and find weapons. Now there's nothing there but straw for the occasional roll between a stable boy and a kitchen maid."

"You and Biased have tried it out?" She pictured the old maid and Shamed and couldn't help but laugh.

He punched her in the arm.

She pushed him then whispered, "Has the trooper who brought the yaks in the middle of the night come back at all?"

"Been here every day. Comes just before dinner. Says he wants to make sure I'm taking good care of his yaks."

"So he might be bringing someone food."

"Might be," Shamed said.

Repentance returned to the kitchen to peel her chignet of potatoes.

Cook stuffed and baked the pork pies, and froze several trays for the Moonlight Festival, but she kept out a couple of trays, fresh and steaming, for dinner. They smelled glorious.

Repentance hated to miss out. But Shamed had said the trooper went to the barn before dinner. So she had no choice in the matter.

"I'm not feeling well," she said, rising from the table before the meal was even served.

"The heat in here?" Cook asked.

"Headache. I think I'll grab a breath of fresh air and then go to bed."

Earlier Shamed had promised to leave the tack room door ajar. He hadn't wanted to, but she'd worn him down. He didn't want any part of any secrets in the barn, and he'd done his best to dissuade her from meddling in matters that didn't concern her.

These things the prince was doing did concern her. She was sure of that. And his schemes meant no good for anyone.

Feeling her way through the dark tack room, she slipped into the barn's central corridor. The yaks knew her scent. She prayed they wouldn't start to bawl and give her away.

Peeking toward the bales of greens at the end of the barn, she saw no one.

She tiptoed along, heading toward the secret room.

Before she got there, the back wall split apart. A door she'd never seen before, its seams blending in with the natural seams of the wall, scraped open.

Repentance dodged into the closest stall. The yak gave a startled little jump. She looked at his face. Bramble.

He sniffed at the large pocket of her work smock.

Oh, please Providence. She hadn't brought him anything.

He snuffled and snorted.

221

"Tonight, then," A man's voice. "I had the brew delivered to the gatehouse an hour ago, and I've ordered their dinner. The guards should be drunk and distracted by the time you leave. Your yak will be tethered down the lane."

"Finally," a second man said.

The first man laughed. "Ah, anxious for the kill, I see."

"Anxious to be done with the evil deed and to get home to my family."

Bramble snuffled at Repentance's pocket.

"Oh, well then, pardon me, dear Consecration, for making you wait. I could have let you kill him the first night, of course. But then I couldn't have allowed you to escape. We had to wait for the prince's feast, you see. It takes a trickle of time, not to mention expertise and cunning, to execute a flawless assassination."

Repentance sucked in her breath and slammed a hand over her mouth. Her heart beat faster than a thumping hare on race day.

Bramble nosed her pocket, throwing her against the door of the stall. A pitchfork that was leaning on the wall nearby, clattered to the floor, but, praise Providence, the door latch held.

"Who's there?" one of the men said.

Repentance crouched in one corner. Bramble hunched over her, still snuffling about for a treat.

Footsteps approached.

"Just the yak knocking over a pitchfork. What about the prince?"

"He'll be in the company of lords and ladies at his dinner— very much in view of many witnesses who are beyond reproach. He'll go, with a select group, to the king's library at precisely nine o'clock and be shocked and grieved to find his uncle dead."

"I don't care about that. I meant what will he do with me? Will he send troopers to search for me?"

"Of course."

"How do I know the prince will keep his word? How do I know that I won't hang for an assassin on the morrow?"

Bramble, finding nothing to eat, snorted crankily.

Repentance held her hands up for him to sniff and lick.

"You can't trust him. Why would you think such a thing? Still ... let me sketch this out for you plainly, Consecration. You can do as he asks and maybe live, or you can refuse and I'll kill you now. After I kill you, I'll go down and take care of your button mate and slavelets. So what will it be? The choice is yours." He laughed. "There you see? You do have a choice. And all those silly anti-slave people, those Deliverance Day pieces of dung marching at the Hall of Justice with their "Free the Lowborns' signs, say we never give you people any choices."

"You leave my children alone."

"Then quit complaining and do the deed. Give me five minutes to get back to the party."

Footsteps padded back down the corridor. The secret door scraped shut.

She held perfectly still while Bramble nibbled her ear and dribbled on her hair.

The double doors at the end of the barn slid along the rolling tracks once, then again. Open and shut.

She waited in the dark.

So the prince had decided the king had sufficiently fallen from favor with the people. An assassination! This was how Lord Malficc was going to take care of the king and move her back to the queen's chamber. The truth hit her like a mudslide.

She pushed Bramble away and slid out of his stall. And then paused in indecision. She wasn't sure she wanted to warn the king. If he was so weak that the prince had ordered the assassination, it would be unwise for her to throw her lot in with his. Besides, he'd accused her and cast her aside, not caring if she lived or died.

But, mad as she was, she didn't want him to be killed. She was fond of him. He'd saved her from the prince, once upon a time. She didn't hate him. But even if she did, she'd still have to warn him. If he died, Malficc would gain the throne. And she was willing to risk anything to keep that from happening.

She turned to go warn the king but stopped before reaching

the door. He wouldn't listen to her. He'd throw her out.

Maybe she could tell Provocation. The king trusted her. Repentance had never been to her rooms but she knew which hallway they were on.

The door to the secret room behind the feed bins began to scrape open.

No time.

Repentance grabbed the pitchfork, sprinted to the end of the barn, and crouched behind the bales of greens.

Justice is hard to come by in the palaces where rich and powerful men decide the course of the world. We all know that's true. But she is just as hard to find in the back alleys. There is no honor among thieves. Wherever people gather, bringing their sinful hearts along, justice will always be hard-pressed and scrabbling for a hearing.

~Judge Bekkett, *Nobody Knows the Trials I've Seen*

CHAPTER 26

An old slave, his pockmarked face looking especially gruesome in the dim light of the barn, shuffled by her hiding place.

Once he was past, Repentance sprang from the shadows and poked him in the back with the pitchfork. "We need to talk," she said.

He stopped and turned around, his arms held out to show he meant not to fight. "Who are you?" he asked warily.

"I want to save you and your button mate and your young ones."

"A pitchfork in the gut is to be my salvation?"

She lowered the fork a trickle. "You can't kill the king. Once the prince takes the throne, he won't leave you for a witness. He'll need someone to blame. You know that. You'll hang for an assassin."

"What are you babbling about? I know nothing of killing the king."

"So the trooper was talking to someone else. Is that it? Another assassin named Consecration is hiding behind that wall?"

The old man narrowed his eyes. "You are entering deep waters, child. Be careful you don't drown."

"You and I are going to the king so we can tell him the whole plot. Because letting the prince ascend to the throne will be worse for me than drowning."

He shook his head. "I'm not going anywhere with you."

She jabbed at him with the pitchfork. "Turn around and start walking. I'm not going to sit here all night and bandy words while you look for a way to disarm me."

He headed for the double doors. She followed, the pitchfork at his back.

"The king will reward you if you tell the truth," she said as they left the barn.

"How would you know that?"

"I know him. He's a just man."

"You are gambling with the lives of my young ones. With my goodwoman's life. Put the pitchfork down and let me go."

"Be a man," she said. "Make your young ones proud. Dare to change the course of history. Maybe your children will see the day when there are no more little slavelets." She spit the hateful word out. Tears stung her eyes as she thought of the bodies of the boys hanging in the square by the slave market. It wasn't right that boys should be born into slavery and killed at the whims of other men.

"You are ill, child. You speak nonsense. Whether I kill the king or not, my young ones are still slaves. What I do tonight won't change the course of the kingdom's history. But it may change the course of my own family's history. If I don't kill the king, the Prince will have me killed and my family as well."

"Think, man!" She jabbed the pitchfork at him.

He jumped forward.

"Think!" she said again. "Why would the prince have a slave for an assassin? He's a rich and powerful man. Why go to the trouble of smuggling you into the palace? Why didn't he have his trooper kill the king?"

He stopped and turned to look at her, the moon throwing

light on the pain in his eyes. "I know they will hang me for an assassin. You cannot let a well-loved king be killed without finding and punishing the killer. If Prince Malficc were to take the throne without punishing someone, the people would never forgive him. I still have hope that he will spare my goodwoman and our young."

Tears slipped down Repentance's cheeks. It was so unfair. "You'll go to Providence with the king's blood on your hands. You don't want that."

"Of course, I don't. Better that than having the prince slaughter my family, though."

She lowered the pitchfork a trickle. "I'm sorry to force you. But I can't let you kill the king. You'll see. It will all turn out in the end. We'll tell the king and he'll believe us."

He closed his eyes for a moment, as if he might be praying, then set off again.

"Up this way," Repentance said, poking him toward the track she always took to the washroom door.

He shook his head. "The prince left the door open on the king's porch. At his library."

He shuffled off across the icy courtyard, bathed blue in the light of the moon.

She followed without argument, anxious to reach the shadows that pooled along the palace walls.

When they arrived at the wall, she breathed more freely.

The slave led the way around the back of the palace, ducking under the windows he passed. He slowed, walking close to the wall, and inched his way up to a door from which issued a sliver of yellow light. The king's library, apparently. Repentance and this assassin were going to walk right in and tell him that his nephew was trying to kill him. And if she had to spear the old slave to make him talk ... well, she was prepared to do that. Maybe. She sent a prayer to Providence. She wasn't above taking help from any quarter at that point.

The slave stopped to peer through the crack in the door. Repentance eased up behind him. The king was sitting at his desk, his back to them.

She prodded the slave with her pitchfork.

He pushed the door open, and stepped into the room.

Repentance plunged in after him.

It happened so quickly—an arm shot out from the side, grabbed her hair, and jerked her off balance. Someone wrenched the pitchfork from her hands.

She cried out as she lurched forward, trying to keep her head from being ripped off her shoulders.

The king stood and turned to face her, his face as white as his hair.

Anger burned in his eyes. And something else. Pity? Disappointment?

She wanted to yell. To warn him. But she was too late. Obviously the old slave wasn't working alone. Others were here to help him.

"What did I tell you, Uncle?"

Repentance looked from the corner of her eye and saw him standing on the far side of his uncle. Prince Malficc. He should have been at his dinner party.

"Release her," the king said.

The trooper let go of her hair.

Two troopers guarded Consecration.

Repentance stood, rubbing her scalp.

"Why?" the king asked, looking at her.

Why? Why indeed? Why was he giving orders and why were the troopers obeying him?

"Why do you think?" the Prince said. "She's proven herself to be vindictive and hot tempered. She's never respected you. Talking back to you. Calling you names at your own table. She thinks nothing of killing you. You are her enemy."

"Me?" She glared at the prince. "It was your plan to kill

him." She looked at the king, then. "Your Highness, I found this man in the yak barn. I overheard him talking with a trooper. They were planning to assassinate you upon order of the prince."

The prince chuckled. "She's a sly one, Uncle. And her tongue moves like hot water over the skating pond—all slippery-smooth. You must at least admire her for that."

The king gave him a hard stare. "Yes, well, I'm glad someone finds the night's activity amusing."

"Your Highness," Repentance said. "You cannot believe that I—"

"You sneak into my library in the darkness with an intruder and a pitchfork, and you expect me to believe you meant me no harm?'

"The pitchfork? No! That wasn't—"

"It doesn't take much discernment to see it," the prince said. "And if I'd not seen her from my window, and gotten here first with the troopers, she'd have succeeded in her wicked scheme. That pitchfork would be buried in your chest, my Lord."

"My scheme? Tell him," she said to the assassin. "Tell the king who ordered you to kill him."

"Yes," the prince said. "Do tell us. You will die either way, but you can save your family if you tell the truth here."

"You're threatening him!" She looked at the king. "The prince is threatening his family."

"Child," the assassin said, looking at Repentance. "It's over. We tried. We lost. The king will die another day."

"No!" she screamed. "You're lying! Do you think the prince is going to save you? You coward. Tell the truth."

"Child, it's not honorable to carry on so. Killing the king was an honorable plan." He spat on the carpeted floor in front of the king.

The trooper in front of him backhanded him. Consecration crumpled under the blow.

"Tell the truth!" Repentance yelled.

He pulled himself up slowly, blood dripping from his lip.

"He has kept our people captive too long and he deserves to die," he said. Then he looked at Repentance. "But you and I will not be the ones to do the glorious deed."

She shook her head, speechless. He wasn't going to tell.

"Now we know," the prince said. "Lock them up."

The troopers looked to the king.

"We know next to nothing," he said. "Who is this man? How did he get into the palace grounds? How is he connected with Repentance?"

"Uncle, please don't let your fondness for the girl fog your vision."

"I don't see a motive. Why would she kill me? What would she gain by it?"

"I have nothing to gain! I would never kill—"

"But you have a confession from the assassin himself." The prince walked over to Repentance and stared down into her face. "Some people are simply motivated by hate, your Highness. They hate, and you can't train it out of them no matter how hard you try. With every suncloth they wash, their hatred grows."

"You're lying. I don't—"

The Prince slapped her. "How dare you accuse me of lying?"

The sting of the slap brought tears. She swallowed them and glared at the prince with every bit of hatred she had.

He stepped aside. "This one is full of hate."

She looked at the king, "I never—"

The king interrupted. "Your expression gives you away, I'm afraid. You stare at me with such malice." He shook his head sadly. "I've told you before that you need to control your tongue and the expressions on your face. And now they betray your heart toward me. I don't know why you hate me, Repentance. I've been kind to you from the start, and you've repaid me with violence at every turn."

"Not so!" she shouted.

"Take them away," he said to the trooper standing by. "I can't stand to hear another word."

"And I shall inform the swingman," Prince Malficc said.

"No, you shall not. I've not sentenced them." the king said.

"Uncle, surely—"

"No more talk! Leave me, all of you."

Two troopers walked them down a brightly lit stairway. Repentance had never been to the dungeons before. But surely they weren't so horrible. Tigen had told her he played in them. He was not afraid.

The air grew cold as they descended, and an icy fear seeped into her soul. She could die in the dungeons, and no one would know. No one would mourn. She stuck her free hand in the pocket of her work smock and worried her big gray buttons back and forth between her fingers.

"The prince won't let you go," she said to the assassin, her breath coming in white puffs. Maybe it wasn't too late for him to change his mind and tell the truth. "He'll kill you and your family, too. It amuses him to wield his power."

Her trooper gave her arm a savage yank. "Enough noise from you. We don't none of us believe you, so you might as well give it up."

A desk squatted at the bottom of the stairs, but no one manned it.

They walked on, reaching a door on the right, twenty feet past the desk. One trooper rapped with his bare knuckles on the wood.

An overlord man opened the door.

"We've two prisoners for you."

He put on a pair of spectacles and inspected the trooper as if to see if he was, perhaps, a young prince, dressed up and playing a joke. "There have never been prisoners here as long as I've been dungeon master."

"There are prisoners now. Come out and show them to their new quarters."

"Hold your yaks, then, while I get the key. Never had need of it afore." He ducked back inside and returned in a moment with a large key.

Crossing the hall he inserted it into a door. "One prisoner in here."

Consecration's trooper gave him a shove. He landed on his face on the icy floor and cried out.

The dungeon master moved to the next door and inserted the key again. "And this one for you, my dear," he said looking intently at Repentance. "I hope you find the accommodations comfortable. If not, don't hesitate to tell me." He laughed, his eyes distorted and eerie-looking behind thick glasses.

Repentance hurried in to keep from being pushed.

The door slammed behind her.

She let her eyes adjust to the dim light in her cell. There were no suncloths but a small window in the door let light in from the bright corridor.

Bitter cold came off the bare ice floor, passing through her slippers and burning her feet. The cell had no furniture—nothing she could climb up on. She lifted one foot and then the other, like a trotting yak, trying to keep her feet off the floor. In one corner she spotted a bit of material bunched up. Lavacloth. She spread it on the floor and sat down.

Her cell was ten feet by ten feet, solid ice. Nothing in it at all except for one square of yellow light lying, like a golden brick, in the middle of the icy floor. She saw a shadow in the corner opposite her and went to investigate. It turned out to be a hole in the floor big enough for a baby to fit through but not big enough for Repentance. A freezing fog rose from it. She couldn't have escaped that way, even if she had fit. Under that hole was the freezing lake. She'd die in an instant if she fell in there.

Repentance returned to her lava cloth and curled up on top of it, hugging herself to stay warm, and staring at the patch of light on her floor.

All she'd wanted was to keep from having her babies stolen,

really. She could have been content on a sunny farm, working hard and minding her own business. She could have even learned to be content in the choking fog, down with the whispering villagers who supposed she was cursed. If only the overlords would have not have forced her to button and breed.

She'd stood up to the overlords.

Had it been worth it?

She'd never have to give sons to the evil warthogs. They could kill her, but at least she wouldn't leave behind any pieces of herself to go on suffering. And she had a little sunlight besides. She'd longed for sunlight ever since she'd read about it in her schoolbooks. And now she had one little square of the lovely stuff, sitting on her cell floor. The yellow light wasn't thrown from the sun directly, but it was still good.

Had it been worth it? She worked her buttons around and around in her pocket. She could have buttoned with Sober. She closed her eyes and pictured his warm smile, and that look ... the one that made her knees feel weak. She could have shared a home with him.

But she wouldn't have been happy. She would have hated herself for giving in. For giving up. For giving away her babies.

A picture of Comfort flitted into her head. She had ruined Comfort's life. Oh, if only Providence would wake up and start looking after the lowborns.

She didn't remember even closing her eyes, but when she opened them back up, she knew she'd been asleep. She didn't know for how long. The little square of light on her floor hadn't moved. It would never move unless someone covered the suncloths in the corridor.

She stretched, looked around the room, then, because she had no reason to keep them open, she shut her eyes again.

Thoughts of her first trip up the mountain—the first time she saw sunlight, and snow, and trees dripping shadows in green meadows—washed across her mind. She remembered the stars, glowing like drops of molten metal on black velvet. Who knew the world was so beautiful?

She slept again, this time waking with a raging thirst.

And other needs. She looked for a waste stool so she could relieve herself. Ah, that's what the hole in the floor was for. It was hard to manage, without touching the ice and burning her skin. She had to hold the lavacloth against the wall and balance carefully as she leaned back.

Exhausted from that meager effort, she slept again and dreamt that she was eating hot sand that burned her mouth and throat.

The key in the lock grated into her dreams and yanked her from the sandy bank at the village swimming hole back into her cold dungeon cell.

Her small square of light grew narrow, and ran ahead of a large golden rectangle, which raced across the floor as the door swung open. The large rectangle finally caught the smaller one and gobbled it up. Repentance felt a stab in her heart as if she'd lost a friend.

"Stand and bow." It was the prince. So he was come to torture her before she died. She was not to die in peace, after all.

Her tongue felt fat and dry, but she managed to speak with venom, all the same. "I don't bow to murderers."

"You are still not ready to admit your guilt?'

She began to hum. She chose one of her mother's favorite tunes. She didn't have to listen to the prince.

He left.

Her square of light returned.

It gave her some comfort to find it always there when she woke.

Some time later the key scraped in the lock again.

She kept her eyes closed so she wouldn't have to witness the death of her square of light.

Common stock or royal prince, lowborn man or high,
There isn't any difference, when Swingman draweth nigh.
~Folk saying on the mountain

CHAPTER 27

"My Lady?" A woman's voice. It sounded trembly and tentative.

Repentance opened her eyes and stared. She knew the face but couldn't remember the name. Someone from the mountain. She squinted in concentration.

"I've brought you soup."

Ah. Her maid, Generosity.

Her tongue felt like a block of wood "We thouldn't be here." Her words came out all lumpy and ill formed. "Thith ith no plathe for uth."

"I know. But don't talk now," Generosity said gently. "Here's some yak's milk. I know you're thirsty. We didn't find out where you were until a few hours ago."

"How long have I been here?"

"Two days. Drink first and then we'll talk."

Repentance drank half of the milk—it was sweet and cooled

her burning throat and shrank her fat tongue. Lowering the flask she noticed that a blotch of shadow was biting into the light on the floor. She looked up at the door. A small head peeped around the jamb.

She smiled in spite of everything. "Why are you here, Tigen?"

"Came to see you," he said stepping into the room.

"Well, I wish I could offer you a proper a place to sit, your highness. This cell is hardly fit for royalty."

Tweaking Tigen's ear, Generosity said, "I told you to wait in the hallway until I could see how she was." Then she handed Repentance a bowl of soup. "You need to eat."

Repentance looked into the bowl. Warm broth with a couple of hunks of potatoes floating in it. Closing her eyes, Repentance prayed. "For your bounty ... of course, it's not bounty, really, is it? For this meager bowl of soup, then, I thank you. You've not given me much in life. I don't expect much in death. And yet I thank you for giving me something, little though it be."

"I've never heard you pray before," Generosity said.

"You've never seen me sentenced to death before, either." She lifted the bowl to her lips and drank.

"The prayer wasn't a very good one, though," Generosity said.

"What was wrong with it?"

"You were accusing Providence of being stingy."

"Did he give me a feast, here?"

"I would have brought more but the guards would not allow it. Prisoners are to be kept barely alive—just enough to face the swing frame. In fact, the prince meant to starve you completely, I think. The king thought the prince had ordered your meals. But Cook didn't even know you were locked up down here."

"Cook didn't know I was here, but Providence did. The reason you didn't bring more was that you could not. Providence, however, could have given more. He chose not to. I'd call that stingy."

Tigen whistled. "Why are you still alive after talking like

that?"

She sighed. Why indeed? Because Providence was in the habit of ignoring her. He'd been doing it all her life. Why would he start listening now?

"I'd call you a lucky leopard," the young prince said in an awe-tinged voice.

"Yes, but you are only in your eighth year, so no one cares for your assessment." She forced a smile and gave his head a friendly pat.

"Providence ought to slap you cross-eyed," Generosity said. "You know it's true."

Repentance lifted her bowl and drank some more before answering. "I'll grant I have not always been his most grateful subject. I haven't had much to be grateful for, though, you must admit. Still, now that I am destined to go and meet him, I'm trying to mend my ways. Hence my prayer of thanksgiving for the soup. I'm sorry you don't approve."

"It's not determined that you're going to meet Providence any time soon," Generosity said. "The king has yet to pronounce a sentence."

Repentance sighed. If her mother were there she'd have said the same thing. She'd kiss her forehead and whisper, "Hush, Repentance, Providence will make it all come out right in the end." She'd heard it so many times growing up. Yet here she was at the end, and nothing was coming out right. She drained her bowl and handed it back to Generosity.

"Did you really try to kill the king?" Generosity asked. "Shamed has been worrying ever since you vanished. Whispering and crying about how he should have stopped you."

Repentance sat up straighter. Shamed might be able to help her. He could go to the king and tell what he knew. She shook her head. All he knew was that there were a couple of strange yaks in his barn and a trooper visiting every day. And maybe someone was hiding in the secret room. He couldn't prove that the men weren't there to meet Repentance. The prince was never near the barn. He was blameless as far as anyone could prove. And if Shamed got involved, the prince would find a way to punish him.

She shook her head. She'd not take Shamed to the swing frame with her.

"Tell Shamed to stop talking about it. It's not safe. He needs to forget he ever saw anything. Lord Malficc—" she broke off, looking at Tigen's sweet, open face.

"What happened?" Generosity asked. "Surely there has been some mistake."

"It's not a story worth telling," Repentance answered, wearily. "I was trying to save the king, not kill him. But I have no way to prove my innocence."

"We'll pray on it," Generosity said. "Maybe Providence will be pleased to save you. In the meantime, I'll work on improving the menu the next time I come. Providence does care about you."

Tigen nodded. "And Generosity and I love you, too," he said shyly. "And we'll get you out of here. You'll see."

Generosity shushed him. "Maybe you shouldn't make such promises, Tigen. We don't know what the will of Providence is."

"I do know," he said.

Repentance reached for him and hugged him tight.

His kindness—his sympathetic smile and childlike confidence—undid her. Tears sprang to her eyes and overflowed. Bless the boy. He loved her. He did. And he would save her, if only
. . . .

If only he were king.

Maybe one day he would grow up to be king. Oh, please Providence, knock his evil brothers aside, and set Tigen on the throne. He was such a good boy. He would free her people and never again would a slave girl, unjustly accused, lie in a dungeon. Never again would a slave boy swing for a runner. Tigen wouldn't stand for it.

She kept holding him and weeping, unable to let him go.

He stood sweetly, patting her back and letting her cry all over him.

She set him away from herself. "I'm sorry! I got you wet." She swiped at his hair, pushing the damp, blonde strands back behind his ear, and curling the wet ends around her fingers. The shaft of light from the door, gave his hair a golden glow. So shiny and pretty.

And then she saw the mark on his neck. Just behind his left ear. It stood tan against his white skin. She brought him closer.

"It's all right." Tigen said. "I don't mind the wet hair." He pulled back from her.

"Hold still, I'm trying to see your neck." She stood and tilted his head. There! A tiny sun—a circle with sunrays all around it.

"It's my birthmark," he said.

"It looks like a sun."

"Of course. They all do."

"You have more?'

"Not me, Silly." Tigen laughed.

"You said 'all'—you said, 'They all look like suns.'"

"We all have suns behind our ears."

"All overlords have this birthmark?"

He laughed again. "Not all overlords. All who are from the royal house."

She reached up and laid a hand on her own neck. Royal house?

"Are you ill?" Generosity asked.

Her mother's sin. Her mother's great sin. She finally knew what it was.

Her mother had been pregnant on her buttoning day. Did her father know? Of course, he wouldn't have said anything. He was in his fifth year. If Mother hadn't buttoned him, he'd have been taken off in the slave carts.

She remembered the king looking at her with that sad look, saying, "You reminded me of someone I knew." And then there was the time he'd said, "Your mother was a beautiful woman." He knew her mother.

Intimately.

That was why he'd tried to protect her.

Dizzy, she stumbled back to sit on her lavacloth. "I'm his daughter?" she whispered.

Generosity shook her shoulder. "Repentance, what's the matter with you?"

She looked up. "I'm sorry. I forgot you were here."

"It's from going two days without food and drink." Generosity laid the back of her hand on Repentance's forehead. "You're ill. I'll bring you better food next time."

"I'm thirsty more than hungry."

"I'll bring you more yak's milk with mountainberry wine."

"I think you'd better bring me something else."

"What do you want?"

"I think you should bring me the king."

Generosity looked worried. "Shall I stuff him in my pocket for you? Repentance, are you having a joke on me, or are you ill?"

"Tigen, can you take a message to your old-uncle for me?"

He nodded.

"You have to make sure your father and your brothers are not around."

He nodded again.

"You have to be really careful. You have to be alone with the king."

"I'm not very good at memorizing. Can you write it down?"

She pulled aside her hair and bent her head forward so he could see the tiny sun birthmark behind her left ear.

Generosity gasped. "Holy Providence."

Tigen stared, wide-eyed.

"Tell him I showed you this mark," Repentance said. "I need him to come talk to me."

She spent the hours, while she waited, thinking about her own father. The father she grew up with. He must have known that she wasn't his daughter, and yet he never treated her differently from his flesh-and-blood children. She remembered him taking her swimming when she was a tiny girl and kissing her tenderly when he put her to bed at night. She remembered his gentle smile. And the way he laid a hand on her shoulder and squeezed when he wanted to encourage her.

Tears slipped down her cheeks when she thought about how well he'd loved her and how much she had hurt him.

And the king ... he'd gotten her mother pregnant, and he'd left her down there to have a baby with no one to help her. And he'd left Repentance down there suffering for so long.

He must have forced her mother. She wouldn't have lain with an overlord by choice. No lowborn would do such a despicable thing. It was unthinkable.

And yet ... her mother had named her Repentance Joyous Forgiveness Abounding Atwater, as if she had repented of some sin. As if she had chosen to give herself to the overlord king and was sorry about it.

She tried to imagine her mother and the king together. He was much older, but he was a handsome man. And her mother ... the king had been right when he'd said she was a beautiful woman. Repentance could understand why he would want her. But why had her mother wanted him? He was an overlord king!

Repentance wondered if she had done the right thing, telling Tigen to get his old uncle. The king had never made a move to claim her for a daughter. He'd left her in the swamp all those years.

He didn't have to claim her. She didn't want anything from him. She only wanted to convince him that she hadn't tried to assassinate him. She wouldn't do such a thing.

The key scraped.

The door swung open.

The king walked in slowly.

Repentance jumped up and bowed her head.

Two guards made to follow him.

"Leave us," he said.

The guards glanced at each other like they thought he might be crazy, but they obeyed.

Repentance stared at him in awe. Her father.

The king's look was not friendly. "Tigen told me you wanted to show me your birthmark."

"I don't need to show you. You already know it's there."

He didn't look like a father should look. He didn't look happy.

"When did you discover it?" he asked, sternly.

Why was he glaring at her?

Why did it matter when she discovered the birthmark?

"I've had it all my life," she said, stalling.

"You try my patience, Repentance. Why show me now? What do you think it means?"

A flash of insight came. If she told him she just found out that she was his daughter, he might think she tried to kill him, not knowing ... never suspecting she was trying to kill her own father.

"I know what it means. I've known all along. Ever since you told me my mother was a beautiful woman. I figured it out then."

"What precisely did you figure out?"

Were those tears sparkling in his eyes? Maybe he did love her. "I figured out that you're my father. And however cold you think me, surely you must know I would never kill my own father. Your Highness—Father—I never tried to assassinate you."

He smiled a sad smile. "I could not sentence you these last three days, because I couldn't see that you had any motive to assassinate me. You are impetuous and you often strike out in anger with no apparent logic. But this assassination was planned."

She nodded. "I never planned to kill you. I found the assassin in the—"

"But now you admit you did have motive. You thought you were my daughter. You planned to kill me and ascend to the throne, so you could free your people." He sighed. "We both know you have little love for me. You think I'm a murderer because I won't change the laws. Because I won't free the slaves, you hold me responsible for the death of every runner who ever met up with the swingman. I was heartbroken when Tigen came to me this afternoon. I wanted to believe you hadn't tried to kill me. I'd grown fond of you, young Repentance, your stubborn temper notwithstanding."

She shook her head. "I ... don't ... I wouldn't—"

"But my fondness for you was what blinded me. I don't know you. I don't know anything about your character. If I look with eyes of reason instead of emotion, I see that you have been a liar from the start. And you've hated me from the start. I wish it wasn't this way, but wanting a thing doesn't make it so." He shook his head sadly then turned to leave.

"You will watch your own daughter swing?"

He looked back at her. "You aren't my daughter."

She stared at him, her mouth open but no words making their way out.

"Your father's name was Lord Baldin. He was the son of my sister. A beloved nephew and a trusted friend."

"Baldin?"

"You have his nose."

She touched her nose.

"We went to the Hot Springs for healing. He was out walking in the woods one morning, and he met your mother. They spent two weeks together."

A fist squeezed her heart. "Not you?"

"He loved her. He planned to go back and take her away to Montphilo where there are no slaves and no one cares who an overlord buttons."

She wasn't supposed to be a slave. She was supposed to have grown up free in Montphilo. She was never meant for the fog and the swamp.

"Before he could go back for her, he was killed. By a runaway slave." He shook his head and gave a bitter laugh. "Yes, you were sentenced to a life of slavery, by a runaway slave. As soon as I saw you, I knew. You look very like your mother, but with your father's nose. For your father's sake, I wanted to love you. Baldin would have wanted it. And I did love you some. You made me laugh ... you made me angry ... you made me young."

"I didn't try to kill you," she whispered.

The look in his eyes turned to steel. "You thought I was your father all that time and you never once spoke to me of the matter. Never hugged me. Never gave me any indication that you loved me. Only now, when you fear dying, you show me your birthmark. You've never wanted me for a father. You've only tried to use me to gain what you wanted." He pushed the door open and walked out.

She lay on her lava cloth, clicking gray buttons in her hand and humming one of her mother's favorite tunes until the lump in her throat made humming impossible. Tears overflowed her eyes. What she wouldn't give to hear her mother's assurances that all would be well in the end. A sob tore itself loose from her soul.

Oh, holy Providence, she'd made a mess of things. Trying to be so smart and never quite pulling it off. She was out of ideas. Nothing would come out right now, regardless of her mother's predictions.

After a time, her sobbing subsided. She scrubbed her wet, chapped face with her sleeve and fell asleep.

An old slave woman came and woke her. The next day? Repentance didn't know. She was parched as if she'd not had a drink in a week.

The old slave set a stool down and sat. "Kneel here in front of me, then," she said. "No, no, with your back to me." She shook out a straight razor as she spoke.

"You slit my throat right here?" Her voice came out in a whisper, like sand sifting over rock. "I thought I was for the swingman."

"And have you ever seed long hair on a body what's on the swing frame?"

"My hair?"

"I'm to take it off."

She twisted so her back was toward the woman.

Shouts floated down the hall.

Running.

The door flew open, flooding the room with light.

"Out, you hag." It was the prince, his blonde hair blown back from running. "And don't you ever even think of touching this girl's hair."

The old woman jumped up, grabbed her stool, and scuttled through the door.

The prince glared at Repentance, his pale blue eyes glittering with hatred. He picked up a strand of her dirty, stringy hair and let it fall again, a sneer of disgust on his face. "You've not been keeping yourself up, my Lady. Such a waste. But we can't let anyone cut your hair. We want you in all your glory when you swing."

"My birthmark! This is all about my birthmark?" She jumped up, intent on scratching his eyes out.

He grabbed her hands and clamped them in his grip. "Of course it's about your birthmark. Once I saw it, I knew either you or he had to die. If he died, there would be no way you could prove you were his daughter and since I very much preferred to have you sleeping nearby in the palace, I went to great trouble to arrange his death and save you. But you wouldn't have it."

"To save me? No one was trying to kill me, but you."

"All you had to do was keep to your own affairs. The entire city was laughing at the king over his pretend concubine. My friends made sure to plant serious doubt in the minds of the most influential people regarding the king's fitness for the throne. A king who is a laughingstock is not an asset to a kingdom. It was the perfect time for me to act. He had lost the respect of the troopers. All you had to do was wait, and the king would have been dead, and you would have had the queen's chamber."

She struggled to free herself.

He pushed her so that she fell back against the wall, burning her forearm. Then he dodged out the door and slammed it.

Repentance sank down on her lavacloth, her knees weak, but she lifted her chin defiantly. She'd messed up his plans at least—the wretched, wicked man. The King lived and the prince would never crawl into Repentance's bed.

There was some comfort to be had in that.

But she was going to swing.

Soon.

The king had ordered it.

The woman had come to cut her hair.

The swingman would come next.

She buried her face in her hands and wept.

To save my honor, careless words were spoken,
    They left me empty, lost, and broken.
But truth was proclaimed, and wounds were healed.
    Love was poured out, and hearts were sealed.
        ~Repentance Atwater, *The Fawlin Palace Poetry Collection*

CHAPTER 28

Footsteps sounded in the hall, and Repentance sat up, tense and ready. She'd been waiting. Her crying was done. She'd walk to the frame with her head up.

The door creaked open.

Generosity came in, followed by Tigen.

Repentance, relieved, let a sob escape.

"I'm sorry I've not been back." Generosity said, reaching down and laying a gentle hand on Repentance's shoulder. "The prince would not allow it. We had to sneak down."

"No, no," Repentance said. "Don't apologize. I'm so happy to see you. I've gotten water and broth and dried bread twice. One of Goodwoman Hardscrabble's girls brought it."

Generosity handed over a bowl of thin soup.

Repentance lifted the bowl in salute. "Providence is in keeping with his own generous nature today, I see."

"He most certainly is," Generosity said, pulling two pork

pies from the big pocket of her work smock.

Repentance took them eagerly. "Now that's an answer to prayer."

"And this," Tigen said, reaching under his sweater and producing a flask. "Yak's milk with mountainberry wine and honey."

"You are my hero, Tigen. This will be a day of celebration." She took a swig of the cool liquid. "What day is it, anyway? I can't keep track down here."

"It's Monday." Generosity's breath came out in a puff of fog.

She'd only been in the dungeon six days. Six weeks would have been more believable.

"I delivered your message for you, too, my Lady," Tigen said proudly.

The memory of that botched plan made the pork pie she was eating turn bitter. But he didn't need to know that. She ruffled his hair. "A fine job you did of it, too."

"Did the king come, then?" Generosity asked, her face aghast. "I thought he'd not come yet. When he sentenced you—"

Repentance shot her a look. "He did sentence me, then? I knew he did. They sent a woman to cut my hair."

"Did you show him your birthmark?" Generosity asked.

"It went wrong. He's convinced I tried to kill him."

We'll think of some way to change his mind." Generosity said. "But you need to keep your strength up. Eat the lovely pork pies Providence has provided."

Repentance had to smile. "With a little help from Cook."

"She is convinced you are a foolish girl but no murderer, and she's determined to do for you what she can. She'll send no extras to the man next door, though. She can't forgive him for wanting to kill the king."

Repentance handed the second pork pie back to Generosity. "Take him this one then, when you leave me."

"The assassin?"

"He must be hungry."

Generosity tucked the pie into her pocket and picked up the

soup bowl.

"Tell him, I forgive him."

"For what?"

"No one would have believed him if he'd told them I was innocent."

Generosity leaned over and kissed Repentance on the top of her head. "Don't give up. Providence will make it all come out right in the end."

Repentance pulled back and looked at the girl's face. She had never told Generosity that her mother used to kiss the top of her head and say that exact thing. Providence alone had known how she was longing to hear those words.

Generosity came three more times, with the ever-present Tigen tripping along behind. They smuggled in good food for Repentance, which she, in turn, shared with the slave next door.

She wanted to ask Generosity for news of the outside world. Particularly she wanted to know when she was scheduled for execution—every time she heard the key grate in the lock she was sure the swingman was coming for her—but she couldn't bring herself to ask.

Between visits, Repentance sat in her dim cell remembering her life in the swamp. Picturing her mother as a young woman with an overlord lover. How devastated she must have been when he didn't come back for her.

But what would have become of her father if her mother had moved to Montphilo with the overlord?

Life was not neatly laid out the way Repentance wanted it to be. She loved her father. And her mother, too. What if they'd never buttoned? That would have left a hole too big to mend, for there would be no Comfort in the world.

It hurt to think about Comfort, but she couldn't stop herself. Childhood memories flooded in nonstop. She and Comfort picking persimmons. Comfort drawing pictures in the mud with a stick, down by the hot springs. Her mother laughing again after Fullness was born. She remembered her father teaching her to catch fish and her mother teaching her to cook them.

She was sorry she'd hurt them. So sorry she would never see them again.

As the memories washed over her, she laughed and wept and prayed.

Yes, she prayed. She wasn't sure that Providence could hear her, but she hoped he could, because she was going to die and she hadn't made anything but a mess of her life. She saw, in that dark cell, that her life was like a bunch of loose marsh grass, scattered on the ground. All it needed was time and wisdom to weave it into a worthwhile basket. She was going to die before she was formed. She hadn't figured out what to do with the pain she'd suffered. She never understood why one man was born a master and another man was born a slave. She had learned from her mistakes, but she wouldn't live long enough to put the learning into practice. In the end her life was worth nothing, then. After she died the world would go on as if she'd never lived. Her parents wouldn't even know to mourn. They wouldn't know she was dead.

But maybe she was looking at things the wrong way. Maybe she wasn't a pile of straw. Maybe her life was one strand of straw in a larger work. She would die alone and unjustly accused. A slave. Unloved. But it might be that in her coming to the mountain and befriending Tigen, she was going to effect change that was worth more than her own personal freedom. Her mother might be right. Maybe everything *would* come out right in the end. Maybe she wouldn't get to see it, because she wasn't part of the end. Maybe she was part of the middle.

The key in the lock jerked her from her thoughts.

She watched the door, sure that this time it would be the swingman. Her heart sped up and drops of sweat sprang forth on her forehead.

The door swished open.

And there, in the light, which flooded the cell, stood Sober Marsh.

She gasped and covered her face with both hands. He was the last person she wanted to see. Or the last person she wanted to see her, tired and filthy as she was.

"Why are you here?" Her voice was muffled.

"I've brought your food." Pulling one of her hands down so she could see him, he made a shushing expression with his lips. "Cook ordered me to bring it and the dungeon master, the nice fellow outside the door here, has been kind enough to allow me to deliver it."

Tigen sashayed in. "No one is outside the door but me. The dungeon master has gone back to his quarters."

Repentance yanked her hand from Sober's grip. "Go away," she moaned.

She would rather die than have Sober see her this way.

And then it hit her.

She was going to die.

And everyone would see her this way—and worse.

When her body hung in the square by the slave market ... she would be naked and missing her fingers and toes. Her eyes would be burned out. And everyone would see. New slaves would be forced to look on her as she swayed in the wind.

She ran to the hole in the corner and threw up.

Sober crossed the room and stood by, holding her hair back and rubbing her shoulders.

As soon as she finished retching, she wiped her mouth and screamed. "Get out!" She stood and beat on his chest. "It's your fault. Your fault! You told. Why did you tell?"

He dropped the soup bowl, grabbed her hands, and held them still. "I never told anything."

"You didn't come to lunch. You were avoiding me."

"My mistress wouldn't let me come. Calamity told her trouble was blowing on the mountain. He told her you were involved and I needed to stay home so no one would connect us."

"You told *someone*." She searched his eyes for the lie she was sure was lurking there. "I never told anyone else that the king was too weak to use me as a concubine. No one knew but you, Sober."

"I wish I could take the blame, if it would ease your pain, Repentance." He put both arms around her and squeezed her against his chest. "I never told anyone," he whispered.

"My Lady?" Tigen said, his voice thin and shaky.

She pushed herself away from Sober. Tigen stood as white as the wall behind him. She shouldn't have screamed. She'd scared the poor boy out of his wits.

"My Lady?" he said again.

"I'm sorry I scared you, Tigen."

"One day ... one day ... I was by Mist Lake, and I heard you talking to someone."

Oh no.

"I heard you say that the king was sick and he only took you because you reminded him of someone he knew."

She groaned. It couldn't have been Tigen.

"Later when Gaylor and Baeler were calling you a whore, I told them that you weren't our old-uncle's concubine."

And so she would die.

She had befriended a little overlord boy and made him want to defend her honor, and now she had to pay with her life. That's how it worked when you went against the order Providence had set.

She would die and what would she leave behind? She'd screamed at Sober, blaming him, and by doing that she'd laid a burden on Tigen that would likely crush him. Now when she was hanged, Tigen was sure to blame himself. He would grow up thinking he'd as much as slipped the noose around her neck.

She reached out to him and he came into her arms. "Tigen," she whispered as she hugged him. "I love you. I don't care who knows it. I don't care that you're an overlord boy and I'm a lowborn girl. I love you because you're good and loving and kind. You didn't do anything wrong."

She wept into his hair for the second time that week.

When she released him he was still white, but he gave a brave, trembling smile. "You're not a lowborn girl, though. You're an overlord lady."

She touched her neck. "Not that anyone can tell."

Color flushed back into his cheeks and he squirmed around, all excited, like a piglet at feeding time. "Everyone will be able to tell soon enough," he said. "We have clothes for you. You will wrap the turban around your head and all people will see is your eyes. Your light eyes. They don't look like slave eyes. You could look like an overlord from Norbank."

"What are you saying?"

"I'll be your slave," Sober said. "And Tigen will be your younger brother. No one will suspect."

"We are to kidnap the prince's son?"

"Only until we get out of the city. We'll send him back when we get to the wall."

She shook her head. "It's too risky. What if you get caught?"

"I'm not leaving you here, so there's no sense in arguing."

"How am I going to get out of the dungeon?"

Sober pointed to Tigen. "Who else knows all the hidey holes in a palace if not the young prince?"

"Tigen, you know a way out of here?"

He puffed his chest out.

"We leave now?"

Sober put a hand on her arm to hold her back. "We'll be back tonight. We don't have much time so listen carefully. When we come back and open your door we won't have a key. We're going to knock the handle off. Tigen knows how to do it. But the floor of your cell is set to slide back into the wall if the door is opened without a key. It's an escape deterrent. The lake lies right beneath your floor, and if you fall in, you'll freeze immediately. Do you understand?"

She nodded. And shuddered. She knew about the lake. Tigen had told her he fished in it.

"When I open the door, you need to be prepared to jump

253

over to me."

"But I can't run away. My family—"

"—will be fine," Sober said, finishing her sentence for her. "I've taken care of everything. We've got to go before the dungeon master gets suspicious. We'll be back with the clothes, and everything you need. Trust me."

And he and Tigen were out the door.

In the quiet after they left, Repentance stared at the square of light on her floor, thinking.

She couldn't run. By law, after he executed her, the king could take a sister or a brother to replace her.

But she was sure he wouldn't hurt them. He wasn't vindictive. He loved her overlord father and he had been learning to love her. He wouldn't take any pleasure in punishing her family after she was dead.

Running was different from an execution, though. He might feel forced into going after her family to publicly humiliate her. To show that no one could escape from him without paying a heavy price. He was so determined to punish disobedience, so as not to appear weak.

And Sober couldn't run, either, or his parents would be forfeit to his mistress.

But Sober said he'd worked it all out. She had to trust him.

He told her to be prepared.

So she would prepare.

Reaching her hand into her pocket, she felt her little parchment book and her char-stick, and she counted her buttons with her fingertips. "One, two, three. There we go," she whispered. "All packed."

Love gives birth to courage. It turns the smallest of lizards into mighty dragons.

~Professor Pottamous Scroll, Harthill University

CHAPTER 29

Sitting on her lava cloth in her dark dungeon cell, she stirred the buttons in her pocket around with her finger, and she laughed and laughed and laughed.

She'd come up the mountain with nothing. Once there, she'd gained beds and books and bathing pools. Now she was to go back down the mountain with nothing. No fancy clothes, no rich foods. Just her grimy self and her three gray buttons.

But she would be free.

Was it possible?

Hours later, a small knock sounded on her door. She jumped up and looked out the square window. Sober stood outside, his finger to his lips.

She positioned herself in the center of the room figuring whichever way the floor slid, the center would be the safest place.

She heard a muffled clunk. The door handle popped off and skittered across her floor. The door swung open.

With a soft, grinding sound, the floor began to slide into the back wall. Mist billowed up from the underground lake beneath the palace.

"Come to me," Sober whispered.

She stepped to the edge of the floor, feeling carefully with her foot, not really able to see with all the fog swirling through the cell.

"Jump!" Sober gave a whispered command.

She hesitated. The mist cleared a trickle—enough for her to see the lake several feet below her, the surface reflecting back the light from the hallway in dizzifying motion.

"Jump!" Sober said again.

She barely heard him over the grinding of the floor. He seemed too far away.

"Repentance, you have to jump now."

She'd waited too long. She'd never make it across.

"Catch this!"

Something hit her hands. The end of Sober's button scarf.

"Got it?"

"It's too far," she said.

"You jump, Repentance. One, two, three!"

He yanked.

She hung onto the button scarf and let it pull her off balance, but she didn't jump in time. She tried at the last moment to push off, but as soon as her feet left the floor she knew she didn't have enough momentum. She was going to land in the lake.

Holding the button scarf for dear life, she gave a little scream. Then she slammed into the ice wall below the doorway where Sober stood. The ice bit into her hands, and she almost let go of the scarf.

Sober grabbed a hold of one wrist. "Tigen, where are you?" he whispered loudly.

"Pull me up," Repentance said, frantically. "My feet are in the lake." Panicking, she tried to scramble up, but when her wet feet touched the wall, they froze to it as quickly as a dampened corner of a suncloth would have done. "Oh, dear Providence, my feet! Sober, my feet are frozen."

"Repentance, look at me," Sober said. "You'll be fine. Stay still."

"I'm here." Tigen's voice came from below her.

Something bumped into her legs.

They heard a splash and a muffled scream coming from the direction of the cell next door.

A look of shock crossed Sober's face. "Tigen, when you open one door, *all* the floors slide back?"

Repentance looked down. Tigen sat in a rowboat, right underneath her, his face white and his eyes round and terrified.

"Never mind," Sober said. "Tigen, you have to catch Repentance when I let her go. Put your arms around her waist and ease her into the boat so I can come down and get her feet loose."

Tigen grabbed her and Sober let her go. Tigen swayed under her weight, the boat rocking crazily underneath them.

"Sit down," Repentance said, in an urgent whisper. "We'll tip!"

He half fell underneath her so they were both lying in the rowboat anchored to the wall by her frozen feet.

Sober dropped down, the boat once again rocking wildly as he swayed and finally got his balance.

He lifted Repentance enough so Tigen could crawl out from under her, and then he set to work freeing her. Scooping icy water from the lake with his hands he dumped it on one foot and yanked it quickly from the wall. "Wrap her feet in lavacloth," he told Tigen, as he freed the next one.

"I'm sorry. I'm so sorry," Repentance said. "I didn't jump. I was too scared."

"You've nothing to be sorry about, Repentance." He reached under her arms and pulled her more fully into the boat, sitting her on the floor in front of the middle seat. "You've hardly had anything to eat in over a week and you're in shock. You've done fine. Rest, now. The lavacloth will warm your feet up in no time. We'll be fine."

He twisted so he was sitting on the middle seat, with his back toward Repentance. Tigen, done wrapping her feet, turned his back on her, as well, so he could face the prow.

"Row straight ahead, Sober," the boy said. "You're all clear until we come to an island halfway out."

Sober rowed, and the boat skimmed under the wall that separated Repentance's cell from Consecration's. Light falling from the small windows in the doors above cut through the murk at regular intervals, making the shadows between feel all the darker.

Something clunked against the boat. Repentance glimpsed Consecration's frozen, white face and quickly looked away in horror.

"He froze that fast." Sober said, looking over his shoulder.

Horror filled her. And pity.

And fear.

She looked at Tigen as he leaned forward in the boat, trying to see through in the blackness and the fog. "Don't lean so far, Tigen. You might fall out."

"I'm the one who brought the boat in, my Lady," he said. "I've done this many times."

They skimmed along in silence after that, bypassing the island Tigen had mentioned, and then heading for the moonlight that seeped in at the end of the palace. They had to crouch down to get out from under the palace wall, the boat barely scraping through.

Silvery, moonlit fog shrouded the lake. Repentance shivered and whispered a prayer of thanks for the fog that hid them.

Sober bumped the dock, tied the boat off, and helped the others out.

Tigen pulled a bundle of clothes from under the bench on the dock. "Wrap the scarf around your head, my Lady—like a turban," he whispered. "And put the robe on over your smock."

The turban was lopsided and lumpy, though she pushed and tucked as best she could with cold, clumsy fingers. The robe, lava cloth woven into thick, velvety material, warmed her instantly and made her feel like an overlord lady despite the dirty work smock beneath.

"But I can't walk," Repentance whispered when Sober directed her to jump down from the dock.

Concern filled his eyes. "Your feet? They're frozen?"

"They're warm, but still wet." The dock was covered with lavacloth so nothing would freeze to it. But she knew as soon as she stepped onto the icy ground her damp feet would stick in place.

Sober grabbed the lava cloth from the floor of the boat and tore it in two. The ripping sounded too loud in the still night. Repentance looked around frantically, sure a skein of troopers would attack at any moment. Sober wrapped each foot, applying the cloth right over top of her shoes.

The three sneaked along the back wall of the palace, staying in the shadows. When they reached the point where the two wings met, Sober made to leave the palace's cover to cross the exposed kitchen courtyard. Repentance yanked him back. "Stop," she whispered.

"We have to get to the yak barns."

She shook her head. "The prince will see us. He watches out the window. He's watching, I'm sure."

"How would you know he's watching?" Sober said. "If he is, he won't recognize you. You look like a noblewoman."

"What would a noblewoman be doing wandering around in the night?"

"We have to go. People are waiting to help us—the longer we make them wait, the greater the danger. Pray Providence you're wrong and the prince is not watching."

She couldn't go. The prince had seen her the last time she'd crossed that courtyard by moonlight. Thinking about being caught and thrown back in the dungeon, she stood trembling. "I can't do it."

Sober took her shoulders and looked at her intently. "Much is at stake. You cannot selfishly sit here and wait to be caught. Your friends have risked their lives to free you."

At the other end of the palace, yellow light splashed into the courtyard when someone opened the kitchen door. Generosity came through the door, grabbed the garbage sled, and started in their direction.

Dragging the sled noisily behind her, she came. She was nearly even with them when she saw them and jumped back, a hand over her heart. "You scared me that much," she whispered, once she'd caught her breath. "I wondered where you'd gotten to. I meant to go around by the lake to see what I could see. Figured I'd take the garbage sled along as an excuse, though it's empty. And then I see movement in the shadows and I think I'm as good as caught by the swingman for sneaking about with an empty garbage sled."

"We're stuck here," Sober said. "Repentance is afraid to move, lest the prince see us from one of the palace windows."

"Get in the sled then, and be quick. Crouch down. I'll pull you to the yak barn."

"The garbage sled doesn't go to the yak barn," Repentance said. "The garbage goes to the other side of the palace."

"But the prince, should he be looking from the palace windows, will not know that, will he?" Generosity said. "He's never taken the garbage to the burn pit, I'll wager."

Repentance and Sober climbed in and lay on the bottom of the sled. Tigen stretched out on top of Sober.

Generosity threw her cloak over the piled bodies in case someone should look down from an upstairs window. She grunted and puffed and panted, getting the sled moving, but once she got them gliding along, they moved at a steady clip, the ice squeaking under the runners, and sounding way too loud in the clear air of the mountain evening.

Repentance looked through a gap, and saw the stars, shining brilliantly in the cold, crisp sky. She remembered the first time she'd seen a starry sky. Sober was lying next to her that time, too. Tears filled her eyes when she remembered how she'd hated him that night. How could she have ever hated him?

The way to the yak barn ran over even ground, fortunately, and Generosity pulled without stopping. Repentance, through her peep hole, counted the barns as they passed. The top of the last barn slid into view and disappeared behind them before the runners slowed and then stopped.

They disembarked on the far side.

Repentance hugged Generosity. "Thank you, my friend," she said softly. Her friend. She had found dear friends on the mountain. She wasn't cursed after all.

"You are most welcome," Generosity answered.

Sober, with Tigen on his heels, peered around the corner of the barn. "No one following," he said over his shoulder. "But we must move on."

"Did I not tell you he was in love with you?" Generosity whispered, giving Repentance another squeeze. "He risks his life for you."

Repentance felt her cheeks flame. "That means nothing. Tigen risks his life as well."

"You make my point for me, Repentance. For we all know young Tigen is utterly smitten." She turned then, chuckling, and pulled the garbage sled back toward the palace.

Sober and Tigen joined Repentance. She took a final backward glance toward the courtyard, wondering if she'd ever see Generosity again.

Sober tugged on one of her arms and Tigen on the other, and the three hustled toward the bluff that overlooked the city.

As they neared the bluff, Shamed separated himself from the dark silhouette of the pine tree, which stood on its brow.

Repentance hugged him. "Thank you, Shamed."

His blush was dark enough to show in the moonlight. Repentance turned away so as not to embarrass him further. She looked over the city, stretching out below the palace. The night was dark, but the city streets were well lit.

"You first, Miss Repentance," Shamed said, as he held up a rope with a loop tied in it. "Step into this."

"What am I first at?" she asked, stepping in.

He pulled the loop up to her thighs. "You're going to sit down on this and I'm going to lower you down the cliff. Hold the rope right here." He showed her where to put her hands and slipped three pickles into her pocket. "Give Bramble my regards."

"Wait! You're going to lower me down? How far is it?"

He shrugged. "I've got sixty feet of rope and you'll hit bottom before I run out."

She tried to think how far sixty feet was but the words meant nothing to her. Her body trembled in fear.

"Keep your hands inside your sleeves so you don't hit the mountain and burn your skin on the way down."

She used her arms to push off from the cliff face as Shamed lowered her, and she made it down with only one small ice burn on the knuckles of her right hand.

She managed to wriggle out of the loop of rope, no easy task with Bramble snuffling at her pockets, and let it go so Shamed could pull it back up.

A minute later, Tigen came over the top of the cliff and began bobbing his way down the face. Shortly after him, Sober followed.

Tigen rode on Bramble, sitting in front of Repentance, while Sober walked as a slave should, leading the yak his mistress sat upon.

They were going, then. They were escaping. They were going to be free. Repentance sucked in a breath—she felt free already.

Sober led the yak down the deserted road that ran along the palace grounds. Soon they would turn and head away from the palace—away from the king and the prince and the sentence of death.

"Where are we going?" Repentance asked. "And how long do we have before they come after us?"

"They shouldn't discover you missing until tomorrow. When Goodwoman Hardscrabble's girl takes you your meal, she'll report the escape."

"So we have to get through the city gates tonight." Repentance said. "Before they start searching. When do they lock the gates? Are we too late?"

She looked at the moon, hanging low in the eastern sky, testifying to the early evening hour.

"The gates are locked at sunset," Sober said. "But they'll open them up for emergencies."

"What's our story, then?" She looked at Tigen. "Traveling at night because the doctor told me I had to get my sick brother to the healing house immediately or he'd die?"

Sober gave her an approving grin. "I like that one better than the one we planned. Only we can't take Tigen out of the city. He has to go back with the yak. He took Bramble out this afternoon as if he were going for a ride. We mean for him to go back tonight saying the beast ran away from him and that's why he's late."

They turned onto the main road, then. The one that ran in front of the palace. Talking ceased. Repentance could see the two huge statues of dragon hunters that guarded the palace gate. She knew a guard shack stood there, too, though she couldn't see it. They were far away, but she, a condemned assassin, was moseying along in plain view, kidnapping the prince's son. It hardly seemed like a good plan.

Long before they reached the palace gate, though, Sober cut into an alley that led down to the next level of the city.

Repentance breathed a little more freely as the palace fell behind. "Tigen, you took Bramble this afternoon? How did you sneak back into the palace without being seen?"

"There was no other way to get the yak out of the palace grounds," Tigen said. "But I had to get back in to take the boat under your cell. Shamed pulled me up the same way we came down."

She hugged him, wrapping her arms around him from behind. "You are so brave, Tigen."

"I'd go with you all the way, too. Only if I don't go back tonight, I'll never be able to go back. They'll know I helped you."

"Of course you must go back. And someday, when you're grown, you'll visit me. And we'll laugh over this adventure."

"Remember the dragons, my Lady?"

"Dragons?"

"The picture I drew in class?"

"Ah, yes, you were a big dragon and you had your wing

wrapped around me."

He nodded.

"And now here you are saving me." She hugged him tighter. "Thank you, Tigen, my brave friend." Her voice broke and she gave her eyes a quick swipe with the back of her hand.

Sober turned to the right onto a major street—this one busy with yak carts going up and down and with people shopping in the stores, which lined both sides of the thoroughfare.

Repentance stiffened, seeing all the overlords.

Some wore hats and vests made from sun cloth, so they looked like giant lanterns bobbing about. Tall posts hung with suncloths and mooncloths were set at regular intervals, too, pouring more light into the street. Repentance shivered, feeling exposed and vulnerable.

She couldn't enjoy the sparkling street, the icy storefronts, or the frozen sculptures scattered willy-nilly along the walkways. All she wanted was to get out of this city. Fast. She pictured in her mind the map carved and painted on the wall of the queen's suite. She had memorized every turn. Two blocks down and three blocks to the right was the slave market with the swing frame in the courtyard. The more distance she put between herself and that, the better.

But Sober walked along at a slow pace, as if there were no place he'd rather be.

"If you were to lead us off the main street," Repentance whispered, "and into an alleyway, you wouldn't hear me complain. For all we know the troopers may be out looking for Tigen now. How long have you been gone, Tigen?"

"There are no troopers looking for me, my Lady. No one in my family will notice me missing until I return. They'll think I'm in the kitchen or some such."

"Still, I'd as soon get off this busy stree—"

A trumpet blast ripped through the thin mountain air. Repentance nearly lost her seat as Bramble jumped and bawled out his fright.

Three more blasts rang out.

"The alarm!" Tigen's whisper was full of dread. "They know you're gone."

CHAPTER 30

Sober dragged the skittish Bramble into the first alley he saw, stopped, and slugged the wall. "Ow!"

Repentance slid off the yak. "You do have a back-up plan, Sober Marsh, don't you?"

He ignored her, looking at his ice-burned knuckles.

"Tigen," she said, taking Bramble's reins from Sober and handing them to the boy. "You go home. If you see troopers along the way, slow them down if you can. Tell them about how your yak ran away and how glad you are to be found."

Sober looked up, a spark of hope in his eyes. "Maybe the trumpet blast is for Tigen. Maybe they've discovered him missing and not you, Repentance."

Tigen shook his head. "The alarm is just for when slaves escape. All the guardsmen come out and line up all along the wall."

"Insist the troopers escort you safely home," Repentance continued as if she'd not been interrupted. "Tell them they must, for you are far too scared to go alone."

He would be able to play that part all too well, she knew. His small face was white with fear, and tears threatened.

"I have help outside the city," Sober said. "A place to stay, food, traveling clothes. But the entire plan hung on our getting out of the city tonight."

"But I know of a safe place in the city," she said. And she'd memorized how to get there, too. "Go Tigen, and Providence go with you." She reached up and touched his soft cheek one last time. "Don't worry about us, we'll make it."

She turned the yak around and slapped his rump to get him moving.

Follow me," she said to Sober, and she took off running.

Three blocks down and another three blocks to the left. Rounding a corner from an alley onto a busier main street, she came to a sudden stop.

Two troopers on the walkway came right toward them.

Repentance spun around and stared into a shop window, her heart drumming against her ribs in utter panic. Sober stood beside her, his head down.

The troopers approached. "Pardon, my Lady," one said.

"Yes, what is it?" Repentance said without turning around. She leaned forward to look into the window, as if she had never seen anything as interesting as the men's under garments displayed there.

"Is this slave with you?" the trooper asked.

"Of course he's with me, who else would he be with?"

"Did you hear the trumpets? A slave has run away."

She turned to look at Sober. "Not mine. He's still here, as you can see."

"Yes, I do see," the trooper said. "Maybe you'd better get off the street, all the same. The runaway could be dangerous."

"Now that is a worthy trickle of advice, sir, and I'm going to take it." She turned and swept up the street, ignoring Sober, as she'd seen overlord women do with their slaves.

She heard him dutifully shuffling along behind her.

They turned into an alley and took off running again. Two more blocks down, one jog to the right—

"Stop!" Someone hollered from the main street.

Feet pounded on the icy ground behind them.

They were only a half a block away from safety, but Repentance jagged to the left. She couldn't go straight to Lord Carrull's with someone following.

They ducked into one alley, crossed a main road, dove into another alley and quickly hid behind a garbage receptacle.

The bell of a yak cart sounded from behind them, and a man, presumably the driver of the vehicle, cursed. "You were born without all your faculties? What are you thinking running into the road like that?"

Footsteps slapped into the alley, going full speed.

Repentance crouched beside Sober, her heart keeping time with the footsteps of their pursuer and feeling like it would burst out of her chest any moment.

The trooper flew past their hiding place.

They crawled out from behind the garbage and took off. She backtracked, re-crossed the road, slipped into another alley and skidded to a halt in front of Lord Carrull's side door.

She stopped, leaning over, trying to quiet her panting so she could hear if they were pursued.

Nothing.

She lifted the knocker and tapped it several times quietly. Each tap sent a deafening echo through the alley. Repentance looked around half expecting to be captured right there on the doorstep— on the edge of safety.

Finally an old slave woman opened the door a crack.

"Thank Providence," Repentance said. "I need to see Lord Carrull." She pushed through the door without waiting to be invited.

The woman, eyes wide with fear, left them in the hall and disappeared into the great room where Repentance had eaten dinner the last time she'd been in the house.

Seconds later, Lord Carrull burst through the door.

He stopped and stared, and then he smiled. "Repentance Atwater from Hot Springs!" He looked as she remembered. Same pale green eyes. Same tan, suede britches. "Running away again? And this time you've brought a friend. How delightful." He clapped his hands together in glee. "I will get a double reward for returning the two of you."

Repentance stood panting. What was wrong with the man? Ah. She remembered. He was playing that part. Whiney overlord letch. He played it so well it was unnerving.

"Stop acting," she said. "We need help! They're after us."

Lord Carrull gave her a hard look, his eyes going from stupidly amused, to dead serious. "Who is after you?"

"Troopers."

"And you've led them to my door? Selfish girl."

"No one saw us come here," she said. "We need a place to hide."

"Don't be ridiculous," Lord Carrull said. "Do you not remember what happened the last time you ran away? I captured you and took you back to Madam Cawrocc."

Sober looked over at her. "The last time you ran away?"

Repentance sighed. She and Sober didn't know each other well at all. There hadn't been much time for talking. That would have to come later. If they managed to survive. For now she needed to deal with the overlord standing in front of them.

"Lord Carrull," she said, "This is my friend Sober. He's assured me that this time it's different. He says my family is safe." She took Sober's hand. "My family is safe. Right?"

He put his arm around her shoulder and pulled her to himself. "They're fine. Everything is taken care of."

She pushed back far enough so that she could look at his face, "How do you know they're safe?"

He shook his head and threw a glance at Lord Carrull. "This is not the place to speak. Come away with me, and I'll tell you all as we go."

"Yes, that is an excellent idea," Lord Carrull said as he strode to the door and yanked it open. "You go back out in the streets. I'm sure some trooper will come along straight away and give you a ride back to the palace."

"Stop!" Repentance said to him. "Why are you being so mean?"

The overlord opened his eyes wide in surprise. "Two slaves, with troopers on their heels, show up at my door. One is a man completely unknown to me. And you think I ought to invite them in for dinner?"

"That would be a start, yes."

Sober pulled Repentance toward the door.

She resisted, locking her gaze on Lord Carrull. "Sober won't turn you in. If he wasn't trustworthy, I wouldn't have brought him here. We need your help."

"You've been on the mountain, what? Three or four months? And you've run away twice. That I know of. You aren't wise, Repentance. I can't afford to help you. I've heard that you are concubine to the king. I can't get involved with you."

Tears sprang to her eyes. "I had no choice. I had to run."

"You always have a choice."

"I'm sentenced to the frame," she said softly.

The lord's eyes flared open in surprise. His expression softened and he shut the door. "Come sit down. I can put you out as easily after I hear your story as before." He motioned them into his great room.

They took seats before the fire.

Lord Carrull rang for his servant. "Cakes and wine, please, Compassion."

When she left, he turned to Repentance. "Now tell me. Why are you sentenced to swing?"

"For trying to assassinate the king."

Lord Carrull pulled back in his chair. "You're having a joke on me. Not even you could be so hotheaded and stupid."

"I do not jest. I'm accused of trying to kill the king."

The lord gave Sober a long, hard look. "And who are you?

Assassin's apprentice?"

"I am her friend." He put his hand on Repentance's shoulder.

She melted under his touch and words. Of course she knew he was her friend. He'd risked his life to save her. But to hear him say it—to have him claim her—sent a flood of warmth spreading out from his hand on her shoulder.

"Well, I won't be able to help you. But you might at least tell me why you did it before you go. Couldn't stand the thought of the king having her so you decided to kill him?" He challenged Sober with his look.

"Stop accusing us," Repentance said. "I didn't really try to kill the king. I was blamed for it, is all. Besides, *you're* the one who owes some explanation. The last I saw of you, I was jumped from behind and whacked over the head!"

Sober took Repentance's hand. "We're leaving."

Lord Carrull gave him a cold look. "Where do you plan to go?"

"Sober, please," Repentance said. "Lord Carrull can help us."

"Did this man capture you and hit you on the head and return you to Madam Cawrocc?"

"Not exactly. He returned me to Madam Cawrocc and *then* he hit me on the head." She turned to Lord Carrull. "Why did you hit me?"

"I hit you to keep you from dying with Cawrocc's gnarled fingers wrapped around your tender neck. But I must admit that I rather enjoyed hitting you. There are few selfish, unthinking, hysterical girls whose skulls I'd rather crack. You were screaming like a hog at the slaughter."

"Cawrocc was threatening to kill my sister."

"Which, of course, she couldn't do, since she didn't own you. Jadin did."

"You knew that?"

"Oh, please!"

"You could have told me, instead of almost killing me."

"I should have simply explained it all, so Madam Cawrocc would have known what good friends you and I were, hmm?"

Sober sank back into his chair. "The two of you are friends? Repentance, could you not have simply made friends in school like other girls? Must you do everything the hard way?"

Lord Carrull broke out in hearty laughter. A moment later Sober was laughing with him.

Repentance did not see the humor of the situation.

Before she could think of a sharp retort, Compassion came with wine and cakes.

Repentance sat staring into the fire and kept her peace while the servant quietly poured and served.

After she left, Lord Carrull patted Repentance's knee and said, "Of course we are friends. And of course our friendship is an odd one. This mountain makes for odd friendships. I am afraid, though, that my friendship will be of little help to you. If you are blamed for trying to assassinate the king—" He shook his head. "Entire villages have been wiped out for less."

Repentance gasped. He spoke the truth. She had learned of several village-wide slaughters in school. But surely the king wouldn't ... he was not evil as some of his predecessors had been. The prince, though, was another matter. She could believe he would kill innocents without blinking an eye.

"Sober?" she asked in a shaky voice. "Tell me how you know my family is safe."

"Last week, Mistress Merricc sent through a request to buy your family."

"Mistress Merricc?" Lord Carrull said. "How do you know her? A fine woman, that."

"I work for her."

"Why didn't you say so earlier? She actually pays her slaves. Lets them earn their freedom. Amazing woman."

Repentance had forgotten that. She looked at Sober. "You gave up a farm where you could earn your freedom, to become a runaway slave with me?"

"Get back to the request to buy Repentance's family, please," Lord Carrull said. "Where is the family now?"

"The king granted Mistress Merricc's request to buy the family." Sober looked at Repentance. "The Hot Spring slavers knew they would get no babies out of your sister or your brothers. They knew no one would agree to button with them. So they were happy to sell. Mistress sent the king recompense for his loss, and paid the Hot Springs slavers the balance. Your whole family is at the farm."

It was all she could do to keep from kissing him. Comfort was in the sunshine and the little boys were cavorting with colts and calves. She'd never dreamed it possible.

"That's why it took me so long to come for you," Sober said. "I had to wait until they were safe before I stole you away."

Was it her imagination or did his dark eyes reproach her?

"Sober—" Tears filled her eyes and she gulped down the lump in her throat. "You asked her to buy my family? How can I ever repay you?"

He shook his head. "I'm not looking for payment."

She pictured Comfort on the farm with her parchments and char-sticks. It seemed too good to be true. "But won't the prince be able to find them? Don't the slavers keep track of their transactions?"

A shadow of doubt flitted into Sober's eyes. "We planned to have you and your family in Montphilo before the prince came looking."

She stared at him, trying to think through all the new information and wondering what her failure to get out of the city would do to her family.

Turning to Lord Carrull, she said, "Now that I'm stuck here, won't the prince go down to the Hot Springs, find my family missing, and track them to Mistress Merricc's farm? Won't he use them to teach me a lesson?"

He shook his head. "You've left me back in the valley. Why are we talking about the prince? I thought the king was after you."

"Both." She squirmed under his scrutiny. "The king sentenced me, but the prince is the one who really wants me dead."

"You could not have made a worse enemy. I suppose you know that." He poured more wine into her glass. "I think you need to tell me everything that has happened since last I saw you. We can't make plans unless we know what we're up against."

Sober and Lord Carrull listened as riveted as her little brothers had always been when she wove danger and dragons into their bedtime stories. The Lord kept her wine glass filled, the flames in the fireplace danced, and Repentance told Lord Carrull of her journey down to the healing house and back up the mountain. She told him about her dream of getting the King to buy Comfort and later her brothers. And how she even hoped he might find and buy her other brothers, the ones that had been taken as weanlings. She explained her plan to become a trusted friend to the king. She told him of the prince's threats to kill the king and of his desire to take more lowborn boys and to build an army to invade Westwold. She recounted her fears, her losses, her mistakes, and her lies. She ended up with her arrival at his door, on the threshold of freedom. She'd be caught and killed or she'd escape. Free from slavery, either way.

"The king would probably let me go," she said in closing, "but the prince needs me dead. Not only do I know he tried to kill the king, but he thinks I'm heir to the throne. He can't let me live."

The room fell silent.

Finally Lord Carrull said, "Well, we can thank Providence you didn't bring the Prince's son to my house with you. Good great dragon guano, child, you're a menace. I can't believe only one person has died in your company so far. Even more, I can't believe you're still alive. Providence must have plans for you." He stood and approached. "May I see the birthmark?'

She turned her head and pushed the edge of the turban back.

"I wouldn't have believed it if I'd not seen it." He went back to his chair shaking his head. "I knew your father well. No wonder the king felt kindly toward you. Lord Baldin was a fine young man, and he and the king were inseparable before he was killed."

She felt a warm glow. Her father—the one who'd raised her—was a fine man, too. Now she had two fine fathers. One a hated slave and one a hated overlord. Both fine men in their own worlds. But she was half overlord! And that made her feel dirty and thrilled all at once. It was confusing.

Lord Carrull looked at Sober. "And what's your story? You ran away from Mistress Merricc to save Repentance? Is that what she'll tell the troopers when they look at her farm and dig into her affairs?"

"I planned to be back before anyone came looking. I promised to go back and run the farm for her as soon as I got Repentance to Montphilo."

Lord Carrull smiled. "An incredible woman, that."

"What now?" Repentance looked at Sober. "The prince is liable to wipe out all of Hot Springs and the farm as well."

"Not if we can get him locked up, first," Lord Carrull said. "I'll see the king the first thing in the morning."

"Will he believe you?" Sober asked. "How well do you know him?"

"He will believe enough to arrest the prince and hold him over for trial, I hope. I'm an overlord. If I bring a charge, it will carry more weight than if a slave brings it. And there's always Tigen. The prince's own son knows his father had a slave hidden in the barn." He nodded. "I think we can convince—"

Behind them the door burst open with force, causing all three to turn and look.

"I'm sorry to interrupt, Lord," Compassion said, breathlessly, "but Starved says a skein of troopers are going door to door. Someone, it seems, reported seeing two runaway slaves fleeing in this neighborhood."

Love, when it came, crashed into me with the churning force of a waterfall. It turned me upside down, shook me all around, and left me standing, dripping and shaking, on the riverbank, not knowing which way was home.

~Repentance Atwater, *Mountain Journal*

CHAPTER 31

The knocker sounded on the front door. "Open up. Business of the king," a trooper shouted.

A male slave joined Compassion in the doorway of the great room, fear in his eyes.

"Take your dishes and follow Starved," Lord Carrull said. Turning to Compassion he added, "Stall as long as you can, then show them in to me here."

Repentance and Sober followed Starved up six stories. He was a young man, not much older than Sober, and he moved quickly.

At the top, the stairs opened up on a great room. As they raced across the room, Repentance registered bookshelves interspersed with maps, and portraits carved into the walls.

Cushioned chairs and settees were clustered around tables made of shiny, dark wood. They held suncloth lanterns.

"Quickly," Starved said, never slowing. He reached a painting on the far wall, a man with a bow facing a dragon, the beast stood, hunched over the man, fire issuing from its mouth. Starved took a knife from his belt and tapped the dragon's eye with the handle. The painted body slid back and to the side, leaving a dragon-shaped hole in the wall. Repentance gasped. Sober steadied her with a hand on her elbow. Starved stepped aside and directed Repentance and Sober to duck through the hole in the wall.

"Stay here until I come for you," he said. "Stay quiet." He reached up and tapped another spot on the wall and the dragon slid over and forward and snapped back into place, leaving not a sliver of light at the seams.

Repentance and Sober stood for a minute staring at the wall. On this side it had the same picture—only this one was facing the opposite direction, like an image in a reflecting rock. Repentance strained to hear any sound coming from the other side. Nothing. She shivered and turned away.

They were in a narrow, windowless room. By the dim light thrown from two small suncloths she saw a settee with two ice-block tables on either end. The tables were covered with lavacloth and strewn on top of them were books. On the opposite side of the room was a door. She crossed over and pushed it open. A relief room with one waste stool and one sink. They were in a hiding place. Not meant to be lived in for long periods, obviously, and not overly comfortable.

She flopped down at one end of the settee, prepared to wait. She tapped her foot, letting off nervous energy. She felt trapped. Surely Lord Carrull would keep them safe. Probably hundreds of slaves had hidden in this very room. And they'd all been let out. Set free.

Sober picked up a book and sat down on the other end of the settee.

Repentance studied his profile. His book was tilted toward the suncloth, his face angled away from her slightly. She was surprised by the depth of emotion that rose in her chest. Sober Marsh was, without a doubt, the handsomest man she'd ever met. She'd known he was handsome, she'd agreed with Generosity on that count. But she had never considered that there was no man handsomer.

Anywhere.

She shook her head, trying to clear it. Now was not the time to be thinking about Sober's dark eyes and broad shoulders. His smile—"So, you saw Comfort before you came to rescue me? How is she?" Her voice shattered the stillness, sounding harsh and demanding and overly loud.

He looked over at her, a pained expression on his face. "Be quiet," he whispered.

A hot flush burned her cheeks.

He must have noticed, because he scooted next to her and whispered in her ear, "They are all fine, trust me. I'll tell you later, when we can speak safely."

He didn't move away from her. Her ear burned where his breath had brushed over it, and her thigh felt warm where his bumped up against hers.

She felt as if the room was getting smaller, making it hard to breathe.

A memory tumbled through her mind unbidden. She did remember him. He dove from the waterfall into the pool below to save Ambivalence Bigrock. Repentance had been—what?—in her tenth year? So Sober had been in his fifteenth. Everyone in the village thought he was the bravest boy.

And he was cute even then, with dark curls and dark eyes and that slightly crooked nose.

So why hadn't anyone buttoned him the following year? Or the one after that?

She wasn't sure she believed he'd been waiting for her. She wanted to believe, but no boy ever waited five years for a button mate. It was too dangerous. The girl you chose might die, for one thing. She'd half thought he'd made that story up to cover up whatever flaws the button girls had seen in him when they turned him down four years in a row. But now, with him sitting right next to her, she found it hard to see how anyone would find him flawed.

He shifted a bit and his hip snuggled against hers. She scooted back, pressing herself up against the corner of the settee, but she couldn't get away from him. He was so big and so near. She bit her lip. What had she been thinking about?

Oh, yes, his flaws.

He hadn't any.

She remembered his earnest look on the slave dock when he pronounced the ancient blessing on her. He, who should have hated her, had blessed her.

She cast back into her memory looking for all that she knew about him. Third son. Only child. Devoted to his mother. She remembered him vaguely from school. She never knew him well. He was one of the big boys. And then he was gone. He lived on the other side of the swamp. She saw him at village meetings. And occasionally when she was fishing. Often when she was fishing, now that she considered the matter. She'd row her boat around a corner in the stream, and there he would be in his skiff. He'd nod his head and smile and say something about the fish or the weather. She'd barely paid him any notice.

He was so overpowering. He took up the whole room. He squeezed the air from it. How had she passed him by so often without notice?

He chuckled. "This fellow is funny," he whispered, tapping the page.

How could he read? She couldn't concentrate on anything but him. His proximity. His smile! It did something to her. Or was it the hot wine she'd had with the cakes downstairs?

She jumped up from the settee and began pacing.

He glanced up from his book and raised his eyebrows as if to ask what was wrong.

She shook her head and continued pacing.

He went back to reading.

She walked behind the settee. His silky hair curled at his collar and she had an urge to reach out and touch it.

If he didn't have any flaws, then he must have been waiting

for someone. But that didn't mean he was waiting for her.

Sure, he had blessed her. And he had befriended her at the palace. But he was the type of man who blessed and befriended everyone. Generosity loved him, and even the older maids and Cook doted on him. Repentance sighed. He hadn't treated her any differently than he'd treated the others. If they'd been in the dungeon he'd have risked his life to save any of them.

She circled the room again.

Sober looked up from his book. "Sit down," he whispered. "You're making me nervous."

She sat on the far end of the settee.

Sober looked over and smiled, his teeth gleaming in the dim light. "You still dislike me so much, eh, Repentance? You can't stand to be stuck in here with me?"

"I never said any such thing," she whispered back.

He leaned toward her. "Why the pacing, then?"

She pulled back.

The door in the wall scraped open.

Repentance held her breath.

Lord Carrull ducked into the room. "They've gone," he said breathlessly. "They suspect nothing. Going door to door. Checking all the houses."

He pulled a handkerchief from his pocket and wiped his brow. "Those stairs." He tucked his handkerchief away. "Well then, what is next on the agenda? Early to bed, I should think. Tomorrow is a big day. I'll go to the king at first light."

"If you say you know us, won't you be in danger yourself?" Sober asked.

Lord Carrull nodded. "I don't intend to tell him I know you. I plan to make it clear that I'm not ready yet to disclose how I got the news I'm going to share with him. If I can get him to call Tigen in, that might be all it will take."

"Oh, I wish Tigen wasn't needed. It's a terrible thing to ask a small boy to tell on his own father. If the prince goes to the swingman, Tigen will always feel responsible."

"It can't be helped. He's your only witness."

"I tried to protect him. I didn't want him to know his father had tried to kill the king. I thought of asking him to tell the king that his father had a slave hidden in the barn, but I was sure the king wouldn't believe it. He knew Tigen and I were friends. I think if you make Tigen tell, the king will assume that Tigen is lying to help me."

"Not necessarily," Lord Carrul said. "Tigen was not a credible witness while you were in the dungeon. He would have spouted off with any tale he could think up, in order to get you out. But now that you are no longer locked up, he has no reason to lie."

"Lord Carrull," Sober said. "If the king doesn't arrest the prince and if the prince hears what you've done, he might kill you."

"I'll have to make sure the prince doesn't hear. What choice do I have? This king is the friendliest toward slaves that we've ever had, and his life is in danger. If Lord Malficc takes the throne we're all going to suffer. I shudder to think."

Repentance sat back in the settee thinking. She'd had it in her mind that if the king believed Lord Carrull, she would have to go back to a life of slavery at the palace. But ... "So, if you aren't going to tell the king you know us, we can still go to Montphilo."

"I'm not going to stop you. If no one ever finds out that you've been here, I'll be happy."

"I can't go to Montphilo," Sober said. "I have a responsibility to my Mistress. She has been good to me and I'll not run off after all she's given me."

"All she's given?" Repentance was horrified. "She's a slaver."

Sober gave her a stern look. "She's risked much to save your family."

"And I'm grateful. But you don't owe her your life. She had no business owning you in the first place. She has no business telling you where you can and can't go."

Lord Carrull made a shushing noise. "Repentance, you still haven't learned, have you? Think first, child, and speak after that."

Sober gave him a dirty look. "What right do you overlords have to put us on the slave dock in the first place? Unless you've been abused by men you don't even know, kidnapped from your home, torn from your family, threatened, and beaten, maybe you ought to not be so quick to judge Repentance."

Lord Carrull started to answer, but stopped himself. "You're right, young man. Right to call me on it and right to stand up for your sweetheart."

Repentance gasped.

Lord Carrull smiled. "My apologies, Repentance. Forgive me for being harsh with you."

Sober turned to Repentance and said gently, "I do owe Mistress Merricc. She saved me when she bought me off the dock. I have to work to repay her the beads she spent on me."

"And now my family? You're working to pay her for them, too?"

His cheeks flushed. "I'm happy to pay, Repentance."

"But we'll be in Montphilo and you won't be there with us."

He smiled. "Are you saying you'll miss me?"

"Of course she'll miss you," Lord Carrull said. "You're her hero." Hearing a noise, he turned toward the secret door. "Ah, Compassion, good. I'm guessing our guests would appreciate turns in the bathing rooms before bed."

Repentance nodded her agreement, and thanked Providence for the maid's timely interruption.

"The beds are made up," Compassion said. "And the hot water is ready in both bathing rooms if the young people are so inclined."

Repentance shot her a smile. "I most certainly am inclined. Thank you, Compassion."

The maid bowed her head slightly. "And the young man?"

"I can think of nothing I'd like better."

The maid nodded and backed away from the doorway.

Repentance followed, feeling a little dizzy. Her family was safe.

There was that to be thankful for.

And Lord Carrull would explain everything to the king. And

she would join her family in Montphilo.

But Sober?

He wouldn't be there. He'd be working to pay her debt.

So there I stood on the riverbank, dizzy and confused. And what did I do? I climbed to the top of the falls and jumped in again. Love—I mean the button mate kind, not the sister kind—is dangerous and scary, but it made me feel, oh, so alive.

~Repentance Atwater, *Mountain Journal*

CHAPTER 32

Repentance woke with a jerk, thinking for a moment that she was in her cell under the palace. But, no, she was in a warm, soft bed at Lord Carrull's house. Relaxing back into the pillows, she thought over the events of the previous evening.

Had Tigen made it safely home? And Comfort! When would she get to see her sister?

She threw off her covers and took the night shade from the sunlamp on the bedside table. Laid over the foot of the bed was a dress. Deep blue, silky material. She took it into the bathing room with her, wondering how Compassion had found a dress to fit her. A lot of slaves traveled through this house. Maybe Lord Carrull kept a variety of clothes on hand for them.

Once dressed, she stepped into the hall, but she couldn't remember which door led to the great room she'd seen the night before. She crossed to the room opposite hers and knocked softly. Getting no answer, she cracked the door open. Sleeping quarters.

Empty. The bed looked like it hadn't been slept in.

At the next door, when no one answered her knock, she again peeked in. The blankets on the bed were rumpled. The door to the bathing room stood ajar and the room was still steamy. She'd apparently barely missed Sober.

She was about to close the door when she saw the gray flannel button scarf in a rumpled pile on the desk. She tiptoed into the room and held the scarf to her cheek. It smelled of Sober. "Why do you keep this?" she whispered.

"I already answered that once."

She spun around, still holding the scarf, her cheeks burning.

"Didn't you believe me?" He leaned against the bathing room door, a brush in his hand. He wore loose flannel trousers—brown—with a tan shirt that looked creamy-white against his dark skin.

Repentance threw the scarf on the desk and backed toward the door. "I'm sorry. I was looking for the library."

He took a step toward her.

"I didn't know you were here. I'm sorry." She backed out the door and fled across the hall to her quarters.

A knock sounded on her door and Sober walked in without waiting for an answer.

"Will you please talk to me?" He sat on the bed next to her. "I really need to know where I stand with you."

Her cheeks were still hot and she didn't want to look at him. "I don't know what to say." She wanted to throw herself into his arms and tell him, "I love you, that's where you stand." But to what end? He'd already told her he wouldn't go with her to Montphilo.

"How about if I ask questions and you answer?"

She nodded.

"Why did you refuse to button me? What was it about me that was so distasteful?"

She looked up and rolled her eyes. "Must we go back to that, Sober? I thought you had forgiven that."

"I did forgive." He took her hand. "I'm merely wondering at

the reason. Was it something about me you couldn't stand? Is it something I can change? Is there hope you'll ever change your mind in the future? How can I know what I need to do, if you won't tell me what I did wrong in the first place?'

She pulled her hand away from him. "Now you're being ridiculous."

He nodded. "I guess I am. How ridiculous of me to think we might make a good button couple. What is it about me that you can't stand?"

"You're serious?"

He sat waiting.

"It had nothing to do with you. If I had been promised to Justice Palmtree I'd have refused the buttoning, all the same."

"Justice Palmtree? He was a more desirable button mate than I was?'

She groaned. "I just meant ... Oh never mind. Sober, I didn't even know you. I didn't refuse because you were lacking. I refused because I couldn't stand the thought of the overlords taking my babies and making them slaves."

He studied her for a moment. "So to protect babies that didn't exist, you sacrificed me to the overlords?"

She winced. He'd never understand. "You're the youngest. You never had to watch your baby brothers carted off. You never had to hear their wailing or your mother's weeping. "

Compassion pushed the door open and stuck her head in. "Oh, there you are, young man. I wondered where you'd gotten to. Well, come on, then. I've laid breakfast out in the library for the two of you."

Repentance silently followed Compassion down the hall, hoping that Sober might drop the whole conversation. She was sure she loved him, but she wasn't sure she could talk to him about it right then.

Two plates and two mugs stood on a low table in front of one of the settees in the library.

"Lord Carrull won't be joining us?" Repentance asked.

"He's gone to the palace." Compassion answered.

A surge of hope filled Repentance's heart. Lord Carrull would fix everything. She was sure of it.

Breakfast was fluffy mounds of scrambled spruce hen eggs with vegetables and sausage mixed in and buttered toast on the side. And to wash it down they had strong coffee with sweetened yak's milk.

Compassion, after pouring and making sure that everything was to their satisfaction, and after asking fifteen times if they were sure there was nothing else wanting, left them alone to eat.

"So," Sober said as if the conversation in Repentance's sleeping quarters had never been interrupted, "if you'd been promised to Justice Palmtree it would have been a little harder to sacrifice him to the overlords than it was to sacrifice me?"

She laughed. "Stop! You're being silly. I never said I wanted to button Justice. I had no intention of buttoning any man. Ever. From the day my first brother was taken, I made up my mind to never, ever button."

"It would have been helpful if you'd have told me that before I passed up every other chance."

"I didn't know you were waiting for me. I barely knew you were alive."

He chuckled. "If only I was as good looking as Justice Palmtree. You knew he was alive."

She picked a piece of tomato from her eggs and flicked it at him.

He swatted it away, laughing.

"Justice was in my school with me every day. You weren't. How was I supposed to know you?" She laid one hand gently on his back. "But I am sorry for what I've put you through. I didn't know they would beat you." Tears stung her eyes. "I didn't know anything, really. I didn't even know Harthill was made of ice." She shook her head, amazed to think of all the things she hadn't known about the outside world on the day of her buttoning ceremony. "All I knew back then was that I would never button and breed for the overlords."

"You knew we'd be taken away on the slave carts and that we'd never see our families again."

Repentance remembered Goodwoman Marsh on the ground, blood running from her broken nose, and shuddered. "I'm sorry," she whispered.

She set her fork down and shoved her food away, her appetite gone. "I was six when they took Tribulation. I hated my mother and father for letting the boys go. I grew up knowing that my parents couldn't protect me—wouldn't even try to protect me—if the overlords came for me."

Sober reached over and brushed the hair back from her forehead. "I wish you had trusted me enough to tell me before the ceremony. I would have liked to have said goodbye to my folks."

"I didn't even tell Comfort. I left her without saying goodbye." She had left a note, though. Sober hadn't gotten that chance.

"But it was your choice."

"Which made it worse. You went as a victim of my selfishness. Your parents could remember you with love. Mine had to live with the shame of what I did."

He took her hand, playing with her fingers for a moment and rubbing her palm with his thumb. "You really didn't know I was alive?" he asked looking up from her hand.

She shrugged and gave him an "I'm sorry" smile. "I know I owe you, Sober. I'll pay you back someday."

"No. You don't owe me anything. I don't expect payment from you. I know that's hard to believe when you've grown up in a world where you owe your entire life to a man with a dragon stick."

"But Sober—"

"No, let me finish this, please. I don't want to own you, Repentance. I rescued you because I couldn't bear to think of the life squeezed out of you by the swingman's rope. I couldn't bear to think of your beautiful eyes with no light in them. It was purely selfish on my part, but not the kind of selfishness you think. I don't mean to use you or take anything from you. I love you and I want you to be safe and free."

She smiled. "You love me?"

He looked confused. "Of course I love you. Was that ever in question?'

"So you're not having a joke on me? You really were waiting for me all those years?"

He looked shocked. "How many times must I say it?"

"I don't understand why you would do that. You didn't even know me. We'd not spoken more than a few words before that trip up the mountain."

"I loved you all the same," he looked at her, his face flushed and his eyes bright. "I've loved you since the day I saw you in the swamp picking persimmons for Comfort, when everyone was saying your mother wasn't right in the head. I heard you singing to Comfort and telling her you'd never let anyone take her away. I wanted to protect you. That's why I put the bunches of swamp bananas on the ground every week just at the time you were out with Comfort looking for breakfast. And the berries and nuts. Didn't you ever wonder why the squirrels loved you so much that they left you mounds of berries in the summer and nuts in the winter?"

She laughed. "You? I used to thank Providence for all that food. I thought he knocked those bananas out of the trees for us."

"No, that would have bruised them. He made me crazy in love with you so I climbed the trees and carried the bananas down and gently laid them on the ground for you."

Repentance blushed. He was crazy in love. She was overwhelmed. She never knew. And even after she caused him so much pain, he still loved her. She swiped at the stray tears that slipped down her face. "And here I was afraid you might want to button with Generosity."

"Generosity?"

"She's very nice," Repentance said. "And she's pretty."

"She is both of those things." Sober said. "But I've never thought of her in that way." He leaned back and closed his eyes, thinking. "Interesting question. Were I not in love with you, would I button Generosity? She's a fine girl. Still a man likes to have a little peace and quiet in his own home of an evening." He opened his eyes and threw Repentance a wink. "And I do believe Generosity could chase a dead man from his grave with all her chatter."

She looked at his happy face and laughed with him at the thought of Generosity talking a dead man from the grave. She kept looking at him after they grew quiet. Where would she be in five years? He would be free eventually. Would he still want her?

It didn't much matter. She understood perfectly what Providence had done to Sober all those years ago because he'd done the same thing to Repentance. Crazy in love. That described it perfectly.

She slid close to him, picked up his arm, ducked underneath it, and laid her head on his chest. He settled his arm around her.

"I love you, Sober," she said.

He bent down and kissed the top of her head. "And now I can die a happy man," he whispered.

She snuggled against him.

"Well, no, that's not true. I'm not perfectly contented, yet," he said. He reached under her knees and pulled her onto his lap. Then he kissed her.

On the mouth.

For a long time.

When he finally pulled away she fell against his neck, feeling a little lightheaded.

He closed both arms around her and held her tight.

"Now you're content?" Her voice sounded gravelly as if she'd not used it in years.

"Not really."

She stiffened in his arms. He hadn't liked it? She'd never kissed anyone before. Maybe she'd done it wrong.

He kissed her again. Longer that time. Finally he trailed little kisses across her cheek to her neck, just below her ear.

"Not nearly content," he whispered. "You're like salt water.

The more I drink, the thirstier I get."

She leaned against his shoulder and sighed. She, at least, was perfectly content.

There is rest for the weary warrior on the sunny slopes of Providence's Mountain, but there is none to be had in this world. You mustn't lie down and sleep. Every time I've thought to take a little nap, I've paid the price. Evil never rests and neither can we.
~Kindness Firtree, *Meditations on the Precepts*

CHAPTER 33

Sober kissed her once more and scooted her off his lap and onto the settee beside him. "Now, leave me be, woman. My breakfast is already cold," he said as he picked up his fork.

She shoved him with her shoulder. "You blame me?"

"I don't see anyone else here distracting me."

They ate in silence, glancing at each other and smiling every so often.

When he finished breakfast, Sober waved at the bookshelves that covered the walls. "Well, then, what shall we do today, Repentance? Read books, read books, or read books?"

She thought sitting on the settee and continuing with that kissing business might be nice, but she said, "Well, I don't know. I was kind of thinking we might read books."

He smiled. "Good idea. We have lots to choose from." Then he added under his breath, "And thank Providence for that."

She landed a light punch on his shoulder. "Because being cooped up with me all day is such a boring prospect?"

He winked at her. "Because my mind is far too creative in thinking about all the ways we could fill the hours as we wait here." He jumped up as if chased by a trooper and proceeded to browse the books on the shelf by the door.

Repentance, wanting to give him some room, wandered over to the shelf by the window.

Compassion came for the dishes.

Repentance smiled at her.

"What is it, then?" Compassion asked, giving Repentance an odd look.

"What do you mean? I've just had my breakfast and now I'm going to read."

"I never thought the cook's food was that good, is all, to make someone look as happy as you look."

Sober chuckled.

"I said something funny?" Compassion asked, throwing him a glance over her shoulder.

"What? Oh, no. I'm just looking at the books."

"Some funny volumes there, eh?"

He smiled at her.

As soon as the door shut, Repentance grabbed a small pillow from the settee and threw it at Sober.

He batted it aside and winked.

He chose a biography, she picked out a folktale, and they spent the next few hours sitting close, reading.

Every time he turned a page, he'd lean down and kiss the top of her head. She wasn't turning her pages as often. She kept drifting off into her own thoughts and having to read each page several times.

"Listen to this," he said.

She closed her book, her finger holding her place, and gave Sober her attention.

He angled his head to read the title of her book. "Oh, my. Are you sure you don't mind my interrupting that important book? The Yak Herder and the Lowland Girl? Sounds enthralling."

She bonked him lightly on the head with the book. "What do you want, Sober?"

"This is a biography of Lord Banniss. Do you know who he was?"

The name sounded familiar. She remembered one of the young princes spitting the name out with venom. "He was some kind of slave sympathizer, wasn't he?"

"He was sent to the swing frame almost a hundred years ago. Mistress Merricc told me about him. But listen to what he said in a speech a year before he was hanged. 'There are some things worth more than life and some lives not worth living. To die as an honest man is better than to live as a liar, to die fighting evil is better than to live with your eyes and ears and heart clamped shut to the pain around you, and to die serving a friend is to die the best way of all."

"That's pretty sad," Repentance said.

"You think so?"

"Considering he died a year later on a swing frame? Fighting evil, I presume. Yes, I think that's sad."

"I found it encouraging. He died as an honest man. And he died serving the slaves he'd befriended. He got his wish and died the best way."

"Why did he have to die at all?"

"That's beyond my ability to answer. It's a harsh world. But if we have to die, it's good to die well. I think Lord Banniss would have heartily approved of you, Repentance." He picked up one of her hands and kissed the palm. "It's better to die fighting evil than to button and breed for the overlord slave traders. You were right about that. You were willing to sacrifice for your beliefs. I'm happy to know you. And Lord Carrull, too. He risks his life to help slaves. I'm convicted. I have been far too complacent."

She frowned. "You didn't know. No one in the village knows anything. We didn't even know a place like Montphilo existed." She remembered her Geography books with the maps ripped out and her History books that told half-truths.

He paused, considering. "I was asleep. I think I could have

known. I should have known. I was simply content to wait upon Providence to deliver us out of slavery, and I never took a stand for what was right."

Repentance shivered. She had never been content. That was her problem. She'd always railed against Providence and the unfair treatment he allowed. She hadn't run away from the village for such noble reasons. She wasn't so much loving her future babies as trying to protect her own heart and trying to strike back at the hated overlords and simply trying to escape the swamp where she always felt like she'd choke on the gray and where she never felt safe for one single minute after the overlords tore her brothers from the family. Her motives were all mixed up together but she knew she was not as noble as Sober was making her out to be.

"I see now," Sober continued, "that I was sitting contentedly by, while slaves were being beaten and hanged. I knew it when I saw those three boys on the swing frame the day we arrived in Harthill. I knew that very moment that Providence had used you to pull me out of the swamp and open my eyes to the evils of the world, because He wanted me to act."

"Act on what?" Lord Carrull said as he entered the room.

Repentance's heart skipped a beat. "You're back. Did the king believe you?"

"I didn't see him." He sat in a chair facing Sober and Repentance. "He was gone. I saw the prince. He says the king has gone away on business. He would not say where."

"That makes no sense," Repentance said. "Why would the king leave now?"

"Particularly when tomorrow night is the Moonlight Festival." Lord Carrull said,

Repentance had forgotten all about the festival. The preparations in the kitchen felt like a lifetime away. The time she spent in the dungeon had driven all thoughts of feasting and thanksgiving far from her.

"The housekeeper would know where the king has gone and why," Sober said. He looked at Repentance. "What is her name?"

"Provocation."

"That's right." Sober nodded. "Provocation. Sharp-eyed, that one is."

"I did see her for a moment," Lord Carrull said. "She said the king was gone on urgent business and wasn't expected back for two weeks."

"Maybe he has gone to the healing house." Repentance hugged her arms around herself as she remembered his racking coughs. He would have to be really sick to miss the Moonlight Festival.

"I've sent a man down to check at the healing house. We'll know by tomorrow evening. I'm afraid, though. We can't rule out the idea that the prince has a hand in the king's absence. He tried to kill him once. Who's to say he hasn't tried again?"

Her heart sped up. "What do we do now? We can't wait two weeks to find out if the king is coming back. Who will stop the prince from taking my family as payment for my disobedience?"

Lord Carrull threw her a worried look. "I'm afraid you're right. I'm less concerned about them than others, though. I can go to Mistress Merricc's farm right now and make arrangements to move your family to Montphilo."

"Is there no way we can go with you?" Repentance asked.

"It's far too risky. Gate guards are doubled and they are searching every cart and wagon." He rose to leave.

Sober stopped him with a question. "You are concerned about others, besides the Atwaters? What do you mean by that?"

Lord Carrull paused, then took a deep breath and said, "I'm afraid when the prince finds the Atwaters gone, he may turn his wrath on the village. It has happened before. More than once."

Sober blanched.

Repentance felt like she'd been kicked by a yak. She lost her breath. The whole village? The Mossybanks? The Gumtrees? Sober's parents?

Lord Carrull shook his head. "Pray Providence for mercy." He turned back at the door. "It's late. I may not make it back before the city gates close at sunset. If not, I'll be here by lunch tomorrow. You two stay up on this floor, keep the window shades drawn, and obey Compassion."

After Lord Carrull left, Repentance couldn't concentrate on her book at all. She spent the afternoon worrying. By dinnertime her stomach was feeling a little sick. Looking for a diversion, she opened the window shade a crack and peered down on the lighted street below. The sun had only just set and little people, six stories down, were still milling around looking into shop windows.

"Here's another one," Sober said. He'd been reading her bits from Lord Banniss's biography all day.

"Sober, how can you read? Aren't you worried about the village?"

He looked up. "I've given it to Providence. Yes, I'm concerned. But what can I do about it now? The best thing I can do in this very minute is read, I think. Worrying about my mother and my father serves no good purpose." He paused, thinking. "Besides, I'm convinced Providence will give us a way out. I don't think he'll let the prince destroy the village."

She wished she could so easily set things aside. But then Sober wouldn't bear the guilt if the villagers were slaughtered. If they suffered the blood would be on her hands, not his.

"Do you want to hear this? It's worth thinking about."

She nodded.

"Lord Banniss's brother—this is incredible—was the one who led the troopers to him. In an interview after his brother was hanged, he said, 'Harding (that's Lord Banniss) thought it was better to die fighting evil than to live. Who was I to argue? When the authorities came threatening me and demanding I tell them where my brother was hiding, I realized there was no sense in my dying to protect him. Harding and I could both get what we wanted. He wanted to die, and I wanted to live.'"

"That's evil."

"But listen to this. A week after Harding was hanged, the brother, his name was Hamchet Banniss, was killed. His throat slit, and *gutter tongue* written on his chest in blood."

"What does *gutter tongue* mean?"

"It's a man who hears back alley secrets and repeats them for the highest bidder."

Repentance shivered and crossed the room to sit next to Sober. "Do you believe all that business about the life spark still glowing on the other side of death? Do you think Hamchet had to face his brother?"

"Worse than that. He had to face Providence. Two brothers die in one week. One dies because of his work saving strangers, one is killed for betraying his brother. Which man would you want to be?"

"Neither! I'd like to live, thanks all the same."

He patted her leg. "You will live for a good long, time, Repentance. But we all do die sometime. That's out of our control. We *can* control some things though. I hope, after I'm gone, that my loved ones—" he paused and waggled his eyebrows at her, "I hope my loved ones will have the comfort of knowing I died like Harding and not Hamchet. Can you imagine? Hamchet only got to live for one extra week and look at what it cost him! He had to present himself to Providence wearing the coward's cloak."

Compassion came with dinner, and Repentance, worried and antsy and not feeling like reading, asked if she might have a new char-stick, as she'd used hers up. She decided to put Hot Springs out of her mind. Sober seemed to know Providence pretty well. Maybe he was right and she didn't need to worry. So, after dinner she fetched her parchment pad from her room and settled down at the desk in the corner. Two hours later she had written a poem about Harding and Hamchet Banniss, the beginning pages of a journal that would chronicle her trip up the mountain and her escape, and she was halfway through a love poem for Sober that she would probably never let him see.

He stood and walked toward her and she quickly covered the poem with a fresh sheet of parchment.

Laying one hand on the back of her neck, he said, "I'm going to bed."

She tipped her head to look at him. "It's early still. We could play a game of bobberchinks. I saw a cup of cubes on the bookshelf by the door."

He shook his head. "It's early, but here we are, stuck alone in this room, and I'm having a hard time keeping myself from sweeping you up and kissing you every two minutes."

Heat rushed into her cheeks. "Would that be such a horrible way to spend the evening?"

"Hmm. Let me check." He kissed her. Finally he pulled away and whispered, "Just as I thought. Trust me, Repentance, I'm not to be trusted."

At the door he turned and winked. And then he was gone.

Repentance looked around the room, which a minute earlier had been warm and cozy, and shivered at the emptiness she felt. She gathered her parchment and her char-stick and went to her own room to soak in a hot bathing pool and then try to sleep. Between thinking about her family and Hot Springs and Sober not being trustworthy, she doubted she'd be able to sleep a wink.

A wink.

She loved it when he winked.

When Repentance entered the library the next morning, Sober was already there. He stood, crossed the room, wrapped his arms around her and kissed her deeply.

Her knees went rubbery, and she had to cling to his shirt to keep her feet.

He broke the kiss but kept on hugging her. "I missed you all night," he whispered into her hair. And then his mouth was on hers again.

Compassion came in. "Oh. My. Oh, my," she said, and she stopped so suddenly the dishes on the breakfast tray rattled against one another.

Sober let Repentance go and she quickly smoothed her dress and patted her hair.

"I'm so sorry," Compassion said. "Excuse me. Please." She began to back out of the room.

Sober chuckled. "Don't leave, woman. Can't you see we're starving? We're so hungry we decided to try to eat one another."

Repentance kicked him. "Sober!"

"Oh, my!" Compassion said.

"She doesn't taste very good, though," Sober said. "So, if you don't mind, I'll take some breakfast."

Compassion set the tray on the low table in front of the settee.

"Is Lord Carrull back yet?" Sober asked her.

"He's not," she answered. Then she toddled out of the room without even pausing to pour the coffee.

Two hours later she'd still not come back for the breakfast dishes.

"You scared her off," Repentance said.

Sober shrugged. "I didn't think she'd be so shocked. Has she never seen two people kissing before?"

Her cheeks felt hot. "That kind of kissing is usually reserved for people who are buttoned."

He twisted on the settee and looked directly into her eyes. "I did some thinking about that last night."

Holding his gaze, she put an encouraging expression on her face, willing him on.

"Will you wait for me, Repentance? I won't be able to join you in Montphilo for seven years."

She ducked under his arm and leaned against his chest. "Seven or seventy, Sober. I'll never button anyone else."

He laughed. "And if I've learned one thing about you, it's that when you make up your mind about not buttoning someone, you follow through."

"This time I've made up my mind to button someone, though." She twisted around and kissed him.

There was a knock on the door and it opened halfway. Starved stuck his head in. "Is it safe to come in?" he asked.

"All safe," Sober said. "Where is Compassion?"

"She's, uh ... busy giving the cook directions for lunch. Sent me for the dishes." After he stacked the dishes, he turned and tripped over the table leg. The tray and all its contents flew from his hands and landed in Sober's lap.

"I'm so sorry."

Sober stood, His pants and shirt were covered in coffee and sticky jelly stains. "I'll go change," he said.

"These feet weren't made for fancy libraries and parlors," Starved said. "I'm more comfortable in the barn than in the house."

"I'll live. Anyway we needed a little excitement. It's been awfully boring sitting around all this time."

Starved laughed. "Compassion had a different tale to tell this morning."

Sober went to his room and Repentance helped Starved clean up. After he left, she browsed the bookshelves, but nothing grabbed her. She stuck her hand in her pocket and, playing with her gray buttons.

A horn sounded in the street.

Another blast followed the first, and Repentance became aware of the fact that she'd been hearing the blasts for some little time. They'd been getting louder and louder over the last fifteen minutes or so.

She went to the window and peeked out.

A crowd clogged the street below, following an open-bed skim wagon, like a slow moving mudslide. An overlord trooper sat in the wagon behind the driver, blowing the horn. It was probably some kind of Moonlight Festival celebration.

Pulling the shade back a little, she saw a woman standing in the wagon bed with the trooper. She was dressed in a thin shift like

Repentance used to wear in the swamp. The wagon drew closer. The woman's hands were tied behind her back and she was turning circles as the trooper hit her with his horn between blasts.

As the wagon drew even with Lord Carrull's house, Repentance could see it wasn't really a woman—not a full-grown one, anyway. It was a girl.

And then the girl turned so Repentance could see her face.

Comfort!

To rush into danger—with no plan and no hope of success—in order to save a friend ... many would call that foolish.

I call it love.

~Professor Pottamous Scroll, Harthill University

CHAPTER 34

Repentance flew from the room, calling for Sober.

Bare-chested and with a towel in his hand, he stuck his head out the door.

"Comfort." She waved back toward the library and beyond. "In the street." She headed down the stairs, crying and praying and not thinking of anything but getting to her sister.

At the front door she paused. Comfort must be cold in her meager swamp clothes. Repentance dove into the cloakroom and snatched a couple of cloaks. Throwing on one, and flipping the hood over her head, she yanked the front door open and fled the house.

She stepped into the slow-moving crowd outside the door, and stumbled, her eyes not yet adjusted to the glare of the sun. Someone jostled her from behind.

"Well, move along, then, child," an old woman said. "You'll not want to stand here like a boulder in the river. The flow will run right over top of you."

Repentance allowed the crowd to carry her along. "I only came out to go shopping," she said to the woman. "What is all this celebration about?"

An eager look sprang into the old woman's eyes. "A swinging," she said. "A perfect way to start off the Moonlight Festival."

Repentance shuddered and stepped to the side, allowing several people from behind to push their way into the space she'd left between herself and the wicked old woman.

"Who'd she run from?" a man beside Repentance asked.

Another man answered, "The prince, I heard. Too bad. She's a pretty little thing."

Repentance pulled her hood farther forward and elbowed through the crowd in an effort to get close to the wagon.

The prince was using Comfort to lure her like a swamp slinker to a beetle, there was not a doubt in her mind. He had chosen well. Repentance would set her sister free or die trying.

She broke through the crowd at the back of the brightly painted wagon. Fabric streamers, blue and purple for the Moonlight Festival, trailed from the sides of the wagon, flipping and flapping in the breeze. The crowd, as if they were going to a party, jostled and laughed.

In the back of the wagon, Comfort stood on display, turning circles. She looked like a rabbit in a snare—all pitiful and terrified. She kept turning as the trooper poked at her. She wasn't like a rabbit in a snare—she was more like a rabbit roasting on a spit, with a slavering mob crushing against the wagon, waiting for a tasty morsel.

Repentance reached out and placed one hand on the smoothly painted wagon. She had no plan. But they were just three blocks from the swing frame. She had no time to think. She would simply jump up and offer the trooper a trade. Her life for Comfort's.

She looked around for the prince. In the front of the wagon was a driver. Lining both sides of the street were troopers walking along the edges of the crowd. They stepped up on porches and stoops every so often, scanning the faces below them. She counted ten on each side of the street. They were looking for her, she knew. And so they would have her. She put her other hand on the wagon bed and made to pull herself aboard.

Someone grabbed her from behind and yanked her back.

She spun around.

Sober.

He wore a workman's shabby cloak with the hood up and the lower part of his face wrapped in his button scarf. She could see just his eyes.

They were enough to break her heart—he looked at her with such love.

"Drop back," he whispered. "When I get her down, you'll have to cut her bonds and get her lost in the crowd and back to Lord Carrull's." He slipped a knife into her hands and shouldered his way in front of her.

Before she had time to protest, he grabbed one of the streamers, ripping it loose, and vaulted onto the wagon right in front of the trooper with the dragon stick. He threw the cloth in the trooper's face and followed it with a solid punch. The trooper fell backwards over the driver's bench.

A surprised roar rose from the mob.

Sober picked up Comfort, dropped her over the edge of the wagon, and jumped down after her.

He shoved Comfort in front of him, pushing his way through the people. Obviously shocked, the people in the crowd parted before them. Several of the men and women around Repentance laughed at the turn of events.

The two closest troopers worked their way through the crowd.

Repentance, struggling to cover the short distance between herself and her sister, took an elbow hard to the ribs but didn't slow down. She had to get to Comfort before the troopers did.

Sober shoved Comfort behind him and pushed his way straight for the troopers. He punched one, and quickly turned on the other.

Comfort pressed back.

The crowd circled around Sober and the troopers like a mob at a hog fight.

The second trooper jabbed Sober in the stomach with the muzzle of his dragon stick. Sober doubled over, and the trooper clubbed him over the head.

Repentance ducked when the dragon stick came down on his head as if she might help him avoid the blow.

Sober staggered. She lost of sight of him when he went down.

He popped back up in a moment, blood streaming from his head.

Repentance watched, horrified.

Sober screamed and charged the trooper that had clubbed him.

The crowd closed in as more and more people pressed forward from behind. Men cried out, shouted direction, laid bets.

"That's it. Don't go without a fight."

"Stay down, boy. It's a lost cause."

Sober's head was no longer visible above the crowd.

"Kick the dirty swine!"

"Let him up. Give him a fighting chance. Let's have a bout to bet on."

"Leave off, boys. You'll want to leave something for the swingman to work with."

Repentance pushed forward, tears clouding her vision.

And then she saw a black braid gleaming blue in the bright mountain sun. It lay over a shoulder clad in thin swamp cloth.

She reached one hand through the people in front of her and grasped that shoulder.

Comfort turned, her eyes full of fear.

When she saw Repentance her eyes snapped wide in shock, and then she began to cry.

Repentance shook her head, and pulled Comfort to her, dragging her through men and women who had eyes only for the fight.

With everyone packed so tightly, she couldn't work the knife to cut Comfort's bonds. She was afraid someone would jostle her and she'd stab her sister. She draped her extra cloak over Comfort's shoulder and lifted the hood over her dark hair. "Stay with me," she whispered. "If anyone stops us, act like my slave."

She wanted to keep her arm around Comfort's shoulder, but overlord women didn't hug their slaves. She gave Comfort one last squeeze and dropped her arm.

The mob pressed forward, and all Repentance and Comfort had to do was stand still, looking forward, pretending to watch the fight, while they allowed people to push around them. In this way they got squeezed further and further back as the people closed in, in front of them.

Slowly, so slowly, they fell away from the fight.

Away from Sober.

Her knees went weak.

But for the crowd she might have fallen. She had no room, thank Providence, with all the people pushing against her, holding her up.

Next to her, Comfort trembled violently. Under the hood, Repentance saw tears streaming down her sister's face.

Something hard slammed into her back.

"Out of the way!" A trooper commanded.

Comfort gave a startled little scream.

Trying to get out of the trooper's way, Repentance pressed against Comfort, squishing her into a woman on the other side.

The trooper pushed past, hurrying toward the fight.

"What are they after?" the woman asked, her eyes locked on the trooper pushing through the crowd.

"Some fight going on," Repentance answered.

"I don't see the slave in the wagon anymore," the woman said, straining to see over the tops of the heads in front of her.

"She's run away," Repentance said.

"Such a pity. I always sell cases of mountain magic at the

swingings." Her face brightened. "They'll catch her yet. She can't get far. They never do."

Comfort jerked and Repentance gave her a warning glance.

The trooper who had shoved his way through shouted out, "Alive! The prince will want to speak to that one."

At the mention of the prince the two troopers stopped beating Sober. "Oh, he's alive, Captain," one said. "A little less cocky now, is all."

The other trooper bent down and came back up a moment later with Sober in his grip.

Repentance stood on tiptoes to look. His face was covered in blood. She gagged.

The woman beside her chortled. "Oh, there may be a double swinging now. Won't that just be too good for business!"

"Where's the girl?" the trooper captain asked. He scanned the sides of the streets, apparently looking for his troopers. Repentance followed his gaze. Several of the men had left their stoops and were working their way toward captain.

"The girl," the captain called. "Where has the girl gotten to?"

The crowd immediately shifted. It began to ooze away from the troopers and Sober.

"Come on, then," the woman standing next to Comfort said. "We'd best be moving. Watching a good fight is one thing. Having a skein of angry troopers searching for a runaway is another altogether."

Repentance moved with the woman back toward the building on their right, pushing Comfort along and looking for an opportunity in the thinning crowd, to get across the street to Lord Carrull's.

"Those troopers," the woman said, "are none too discriminating about batting people out of their way when they are thinking of saving their own hides from the swingman."

The woman reached the wall. "Here we are, safe and sound." She fell into the doorway of a pub.

Repentance turned toward Lord Carrull's house. There, on

his steps, stood a trooper.

She swerved and pushed Comfort toward the pub.

"Hush," she said when Comfort started crying. "Stay with me. It will be fine. It will all be fine." The picture of Sober's bloody face rose in her mind. Nothing would ever be fine again, she was pretty sure. "Everything will be fine," she repeated.

"Find her or you all swing," the captain said. "She can't have gotten far."

His troopers scattered, and he looked up. Directly into Repentance's eyes.

She dropped her gaze and pushed into the pub. In the dimness she barely made out tables and chairs and a long bar at the back of the room.

"Ah, there you girls are," the woman from the street said. She stood behind the bar. "Come have yourself a jug of mountain magic. It will perk you right up of an afternoon."

Someone else stumbled in through the doorway behind Repentance. She turned to look. Two overlord men. "Wild out there," one said.

"In truth," the other answered. "How fortunate that we can sit out for a trickle in this comfy little pub."

Comfort, pasty-faced and dull-eyed, sagged, and Repentance steered her to the bar. "Where is your relief room?" she asked the Pub Mistress. "My slave has taken ill."

Comfort's head was down and she was holding her stomach, so the mistress caught only the top of her hood. She waved at a door to the side of the counter.

Repentance led Comfort into the small room with its sink and its stool, and locked the door behind them. Sitting Comfort on the stool, she whipped out her knife. "You're going to survive this, Comfort." Tears sprang to her eyes. "I'm so sorry I caused you so much trouble."

The confusion in Comfort's eyes didn't lift any. "What was Sober doing out there?"

Repentance lifted the cloak and started sawing at the ropes

on Comfort's wrists. "I'll tell you everything later. Where are the others? Mother and Father and the boys?"

Her sister shook her head. "I don't know. The troopers dragged me from my bed this morning. We were on a farm. We were going to move to someplace called Mont ... Mont ... "

"Montphilo," Repentance said. She finished cutting through the ropes and pulled Comfort against her in a serious hug. "We'll figure it out." She sighed. "One step at a time, though, is all I can see right now. First we have to figure out how to get across the street without discovery."

"What's across the street?"

"Safety." She picked up Comfort's braid. "I have to cut your hair."

Comfort's hand flew to her head. "No!"

"They'll be looking for you. They'll never think you've had time to cut your hair." The knife was sharp. The braid fell neatly into her hand. She shoved it into her pocket, unwilling to leave any evidence behind in the relief room.

Comfort's hair hung above her shoulders in a shaggy mop. Repentance gazed at her. Any trooper who had taken the time to look at her before would know her still. And she was sure they had all looked. Her face was pasty, and her eyes were full of fear but she still had that beauty that made men notice. "Comfort, remember when we were little and you used to make that face like someone born accursed?"

A glint of recognition entered Comfort's eyes and she twisted her face into a grimace with one side of her mouth hanging down and one eye popping open wide. She looked like one born under the wrath of Providence himself.

They stumbled from the relief room. The Pub Mistress looked up and jerked back at the sight of Comfort. "Is she not feeling better then?" she asked.

"A little, but I'd best get her home."

"Please do. She'll scare away business, that one will."

Repentance led the way. When she got to the front of the

pub she peeked out the window. The crowd was gone.

One minute. That was all it would take for her to get to Lord Carrull's. Less than a minute. She said a prayer and pulled open the door.

And there, with his hand on the knob stood the trooper captain.

Against the backdrop of darkness in an evil world, the selfless deeds of friends blaze brighter than stars in a moonless heaven. With sorrows and trials come opportunities to sacrifice for one another, and both the givers and the receivers benefit. Nothing fills bruised hearts with joy like sacrificial love.

~Lord Willikk, *Look to the Night Skies*

CHAPTER 35

In the space of a second, Repentance took in the grim set of the trooper's mouth and his hard eyes—they were like chunks of ice-cold jade.

She stepped back, dropping her eyes.

He moved forward, blocking the doorway.

Repentance shrank into her hood. The troopers had, no doubt, all studied her picture. They'd been scanning the crowd for her. The sketches were never completely accurate or clear, thank Providence.

Comfort made a gurgling noise, and the trooper shifted his weight and leaned around Repentance.

Turning slightly, Repentance saw Comfort, with her hair draping down in front of her face and her tongue sticking out of her mouth, giving the trooper a slobbery smile.

"How is that you were not drowned at birth?" he said with disgust.

Comfort bobbed her head and giggled like an imbecile.

The captain suddenly jerked forward as if he'd been hit from behind.

"Oh, do excuse me. I didn't mean to bump you." Lord Carrull's maid, Compassion, slipped in the door and stood beside the Captain, looking sorrowful.

He turned and laid a stinging slap across the old woman's face.

Repentance gasped.

Compassion grabbed her cheek and sidled away, pulling the trooper's attention after her, away from the door. "I'm so sorry, sir. I meant no harm. Clumsy old thing that I am. I'm so sorry."

"Not nearly as sorry as I'd like to make you," he answered, his face twisted into an ugly sneer.

Repentance slipped behind the man and out the door, pulling Comfort behind her.

"Unfortunately, I have more pressing matters at hand."

The door swished shut.

Repentance forced herself to walk.

Without looking back.

Across the street.

Up the steps.

Into the house.

The door slammed behind them and Repentance fell upon Comfort, hugging her and crying and laughing all at once. What a brilliant sister was Comfort. It made sense that in studying people's faces she would learn to duplicate them not only on parchment but with her own face as well. But where had Comfort found the courage to grin at the captain that way?

"Were you scared?" Repentance asked.

"He was looking at you like you were swamp muck on his good sandals. I knew that if I didn't distract him, we'd be in trouble."

"And you were right in that assessment." Repentance hugged Comfort for the fiftieth time. "Because if he'd looked any longer he would have seen I wasn't swamp muck. He'd have seen I was the one the prince wanted him to find."

Compassion came home, her cheek bruised.

"Oh, Compassion, are you hurt badly?" Repentance asked. "We were dead, but for you!"

"Upstairs into the hidden room," Compassion said, breathlessly. "They'll be searching door to door."

The door burst open behind her. "They've taken him to the palace," Starved said. He won't swing tonight. Tonight will be for tor—" he threw a pitiful look at Repentance. "—tonight they will interview him."

Repentance stopped, her foot on the bottom step. They were going to torture him!

"He said an odd thing," Starved reported. "And I think he wanted me to pass it on. When the troopers threw him in the wagon, one of them said, 'It's the frame for you come sunup, or there's no ice on the mountain.' And Sober answered, 'Then I'll look forward to the sunup. I would have those I love, know I die content.' And then he looked straight at me and winked."

"Upstairs," Compassion said, shooing them from the hall.

A dull ache spread through Repentance. Sober had jumped right onto that wagon, thinking no more about it than he'd thought about diving into the waterfall to save Ambivalence. And it was her fault. All of it. From the very beginning.

She could have buttoned him. Why did she think she had to be the one to stand up to the overlords and refuse to give them slave babies? Why, in the name of Providence, had she hated the village so much? She'd felt lost there. As though she didn't belong. But if she'd have buttoned Sober she would have belonged.

Things were more complicated than that, though. Ever since the troopers had taken Tribulation she'd been afraid they'd come for her and her parents would let her go without a fight. When her mother had taken to rocking and humming Repentance had sworn to protect Comfort, but she'd grown up knowing she couldn't do it. And she hated that feeling of helplessness and hopelessness. Whether she buttoned or not was the one thing she was able to control in her life.

Once in the hidden room, Comfort asked a million questions. What was Sober doing at the wagon? How did Repentance know she was there? Why had the troopers taken her away from the family?

"Where were you when they took you?" Repentance asked.

"A fat woman, Mistress Merricc, do you know her?"

Repentance nodded.

"She bought us. The whole family. And she took us to a farm. Oh, Repentance, we saw the sun and the moon and the stars. We thought the world was wonderful. But then ... but then ... "

"Where are Mother and Father and the boys?"

Comfort gave Repentance a pitiful look and tears overflowed. "I didn't see them today. The troopers came and pulled me from bed and loaded me on the wagon. Mistress Merricc told them she owned me, and they couldn't have me without compensating her." She shivered and put her hands over her face. "Her old slave, Calamity, tried to pull her back to keep her from getting beaten by the troopers, and one of them asked him what he thought he was doing placing hands on an overlord woman. He knocked Calamity to the ground and he ... and he ... " she broke down sobbing.

Repentance hugged her, rocking her back and forth. "Never mind. Don't tell it."

She thought of Calamity with his wide, gap-toothed grin, sucking down Cook's potato soup.

"His dragon stick," Comfort mumbled, her face buried in Repentance's chest. "And he was screaming, and you could smell the burning flesh ... "

Oh, Calamity. Poor old Calamity.

Repentance felt a raging anger flow over her. If there were a trooper in the room just then, she felt sure she could rip his face off with her fingernails.

But as she patted Comfort's back her anger drained away and was replaced by a sense of hopeless dread.

Calamity was dead.

And Sober would soon join him.

She had no idea where her family was and Comfort wasn't even safe. Here they were, huddled in a small, hidden, tomb-like room. Freedom felt like myth and make-believe.

Maybe Comfort could yet be saved. Maybe Lord Carrull would be able to smuggle her out of the city.

When Lord Carrull finally arrived, Repentance dove on him with questions. Where were her parents? What was going on outside?

He ignored her, staring at Comfort in shock.

"Why is she here?" he whispered. "How can this be?" He looked at the faces of the people around him. Repentance, Comfort, Compassion, and Starved all stared back. "Where's Sober?" he asked.

"The troopers took him while he was saving Comfort," Repentance said.

His face reddened, and he clenched his fists. He stepped toward her as if he might strike her. "Sober left this house, kidnapped this girl from the troopers, and he brought her back here?"

"I brought her here," Repentance whispered.

"So whereas the prince did have a young woman who knew nothing about your whereabouts or my work, he now has Sober—a young man you brought to my house. A young man who has seen the secret room and who knows I steal slaves and smuggle them to freedom."

Repentance jumped up. "You wanted us to leave my sister to die? Just to save your sorry skin? Well, you needn't worry. Sober will never tell about your secret room. He knows Comfort and I are hidden here. He'll never give us up."

Lord Carrull looked at her sorrowfully. "I pray Providence you're right. You are, though, completely unaware of how persuasive the interrogators can be. I dare not chance it." He jumped into action, handing out orders. "Starved, the yak wagon, we'll be traveling all night. Compassion, pack food. For them," he indicated Repentance and Comfort, "and for us."

Repentance stared with her mouth hanging open. "What about Sober? Are you going to abandon him?"

A look of pity crossed his face, followed quickly by resolve. "I can do nothing for Sober. I'm sorry about that. I liked that young man, so don't try to blame me. He has you to thank for his fate. You fight when you have no way to win, and you seem determined to drag others down with you."

She winced.

Comfort stood and hugged Repentance.

Lord Carrul's expression softened. "I know you don't mean any of it, Repentance. Sober knows it, too, I'm sure. He was full-force in love with you, that one. Any fool could see it." The lord studied her face. "And it's easy to understand why. You're stubborn as stone, but when you blurt out your opinions there's usually a lot of truth in them. You're full of vim and vigor, and there's something attractive about that in this world where we so often feel beaten down by forces so much bigger than we are."

She shook her head. Because he loved her, Sober would swing. There was nothing noble or good about her.

"I'm sorry I can't help you or your sister, now," Lord Carrull said. "You're welcome to hide out here. It will be safer than on the street. And you are right about one thing: Sober will not give you up without a fight. If Sober doesn't talk, my friends will get me word, and I'll be able to come back. Then I'll be able to help reunite you with your family."

"My family?" She looked at him hopefully. "You saw them at Mistress Merricc's farm?"

"They are safely on the way to Montphilo."

Relief flooded her and she couldn't speak.

"You were at the farm?" Comfort asked.

"Not so as anyone would have known. I spent the night there. I didn't meet your family because I was trying to avoid any ties to your sister or Sober. But I did see your family leave, and they will get to Montphilo safely. I promise. No one was chasing them. The troopers left with you, confident that you were all the bait they needed."

Repentance nodded. They were right about that.

After the others left, Repentance sank to the floor and wept. If she lived, by the time she left the hidden room Sober would be dead.

He would be dead by sunrise. And maybe all of Hot Springs along with him. She wouldn't put it past the prince to wipe out the village in a rage. The pain in her chest rose into her throat and she felt like she might choke on it.

Comfort knelt next to her, patting her back, as her own tears splattered on Repentance's neck.

After she was cried out, Repentance sniffed and swallowed and wiped at her swollen eyes with the sleeve of her gown.

Comfort rose and moved to the settee. She sat down with a heavy sigh. "Will we ever get out of this room?" she asked. "Or are we locked in forever?"

"We aren't locked in. All we have to do is poke the dragon in the eye if we want to get out."

Comfort gave her an "are you mad?" look.

"The door will open," Repentance said, "But we have nowhere to go. This is the safest place in the city for us."

She looked at the door. It struck her that one of the reasons she was so desperate to leave the swamp was that she never felt safe there. She'd always been afraid that one day the overlords would come for her, or someone she loved. No one was safe in the swamp. She thought she'd rather get into the slave cart of her own free will than have to keep living in fear that they would come for her one day.

But she would never really be safe unless she was free. And she would never be free if she left Sober to die alone.

"But that man," Comfort said. "Lord Carrull. He will come back for us? Someday?"

Repentance crawled over to Comfort and leaned against her knees. "He will come back for you. I ... may not be here."

"Where will you be?" Her sister's tone was high-pitched and

anxious.

"Sober saved me by breaking me out of the dungeon two days ago. Then he saved me again this afternoon by jumping on that wagon and setting you free. I have to try to save him."

"How will you do that? Where will you go?"

"I'll have to go to the palace. It's the Moonlight Festival. I'll be able to sneak in." She pulled over the trunk of clothes Starved had brought in. "I wonder what kind of disguise I can come up with."

Comfort joined her. "I'll come with you."

"You'll stay here," Repentance said matter-of-factly.

"Sober saved my life, too. I want to help him." She gave Repentance her stubborn look. "Besides, there is not a way in the swamp ... no way on this Providence-forsaken mountain, are you leaving me in this room all by myself."

Repentance sighed. And nodded. She'd left Comfort once. She couldn't do it again. But then again she couldn't very well take her into the dungeon, either. She needed to think. There had to be a way for her to keep Comfort safe.

If you fail to take a weapon when you beard the lion in his den, you should hardly be surprised when he decides to eat you for dinner.
~Professor Pottamous Scroll, Harthill University

CHAPTER 36

The trunk was full of fine overlord clothes and rough slave clothes all mixed together. Costumes Lord Carrull had apparently collected as disguises for the slaves he smuggled out of the city.

Repentance considered a pair of flannel trousers.

Comfort rubbed her cheek against a velvet gown. "I never imagined material this soft. And look at this!" She rubbed her hand over the nap, changing the material from dark to light and back to dark again.

Repentance nodded absently. "But look at these." She held up the trousers. Aren't they nice?"

Comfort wrinkled her nose. "You're going dressed as a boy?"

"I was thinking you might. You have the short hair already. We'd just have to trim it a bit."

Comfort put a hand to her ill-cut hair, looking like she might cry.

Repentance hugged her. "I know. I know. It's too much.

You've been dragged off and paraded in front of a mob. You've been scared and threatened and pushed and pulled and forced here and there." The thought of Calamity flashed into her mind. "You've seen unspeakable brutalities. And on top of all that, I chopped off your beautiful hair. It will grow back, though." *If we live.*

"I'm being silly. A bad haircut is the least of our troubles."

"It's the final indignity. Anyone with any heart at all would be overwhelmed by it. But you're right. In the end it matters for nothing whether we have long hair or short. I think we should both go as boys tonight. The troopers will be looking for two girls."

Comfort looked at her, eyes round. "You're going to cut your hair?"

"You're going to cut it for me."

Three hours later a royal overlord boy, dressed in tan suede knickers with a matching jerkin, slipped out of Lord Carrul's house by way of the alley door. His slave, a well-dressed boy in flannel trousers with leather boots and a wool vest, followed a few steps behind. Darkness had already fallen.

The jerkin Repentance wore was a little out of fashion, being a size too big and loose-fitting, but it covered her shape without showing any curves and the largeness of it made her look small—like a boy in his twelfth or thirteenth year. And that was good as her voice was not deep enough to sound like it belonged to one who had already ripened into manhood. Her hair was cut shorter than Sober's. When she'd looked in the reflecting stone she couldn't believe how large her eyes seemed in her small face. But it had to be that short. If she turned her head the right way her birthmark was visible. The troopers were looking for a runaway female slave. And if she knew the prince, he hadn't bothered to tell anyone that the slave bore the royal birthmark.

She would pass this night as a member of the royal house come over from Norbank for the feast—a nephew to Lord Baldin—

and her birthmark may be needed to purchase her way into the palace.

Of course, she traveled with her slave.

Comfort, once she accepted the idea, played her part to the full. She'd smudged a little ash into her cheeks and chin to make herself look work worn and she held her mouth in a tight line—no sign of Comfort's plump, red lips in Vengeance, the slave's, serious face.

Comfort walked a step behind her master. They turned the corner onto the main thoroughfare, which was clotted with small groups of people. The sound of singing drifted from the pub. The mountain magic was flowing, apparently, despite the lack of a good swinging to get everyone in the mood for drink. She and Comfort fell in behind a trail of people, working their way to the palace.

As they wound through the city streets more and more people filed in from side streets. Many of them were wrapped in lava-cloth cloaks or shawls and Repentance mentally kicked herself for forgetting how chilly the mountain could get once the sun went down. She shoved her cold hands into the pockets of her jerkin.

By the time they reached the palace gates, they were shuffling along with a good-sized throng. There were not many richly dressed overlords in the crowd. Most of those rode in carts. Repentance hoped since she was just a boy people overlook the fact that an overlord noble was walking alongside the commoners. She was obviously a foreigner with her dark complexion. She hoped the people in the crowd would allow for her presence, figuring that overlords in Norbank did things differently from overlords in Harthill. A few people gave her odd looks, but most simply shrugged and moved on. They were looking forward to a night of food and drink and goodwill, and they apparently didn't have time to wonder about the young nobleman in their midst.

Two troopers stood at the palace gates, watching the crowd.

A prickly feeling ran over Repentance when she saw them and the collar of her white silk shirt felt too tight. She forced herself to slow her breathing. Surely no one was expecting her to break into the palace grounds. Not after she'd gone to such extremes to run away.

She and Comfort followed the crowd, shuffling through the gates without incident. On feast nights all were welcome, apparently.

They traveled up the long drive. As she drew nearer the palace, Repentance surveyed the set-up. She came to the slave tables first—several of the palace slaves were already seated. As she moved on, she passed the poor overlord tables, and then the rich overlord tables. Finally she arrived at the tables for royalty. Past those, right in front of the palace's main entrance, was the platform—still vacant, thank Providence—where the king and his family should sit.

In between the royal tables and the royal platform was a bonfire, on both sides of which jugglers entertained a mixed crowd that looked to be mostly comprised of slave children and poor overlord children.

Repentance, with Comfort following dutifully, circled back toward the slave tables. It wouldn't do for an overlord prince to mix with the slaves, so she stayed in the main walkway. There were booths set up on both sides. Over the curtained doorways hung signs that said things like, *Madam Menntiss, Moon Magician: five beads for your future,* or, *Madam Lilliberrn, Lunar Enlightenment: if you don't like your fortune you keep your beads in your pocket.* One booth sold jewelry—bracelets dangling with moon charms and necklaces made of blue moonstones. Another sold mooncloth.

Just past Madam Lilliberrn's booth, was a booth with no sign and no curtain hanging in the doorway. She casually peeked in and found it empty. Drawing off to the side of that booth, she surveyed the slave tables.

And there he was. Shamed. He sat next to Blustering, halfway down one of the tables. They both had jugs in front of them and they were in the middle of an animated conversation.

Repentance whispered to Comfort, "Do you see that slave right there—the one closest to us?" She nodded toward Shamed. "I need you to get him for me. Tell him Tigen needs to see him. Don't let anyone else hear. I'll be waiting right behind this booth."

"Tigen needs him," Comfort repeated.

"And wait there until he comes back. We don't want a crowd here, drawing attention. Sit with the other slave, his name is Blustering, and drink a jug with him."

When Shamed arrived a few minutes later, he glanced around. Not seeing Tigen, he started to leave.

"Wait, Shamed," Repentance said.

Shamed looked at her. "Excuse me?"

Repentance looked at him intently. "Don't you know me?"

"Should I know you? There's something familiar about you." Shamed squinted, then gasped. "Do you have a sister? You look like a lady I once knew."

Repentance put her finger to her lips to quiet him. "I am the lady you once knew," she whispered. "A lady you once helped. I'm hoping you'll help me again."

"Repentance! Your hair!" Then he stepped back, aghast. "What are you doing here?"

"Where is Sober?"

A pained look crossed Shamed's face. "He's in the dungeon. Generosity took him a bowl of soup earlier. She said he's broken up bad."

"I need to get to him."

His eyes shot wide open. "You need to get out of Harthill. The king is gone, who knows where, and the prince has whipped his troopers into a frenzy looking for you. Word is ... " he faltered.

"Tell me!"

"Word is that Sober is to swing at first light. I've also heard that the Hot Springs slavers have been moving the strongest villagers out, taking them on slave carts for auction. They don't want to lose all their inventory."

Repentance put her hand to her mouth to hold back the bile that was rising in her throat.

"You need to get away, Repentance, but whatever you do, don't go back to Hot Springs."

She swallowed. "I can't do anything for the people in the

village. But I can free Sober."

A look of horror filled Shamed's face. "If you stay here, you'll swing with him and I can tell you this, true as true, Repentance. If he thinks you're safe, he'll die happy. If you want to torture the man, get yourself caught and swing by his side."

"Do you know if the boat is still docked at Mist Lake?"

"You're crazy!"

"Is it there?"

"Broken up and burned the day after you escaped. Are you trying to kill yourself? The place is thick with nobles and troopers."

Repentance nodded, stepped forward and hugged him. "I know. And I hate to ask you this when you've already done so much for me, but I have to ask you to do something more."

He looked at her, waiting.

"The boy who gave you the message to meet Tigen?"

He glanced at Comfort, still at the slave table, talking to Blustered.

"That's not really a boy. It's my sister, Comfort."

He shook his head. "Why would you bring her here?"

"She wouldn't stay behind. Listen to me, I don't have a lot of time. She belongs to Mistress Merricc. If something happens to me, and I don't come back for her tonight, will you hide her in the barn for a couple of weeks? At your first opportunity, let whoever comes from Mistress Merricc's farm know that you have Comfort. They'll smuggle her out."

"Calamity's so old he can barely find his own mouth with a spoon. How will he smuggle a slave out of the city?"

She winced. "Calamity is dead."

"What?"

"Will you watch out for Comfort, please? If the prince catches me tonight he won't care about Comfort. No one will be looking for her. After a couple of weeks things will calm down and Mistress Merricc will be able to get her out."

He nodded. "I'll try."

She kissed his cheek. "I know you'll do your best. Go back

now and keep her busy so she won't try to follow me."

"What are you going to do?"

"I'm going to sneak into that dungeon, open Sober's door, and sneak back out again."

"Providence smiles on courage. Are you being courageous or just plain foolish, is the question." Shaking his head, obviously putting her in the latter category, he turned to leave.

"Shamed?"

He turned back.

"Tell Comfort I love her."

She strode off without a backward glance, a few stray tears freezing in her eyelashes.

As she neared the bonfire, the sound of musicians warming up their instruments filled the chilly mountain air. The jugglers had traded in their balls and were throwing flaming torches back and forth. Repentance saw a familiar face in the crowd of children watching. Tigen. He was up front and laughing. Always in the middle of the action, that one.

She wished she could talk to him one last time.

Swallowing that desire, she ducked around back of the palace and entered through the washroom.

Peeking around the doorway into the kitchen, she saw a snake's nest of activity. Cook bustled about in the middle of it all, giving orders to scores of slaves with pitchers and slaves with trays. Repentance moved over to the hall door, praying for the traffic to slow down enough so she could sneak down the hall and into the great room above the dungeons.

"Who are you?" someone said from behind her.

She nearly jumped from her boots.

Turning, she found Tigen, gazing at her intently.

"I saw you come around back of the—" he broke off with a gasp. "My Lady?"

She shook her head. "How can you know me?"

"You look like a boy."

"I'm supposed to look like a boy. I don't want anyone to

know I'm here."

"Why *are* you here?"

"I need to get into the dungeon."

"What for?"

"Sober."

He nodded. "Wait."

Before she could answer, he disappeared into the kitchen. He reappeared in a few moments, handed Repentance a jug of mountain magic, and disappeared a second time. He returned with a tray of food. "Come on. We can pretend we're taking food to the dungeon master."

"I can't walk down that hallway. Look at all those slaves."

"Slaves don't look ever look at overlords they don't know," Tigen said. "They'll look down at the floor when you walk by."

She bent and kissed his cheek. He was so smart and so good.

He grabbed a short paddle from the tool bucket in the washroom and tucked it under his arm. "We need something to knock the door handle off."

She was skeptical. "That's how you got the door open when you rescued me?'

He nodded. "You hit the door handles dead center, and they pop right through the door into the cell." He stepped into the hall. She followed, ignoring the slaves they passed and being ignored in turn. Into the great room they went and across it to the stairway, which led down into the cold dungeon.

"When we get down halfway, let me go ahead to make sure the corridor is clear." Tigen said.

They headed down the stairs, Repentance's throat constricting as the air grew colder and the memory of empty hours in her frigid, dark cell flooded her mind. They got to the landing where the stairs switched back, and Tigen stopped. He handed Repentance the stir paddle, took the jug of Mountain Magic, and motioned for her to stay put while he descended alone.

"What's this, then?" a man's deep voice floated up the stairs.

Tigen gave a little squeal. "You surprised me," he said. "Why are you sitting in the cold hallway?"

The deep voice answered. "The last dungeon master never sat in the hallway, did he? He was always in his quarters, wasn't he? That's why his quarters are my quarters now."

"I didn't know. Well, I brought you a trickle of food and drink for you to celebrate the feast."

"Food and drink, you say?"

"Come, open your door and I'll put it in your quarters," Tigen said. "You don't want to eat it out here in the cold."

"And why are you suddenly so concerned about what I eat and where?

"Cook said it wouldn't do to forget anyone on Feast night."

"Cook sends little boys to do her bidding these days, eh? Where's the slave girl what usually brings my food? I'm supposing you are up to some mischief of the kind what will end with my body swinging at the end of a rope."

Blood pounded in Repentance's ears.

"If you aren't hungry now I'll leave it in your quarters," Tigen said. "You can eat it later."

Repentance crouched on the step before the landing and craned her neck, peering around the corner of the stairs. She could see Tigen's back as he stood before a desk. As soon as he got the man into his quarters, she could shoot down the stairs and past him.

"That makes a likely compromise," the dungeon master said. "I'll take you into my quarters and you can leave the food for later."

Repentance moved her paddle to her left hand, grasped the railing with her right, and prepared to launch herself down the stairs.

But Tigen never moved away down the hall. Instead a big man burst into view, pushing Tigen aside, and charging up the stairs.

He was on her before she could even turn around, let alone try to run away. "Got you!"

She yelped in pain as he twisted one arm up behind her back.

There comes to every man a moment when the choices set before him are intolerable. To choose one course will tear the heart out six ways and to choose the other will tear it out seven. A man in this circumstance needs no lecture. He needs pity and prayer.
~Meticulous Mudslide, *An Old Man Remembers*

CHAPTER 37

Holding her arm twisted up behind her back, the dungeon master shoved Repentance ahead of him as he descended the stairs. "Two demons playing tricks on the dungeon master!" he yelled. His breath came hot against Repentance's cheek. He smelled as if he'd already had a trickle of Mountain Magic. "I know all about the deeds and doings of mischievous little boys. I'm having none of your nonsense, thanks all the same."

With her free arm, Repentance tried to stick her paddle in between the man's feet to trip him.

The dungeon master saw and gave an extra jerk, pulling her arm farther up behind her.

She cried out.

Tigen, an indignant look on his face, threw the platter and jug at the man. With a wild scream, he scrabbled onto his back and pummeled him with his small fists.

The dungeon master shoved Repentance away. She slammed into the wall beside the desk, the ice burning her cheek on contact.

She spun off the wall and turned in time to see the man reach one beefy hand over his shoulder, pull Tigen off his back, and toss him down as easily as her father, in the swamp, would have peeled off a leech and shaken it back into the water.

Tigen's head hit the corner of the desk with a sickening, hollow-sounding clunk. He landed on the floor, a puddle of scarlet blood spreading out from his head.

"You've killed him!" Repentance screamed. Ice crystals immediately formed at the edges of the puddle. "He's freezing to the floor!"

The dungeon master grabbed Tigen. Strands of frozen hair broke as he lifted and laid the limp little body on the desk. He leaned over the boy. "Still breathing," he said.

Tigen's head flopped to the side.

The dungeon master gasped when he saw the birthmark behind the boy's ear. "A prince! Providence have mercy. I'm an honest man just trying to do my job and keep my life in the process." He leaned over Tigen, searching his face. "Wake up! You must! Why do you young princes want to bring this trouble crashing down on my head?"

Repentance took aim with her paddle and brought a little more trouble crashing down on his head.

He slumped over Tigen on the desk.

She shoved him, so he was draped over the boy's legs. Looking closely, she saw Tigen's chest rising and falling steadily. She would carry him out of the dungeon after she saved Sober. They could drop him in the kitchen. Cook would know how to help him.

She ran past the dungeon master's quarters to the first cell door and opened the window. She could see nothing outside of the little square of light on the cell floor.

"Sober?" she whispered. "Are you in here?"

"Repentance?" his voice was weak. "No, no, no. Tell me I'm dreaming. Tell me you aren't really here."

"That's a fine way to greet your rescuer and future button mate. Get up, Sober, we have to hurry."

He groaned. A moment later he was at the window. His face was battered— dried blood matted in his hair, his nose was bent and swollen, both eyes were black and puffy. He looked at her, shock registering in his eyes. Reaching one hand out, he touched her head. "Your hair."

"It will grow again. Stand back, now, I'm going to open your door."

"You can't open my door." He spoke slowly and was obviously having a hard time understanding what was going on.

She held up her paddle so he could see. "I can." She stepped back to take aim at the door handle. "Move away, Sober."

"No!"

"We don't have time to waste. Tigen is hurt."

"If you open my door, the other prisoner dies."

Another prisoner? "But if I don't open your door, *you* die."

He reached through the window and cupped her face in his hands. "Yes. I die. Let me die. Go save the king."

"The who?"

"He's in another cell. Find him. Set him free. He'll help you. He'll save Hot Springs."

She shook her head. "I can't do that. You can't ask me to do that, Sober."

He rubbed one thumb over her cheek. "I know you can do this. I know you will do this for me. Let me go to Providence bravely and not crawling like a coward. My parents, Repentance. They're still in Hot Springs. Along with a couple of hundred more."

His eyes, in his swollen, bloody face, were filled with love and sorrow. But they also held a determined light

Tears streamed freely down her cheeks. "You're asking me to kill you."

"No. Don't think that." He brushed his hand over her short hair. "I'm asking you to save my parents. I know I'm laying a heavy burden on you, but I'll die happily, knowing you love me and knowing my death will help so many people."

She shook her head.

"Please, Repentance."

Maybe she could free them both. It took the floor a few seconds to slide back. If the king's cell was close by, she might be able to knock the door handles off both doors.

She crossed to the cell opposite Sober's and slid the window open. "Your Highness?"

No answer.

She went to the next cell, and the next. Back and forth across the hall.

She was met with silence at each door.

At the last cell, when she slid the window open, she heard someone coughing.

"Your Highness?"

"Repentance, is it you?" She heard him scrabbling around. "It can't be. No, it can't be. No one knows I'm here. He brought me down in secret and shoved me in the last cell. No one knows, not even the dungeon master. I'll die here and no one will ever know."

"I have to get you out." she whispered. "The prince is going to destroy Hot Springs."

He hobbled to the window. His face was gaunt, but he hadn't been beaten. "You are real? Not a dream?" He reached out to touch her. "Tell Provocation. She'll get my troopers. Don't go to the dungeon master, he won't believe—" he broke off, coughing.

The dungeon master! She could use his key and open both doors. She was as dumb as a catfish! "I'll be right back," she said to the king, and she turned toward the desk and the unconscious dungeon master.

She took two steps and came to a sudden halt.

Coming down the stairs were a pair of men's legs in silk britches. The top of the man was hidden from view, but she didn't need to see. She knew who it was.

No time for the key. And no way could she open both doors with the paddle. She looked at Sober's door ahead of her. She could make it. She could leave the king and save Sober.

From the dungeon master's desk she heard the familiar

voice. "What's all this?"

Her heart failed.

She had the paddle, though. The prince was not a strong man. He had other people do his fighting for him. With the paddle, she and Sober could knock the prince over the head and escape. But Sober didn't want to live like Hamchett Banniss—living while others died.

"Repentance," the king said. "I'm sorry I didn't believe you, child."

The king deserved to die. He kept slaves. Sober had done nothing wrong. He was nothing like Hamchet Banniss.

"Are you drunk?" the prince demanded, yanking the dungeon master's head up.

The prince's voice brought her back to the truth. If she and Sober escaped and the king died, the prince would take the throne. And all the people of Hot Springs would pay the price.

Sober didn't want to live, carrying that weight on his conscience.

"You'll swing for this," the prince said dropping the man's head.

The injured man slipped off the table onto the floor and lay there moaning.

The prince bent over Tigen. "I told you!" he said to his unconscious son. "I said that your fascination with slaves would bring you no good." He shook his head in disgust.

He didn't even care if Tigen was alive or dead.

Rage filled Repentance.

She backed up. "Stand away from the door," she whispered to the king.

She had no time for troopers, and no help would be forthcoming from the dungeon master, but she would free the king and knock the prince over the head with her paddle. She would save Hot Springs. For Sober.

The prince looked up, then. Straight down the hall and into Repentance's eyes.

He flashed a wicked smile.

"Well, Repentance. I'm happy to see you again."

"Sober," she whispered, tears streaming down her face. "Forgive me."

"Get back away from the door," she called to the king. Then she raised her paddle and swung at the door handle with all her might. The paddle connected and a shock ran up her arms and rattled her teeth.

The door flew open.

The prince laughed. He stood at the end of the hall, clapping his hands and laughing. "You keep on surprising me, Repentance. You just killed your farmer."

She stared at him. She could hear the words, but she wasn't sure what they meant.

"Repentance, help me." The king was backed against the far wall in his cell, his floor receding.

What had happened? Something was terribly wrong, but she wasn't sure what exactly. She tried to replay events, but all that came to her were pieces of pictures and phrases. Sober telling her to free the king. His sad smile. His hand on her cheek.

"Repentance!" the king called.

She jerked back to her right mind. She'd chosen to save the king.

She held out her paddle. The old man came to the edge of the receding floor and grabbed a hold.

She counted to three.

He jumped and she yanked.

He was so frail—so light—that he flew across the void and slammed into her. They both went down onto the floor. The back of her head bounced on the hard ice. Lights flashed before her eyes. She blinked several times, trying to clear her vision.

The king lay on top of her, coughing. The prince was still laughing. The ice floors under the cells receded fully into the walls with a scrape and a click. She looked down the hall at Sober's window. It gaped at her. Empty.

She tried to roll the king off of her, but before she managed that, the prince arrived. He looked down on her, gloating.

Repentance blanched.

The dungeon master stepped up behind the prince, rubbing the back of his head. He peered over the prince's shoulder with bleary eyes. "Still here, then," he said. "No one has escaped?"

"No credit goes to you on that account," the prince said with a sneer.

He used his foot to roll the king off Repentance.

The old man hit the ice and cried out.

The dungeon master, seeing the king's face, gasped.

The prince dug his toe under the king and rolled him over again, moving him toward the open water under his cell.

Repentance bit her lip, trying to think. This was not going to happen. Sober did not die for nothing. She was not going to lie there and watch the prince throw the king into the lake.

The king pulled his feet up, bracing them against the wall. He tried to say something but only succeeded in breaking into a spasm of coughing.

The prince leaned over to yank the king's feet from the wall.

"Arrest him," the king managed between coughs.

Repentance lay still, not wanting to draw attention to herself. Where was the paddle? She looked out of the corner of her eyes.

The dungeon master, obviously afraid to touch the prince, said, "That's the king."

The prince threw a look over his shoulder at the man. "I am aware. Do you want to help me and live, or will you stand there and make me do all the work myself?"

Repentance felt around the floor, her hand burning. Finally her search was rewarded when she brushed the paddle with her fingertips.

"Are you sure you want to throw the king in the lake?" the dungeon master asked.

"You, my dear dungeon master, just made the wrong choice," the prince said. "Did you never learn that it's dangerous to question those in authority over you?" He turned back, bent down, and grasped the king's legs.

Repentance had the perfect opportunity. She slammed her heel into the center of the prince's face. His head jerked up.

He stood, blood gushing from his nose. "You will die for that."

"I'll die either way," she said. She closed her hand around the paddle, rolled over, sprang from the floor, and took a swing at his head.

The paddle connected, and the prince slumped and landed, unconscious, on top of the king.

The dungeon master stepped forward. Repentance waved the paddle at him.

"I'm not going to hurt you," he said. "I'm trying to help."

"Move back."

"I swear," he said. "I didn't know the king was locked up here. The prince brought him down with a bag on his head, packed him into this end cell, and wouldn't let no one near him. He brought the prisoner's meals his own self."

From under the prince came the sound of the kings racking coughs.

"Get the king off the cold floor," Repentance said, weakly.

The dungeon master pushed the prince aside and picked the king up as if he were a small child.

As the king came up, the prince's unconscious body rolled off his legs, balanced for a moment in the cell doorway, then started to roll over into the lake.

"No!" Repentance yelled.

The dungeon master threw the king over his shoulder and reached for the prince.

Missed.

They heard a splash. Nothing else.

Repentance peered into the lake. The prince floated facedown, perfectly still.

"Pull him up," she said.

The dungeon master shook his head. "With what? By the time I get the hook, it will be too late. He's dead already. There's no coming back once you hit that water."

Repentance looked at Sober's door and started shaking.

The dungeon master set the king on his feet. "Can you stand, your majesty? I had no idea you were a prisoner here. No idea at all."

The king gave him a searching look, "I ordered you to arrest him."

"I was thinking how best to obey, your highness. I was waiting for my opportunity to arrest him."

The king turned away without answering. "Come, Repentance," he said, between coughs. "We need our wounds attended to."

She walked to Sober's door.

She had to look.

And there he was, at just that moment, floating through the shaft of light that poured through the window in the door. Frozen. Stiff and white. His swollen eyes were forever frozen shut. Never again would he wink at her.

She shuddered, her heart screaming for a chance to talk to him one last time, for a chance to tell him goodbye.

But there he was, cold and lifeless.

Her last look was not upon the vibrant handsome face she remembered but upon a face she didn't even recognize—beaten and frozen and mottled and dead. He was past all pain, at least. His gray flannel button scarf floated around his head like a crown and trailed across his mouth and nose.

When she saw that, a foggy memory drifted into her mind. She remembered lying beside Sober in the slave cart, sharing her blanket and dreaming that his button scarf would suffocate her. And there it lay, floating across Sober's misshapen face. She felt like all the air had been sucked from her lungs. *Yes, I will take the scarf,* a voice screamed in her head. *Oh, please. I didn't know what I was doing. I want to be his button mate. I want to take the scarf.*

The king looked over her shoulder. "What is this about?"

"Sober Marsh," she said, moving aside so he could look in the window. "He was such a good man." Tears dribbled down her cheeks.

"Your farmer?"

"My friend," she whispered.

"Come," the king said. "We'll take care of what we can tonight. We'll have to wait for time to heal the rest."

"I came to save him," Repentance said. "I wanted to save him. I was supposed to save him."

"Come away, Repentance." The king took hold of her elbow and steered her from the door.

Tears washing down her face, she did again as she had done months earlier. She mouthed the words, "I'm sorry," and she turned her back on Sober Marsh.

To die as an honest man is better than to live as a liar, to die fighting evil is better than to live with your eyes and ears and heart clamped shut to the pain around you, and to die serving a friend is to die the best way of all.

~Lord Harding Banniss, *Letters to a Young Man*

CHAPTER 38

The king led the way, shuffling along, stopping often to cough. The dungeon master followed, carrying the unconscious Tigen. Repentance watched her feet as she walked, but what she saw was Sober, dead and frozen. So cold. He must be so cold.

At the top of the stairs, the king stopped to instruct the dungeon master, "Take the boy to his quarters. I'll send a doctor."

The dungeon master strode off, and the king turned to Repentance. "Do you remember where the family parlor is? Across the hall from my small library?"

She remembered the dungeon. Everything else was shrouded in fog.

"Can you hear me?" he asked.

Sober was dead.

"I'll take you," the king said kindly. He took her hand and led her through the great room and down the wide hallway to a small parlor. "Wait for me here."

She wandered to the window. Outside, the Moonlight Festival celebrants feasted and laughed and danced, completely unaware. Repentance had an urge to run into the courtyard crying, "He's dead, he's dead. The universe has been torn open and can never heal. Stop your dancing. Weep and wail. Sober is dead and there can never be joy again."

She stood at the window, tears streaming down her face.

If she hadn't run out of Lord Carrull's house without a plan, he might still be alive. Why had she run out so foolishly?

If only he'd never come to rescue her. If only they'd never fallen in love. If only she'd buttoned with him in the beginning and had never come up the cursed mountain in the slave cart.

If only, if only, if only.

How far back did she want to go with the blame? If only the overlords had never enslaved the lowborns. It was no good. Time moves forward. Going back and assigning blame all around would do nothing to bring Sober back.

She sat on the floor and leaned against the wall, letting the cold bite through her leather jerkin. She wanted to feel something besides the ache that filled her chest.

She couldn't bring him back, but she could hold him in her memory. His face, his smile, his arm resting on her shoulders as they sat reading. She closed her eyes and for a moment she thought she felt him sitting next to her. She thought she might lean over and rest her head against his shoulder.

She buried her face in her hands and wept.

The door swished open, and Repentance wiped her face and looked up.

The king hobbled in, leaning on Provocation's arm.

Behind them came a girl with a tray. She poured hot wine into a cup and handed it to Repentance.

"Come here, child," the king said to Repentance. "Let Provocation see to your burns."

She touched her cheek and then looked at her blistered fingers and winced, feeling the burns for the first time. She pushed herself off the floor and sat on a settee across from the king.

Giving him a hard look, she said, "I never tried to kill you. That slave and I were coming to tell you that the Prince was trying to kill you."

"I found that out. After you ran away with your young man—it was the farmer that helped you, wasn't it? Sober?"

Her young man. Oh, holy Providence. *Why give me the young man, only to snatch him away so quickly?*

"After you ran away with your young man, the prince came to tell me of his plans for hunting you down. I told him to leave you. I told him ... " he sighed. "I told him I had no heart to see my own kin swinging on the frame." He covered his face with his hands. "What a fool I was. Malficc was surprised that I'd seen your birthmark. I told him of course I had. Why did he think I took you away from him? I'd seen the birthmark on the first day I met you."

He paused to take a swig from his medicine flask. "Malficc thought I was saying I was your father. That night he came into my room and knocked me over the head. I woke up in the dungeon."

Provocation, slathering a cool balm on Repentance's cheek, broke in. "I blame myself. I should have known. But why would he lock you up? Even if you did think Repentance was your daughter, you still thought she was an assassin. We all did."

"Because I was going to let her go, and she was a threat to him. As long as she lived he couldn't be sure she wouldn't come take the throne from him someday. Or so he thought."

"So his plan was to keep you locked up until you died?" Repentance asked. "And tell everyone you were away on business?" That seemed like a foolish plan.

"His original plan was to have the slave kill me, and have you for a concubine. With me dead, even if you thought your birthmark meant you were my daughter, you'd not be able to prove it. When you spoiled that plan, by coming with the assassin to warn me, he decided to hand you over to the swingman and let me live. For a while, anyway. When I told him to let you go, he had to change his plan again. He put me in prison and went after you. Once he found you, he was going to kill me and claim you got loose and succeeded in assassinating me. I would be dead, you would go to the swingman, and he would ascend to the throne."

The king rubbed his forehead as if it ached and then added in a whisper, "He took great joy in the dungeon, telling me exactly how he was going to do it all."

"He told us you'd left early in the morning to go to Hot Springs," Provocation said. "I wouldn't have taken his word for it. You never left before without waking me. But the footman told me he'd put you in the coach himself."

"The footman will pay for his misplaced loyalty," the king said. "As will all the of Lord Malficc's friends."

"And the troopers," Repentance said. "There was one in the barn. He threatened to kill Consecration's children if he didn't assassinate you."

The king sighed. "We'll sort it all out. Everyone who played a part in this scheme will be punished appropriately. I promise you that."

"Why didn't you tell the prince I wasn't your daughter?" Repentance asked.

"I did. Not that I expected it to do me any good. He had sent an assassin after me and then he'd imprisoned me. He couldn't let me live. But I thought he might let you live if he knew you weren't my daughter. He didn't believe me, though. He thought it was a ploy to spare your life. Besides, by then he hated you for besting him and he was determined to hunt you down and kill you, along with your entire village."

There was a knock on the door and Generosity came in. "The doctor says Tigen has lost much blood. If he's still alive in the morning, we should have every hope he'll live, but he cannot say if Tigen is strong enough to make it through the night."

Repentance said a quick prayer. Not Tigen, too.

The king nodded at Generosity. "Thank you."

She stood there still.

"Something else?" the king asked.

"One of Repentance's friends from the village came to the festival tonight. I thought she might be wanted." She hesitated. "Shall we wait?"

"Bring her in, Generosity. Friends are helpful in times like these."

Comfort pushed past Generosity, bobbed her head at the king, and threw herself into her sister's arms.

Repentance hugged Comfort, weeping, and shushing and petting her all at once. Comfort was safe.

There was that to be thankful for.

Comfort held on to her and cried with her, as they followed Generosity to the queen's chamber.

Repentance crawled into bed beside her sister, utterly exhausted and numb, and sobbed into her pillow while Comfort rubbed her back.

She finally drifted to sleep.

The next thing she knew, Generosity was waking her and asking if she felt well enough to eat in the kitchen. A certain stable boy, she said, Shamed, by name, had been asking after them and all the servants wanted to see Repentance again.

"Do they not know that Sober is dead?" Repentance asked. "How can they eat?"

"I'll come with you, Generosity." Comfort crawled out of bed. "Give me a moment to wash and dress." She tucked the blanket around Repentance's shoulders. "You stay here and sleep. I'll bring you back some coffee." She ducked into the bathing room.

Repentance looked at Generosity. "Is ... " she was afraid to ask. "Is Tigen alive?"

Generosity's flashed a wide smile. "It'll take more than a bonk on the head to put that young beast down, and that's giving it true."

"Where is he?"

"He's in his quarters. His mother is with him."

"And his brothers, no doubt." Repentance shivered. And then pity washed over her. The Prince's children would suffer when they learned of their father's betrayal. Sober had been right. Everyone dies. It was better, then, to die well. At least Repentance could hold on to the comfort of knowing that the man she lost had died bravely and with honor. He wasn't wearing the coward's cloak before Providence.

He had chosen to die with honor, and she had to choose to live with honor. So she had better start living. Comfort and Generosity left, and Repentance sighed, and forced herself out of bed and into the bathing room. When she was dressed, she still felt that she couldn't face anyone. She wandered out of the palace by the front door, circled around to Misty Lake, and sat on the bench at the dock, the foggy gloom fitting her mood.

It also brought her close to Sober. He was in the lake somewhere. Under the palace. His body was, anyway. His life spark was safe with Providence. She was sure of that. Providence would never turn his back on his faithful friend Sober Marsh.

"Ah, here you are." The king stood at the bottom of the steps. "May I sit with you a moment?"

She scooted over.

He hobbled up the stairs, leaning on a cane. "I'm sorry to interrupt your solitude. I saw you go by my library window and I wanted to talk to you privately." His face was bruised and he looked thinner than when she'd last seen him.

She nodded, waiting silently.

He folded and unfolded his hands a couple of times. Then he cleared his throat and wiggled on the bench. Finally, he said, "I find myself wondering why you saved me ... I didn't sleep last night, going over it in my mind. I sentenced you to the swing frame. I was keeping you as a slave. You had every reason to hate me. The young farmer, on the other hand, you loved. Am I correct in that?"

She nodded.

"So you made an incredible sacrifice. Why did you save me and let him ... ?"

She sighed. "I could have saved Sober. We could have clubbed the prince over the head and escaped." She looked at the

344

king. "But you would have died, and the prince would have ascended to the throne. It never occurred to me that we could roll him into the lake. It all happened so fast. But even if we had murdered him, the young Lord Gaylor would have taken the throne. Either way, the village of Hot Springs would have been destroyed."

"So you sacrificed the one you loved to save your village?"

She gave a little nod. "I sacrificed one I loved, and one that loved me, to save many who have cursed me."

The king cocked his head. "I don't understand."

She shook her head. "It's not important. Have you heard of Harding and Hamchet Banniss?"

The king nodded. "Very famous brothers."

"Sober wanted to die like Harding, not Hamchet."

The king nodded. "I see."

"I was about to open his door when he told me you were in another cell. He made me go save you."

"Can you forgive me? Will you ever forgive me for not believing you?"

She reached over and gave one of his hands a squeeze. "I was not trustworthy. I don't blame you for not believing me." She started to cry. "I'm more to blame than anyone. If I'd buttoned him in the beginning none of this would have happened."

"But if you had buttoned the farmer in the beginning, I'd have never met you. And I'd be the poorer for it."

She wiped her eyes and gave him a sideways look.

He chuckled. "Your face. Always your expression gives you away. Yes, Repentance, I mean it when I say I am richer for having known you." He put one arm around her shoulder. "I want to tell you the stories of two lowborn women. A long time ago an overlord king buttoned a lowborn woman. That woman was not faithful. She defiled the button bed. So the king, in a fit of rage, cut off her head, killed everyone in her village, and took the rest of the lowborns as slaves."

Repentance sniffed. "I never understood why I had to pay the price for something that happened so long ago and had nothing to do with me."

"The ways of Providence *are* hard to understand," the king said. "Why did he give the overlords the strength to enslave the lowborns? And why now, after so long ...? Yesterday a lowborn woman made a great sacrifice to save the life of an overlord king. That king, in a fit of gratitude that matched his predecessor's fit of rage, decided that all slaves in the kingdom would go free."

Repentance pulled away to look at his face. Was he having a joke on her?

He nodded. "I may be assassinated for it. The rich overlord nobility will hate me. And the kingdom will go through some hard times as the bead flow is interrupted and readjusts. I'm well aware of these things. But what is a man to do? I have always prided myself on being a fair-minded man and one who pays his debts."

She threw her arms around him and kissed his wrinkled old cheek. Then her smile faded. She wished Sober could have known what his sacrifice would bring about.

A sob escaped her. "Have you gotten the ... bodies from the lake, yet?"

He nodded. "My men went down several hours ago."

"I'd like his button scarf, please. Did you recover it?"

The king smiled and patted her knee. "You shall have that button scarf, Repentance. Come with me."

She hesitated. She didn't want to see Sober's body again. She'd been trying to wipe the memory of his frozen corpse and misshapen face from her mind. She wanted to remember him the way he looked at Lord Carrull's house.

"Come, Repentance," the king said. "You'll catch cold sitting out here. We'll have a cup of hot wine and get the scarf."

She didn't feel like drinking hot wine with anyone. "I'm afraid I won't be very good company."

"I won't make you talk to me," he answered, holding out his hand to her. "But ... I do know someone who would like to talk to you. He's injured and I know a visit from you would cheer his heart and speed his recovery."

Tigen. She really wanted to see him. But—"I don't want to see his brothers."

"I'll make sure no one bothers you."

Together they walked slowly back into the palace.

Once inside the king asked, "So will it be the patient first, or the hot wine?"

"I want to see Tigen," she said.

He led her to a room on the first floor. "When you are done, come find me in my small library, and we'll see to that wine."

She opened the door and slid in quietly in case the boy was asleep.

The chamber was softly lit with mooncloth.

She looked at the bed and gasped. Whoever was in the bed was much bigger than Tigen.

Hearing the gasp, he turned his head.

"Sober!"

Gladness comes after the battle,
and the old wounds and the myriad scars
make the victory all the sweeter.
~Lawful Atwood XV, in the year of emancipation

CHAPTER 39

He smiled.

She stared, dumbstruck.

His head was bound in white bandaging, stained red at the ear, and his face was swollen and bruised.

He was still the handsomest man she'd ever seen.

"But I saw you. You were frozen. I saw the floor gaping open." Tears sprang to her eyes as she stepped to the bed and picked up one of his hands, needing to touch him to see if he was real.

"I was pretty weak-minded. But after I told you to open the king's door, it occurred to me that I could take my trousers off, dip the ends of the legs in the lake and freeze them, like a sling, across one corner of my cell."

She swiped at the tears on her cheeks. He was so smart. "It makes one wonder what amazing things you might come up with when you aren't half-dead."

"I had to move quickly. The floor was sliding by the time I

got the pants frozen in place. I barely made it, and I managed to burn my skin pretty thoroughly in the process."

She gently touched his bandaged arms with her own blistered fingers. "Who was in the water, then? I saw someone," she shivered, "—a dead someone—with your button scarf."

"No, no, no. Don't cry." He pulled her fingers to his mouth and kissed them. "That wasn't me. That was the Prince's assassin—Consecration. I had climbed into the sling seat I'd made with the pants, just in time. The floor slid all the way into the wall, and all that was under me was lake. My back was burning, and I was trying to wrap my lava-cloth blanket around me so I could lean against the wall for a little stability. I was wobbling all over in the sling, trying not to fall, and my scarf slipped off."

Repentance sat gingerly on the edge of the bed. "I can't believe you were saved by such a flimsy sling. But why didn't you call to me? I looked in the window."

"I must have lost consciousness. I was dizzy. My leg wasn't splinted, and I was in a lot of pain. I remember getting the lava cloth wrapped around me and my scarf falling, but I remember nothing from that point until I woke up to dead silence a few hours ago." He shuddered. "If I never feel that way again, I'll be happy. I was still hanging in my cell, so I assumed you had not been successful in freeing the king. I thought you must be dead. When the king's troopers finally came and told me—" He broke off, his words catching in his throat.

She leaned against his chest and he kissed the top of her head with its short, short hair. "When the King's men went down this morning to retrieve our bodies, they found that the prince was done with his, but I was still using mine. They found the assassin's body, too. I'm sorry for the old guy. He was kindly holding onto my button scarf for me.

"Oh, the button scarf." He rolled to one side and came back with the scarf in his hand. "Repentance Atwater, will you finally take my button scarf?"

Two weeks later, Repentance sat in her silk buttoning blouse, facing the crowd in the ballroom. On the mountain they didn't have one Button Day a year—people buttoned whenever they wanted to. She smiled. Sober had barely been willing to wait long enough for them to gather their families.

His mother was in the front again, this time smiling.

The servants were a few rows back—Cook, crying; Generosity, beaming; Shamed ... sitting awfully close to Comfort!

Lord Carrull sat with his arm around Mistress Merricc—both looking quite pleased.

Her mother and father were up front with the little boys. Mother was humming happily, no doubt. She'd had no hair to braid that morning since both of her daughters were nearly bald, but she had sewn Repentance's three gray buttons onto her silk blouse. And she'd petted Repentance's head and told her how handsome and kind her overlord father had been and how good her lowborn father was and how much he loved her even though he'd always known she was not his own daughter by blood.

Repentance smiled at her father. He sat up even straighter and thrust his chest out a little farther.

Skoch sat on the other side of her father. When he'd heard that the king was freeing the slaves, he'd smiled and said, "There you are m-m-my Lady. Hot Springs, with its gift of dragon breath, has melted the icy towers of Harthill."

And he was right.

He looked friendless as he sat waiting for the ceremony to begin and Repentance reminded herself that she needed to introduce him to her brothers. His young students had left with their mother to stay with her parents in Norbank. All except Tigen. He wanted to stay with the king, and the king wanted him to stay. His mother had put up no fight. Repentance was torn about that. She was happy that Tigen would remain at the palace but so sad that he had such parents. How could they care so little? How could mothers give up their little boys without a fight?

Tigen seemed to have no mixed emotions in the matter. He sat in front of Skoch, a look of pure joy on his face. He'd been a little jealous when Repentance had told him she meant to button Sober. He'd thought she might wait for him to grow up. She explained that she couldn't button him because, though she loved him, she knew Providence had much more important work for him. She was sure there were other ladies in the kingdom in need of saving, and Tigen, being so brave and so good, was just the boy for the job. He wouldn't be ready to settle down with a button mate for a long while yet, she figured. It was a sacrifice, but she was willing to let him go for the good of the kingdom. She told Tigen all of that, and then she gave him a serving of fruit fluff filling, and by the time he was done licking his bowl he'd accepted the idea of her buttoning Sober. If it couldn't be him, Sober was the next best choice, after all.

The king, next to Tigen, nodded at her, conveying a measure of love in that small gesture. Tears filled her eyes. Had anyone told her six months earlier that she would love the overlord King Fawlin, she would have scoffed. And, yet, here she was.

The drumming began—

And stopped before Sober came out.

Provocation entered the room from the back, whisked over to the king and whispered in his ear.

He nodded.

Provocation stopped to talk to the Atwaters. They both stood and followed her out.

Repentance shot a quizzical look at the king.

He grinned.

Grinned? She'd never seen him grin before.

She mouthed the word, "What?" at him.

He stood and approached her. "Just wait. I have found—I have the best button present for you."

Her parents came back into the room, tears streaming down her mother's face.

Behind them came two boys, maybe twelve or thirteen. A

little younger than Shamed.

She put her hand to her mouth. Twelve or thirteen! It was all she could do to keep from jumping up to hug them. The ceremony was about to start, though, and that was a good thing, because the boys looked overwhelmed and uncomfortable as it was.

Everyone settled back into their seats, her parents flanked by four boys.

The drums started up again and Sober came through the door behind her. Repentance saw him through a fog of happy tears. He limped—he always would—and he was leaning on a cane as he danced with his scarf, and yet he managed to look graceful. Repentance brushed her tears away and looked into his eyes thinking she might see some sorrow left over from the things he'd suffered. She found nothing but joy.

He winked at her, and she grabbed the scarf and let him pull her up.

Looking into his eyes she repeated her vows as she buttoned his scarf to her blouse.

> *With my heart I'll love you,*
> *With my hands I'll serve you,*
> *By your side, I'll abide, forever and always.*

Sober hooked his cane into his trousers pocket to free his hands, and he buttoned himself to her.

> *With my heart, I'll hold you,*
> *With my arms, enfold you,*
> *Beside you, I'll guide you, for now and for always.*

And then he kissed her.

She could hear cheering and hooting and hollering, but it all sounded strangely far away. Sober broke the kiss and whispered in her ear. "How soon are we allowed to leave these revelers and have some time alone?"

They were going to Mistress Merricc's farm for the Button

Night. There, a small cabin stood at the end of a lake. Not a swampy lake. Not a freezing lake. A warm, clear lake where ducks and loons raised their families and otters played all the day. Repentance had never seen it, but Sober had told her about it and it sounded like the perfect place to spend a Button Night. It sounded like the perfect place to start a family.

She shivered at that thought. She'd have babies.

"Are you cold?" he wrapped an arm around her shoulders and hobbled toward the crowd of well-wishers.

She put an arm around his waist. "After that kiss? How could I be cold?"

Moonlight filtered into the cabin through the gauzy curtains at the window. Repentance listened to the night sounds—frogs singing love songs in the lake, an owl sounding off with a lonesome hoot.

Sober, snoring softly, lay snuggled against her back in the big bed, one arm wrapped around her.

She twisted under his arm and nestled her head against his warm chest. His heart tapped against her ear with a happy little stutter, sounding as familiar as the dripping of the trees in the swamp.

He woke and squeezed her tightly to his chest and kissed the top of her head.

"I'm sorry I woke you," she said.

"Don't be. I'll be happy if I never sleep again. Sleep means time lost that could be better spent with you."

She thought of her father dragging out to fish in the mornings after sleepless nights filled with squalling babes. "Just you wait until the babies come. You'll be begging for sleep."

He stopped rubbing her back. "We'll have babies?"

She laughed and pushed herself off his chest to look into his face. "Of course we'll have—Did your parents never explain how babies come to be?"

He gave a deep chuckle. "Funny girl. Yes, now that you mention it, I think my parents did tell me something about it."

She snuggled into his neck. "We'll have a son." She was sure of it. He'd be born in a soft bed in a room lit by suncloths, and he would be no man's slave. "We'll call him Gladness."

And there would come rejoicing.

"Gladness sounds about right to me." Sober kissed her head again. "Maybe you'd better show me one more time exactly how the babies come about. I might have misunderstood."

Laughing, she lifted her face and kissed him back.

Yes, there would come rejoicing.

#